E

I THEE WED

I THEE WED

Amanda Quick

BANTAM BOOKS

New York   Toronto   London   Sydney   Auckland

I THEE WED

A Bantam Book / April 1999

Book design by Dana Leigh Treglia

Library of Congress Cataloging-in-Publication Data
Quick, Amanda.
I thee wed / Amanda Quick.
p.   cm.
ISBN 0-553-10084-X
I. Title.
PS3561.R44I18   1999
813'.54 — dc21   98-37168
CIP

Published simultaneously in the United States and Canada

Bantam Books are published by Bantam Books, a division of Random
House, Inc. Its trademark, consisting of the words "Bantam Books" and
the portrayal of a rooster, is Registered in U.S. Patent and Trademark
Office and in other countries. Marca Registrada. Bantam Books, 1540
Broadway, New York, New York 10036.

PRINTED IN THE UNITED STATES OF AMERICA

BVG   10   9   8   7   6   5   4   3   2   1

I THEE WED

CHAPTER ONE

Someone else got to the apothecary first.

Edison Stokes crouched beside him in the gloom of the dark little shop. He glanced at the hilt of the blade that was sunk deep in the old man's chest. Removing the knife would only hasten the inevitable.

"Who did this?" Edison gripped the gnarled hand. "Tell me, Jonas. I swear he will pay."

"The herbs." Blood burbled from the apothecary's mouth. "He purchased the special herbs. Lorring instructed me to send word if anyone sought to—"

"Lorring got your message. That's why I'm here." Edison leaned closer. "Who bought the herbs?"

"Don't know. Sent servant for them."

"Can you tell me anything that will help me find the man who did this to you?"

"Servant said—" Jonas broke off as more blood filled his mouth.

"What did the servant say, Jonas?"

"Had to have herbs immediately. Something about leaving town to attend a house party—"

Edison felt the apothecary's hand grow lax. "Who is giving the house party, Jonas? Where is it to be held?"

Jonas closed his eyes. For a few seconds Edison thought there would be no more information.

But the apothecary's bloodstained lips moved one last time. "Ware Castle."

CHAPTER TWO

The Bastard was here at Ware Castle.

Damn the man. Emma Greyson clenched one gloved hand into a fist on the balcony railing. Of all the thoroughly rotten luck. Then again, it was all of a piece, she thought. Her luck had been rotten for some time now, culminating in complete financial disaster two months ago.

Nevertheless, discovering that she would have to spend the next week trying to avoid Chilton Crane was really too much.

She drummed her fingers on the ancient stone. She should not have been so startled to see Crane arrive that afternoon. After all, the Polite World was a relatively small one. There was nothing odd about The Bastard being among the many guests who had been invited to the large house party.

She could not afford to lose this post, Emma thought. Crane might not remember her, but the only sensible thing to do was to stay out of his path for the duration of the house party. With so many people about, it should be a simple matter to disappear into the woodwork, she assured herself. Few took any notice of paid companions.

A slight whisper of movement in the darkness below the balcony jerked her out of her glum reverie. She frowned and peered more closely into the deep shadows cast by a high hedge.

One of the shadows shifted. It moved out of the darkness and glided across a moonlit patch of lawn. She leaned forward and caught a glimpse of the figure who moved like a ghost through the silver light. Tall, lean, dark haired, dressed entirely in black clothing.

She did not need the brief glint of moonlight on his austere, ascetic cheekbones to recognize the man below.

Edison Stokes. By chance she had been returning from a walk yesterday afternoon when he arrived at the castle. She had seen him drive his gleaming phaeton into the courtyard. The sleek carriage had been drawn by perfectly matched, well-trained bays.

The huge creatures had responded to Stokes's hands on the ribbons with calm precision. Their willing obedience indicated that their master relied on technique and skill rather than whips and savage bits for control.

Later Emma had noticed that the other guests watched Stokes with sidelong glances whenever he was in the room. She knew their ferret-like interest meant that he was very likely both extremely wealthy and extremely powerful. Quite possibly extremely dangerous.

All of which made him extremely fascinating in the minds of the bored and thoroughly jaded elite.

The shadows shifted again. Emma leaned a little farther out over the balcony. She saw that Stokes had one leg over the sill of an open window. How very odd. He was, after all, a guest in the castle. There was no need for him to skulk about this way.

There was only one reason why Stokes would choose such a clandestine approach. He was either returning from a tryst with the wife of one of the other guests or he was about to conduct one.

She did not know why, but she had expected better of Stokes. Her employer, Lady Mayfield, had introduced them last night. When he had inclined his head very formally over her hand, her intuition had sparked briefly. This was not another Chilton Crane, she had told herself. Edison Stokes was more than just another debauched rake in a world that already teemed with an overabundance of the species.

Obviously she had been wrong. And not for the first time lately.

A burst of raucous laughter spilled from one of the open windows farther along the east wing of the castle. The men in the billiard room sounded quite drunk. Music poured forth from the ballroom.

Down below her balcony, Edison Stokes vanished into a darkened chamber that was not his own.

After a while Emma turned and walked slowly back into a dimly lit stone passage. She could safely retire to her bedchamber, she decided. Lady Mayfield would be in her altitudes by now. Letty was extremely fond of champagne. She would never notice that her paid companion had disappeared for the evening.

The sound of muffled voices on the little-used back stairs brought Emma to an abrupt halt midway along the corridor. She paused and listened intently. Soft laughter echoed. A couple. The man sounded disgustingly cup-shot.

"Your maid will be waiting up for you, I assume?" Chilton Crane mumbled with ill-concealed eagerness.

Emma froze. So much for her hopes that her luck would improve. The glow of a candle appeared on the wall of the staircase. In another moment Crane and his companion would emerge into the hall where she stood.

She was trapped. Even if she whirled and ran as fast as she could, she would not be able to make it all the way back down the corridor to the main staircase.

"Don't be silly," Miranda, Lady Ames, murmured. "I dismissed the girl before I went downstairs this evening. I certainly did not want her in the way when I returned."

"There was no need to get rid of her," Chilton said quickly. "I'm certain we could have found some use for the chit."

"Mr. Crane, are you by any chance suggesting that my maid join us under the covers?" Miranda retorted archly. "Sir, I am shocked."

"Variety is the spice of life, my dear. And I have always found that females who are dependent upon keeping a post in a household are extremely willing to do as they are told. Eager, in fact."

"You will have to indulge your taste for the serving classes some other time. I have no intention of sharing you with my maid tonight."

"Perhaps we could look a bit higher for someone to make up a threesome. I noticed that Lady Mayfield brought along a companion. What do you say we arrange to summon her to your bedchamber on a pretext of some sort—"

"Lady Mayfield's *companion*? Surely you don't mean Miss Greyson?" Miranda sounded genuinely appalled. "Never say that you have a mind to seduce that bland creature in spectacles and caps. And that dreadful red hair. Have you no taste at all in such matters?"

"I have often found that drab clothing and spectacles can conceal a surprisingly lively spirit." Chilton paused. "Speaking of Lady Mayfield's companion—"

"I'd rather not, if you don't mind."

"There is something oddly familiar about her," Chilton said slowly. "I wonder if I have encountered her elsewhere."

Panic uncoiled in Emma's stomach. She'd had reason to hope that Crane had not recognized her earlier when, trapped in the music room, she had been forced to walk right past him to escape. He had glanced only casually in her direction.

She had told herself that men such as Crane, who enjoyed forcing themselves on their hosts' hapless maids, governesses, and paid ladies' companions, did not commit their victims' features to memory. Furthermore, her hair was now a different color.

Fearful that a previous employer, who had dismissed her for insubordination, might have warned her acquaintances about that insolent, *red-haired* female, she had worn a dark wig during the short period of her employment at Ralston Manor.

"Forget Lady Mayfield's companion," Miranda ordered. "She is a boring little thing. I assure you I can entertain you in a much more interesting fashion than she can."

"Of course, my dear. Whatever you say." Chilton sounded vaguely disappointed.

Emma edged back a step. She had to do something. She could not stand here like a cornered hare and wait for Miranda and Crane to emerge from the stairwell.

She glanced over her shoulder. The only light in the darkened hall came from a single wall sconce halfway along the corridor. Heavily timbered doors sunk deep in the stone marked the entrances to the various bedchambers.

She whirled, picked up her skirts, and hurried back along the stone corridor. She would have to hide in one of the rooms. The castle was very full, and each room on this floor had been assigned to a guest. But surely they would all be empty at this hour. The night was young. Ware's friends were still downstairs, enjoying the dancing and the flirting.

She paused in front of the first door and turned the knob.

Locked.

Her heart sank. She rushed to the next door. It too refused to budge.

Panic ate at her. She went to the third door, seized the knob, twisted. And breathed a ragged sigh of relief when it turned easily in her hand.

She slipped quickly into the room and shut the door very quietly behind her. She surveyed her surroundings. The bright moonlight pouring through the window revealed the heavy curtains of a large, canopied bed. There were towels on the washstand. The dressing table was littered with elegant little bottles. A woman's lace-trimmed nightgown lay across the bed.

She would wait here until Chilton and Miranda disappeared into one of the other bedchambers. Then she would make her way back to the rear stairs.

She turned, put her ear to the door, and listened to the footsteps moving down the hall. They were coming closer.

A dreadful premonition seized Emma. What if she had stumbled into *Miranda's* bedchamber?

The footsteps paused in front of the door.

"Here we are, Chilton." Miranda's voice was muffled by the heavy door. "Just let me get my key."

Emma stepped back from the door as if it had turned red-hot. She had only seconds. Miranda believed her door to be locked. She was no doubt busily rummaging about in her reticule, hunting for the key.

Emma searched the moonlit room with desperation. There was no space under the bed. She could see that traveling trunks had been stored there. That left only the massive wardrobe. She ran toward it. Her soft kid evening slippers made no noise on the carpet.

Crane's drunken laughter echoed on the other side of the door. Emma heard the soft *ting* of metal on stone.

"There now, see what you made me do?" Miranda said. "I dropped it."

"Allow me," Chilton said.

Emma yanked open the heavy wardrobe, pushed her way through a forest of frothy gowns, and climbed inside. She reached out and pulled the door closed behind her.

She was instantly enfolded in utter darkness. A man's arm wrapped around her waist. She started to scream. A warm palm clamped around her mouth. She was pulled roughly against a strong, rock-hard chest and pinned there.

Terror crashed through Emma. The problem of being recognized paled into insignificance compared to her new predicament. No wonder she had found the door of this bedchamber unlocked. Someone else had already sneaked into the room.

"Silence, please, Miss Greyson," Edison Stokes whispered directly into her ear. "Or we shall both have a great deal of explaining to do."

He had recognized her when she jerked open the door of the wardrobe. From his vantage point behind what he took to be a stylish carriage dress, Edison had seen the moonlight glint fleetingly on a pair of gold spectacles.

In spite of the untenable situation, an odd sense of satisfaction drifted through him. He had been right about Lady Mayfield's dowdy little companion after all. The moment he was introduced to her, he had realized that she was not possessed of any of the qualities one expected to find in a female who had pursued such a career.

Her manner had been properly reticent and self-effacing. But there had been nothing meek or humble about those very perceptive, very clever green eyes. The fires of intelligence, determination, and spirit burned in their depths.

A most formidable lady, he remembered thinking at the time. And attractive into the bargain, although she had obviously done her best to conceal that fact behind the spectacles and an unfashionable bombazine gown, which looked as if it had been dyed several times.

Now he learned that she amused herself by hiding in wardrobes located in other people's bedchambers. How very intriguing.

Emma shifted impatiently in his grasp. He was suddenly very aware of the firm, rounded curves of her breasts pressed against his arm. The clean, faintly herbal scent of her body made him realize just how small, confined, and exceedingly intimate the wardrobe was.

She had obviously recognized him, had declined to panic, and was no longer actively struggling. Cautiously he took his hand away from her soft mouth. She made no sound. It was clear that she was no more eager to be discovered than he was. He wondered if he was sharing the wardrobe with an enterprising little jewel thief.

"Really, Chilton." Miranda no longer sounded amused. "You'll ruin my gown. Kindly do not paw me. There is no hurry, you know. Allow me to light the candle."

"My dear, you inspire such passion, I vow I cannot wait another moment for you."

"You can at least take off your shirt and your neckcloth." Miranda was clearly growing annoyed. "I am not one of your lusty little chambermaids or insipid ladies' companions to be taken up against the wall."

Edison felt a tremor go through Emma. His hand brushed against hers, and he realized she had locked her fingers into a fist. Rage or fear? he wondered.

"But it took my valet forever to tie this particular knot," Chilton whined. "Called the Antique Fountain, y'know. Quite the latest style."

"I shall remove it for you now and retie it for you before you leave," Miranda murmured in honeyed tones. "I have always wanted to play valet to a gentleman such as yourself. A man of such magnificent endowments."

"Is that a fact?" Chilton sounded somewhat mollified by the compliment. "Well, if you insist. But be quick about it. Haven't got all night, y'know."

"But we do have all night, my dear sir. That is just my point."

Clothing rustled softly. Miranda murmured something that was inaudible. Chilton groaned. His breathing became loud.

"My, you are eager tonight," Miranda said. She did not sound pleased by the discovery. "I hope you will not prove to be too eager.

I cannot abide a gentleman who does not wait for the lady to go first."

"The bed," Chilton muttered. "Let's get on with it. I didn't come here to make casual conversation, y'know."

"Just let me take off your shirt. I do so love the sight of a manly chest."

"I'll get out of my own bloody damn shirt." There was a short pause. "There, that takes care of the thing. Let's have at it, madam."

"Damnation, Chilton, that is enough. Let me go. I am not some cheap whore in Covent Garden. Take your hands off me. I have changed my mind."

"But, Miranda—"

Chilton's voice broke off on a hoarse grunt followed by a long, drawn-out groan.

"Bloody hell," he finally muttered. "Now see what you made me do."

"You have certainly ruined my sheets," Miranda said, contempt thick in her voice. "I brought them with me from London so that I could be assured of sleeping on good linen, and now look what you've done."

"But, Miranda—"

"I can certainly understand now why you prefer women who are in no position to demand any great skill from their lovers. You have all the finesse of a seventeen-year-old youth with his first woman."

"It was your own fault," Chilton mumbled.

"Leave at once. If you stay any longer, I shall likely expire from boredom. Fortunately, there is still enough time for me to find a more *talented* gentleman to entertain me for the rest of the night."

"Now see here—"

"I said, get out." Miranda's voice rose in a sudden shriek of pure rage. "I'm a lady. I deserve better. Go find a chambermaid or that whey-faced companion of Lady Mayfield's if you want to amuse yourself. Given your pathetic lovemaking skills, those are the only sorts of females who would take any interest in you."

"Maybe I'll do just that," Chilton retorted. "I'll wager I'd have a lot more fun with Miss Greyson than I just did here with you."

Emma flinched beneath Edison's restraining arm.

"I've no doubt of that," Miranda snapped. "Get out of here."

"I once had a bit of a romp with a lady's companion at Ralston Manor." Chilton's voice abruptly hardened. "Right little bitch, she was. Didn't know when to stop struggling."

"Never say that some poor little companion actually took a notion to refuse your elegant lovemaking techniques, Chilton."

"Got her comeuppance, she did." Chilton seemed oblivious of the sarcasm that dripped in Miranda's voice. "Lady Ralston found us together in the linen closet. She dismissed the stupid little creature out of hand, of course."

"I don't care to hear the details of your conquest of a paid companion," Miranda said coldly. She had her temper back under control.

"No references, naturally," Chilton added with vindictive satisfaction. "Doubt if she ever got another post. Probably starving in some workhouse by now."

Emma was shaking violently, and her breathing was as tight as the fists she had clenched at her sides. Fear or rage? he wondered again. Something told him it was the latter. He began to worry that she would fling open the wardrobe door and confront Crane. It might prove entertaining but he could not allow it. Such a move would not only bring disaster down on her, it would ruin his own plans.

He tightened his grasp on Emma, trying to convey a silent warning. She seemed to comprehend. At least she did not attempt to launch herself out of the wardrobe.

"If you do not leave at once, Chilton, I shall summon my footman, Swan," Miranda said icily. "I am sure he will have no difficulty removing you."

"See here, there's no need to call that great, hulking brute," Chilton growled. "I'm leaving."

Footsteps thudded on the floor. Edison heard the outer door open and close.

"Bloody, stupid fool." Miranda's voice was soft with disgust. "I'm a *lady*. I don't have to put up with anything less than the best."

More footsteps. Quieter this time. Miranda was crossing the room to her dressing table. Edison hoped she would not decide that she needed an item from the wardrobe.

There were a few more small sounds: the click of a comb on the wooden surface of the table, the stopper of a bottle being removed and replaced. Then came the whisper of expensive satin skirts. More soft footsteps.

The bedchamber door opened once more. When it closed again, Edison knew that he and Emma were alone at last.

"I think, Miss Greyson," he said, "that after having shared such a remarkably intimate experience, you and I would do well to deepen our acquaintance. I suggest that we find a more comfortable place where we can conduct a private conversation."

"Bloody hell," Emma said.

"My sentiments precisely."

CHAPTER THREE

Bastard." Emma was still seething when she stalked outside into the heavily shadowed gardens a few minutes later. "Dreadful, slimy, disgusting little bastard."

"I have often, with some justification, been accused of being a bastard," Edison said neutrally. "But few people call me that to my face."

Startled, Emma came to a halt beside an overgrown topiary hedge. "I never meant to imply —"

"And no one," he continued deliberately, "has ever called me a *little* bastard."

He was right. There was nothing small about his person, Emma thought. In addition to size, there was an entirely natural, wholly masculine elegance about Stokes, which many men in the ton must envy. The eye followed him the way it did a large cat on the hunt.

Chagrined, she said, "I was referring to Chilton Crane, not you, sir."

"I am happy to hear that."

"I had a word with Mrs. Gatten, the housekeeper, earlier this afternoon after I realized that Crane was here at the castle," Emma said. "I warned her not to send any of the young maids to his room alone, regardless of the pretext. I also told her to make certain that the females on her staff worked in pairs as much as possible."

"I am in complete agreement with your assessment of Chilton Crane," Edison said. "I assume from your reaction to him that you were the unfortunate lady's companion in the Ralston Manor linen closet?"

She did not answer. There was no need. He knew perfectly well that he had hit upon the truth.

Emma took a few steps deeper into the overgrown garden. She felt, rather than heard, Edison follow.

The Ware Castle gardens were an untidy sight during the day, and at night the massive hedges, untrimmed bushes, and runaway vines resembled a sinister jungle. The only light was that of the moon. It poured over the scene, bathing everything in disturbing shades of silver and darkness. The eerie glow transformed Edison's face into a grim mask with glittering eyes.

Oh Lord, Emma thought. He knew everything now. The events at Ralston Manor, how she had been sacked, the whole lot. She must do something or all was lost. She could not afford to lose her present post until she had devised a scheme to recover from the financial disaster that had overtaken her and her sister.

It was too much. Emma wanted to scream with frustration. Instead, she forced herself to think logically. There was no point trying to explain away what Edison had heard. People were always eager to believe the worst when it came to a lady's reputation.

And even if she could put a better face on the incident at Ralston

Manor, there was still the little matter of the fact that he had just found her concealed in Miranda's wardrobe.

The only point in her favor was that she had not been alone in that wardrobe. She rallied at the thought. It would no doubt be as difficult for Edison to explain what he had been doing in there.

"I commend you on your restraint, Miss Greyson," Edison said politely.

She glanced back at him over her shoulder and frowned. She knew that she had emerged from the wardrobe somewhat the worse for wear. Her cap was askew. Several tendrils of hair had escaped. She could feel them around her face. Her gown was wrinkled from having been crushed against his thigh.

But Edison looked as coolly elegant as he had earlier in the day. Every hair was in place. His coat was not even mussed. His cravat was still crisply tied. It really was most unfair, Emma thought.

The memory of their enforced closeness in the wardrobe sent an unaccountable prickle of sensation down her spine.

"Restraint, sir?"

"You must have been sorely tempted to leap out of the wardrobe and take a poker to Crane's thick skull."

She flushed and turned away. She did not trust his enigmatic smile. Nor did she know what to make of the too-even tone of his voice.

"You are correct, sir. It was difficult to resist."

"Nevertheless, I am glad that you did so. It would have proven a trifle awkward for both of us."

"Indeed." She fixed her gaze on a thick mass of cascading vines. In the moonlight they looked like a horde of snakes creeping across the gravel path. She shuddered. "Very awkward."

"Just what were you doing in Lady Ames's bedchamber, Miss Greyson?"

She sighed. "Isn't it obvious? I heard Crane and Lady Ames coming up the back stairs. I wanted to avoid them, so I ducked into the

17

first unlocked bedchamber I found. It happened to be Lady Ames's room."

"I see." He did not sound entirely convinced.

Emma halted abruptly and spun around to face him. "What about you, sir? Care to tell me why you were concealed in the wardrobe?"

"I was searching for something that was stolen from some friends of mine," he said vaguely. "I was given information that indicated the item might be here at Ware Castle."

"Rubbish." Emma glared at him. "Do not think that you can fob me off with such a banbury tale, sir. Lady Ames is obviously as rich as Croesus. She has no reason to take the risk of stealing anything."

"Appearances can be deceiving among the ton. But as it happens, I do not consider Lady Ames a suspect."

"Then how did you come to be in her room? I saw you sneak into the castle through a window on the floor below a few minutes earlier, you know."

His brow rose. "Did you, indeed? How very observant of you. I had thought that I was unseen and unnoticed by anyone. I used to be rather good at that sort of thing. Perhaps my skills have grown rusty." He broke off abruptly. "Never mind. Concerning my presence in Lady Ames's chamber. There is a simple enough explanation. I was trying to avoid you."

"Me?"

"When I arrived on that particular floor, I caught a glimpse of someone standing out on the balcony at the far end. I knew that whoever she was, she would certainly see me when she walked back into the corridor. I used a picklock to open one of the bedchamber doors and let myself inside. I planned to wait there until you had vacated the hall before I continued my search."

"What a tangle." Emma folded her arms beneath her breasts. "Nevertheless, I suppose I must be grateful to you, sir."

"Why is that?"

She shrugged. "If you had not picked the lock on Lady Ames's door, I would not have found it open, and there was nowhere else to hide in that hallway."

"I am always delighted to be of service to a charming lady."

"Hmm." She studied him with a sidelong glance. "I don't suppose you would care to tell me exactly what it was that you were searching for tonight?"

"I'm afraid not. It is a personal matter."

I'll wager it is, Emma thought. Whatever this was about, one thing was swiftly becoming very clear. Edison Stokes had every bit as much to hide as she did. "Your story is inventive, to say the least, Mr. Stokes."

He smiled faintly. "And your predicament is delicate, is it not, Miss Greyson?"

She hesitated and then inclined her head. "Obviously. I will be frank, sir. I cannot afford a scandal that would cause me to lose my post as Lady Mayfield's companion."

"Do you think that is likely?" Edison sounded politely dubious. "For all her wealth and position in Society, Lady Mayfield does not strike me as being too high in the instep."

"Nevertheless, I dare not risk putting any strain on her sensibilities. Lady Mayfield has been extremely kind to me. I am fortunate in that she likes to style herself an eccentric. She is better able to tolerate my little lapses than some of my previous employers were, but—"

"Little lapses?"

Emma cleared her throat. "I have lost three positions during the past few months, sir. As you just heard, one of them was because of Chilton Crane. But I was dismissed from the other two because of my inability to resist voicing my opinions on occasion."

"I see."

"Letty is very open-minded about some things—"

"Letty? Ah, you refer to Lady Mayfield."

"She insists I call her by her given name. As I said, she is eccentric.

But I cannot expect her to keep me in her service if she is confronted with a serious charge against my virtue. To do so would make her a laughingstock in the ton."

"I understand." Edison pondered that for a few seconds. "Well then, Miss Greyson, it would seem that both of us have good reason to keep our personal affairs confidential."

"Yes." She relaxed slightly. "May I assume that you are willing to keep silent about the incident in which I was involved in Ralston Manor if I agree not to tell anyone that you have come to Ware Castle to prowl through the guests' bedchambers?"

"Indeed. Do we have a gentleman's agreement, Miss Greyson?"

"What we have," Emma said, her spirits lightening swiftly, "is a gentleman's and a *lady's* agreement."

"I beg your pardon." He inclined his head with grave respect. "A gentleman's and a lady's agreement, of course. Tell me, does your emphasis on the matter of equality mean that you are, perhaps, a reader of Mary Wollstonecraft and her ilk?"

"I have read Wollstonecraft's *Vindication of the Rights of Women,* yes." Emma raised her chin. "I found it filled with a great deal of sound reasoning and common sense."

"I will not quarrel with your conclusions," he said mildly.

"Any female who finds herself entirely alone in the world soon comes to a deep and abiding appreciation of Wollstonecraft's notions on the importance of female education and rights," Emma added for good measure.

"Is that the situation in which you find yourself, Miss Greyson? Are you entirely alone in the world?"

It occurred to her that the conversation had suddenly become remarkably intimate. Then again, as he had pointed out earlier, they had already shared an even greater intimacy in Lady Ames's wardrobe. Emma devoutly hoped that she would not continue to blush every time she recalled the feeling of being crushed against his very solid, very warm body.

"Not entirely. I am fortunate in that I have a younger sister. Daphne attends Mrs. Osgood's School for Young Ladies in Devon."

"I see."

"Unfortunately, next quarter's fees are due at the end of the month. *I simply cannot lose this post.*"

He looked thoughtful. "Tell me, Miss Greyson, are you completely without resources?"

"At the moment, yes." She narrowed her eyes. "But I shall not be without them indefinitely. Some of my financial plans failed to materialize on schedule two months ago. But I am hopeful that they will come to fruition any day now."

"And if they don't?"

"I shall think of something else."

"I do not doubt that for a moment, Miss Greyson." Edison's amusement was tinged with respect. "It is obvious that you are a lady of spirit and fortitude. May I ask what happened to your other relatives?"

"My parents died when Daphne and I were very young. Our grandmother raised us. She was a very scholarly woman. It is because of her that I have read Wollstonecraft and others. But Granny Greyson died a few months ago. There was very little money. Just the house."

"What happened to the house?"

She blinked, startled by the manner in which he had pounced upon the one crucial factor in her tale. Belatedly she recalled the murmurs she had heard among the other guests. Stokes was said to be a man with wide-ranging financial interests. Obviously he had a head for business.

"Yes. The house." She gave him a rueful, humorless smile. "You have come straight to the heart of the problem, sir."

"Are you going to tell me what happened to it?"

"Why not? You have no doubt already guessed the answer." She steeled herself. "The house was all that Daphne and I had in the world. That house, sir, and the small farm attached to it, was intended to keep us and shelter us."

"I take it that something extremely unfortunate happened to the house?"

Emma dug her nails into her own arms. "I sold the house, Mr. Stokes. I took out the few pounds required to pay for a quarter's room and board at Mrs. Osgood's School for Young Ladies, and I put all of the rest into a most unwise investment."

"An investment."

"Yes." Her jaw tightened. "I followed a hunch. Usually my intuition is quite reliable. But with each day that passes, it becomes increasingly clear that I may have made a serious mistake."

There was a short silence.

"In other words," Edison said eventually, "you lost the lot."

"Not necessarily. I still have hopes—" She broke off. "All I require is some time and a bit of luck."

"I have always found luck," he said with a chilling lack of inflection, "to be an extremely unreliable foundation for any scheme."

She scowled, already regretting the strange impulse that had induced her to confide so much information of a personal nature. "I do not need any lectures from you, sir. It is very easy for a man of your wealth and power to make depressing pronouncements on the subject of luck, but some of us have little else with which to work."

"Your pride reminds me uncomfortably of my own," he said softly. "Believe it or not, I know what it is like to find oneself alone and penniless in the world."

She choked back a skeptical laugh. "Are you saying that you were once poor, Mr. Stokes? I find that extremely difficult to believe."

"Believe it, Miss Greyson. My mother was a governess who was turned off without a reference when a guest in the house where she worked seduced her and got her with child. The moment the rakehell who was my father discovered that she was pregnant, he abandoned her."

Shock reverberated through her. She opened her mouth, closed it, and then opened it again. "I am sorry, sir. I had not realized—"

"So you see, I do have some feeling for your situation. Fortunately, my mother was able to avoid the workhouse. She went to live with an aging aunt in Northumberland. The aunt died shortly thereafter, leaving enough of an income to allow us to scrape along. My grandmother on my father's side occasionally sent some money to us."

"That was very kind of her."

"No one who knows her," he said very evenly, "would ever make the colossal blunder of calling Lady Exbridge kind. She sent the money because she felt that it was her duty to do so. My mother and I were an embarrassment to her, but she is extremely conscious of what she likes to call family responsibility."

"Mr. Stokes, I do not know what to say."

"There is nothing to be said." He made a dismissing gesture with one hand. "My mother died of a lung infection when I was seventeen. I do not think that she ever gave up hoping that my father would one day decide that he really did love her after all and that he would want to claim his bastard son."

The superficial cloak of casual unconcern in his voice could not entirely conceal the ice beneath his words. His poor mother was not the only one who had hoped that the rake who had sired him would someday come to care for his illegitimate offspring, she thought.

Somewhere, somehow, Emma realized, Edison had found a way to chill the rage that burned within him. But the old anger, while it might be controlled now, would never completely disappear.

"Your father, sir." She paused delicately. "May I ask if you ever met him?"

Edison gave her the sort of smile she might have expected from a large wolf. "He visited me once or twice after his wife and heir died in childbirth. We never became what you would call close. He died when I was nineteen. I was abroad at the time."

"How sad."

"I think that is quite enough on that subject, Miss Greyson. The past is no longer important. I mention it only to reassure you that I do empathize with your plight. Tonight, all that matters is that you and I have made a pact to protect each other's secrets. I trust that I may depend upon you to uphold your end of the bargain."

"You have my word on it, sir. Now, if you will excuse me, I should return to the house. No offense, but I really cannot afford to be seen with you or any other gentleman out here alone in the gardens."

"Yes, of course. The virtue problem."

Emma sighed. "It is a great nuisance having to worry about one's reputation all the time, but it is a vital asset in my line of work."

His hand closed gently but quite firmly around her arm as she started to slip past him. "If you don't mind, I have one more question."

She glanced at him. "What is that, sir?"

"What will you do if Chilton Crane remembers who you are?"

She shuddered. "I do not think he will. I wore a wig and did not have any spectacles when I worked at Ralston Manor."

"But if he does recall your face?"

She straightened her shoulders. "I shall think of something. I always do."

His smile was quick and, for the first time, quite genuine, she thought.

"I can well believe it," he said. "Something tells me that in spite of your present financial situation, you are never entirely without resources, Miss Greyson. Run along. I shall keep your secrets for you."

"And I shall keep yours. Good night, Mr. Stokes. Good luck to you in your search for your friend's missing possession."

"Thank you, Miss Greyson," he said with unexpected formality. "Good fortune to you in your efforts to recoup your lost investment."

She searched his face in the shadows. A strange man and, quite likely, a dangerous one under certain circumstances, she decided. But her intuition told her that she could rely on his word of honor tonight.

She only wished she could depend upon her intuition.

CHAPTER FOUR

Devil take it, where's my tonic, Emma? I have the most rotten headache this morning." Letitia, Lady Mayfield, propped herself up against the pillows and glowered at the tray of chocolate the maid had just deposited in front of her. "A bit too much of Ware's French champagne, I expect. I shall be more cautious tonight."

Unlikely, Emma thought as she picked up the tonic bottle and carried it to the bed. Letty was anything but cautious around champagne.

"Here it is, Letty."

Letty's slightly rheumy gaze fell on the bottle in Emma's hand. She seized it with alacrity. "Thank God. Don't know what I'd do without my tonic. Works wonders."

Emma suspected that the stuff contained a stiff dose of gin mixed with several other vile ingredients, but she refrained from mentioning the fact. She had grown rather fond of her latest employer during the past few weeks. She had even begun to view Lady Mayfield as something of an inspiration. Letty, too, had once had nothing.

She had started life as Letty Piggins, the daughter of an impoverished Yorkshire farmer. She was fond of saying that years ago, when she had arrived in London as a young woman, her only assets had been her virginity and a magnificent bosom.

"I invested my assets wisely, my gel, and look where I am today. Let my story be a lesson to you."

From what Emma could gather, Letty, with assets framed to their best advantage in a low-cut gown, had caught the eye of elderly Lord Mayfield. They had been married by special license. Mayfield had died three months later, leaving his young wife with a title and a fortune.

But Emma's admiration for her new employer was not due to Letty's having managed to snag a wealthy husband. It was the fact that she had spent the past three decades continuing to invest wisely, this time with money rather than her physical attributes. Letty had more than tripled the inheritance that Mayfield had left to her.

Definitely an inspiration, Emma thought.

Letty poured a large dose of the tonic into a mug and downed it swiftly. She burped genteelly and then sighed with satisfaction.

"That should do the trick. Thank you, my dear." She handed the bottle back to Emma. "Mind it for me until tomorrow, will you? I shall probably need it again. Now then, tell me what quaint, rustic entertainments Ware plans to inflict upon us today."

"When I went downstairs earlier," Emma said, "the housekeeper told me that the gentlemen will attend a local race meeting this afternoon. The ladies are going to try their skills at archery and other games."

Letty looked briefly wistful. "I'd rather go to the races but I suppose that won't be possible."

"It would certainly shock the local gentry to see a lady placing wagers alongside the farmers and the gentlemen from Town," Emma agreed cheerfully. "By the bye, Cook told me that breakfast will be served late again."

"Should hope so." Letty massaged her temples. "Doubt if I'll be able to stir from this bed for at least another hour. Can't face the thought of eating until noon at the very earliest. Doubt if any of the others can, either. We were all thoroughly foxed by the time we dragged ourselves off to bed."

"I do not doubt it."

Letty squinted. "Suppose you were up bright and early, as usual?"

"I have always been an early riser," Emma murmured. "I'm well aware that in your considered opinion nothing interesting ever happens in the morning, but some of us are stuck with mornings."

There was no point explaining to Letty that she had arisen even earlier than usual because she had slept quite poorly. Oddly enough, it was not her concerns about Chilton Crane that had kept her awake. Her thoughts had been consumed by her late night encounter with Edison Stokes.

It made a change, she told herself philosophically. Usually when she was unable to sleep it was because the specter of her shaky financial predicament hovered over her bed. Edison Stokes was certainly a good deal more interesting than her own uncertain future.

It occurred to her that, given her rather dangerous agreement with him, it would behoove her to learn as much as possible about Stokes. Letty was always an excellent source of information on the wealthy and the powerful.

Emma cleared her throat. "I had a brief chat on the stairs with Mr. Stokes last night. He is an interesting gentleman."

"Hah. Money has a way of making any man appear interesting," Letty said with relish. "And Stokes has got enough to make him downright fascinating."

Emma probed cautiously. "Investments, I suppose."

"Of course. Hadn't a penny to his name when he was a lad. Born on the wrong side of the blanket, dontcha know. The Exbridge heir was the father. Got some silly little governess pregnant."

"I see."

"Lady Exbridge has never forgiven her grandson, of course."

"It was hardly Mr. Stokes's fault that he was born out of wedlock."

Letty made a face. "Doubt if you'll ever convince Victoria of that. Every time she sees him, she has to face the fact that her son, Wesley, never got himself a legitimate heir before he broke his fool neck in a riding accident. It eats at her, y'see."

"You mean, she has focused her anger at her son onto her grandson?"

"I suppose. It wasn't just that Wesley got himself killed before he did his duty by the title. He also managed to lose the estates in a series of card games just before he died."

"It sounds as though this Wesley at least possessed the virtue of consistency."

"Indeed. He was a complete disgrace. In any event, young Stokes returned from abroad with a fortune about that time. He saved the lot from the creditors and restored the Exbridge finances. Saved Victoria from bankruptcy. Naturally, she cannot forgive him for that, either."

Emma raised her brows. "I'll wager it did not stop her from taking the money, however."

"Of course not. No one ever called Victoria stupid. Haven't actually seen much of her in years. We were never close friends but we had a nodding acquaintance. After Wesley died she shut herself away in that mansion of hers. Never accepts invitations. I believe she attends the theater occasionally, but that's about it."

"Obviously her grandson is more socially inclined."

"Actually, he's not." Letty looked briefly thoughtful. "Don't know a single hostess in London who wouldn't kill to get him to attend a soiree or a ball, mind you. But he doesn't generally go in for that sort of thing. Rather odd that he'd show up here at Ware's house party."

"I expect he was bored. Gentlemen seem to become that way at the drop of a hat. They are forever seeking fresh sources of amusement."

"Not Stokes." Letty gave her a knowing look. "Only one reason why he would have bothered to accept Ware's invitation."

Emma held her breath. Was it possible that Letty had guessed Stokes's true reason for being at the castle?

"What is that?" she asked.

"Obviously he's shopping for a wife."

Emma stared at her. "A *wife*."

Letty snorted. "The man clearly needs some guidance in the matter. He's hardly likely to turn up any suitable innocents from good families here. Basil Ware gave a house party in order to have a bit of fun."

"True. The only single females he invited are wealthy widows, such as Lady Ames. Not the sort to appeal to a man who's looking for a virginal bride with a spotless reputation." She could hardly explain that she knew for a fact that Edison was not in the market for a bride. At least not at that particular moment.

Of course, once he had accomplished his mission, he might well decide to inspect the wares on the marriage mart.

A knock on the door interrupted her thoughts.

"Enter," Emma called. She smiled at the harried looking maid who appeared. "Good morning, Polly. Come in."

"'Morning, Miss Greyson."

Letitia looked hopefully at the tray in Polly's hands. "I trust that's my coffee?"

"Yes, ma'am. And some toast, just like ye said." Polly set the tray down on a table. "Will there be anything else, ma'am?"

"Yes, you can take away this ghastly chocolate," Letty said. "Don't know how anyone can start the day with bloody hot chocolate. Coffee's the only thing that works for me."

"Yes, ma'am." Polly hurried to the bed to collect the chocolate tray.

Letty glanced at Emma. "Have you had coffee or tea yet, my dear?"

"Yes, thank you, Letty. I got some earlier when I went downstairs."

"Humph." Letty's eyes narrowed. "How are you making out up there alone on the third floor?"

"Quite well," Emma assured her. "Don't worry about me, Letty. Mrs. Gatten gave me a pleasant little room. It's quiet and out of the way."

In truth, she hated the small, stark bedchamber on the third floor. There was something depressing about it. No, it was more than that, she thought. There was an eerie sense of malevolence there. She would not have been surprised to learn that at some time in the castle's history someone had been violently dispatched in that little room.

Polly looked at Emma. "Beggin' yer pardon, ma'am, but the housekeeper put ye there on account of that was Miss Kent's room. I reckon Mrs. Gatten figured if it was good enough for her, it would suit you."

"Who is Miss Kent?" Emma asked.

"She was companion to Lady Ware, the master's late aunt, who was mistress here at the castle until she died. Lady Ware hired Miss Kent to keep her company during the last few months of her dreadful illness. Then she disappeared."

"Lady Ware?" Letitia shrugged. "Hardly surprising. Most dead people have the decency to disappear once they've cocked up their toes."

"I didn't mean Lady Ware, ma'am." Polly looked flustered. "Of course the mistress is dead and buried, God rest her soul. It was Miss Kent who upped and vanished like a ghost."

"Not much else she could do, either, under the circumstances," Emma pointed out dryly. "With her employer dead, there was no one left to pay her wages. I expect Miss Kent is working in some other household now."

Polly shook her head. "Not bloody likely."

Emma frowned. "What do you mean?"

"Left without a reference, Miss Kent did."

Emma looked at her. "Why on earth would she do such a thing?"

"Mrs. Gatten thinks it was on account of Miss Kent went and made a fool of herself with the master. Let him under her skirts, she did. And then they quarreled somethin' fierce."

"What did they quarrel about?" Emma asked.

"No one knows. Happened late one night a few days after Lady Ware died. Next morning she was gone along with all of her things."

"Oh dear," Emma whispered.

"Real strange it was, if ye ask me." Polly was clearly warming to her tale. "But she'd been acting odd since that night."

"Odd?" Letty looked briefly interested. "Whatever do you mean, gel?"

"I was the one who found her, ye see. Lady Ware, that is." Polly's voice dropped to a confiding tone. "I was takin' a tray o' tea to her chamber, this chamber, it was—"

Letty's eyes widened. "Good Lord. Do you mean to say that this was Lady Ware's personal bedchamber? The one in which she died?"

Polly nodded vigorously. "Aye. Anyway, as I was sayin', I was bringin' her some tea. As I was comin' down the hall, I saw Mr. Ware comin' out o' this room. He looked real serious. When he saw me he said that Lady Ware had just died in her sleep. Said he was goin' to make arrangements and notify the household."

"Well, it was not as if her death was not expected," Letty said philosophically.

"No, ma'am," Polly agreed. "We all wondered how she'd hung on as long as she had. Anyhow, I came on in here. I was pullin' the sheet up over Lady Ware's face when the odd thing happened."

"Well?" Letty prompted. "What was this odd thing?"

"Miss Kent comes flyin' out o' the dressing room." Polly angled her chin toward the door that separated the smaller chamber from the main portion of the bedchamber. "Real upset, she was. She looked like she'd just seen a ghost."

"Perhaps she had," Letty said. "Lady Ware's."

Emma frowned at her. "Surely you don't believe in specters, Letty."

Letty shrugged. "When you get to be my age, you learn that there are all sorts of strange things in the world, gel."

31

Emma ignored that. She turned back to Polly. "Mayhap Miss Kent was simply upset by Lady Ware's death."

"What was she doin' in the dressin' room?" Polly asked in what was obviously meant to be a rhetorical question. "Know what I think?"

"I'm sure you're about to tell us," Emma said.

Polly winked. "I think her and the master were havin' themselves a bit o' sport back there in the dressin' room when Lady Ware died. Expect it gave Miss Kent a nasty turn when she came out and saw that Lady Ware had passed on."

Letty looked amused. "Poor woman. Discovering that her employer had died while she herself was having a tumble in the adjoining room was no doubt disconcerting."

"Not to mention the shock of learning that she was suddenly un-employed," Emma muttered.

"Like I said, a few days later, she was gone." Polly's expression turned suitably serious again. "Mrs. Gatten told me that Miss Kent would likely never get another post. Respectable ladies wouldn't think of hirin' a companion who hasn't got a decent reference from her last post, she said."

There were ways around that problem, Emma thought. But she decided it would be best not to mention them in front of her current employer.

Letty shook her head with an air of worldly regret. "A young woman must take proper care of her assets. Got to invest 'em with an eye to the future. Any gel who'd throw away her virtue and her reputation on a brief affair must expect to come to a bad end."

"Still, it was a pity," Polly said from the door. "Miss Kent was good to Lady Ware. Used to sit with her for hours even though the mistress was not in her right mind most of the time on account o' the opium she took for the pain. Miss Kent just sat beside her and worked on her embroidery. A great one for needlework, was Miss Kent."

A short silence fell after the door closed behind Polly. Emma used it to contemplate the risks of the career she had chosen.

"A common enough tale, I'm afraid," Letty said eventually. "Not much chance that she found a new post as a companion, that's for certain, not without a reference from her last employer. So depressing when a young woman squanders her assets."

"Hmm," Emma said. She thought about the references she had written for herself in recent weeks. "Sometimes one can invent an illusion of assets."

Letty's thin, gray brows rose. Wry amusement glinted in her bright brown eyes. "If a gel's smart enough to do that, then she'd best use the illusion to marry a wealthy old fool in his dotage. Take it from me, once that is accomplished, one is free to enjoy life."

Emma thought of giving herself to a man she could neither love nor respect. She clenched her hands in her lap. She would forge a better fate for herself and for Daphne.

"I do not have any plans to marry, Letty."

Letty half closed her lashes and eyed her speculatively. "Is it that you no longer have your chief asset to barter or is it that you don't care for the notion of selling it in the marketplace?"

Emma gave her a brilliant smile. "If it transpired that I no longer possessed my virtue, I would certainly not admit it and risk losing my post as your companion, now, would I?"

Letty gave a crack of laughter. "Very well done, my dear. So you don't care for the notion of bartering your assets for a wedding ring, eh?"

"My fortunes may have fallen quite low of late," Emma said. "But not so low that I am tempted to go into trade."

The London newspapers arrived shortly before noon. As was the case with most gentlemen in the country, Basil Ware subscribed to a wide variety, including *The Times*.

Emma had spent the past hour alone in the library feverishly awaiting the arrival of the post. The household was finally astir, but thus far, few of the guests had ventured downstairs. When Mrs. Gatten, plump and placid, walked into the room with the papers in her work-worn hands, Emma practically pounced on her.

"Thank you, Mrs. Gatten." She scooped the newspapers out of the housekeeper's grasp and rushed to the window seat.

"Yer welcome." Mrs. Gatten shook her head. "Never seen anyone so eager to read the papers. Not like there's ever any good news in 'em."

Emma waited impatiently until the housekeeper had left. Then she jerked off the useless spectacles and set them aside. She tore through the newspapers, anxiously searching for the shipping news.

There was no new word of the fate of *The Golden Orchid,* the ship in which she had invested nearly everything she had got from the sale of the house in Devon. The vessel was now more than two months overdue.

Presumed lost at sea.

Emma had first read the dreadful words in the shipping columns six weeks ago, but she still could not bring herself to give up hope. She had been so certain that the single share she had purchased in *The Golden Orchid* would prove to be a shrewd investment. Her intuition had never been stronger than it was on the day she had risked everything on the vessel.

"Bloody ship." She tossed aside the last of the papers. "That is the very last time I shall follow a hunch."

But she knew, even as she took the oath, that she was lying to herself. Sometimes her hunches were simply too strong to be ignored.

"Good day to you, Miss Greyson. The name was Miss Greyson, was it not? I'm afraid I haven't seen much of you since you arrived."

Emma jumped at the sound of Basil Ware's voice. She seized her spectacles and shoved them back on her nose. Then she turned to the gentleman who stood in the doorway.

"Mr. Ware. Good day, sir. I did not hear you come in."

Basil Ware was an attractive man in a ruddy, open, outdoorsy sort of way. He looked especially good in the riding jacket and breeches that he wore this morning. He was seldom without his riding crop, which he carried the way other men carried walking sticks. In spite of his years in America, he was, she thought, the quintessential English gentleman, genial and fond of sports, very much at home with his hounds and his horses and his shooting companions.

According to Letty, Basil Ware had followed the path of many a younger son. Alone and impoverished, he had gone off to America to make his fortune. He had returned to England early last year when he had learned that his aunt was dying and that he was her sole surviving heir.

Upon taking up his inheritance, Basil had moved into the glittering circles of the ton with ease and a charming grace that had made him extremely popular.

"Is there anything of interest in the papers?" Basil asked as he sauntered into the room. "I confess I haven't kept up with events in London during the past few days. Been a trifle busy what with entertaining my guests."

"I saw no news of any great import." Emma got to her feet and smoothed her dull brown skirts.

She was about to excuse herself when a large, hulking figure garbed in Lady Ames's distinctive blue and silver livery appeared in the doorway.

Swan, Miranda's personal footman, bore no resemblance to his graceful namesake. His neck was so thick that it was almost nonexistent. The planes of his face were flat and broad. The fabric of his expensive livery was stretched very snugly across the bulging muscles of his chest and thighs. His hands and feet made Emma think of a bear she had once seen at a fair.

No wonder Chilton Crane had scrambled out of Miranda's bedchamber last night after she had threatened to summon her footman, Emma thought.

Still, there was an honest, earnest expression in Swan's eyes that Emma found reassuring. Swan was no brute. He simply had the misfortune to look like one. From what she had observed, he was devoted to his mistress.

"Beg pardon, sir," Swan said in a voice that bore a striking resemblance to a rusty razor. "I have a message for you from my mistress. Lady Ames asked me to tell you that she will be happy to entertain your lady guests while you're off at the races with the gentlemen."

"Excellent. I shan't have to worry about the ladies growing bored while I'm away with the men, eh?"

Swan cleared his throat. "I also have a message for you, Miss Greyson."

"Me?" Emma was dumbfounded. "From Lady Ames?"

"Yes, ma'am. She instructed me to invite you to join her and the other ladies in the amusements she has planned this afternoon. She said she did not want you to wander off by yourself the way you did yesterday."

"Quite right," Basil declared jovially. "As Lady Mayfield's companion, you're a guest here, same as the others, Miss Greyson. By all means, join Miranda and the ladies today."

It was the very last thing she wished to do, but she could not think of a polite way to refuse. "Thank you, Mr. Ware." She summoned a small smile for Swan. "Please tell Lady Ames that I am very grateful for her consideration."

"My mistress is the kindest and most thoughtful of ladies." There was something close to reverence in Swan's harsh voice. "I am honored to serve her."

Oh dear, Emma thought. The poor man is in love with her.

Chapter Five

The tea was an unusual blend, Miranda had explained. It was mixed to her order by a merchant located just off Bond Street. She had brought enough with her to Ware Castle to allow the others to sample it.

"I could hardly leave the tea to dear Basil, now could I?" Miranda had said when the first cups were poured for the ladies. "Men know nothing about that sort of thing."

Very slowly Emma put down her cup. She dared not move quickly. The sudden sensation of dizziness made her slightly nauseated. She would be mortified if she became ill right here in front of the fine ladies gathered in the circle around her.

Fortunately, none of the others noticed her predicament. They were all engrossed with the new entertainment Miranda had suggested. A guessing game of some sort.

Miranda glittered in her role as hostess for the afternoon. Her glossy black hair was upswept in the newest style. The vivid blue of her gown matched her eyes. She was not exceptionally beautiful, Emma thought, but she seemed to sparkle. Somehow, regardless of whatever was going on around her, Miranda managed to be the center of attention.

Her faithful footman, Swan, watched her with an adoration that Emma found painful to behold.

"Who can tell me what card I have turned facedown on the table?" Miranda asked brightly. "Suzanne? Will you try?"

"An ace of clubs?" Suzanne, Lady Tredmere, hazarded.

"No." Miranda looked expectantly at the next lady in the circle. "Your turn, Stella."

"Let me think." The tall, blonde woman pretended to deliberate for a few seconds. Then she laughed. "I haven't the vaguest notion, Miranda. A three of diamonds, perhaps?"

"I fear not." Miranda's smile had a fixed intensity. "Who will be next? What about you, Letty?"

"I have never been much good at this sort of thing," Letty said. "I take an interest in cards only when there's money at stake."

"Give it a try," Miranda urged.

Letty sipped tea and eyed the card. "Oh, very well. Let me think a moment."

Emma took a deep, shaky breath and tried to collect herself. What was wrong with her? She enjoyed excellent health. In fact, she had felt perfectly fine only a moment ago.

Although she had not been eager to join the ladies when they went outside for the archery contest, Miranda had insisted and she had done her best to be polite. She had dutifully participated in the charades that had followed the archery, and now she was attempting to engage in the silly card game.

Surprisingly, Miranda had been almost cordial to Emma today. A

bit condescending, perhaps, but not unfriendly. She had been especially eager for her to take part in the card game.

"King of hearts," Letty proclaimed.

"Wrong. Miss Greyson?" Miranda turned to Emma. "It's your turn
to guess."

"I'm sorry, I—" Emma broke off, trying to concentrate on not embarrassing herself or Letty. "What was it?"

"That's what I am asking you, Miss Greyson," Miranda said, a trace
of impatience in her voice. "I assumed you wished to play the game."

"Yes, of course." Emma swallowed heavily against the rising nau-
sea and stared at the card on the table.

All she had to do was name a card, any card. Miranda's game was
not one that required skill. Chance alone was involved. Certainly no
one expected her to come up with the correct answer.

She looked up from the card, straight into Miranda's ice blue eyes.

And suddenly she *knew* what card lay facedown on the table.

"An ace of hearts," she murmured politely.

A flicker of what could have been surprise or even excitement
flashed in Miranda's gaze. She reached out and turned over the card.
"You are correct, Miss Greyson. The ace of hearts it is."

"A lucky guess," Emma said weakly.

"Let's try it again." Miranda picked up the deck of cards and quickly
began to reshuffle it. "Swan, please pour more of my special tea for
everyone."

"Yes, ma'am." Swan, who as usual was stationed close to Miranda,
picked up the large silver pot.

Cynthia Dallencamp eyed the footman with an expression of avid
sexual interest as he dutifully refilled her cup.

"Wherever did you get Swan, Miranda?" she asked as if the footman were invisible. "He really is the most amusing creature. I do like
size in a man, don't you?"

Swan flinched but he gamely went on to the next cup. In spite of
her own problems, Emma felt very sorry for him.

"He came to work for me at the start of the Season." Miranda quirked a black brow. "I assure you, he is extremely useful to have around the house."

"Indeed," Cynthia murmured. "Would you consider lending him to me for a day or so? Just long enough for me to determine if everything about him is as large as one would hope. I vow, it is so very difficult to find a man who is big enough to give one satisfactory service in *every* respect."

Several of the ladies dissolved into laughter at the blatant sexual innuendo.

Swan turned a deep, painful red as he stopped beside Emma. She noticed that the teapot shook in his hands. She feared that when he poured her cup he would spill the brew and invite more laughter together with the withering anger of his employer.

"No, thank you," Emma said quickly. "I've had enough."

"But I insist," Miranda said sharply. "It's an excellent tonic."

"Yes, I'm sure it is." It dawned on Emma that it might be the unusual tea that had made her ill. She glanced covertly around the circle. None of the others seemed the least bit bilious.

"Pour Miss Greyson's tea, Swan," Miranda snapped.

"I vow," Cynthia murmured in a voice everyone could hear, "I quite like the way Swan's livery fits, don't you, Abby? It certainly sets off his best features. The view from the rear is especially interesting."

Hot tea splashed on Emma's fingers. She flinched and jerked her hand out of the way. She heard Swan's small, anguished gasp.

"You clumsy idiot," Miranda hissed. "Look what you've done, Swan. You spilled tea on Miss Greyson."

Swan went rigid.

Emma pulled herself together with an effort of will. "Swan did not spill the tea, Lady Ames. I moved the cup just as he started to pour. It was my own fault that I got a few drops on my hand. There is no harm done. I was about to excuse myself, in any event."

Swan looked pathetically grateful.

"Where are you going?" Miranda demanded, instantly distracted from her rage. "We have only begun to play."

"I believe I will retire to my room, if you don't mind." Emma rose cautiously. She was relieved to note that so long as she moved slowly, she could deal with the dizziness. "You have been most kind to include me in your entertainments but for some reason, I . . . I am not feeling quite myself at the moment."

Letty scowled in concern. "See here, are you all right, Emma?"

"Yes, of course." She smiled weakly and clung to the back of the chair for support. "Just the headache."

"Dear me." Miranda's smile could have been carved from a glacier. "I believe we have quite overwhelmed poor Miss Greyson with a little too much excitement. She is not accustomed to participating in social amusements with those who move in elevated circles. Is that the case, Miss Greyson?"

Emma ignored the sarcasm. "Indeed."

She turned carefully and walked slowly out of the library. The staircase on the other side of the vast stone hall looked very far away. She braced herself and started toward it.

It seemed to take forever to climb all the way up to the third floor. But by the time she had reached the landing, she thought she was feeling a trifle better. Nevertheless, she longed to lie down until the last of the ill effects of the tea had worn off.

There was no one about in the hall. Hardly surprising, she thought. She had this wing to herself. She was the only guest who had been assigned a chamber in this corridor. The other dingy little rooms here appeared to be used primarily for storage and linens.

She was definitely feeling steadier by the time she got her key into the lock of her bedchamber. She pushed open the door and walked into the small, cramped quarters.

She glanced around the Spartan chamber with its small bed, tiny washstand, and narrow window. The only hint of warmth or decoration came from the framed bit of embroidery that hung on the wall above the washstand.

Emma took off her spectacles and lowered herself gingerly onto the bed. She adjusted the pillows behind her head and eyed the framed needlework. It was a simple garden scene. Probably Sally Kent's work, she thought. Polly had said that Sally was forever at her embroidery.

Emma wondered absently why the unfortunate Miss Kent had left the bit of needlework behind. She was still mulling over the question when she slipped into a light, fretful sleep a few minutes later.

She awoke quite suddenly to the muffled sound of a woman's fearful cries.

"Please, Mr. Crane, I beg you, don't do this to me. I'm to be married, I am."

"Well then, you'll have good reason to thank me for teaching you a few things about the pleasures of the marriage bed, won't ye, gel?"

"No, please, you must not. I'm a good girl, I am, sir. Please don't hurt me."

"Shut your mouth. If anyone hears you and comes to investigate, you'll be turned off without a reference. That's what happened to the last female I tumbled in a linen closet."

Polly's small shriek of fear and desperation was cut off abruptly.

Emma did not wait to hear any more. A white-hot rage poured through her. She rolled off the bed, vaguely relieved to note that her head was no longer spinning.

She seized the handle of the heavy iron bedwarmer and ran to the door. She stepped out into the hall, just in time to see a door halfway down the corridor closing. A little white muslin cap lay on the floor where it had fallen.

She picked up her skirts and rushed forward. When she arrived in front of the chamber, she heard muffled thuds.

Bedwarmer held on high, she twisted the ancient iron knob. It turned easily in her grasp. She took a breath and prepared to open the door as quietly as possible. She did not want to give The Bastard any time to react to her presence, if she could help it. Everything depended on timing.

She waited until she heard a particularly loud thud and Polly's moan of despair. Then she pushed hard on the door. It swung silently inward to reveal a small, dingy storage room illuminated by a single narrow window set high in the wall.

Crane's back was to Emma. He had already managed to pin Polly to the floor and was working on the fastenings of his trousers. He did not appear to hear Emma enter the closet.

She moved forward, bedwarmer raised.

"Stupid little bitch." Crane was breathing very hard. His voice was tight with excitement. "You should be glad enough to have a gentleman bother to lift your skirts."

Polly's wild, terrified eyes swept to Emma's face. Desperation and despair glistened in her gaze. Emma knew exactly what she was feeling. Rescue from her present dire straits might well mean dismissal, an equally disastrous fate, given the shortage of decent occupations open to females.

"Glad to see you've got some fight in you." Crane used his weight to hold Polly hard against the wooden floor while he opened his trousers. "Makes it more interesting."

"I trust you'll find this equally interesting," Emma whispered.

She brought the bedwarmer down hard on the back of his head.

There was a sickening thunk. For an instant, time seemed to stand still.

And then without so much as a gasp or a groan, Chilton Crane crumpled silently.

"Dear God, ye've killed him," Polly breathed.

Emma looked uneasily at Crane's motionless body. "Do you really think he's dead?"

"Oh, yes, I'm sure of it, ma'am." Polly scrambled out from beneath Crane. The flicker of relief in her eyes was quickly overwhelmed by an expression of congealing horror. "Now what will we do? They'll hang us both for murdering a fine gentleman, they will."

"I'm the one who hit him," Emma pointed out.

"They'll blame me, too, I know they will," Polly wailed.

She might very well be right. Emma shook herself free of the panic that threatened to freeze her where she stood. "Let me think. There must be something we can do."

"What?" Polly asked, clearly frantic. "What can we do? Oh, ma'am, we're both as good as dead, we are."

"I refuse to hang because of The Bastard. He's not worth it." Resolutely, Emma bent down to grab Crane's ankles. "Help me drag him to the staircase."

"What good will that do?" Nevertheless, Polly leaned over to grab Crane's wrists.

"We'll push his body down the stairs and say that he tripped and fell."

Polly brightened. "Do you really think it will work?"

"It's our only chance." Emma heaved on Crane's ankles. "Oh dear. He's awfully heavy, isn't he?"

"As big as the plump new pig me pa bought at market last week." Polly shoved hard against Crane's weight.

The body moved a few inches toward the door.

"We've got to work faster." Emma took a firmer grip on Crane's ankles and hauled with every ounce of strength she possessed.

"Would you ladies like some help?" Edison asked quite casually from the doorway.

"*Sir.*" Polly yelped and dropped Crane's wrists. She took a step back, her hand at her throat. Tears welled in her eyes. "We're doomed."

Emma went very still but she did not let go of Crane's ankles. It was too late to panic, she told herself. If Edison intended to turn her over to the authorities, she was already dead.

She looked at him over her shoulder. His enigmatic eyes told her very little. But when she saw his gaze go briefly to the bedwarmer, she knew that he understood exactly what had happened.

This was a man who was not overly concerned with fine points of law, she told herself. He climbed through windows, hid in wardrobes, and made deals of a less than scrupulous sort with ladies such as herself.

"Yes," she said. "We could certainly do with some assistance, Mr. Stokes. Mr. Crane, here, attempted to force himself on Polly. I hit him with the bedwarmer, as you can see. It appears that I struck him a bit too hard."

Polly moaned. "She killed him."

Edison ignored her. "Are you certain that he's dead?"

Polly whimpered. "He collapsed real sudden like, sir."

"He does feel quite limp," Emma agreed.

"Let's make certain of our facts before we do anything so rash as to toss him down a flight of stairs," Edison said. "Not that he doesn't deserve it."

He closed the door behind him. Then he crossed the small room to where Crane lay on the floor. He went down on one knee and pressed two fingers to Crane's pale throat.

"A strong pulse." Edison looked at Emma. "A very hard head, no doubt. He will live."

"He will?" Emma dropped Crane's ankles. "Are you certain?"

"Quite certain."

"Oh, ma'am." Hope leaped in Polly's face. "We are saved." The hope vanished again in the next instant. "But when he comes to his senses, he'll surely complain to the authorities. He'll say you attacked him with that bedwarmer, Miss Greyson."

"No one," Edison said calmly, "least of all Chilton Crane, will be complaining to the authorities. I think both of you have done enough. You must be quite exhausted after all your efforts. Allow me to tidy up in here."

Emma blinked. "How do you intend to do that, sir?"

"I've always found that the simplest stories work the best, especially when one is dealing with creatures who possess simple minds."

"I don't understand," Emma said. "What will you do?"

Edison bent down, grasped Crane's inert body, and hoisted him over one shoulder with astonishing ease.

"I shall take him to his bedchamber," he said. "When he awakens, I will tell him that he suffered an accident. In my experience, people who have been knocked unconscious, however briefly, rarely recall the precise events leading up to the event. He'll be obliged to believe whatever I tell him."

Emma pursed her lips. "He did not see me before I struck him, but he will surely remember that he dragged Polly in here and that he was attempting to abuse her when he had his, uh, accident. He may very well know that my chamber is on this floor. Mayhap he will guess that I—"

"All will be well," Edison said quietly. "Leave this to me. The only thing you and Polly must do now is keep silent about what went on here in this closet."

Polly shuddered. "I won't say a word. I'd be afraid of what my Jack might do to Mr. Crane if he found out what almost happened here."

"Rest assured, I won't discuss the matter," Emma said crisply. She frowned at the sight of Crane's body draped across Edison's shoulder. "But getting him downstairs to his own bedchamber will not be easy. Someone will surely notice you on the stairs."

Edison looked unconcerned. "I shall use the back stairs."

A profound sense of relief swept through Emma. "I must say, this is really very decent of you, Mr. Stokes."

He raised his brows and gave her a disturbingly thoughtful look. "Yes, it is, isn't it?"

Chapter Six

Chilton Crane moaned weakly on the bed. "My head."

Edison turned away from the window where he had been keeping an impatient vigil. He drew his watch out of his pocket, opened the gold case, and glanced at the time.

"I do not think you were badly hurt, Crane. You were only unconscious for a moment or two. You were extremely fortunate not to break your neck in that storage room. Whatever possessed you to go in there in the first place?"

"Huh?" Crane stirred. His eyes fluttered open. He blinked several times and glared at Edison in evident bewilderment. "What happened?"

"Don't you recall?" Edison managed an expression of mild surprise. "I was on my way to my chamber when I heard unusual sounds coming from the floor above. I went up to investigate. I was just in time to see you open a storage room and enter it. You tripped over an old trunk that had been placed just inside."

"I did?" Crane gingerly touched the back of his head.

"You must have struck your head on a shelf as you went down," Edison said smoothly. "I am told that head injuries can be a bit tricky. You'll no doubt want to spend the rest of the day here in bed."

Crane grimaced. "I've got a blinding headache, that's for certain."

Edison smiled thinly. "I'm not surprised."

"I shall have Ware send for the doctor."

"You must do as you please, of course, but I certainly would not want to trust my head to a country doctor."

Crane looked alarmed. "You're right. Quacks, the lot of 'em."

"What you need is rest." Edison snapped his watch closed and dropped it back into his pocket. "You must excuse me. Now that you've recovered, I shall take myself off. Ware has invited the gentlemen to the billiard room."

Crane frowned. "Could have sworn there was a maid in that closet. Nice, full-bosomed gel. I remember thinking she would be well suited to a quick toss. I wonder if she—"

Edison paused, his hand on the doorknob. "Good God, sir, are you about to tell me that one of the chambermaids refused your advances? How very amusing. I can only imagine what the others will say when you recount the events over port this evening."

Crane flushed a dull, unsightly red. "That's not what I meant. It's just that I was certain there was someone about—"

"I can assure you that there was no evidence of anyone else around when I found you, Crane. I saw only the trunk on the floor. Shall I summon your valet for you?"

"Bloody hell," Crane muttered. "Yes, please, by all means get Hodges in here. He will know what to do for my poor head. Devil take it, what an evil day this has been. I lost a hundred pounds at that race meeting and now this."

"I rather think," Edison said very softly, "that you should be grateful you did not break your neck when you tripped and fell."

Edison made his way back to Emma's bedchamber, careful not to allow himself to be seen on the spiral stairs. He knocked softly. The door was opened at once.

"For heaven's sake, get in here before someone comes along, sir."

Amused by her sharp tone, Edison obeyed. Once inside, he turned to watch her lean out into the corridor to check the hall. When she was satisfied that no one had spotted him, she hastily shut the door and spun around to face him.

"Well, Mr. Stokes? Did Crane believe your tale? Is he convinced that he tripped over a trunk?"

Edison studied the chamber, absently inhaling the scent of herbal soap. It was the same fragrance he had savored last night in the close confines of the wardrobe. He was acutely conscious of the bed in the alcove.

He forced his attention back to the matter at hand. "Whether or not Crane is convinced by the details I gave him, I cannot say. But he has no wish to admit that a lowly chambermaid might have rejected his advances or that she might have overpowered him in an attempt to escape. Regardless of what he believes, he will not contradict my version of events."

Emma's brows arched above her gold spectacles. "Very clever, sir. Polly and I shall both be eternally grateful."

"You were the heroine of the day, Miss Greyson, not me. I do not like to think of what would surely have occurred in that chamber if you had not intervened with the bedwarmer."

Emma shuddered. "I am not the least bit sorry that I struck him so hard, you know. I cannot abide that man."

"I assure you that Crane will eventually pay for his actions."

She looked startled. "He will?"

Edison inclined his head. "I shall see to it. But these things take time to carry out properly."

"I don't understand."

"Have you not heard that revenge is a dish that is best served cold?"

Her eyes widened. "I do believe you mean that, sir."

"You may depend upon it." He crossed the small distance that separated them and came to a halt directly in front of her. "I only wish, Miss Greyson, that I had been close at hand when you encountered Crane in that linen closet in Ralston Manor. My vengeance would have been very swift, indeed."

"I used a chamber pot on his head on that occasion." She grimaced. "I did not succeed in striking him unconscious, only in dazing him. I must say, The Bastard has an extremely thick skull."

He smiled. "Are you saying that you, ah, managed to save yourself from Crane when he assaulted you at Ralston Manor?"

"He did not succeed in forcing himself on me, if that is what you are asking." She rubbed her arms briskly. "But he did cause me to lose my position. When my employer opened the door of the linen closet, we were both still on the floor. It was an awkward scene, to say the least. Lady Ralston naturally blamed me."

"I see." He inclined his head. "Allow me to tell you that you are an extraordinary woman, Miss Greyson."

Emma stopped rubbing her arms. She dropped her hands to her sides and gave him a tremulous smile. "Thank you for what you did this afternoon, sir. Indeed, I do not know what to say. I am not accustomed to being rescued."

"It is obvious that you do not require rescue very often, Miss Greyson. I don't believe that I have ever met anyone quite like you."

Her eyes were luminous and disconcertingly perceptive behind the lenses of her spectacles. He sensed that he was being assessed and weighed in the balance. He wondered if he would pass whatever test she was giving him.

"The feeling is mutual, sir."

"Is it, indeed?"

"Yes." She sounded oddly breathless now. "I am quite certain that I have never met anyone like you, either, Mr. Stokes. My admiration for you is quite unlimited."

"Admiration," he repeated neutrally.

"And my gratitude also knows no bounds," she assured him hastily.

"Gratitude. How nice."

She clasped her hands together very tightly. "I promise you that I will never forget what you did for me today. Indeed, I shall make it a point to remember you in my evening prayers."

"How very thrilling for me," he muttered.

Her brows snapped together. "Mr. Stokes, I do not comprehend. If I have said anything to annoy you—"

"What the devil makes you think that I'm annoyed?"

"I suppose it is the way you are glaring at me. Oh dear, this is not going at all well, is it? Perhaps I should not try to explain myself further. I have not had much experience with this sort of conversation."

"Neither have I."

She raised her eyes to the ceiling in silent exasperation. Then, in a quick, wholly unexpected movement, she went up on her toes, braced her hands on his shoulders and brushed her mouth lightly against his.

Edison froze, afraid that if he moved he would shatter the spell.

It was Emma who broke the embrace. She gasped and blushed furiously as she stepped back. "Forgive me, sir, I did not mean to embarrass you with my boldness. I apologize. I have obviously disconcerted you."

"I'll get over it."

"That is the way the heroines in the horrid novels always thank the dashing heroes," she said rather gruffly.

"Is it? I can see I shall have to broaden my literary tastes."

"Mr. Stokes, please, you really must leave now. If anyone were to come upon us—"

"Yes, of course. The virtue problem."

She glared at him. "You would not find it amusing if your own living depended on your reputation."

"Quite right. It was a thoughtless jest." He followed her gaze to the door. He had no right to put her post as Lady Mayfield's paid companion in jeopardy. If he got her dismissed without a reference, he would be no better than Chilton Crane in her mind. "You may ease your mind. I am on my way."

She touched his sleeve as he stepped around her. "What brought you to this floor at that particular moment?"

He shrugged. "I noticed Crane making his way up the stairs. I was aware that your chamber was up here. I feared that he might have recalled where and when he had last seen you and had decided to . . ." He let the sentence trail off unfinished.

"I see. Very observant of you, sir."

He did not respond. There was no point telling her of the icy rage that had stormed through him when he had caught sight of Chilton on the rear stairs.

Emma took her hand off his sleeve and rubbed her temples. "Heavens, what a day this has been."

Edison smiled slightly. "I just heard a very similar complaint from Crane."

"Did you? Hardly surprising. After that blow to his skull, he is no doubt also feeling somewhat dazed and out of sorts."

Alarm shot through him. "Are you feeling ill, Miss Greyson?"

"Not any longer, thank heavens. But I was rather unwell earlier. That is the reason I was up here resting in my room and thus heard Crane attack Polly."

"Something you ate, perhaps?"

Emma wrinkled her nose. "Something I drank. Lady Ames insisted we all try her special herbal tea and then she forced us to play some silly guessing games."

Edison felt as if he had just shot to the surface of a deep lake and could suddenly see the shore.

"Lady Ames fed you a special tea?" he repeated very carefully.

"Ghastly stuff." Emma made another face. "I cannot think why she would enjoy it. I don't believe any of us actually finished a full cup. I could barely concentrate on her silly games."

Edison reached out and grasped her. "Describe these games to me, please."

Her eyes widened. She glanced uneasily at his hands on her shoulders. "I played only one of them. Lady Ames put a card facedown on a table. We all took turns trying to guess which one it was. I won, but I was feeling so unwell that I could not continue."

"You won?" Edison watched her. "You mean you guessed correctly?"

"Yes. Pure chance, of course. I have always been rather good at that sort of thing. Lady Ames wanted me to continue with the game. Indeed, she got quite annoyed with me when I insisted upon going up to my room. But I really had no choice."

"Bloody hell." Neither he nor Lorring had even considered the possibility that the thief who had stolen the recipe for the elixir might be a woman, Edison thought. It occurred to him that if he was, indeed, after a lady, a female assistant might prove extremely useful in his inquiries.

"Miss Greyson, last night you told me that you are working as a paid companion in order to recover from recent financial reverses."

She grimaced. "Only necessity would convince any woman to take such a post."

"What would you say to an offer of a second, more lucrative position?"

For an instant she looked utterly baffled. Then she flushed furiously. A cold light washed every trace of warmth out of her eyes.

Beneath the sudden hostility lay something else, Edison thought. She looked both hurt and strangely disappointed.

Nothing he had learned during his years of study in the gardens of Vanzagara, he reflected, had ever been of any use when it came to comprehending women.

"No doubt you feel that I should be flattered by such an outrageous offer, sir," she exploded softly. "But I assure you I am not yet *that* desperate."

"I beg your pardon?" Belatedly realization dawned. He groaned. "Oh, I see. You thought I was offering you a carte blanche?"

She stepped out from under his hands, turned her back to him, and clenched her fists at her sides. "You and Lady Mayfield have a good deal in common, sir. She thinks that I ought to sell myself in marriage. You are suggesting a less formal contract. To me it is all one and the same thing. But I have no intention of taking either route. I will find another way out of this mess. I swear it."

He studied the determined line of her spine. "I believe you, Miss Greyson. But you mistook my meaning. I was not offering to make you my mistress. I was proposing to give you a position as my assistant."

She glanced over her shoulder, green eyes narrowed. "Your *paid* assistant?"

He had her now. "You would not have to give up your current post with Lady Mayfield in order to enter my employ. In point of fact, your present position with her puts you in an ideal situation to perform your new duties for me."

A shrewd gleam danced in her vivid green eyes. "Are you saying that I would have two posts? That I could collect wages from both you and Lady Mayfield? Simultaneously?"

"Exactly." He paused deliberately. "I am not a clutch-fisted employer, Miss Greyson. I will reimburse you quite handsomely for your services."

She hesitated a few seconds longer. Then she swung fully around to face him. Hope bloomed in her face. "Could you be a bit more specific about what you mean by *quite handsomely,* sir?"

He smiled slowly. The trick now was not to frighten her off by promising her a vast sum that would arouse her suspicions. He knew that as a professional companion she earned only a pittance, however. He wanted to dazzle her a bit.

"Shall we say double your current wages?"

She drummed her fingers on the bedpost. "My current arrangement with Lady Mayfield includes room and board as well as a quarterly stipend."

"Obviously I am not in a position to offer room and board."

"Obviously. Also, you will not need my assistance for long."

"True. Only for the rest of the week, at most, I should imagine."

A crafty gleam lit her eyes. "If you need my help so much, sir, let us say *triple* my current wages for an entire quarter."

He raised his brows. "Triple your *quarterly* wages for a week's work?"

She looked instantly uneasy, no doubt fearful that she had been too bold in her demands. "Well, you did say that you needed my services, sir."

"True. You drive a hard bargain, Miss Greyson. Perhaps you ought to hear the requirements of your new position before you accept."

"To be honest, sir, I am not terribly particular at the moment. So long as you will guarantee to pay me three times what Lady Mayfield pays for the quarter and not require me to warm your bed, I will take the post."

"Done. Now then, all I shall demand of you, Miss Greyson, is that you comply with Lady Ames's requests to drink her special tea and play cards."

She pursed her lips. "Is it absolutely necessary to drink the tea?"

"Just a bit of it. Only enough to convince her that you have taken some."

Emma sighed. "This may sound impertinent, under the circumstances, but would you mind very much explaining what this is about?"

He held her eyes very steadily. "I have reason to believe that Miranda thinks she is performing some experiments on you with her potion."

"*Experiments?*" Emma's hand went to her stomach. She felt queasy all over again. "That dreadful tea is some sort of poison?"

"I assure you, there is no reason to think that it will harm you."

She narrowed her eyes. "What, exactly, is it supposed to do to me?"

"According to the legend—"

"Legend?"

"Nothing but occult nonsense, I promise you," he said quickly. "I told you that I was searching for something that had been stolen. That object is an ancient volume from the Garden Temples of a distant island called Vanzagara. It is known to the monks of the temples as the *Book of Secrets.*"

"Vanzagara." Emma frowned. "I have heard of it."

"I'm impressed. Not many people have."

"My grandmother was very fond of the study of geography."

"Yes, well, I am conducting my inquiries on behalf of the man who discovered Vanzagara several years ago. He is a very good friend of mine."

"I see."

"His name is Lorring. Ignatius Lorring. And he is dying."

She searched his face and he knew that she sensed the quiet sorrow in him. The knowledge made him uneasy. He would have to be on guard against Emma's unusually perceptive nature, he thought.

"I'm sorry," she murmured.

"Lorring's last wish is to recover the stolen book and return it to the monks of Vanzagara." Edison hesitated. "He feels guilty, you see."

"Why?"

"Because he is the one who discovered the isle and made it known in Europe. It is because of him that outsiders have traveled to Vanzagara. He feels that if it had not been for him, the isle might have remained isolated for many years. No thief would have gone there to steal its greatest treasure."

"Does he know who stole the book?"

"No. But there are rumors that the thief took the *Book of Secrets* to Italy and sold it to a man named Farrell Blue. The tales make sense because Blue was one of very few scholars who would have had even a remote chance of deciphering the old language in which the recipes are written."

"I notice that you refer to this Mr. Blue in the past tense," Emma said warily. "I assume there is a reason for that?"

"He died in a fire that consumed his villa in Rome."

"Not exactly an auspicious event. About this business of the occult, sir—"

"As I said, utter rubbish. But according to the legend, the brew is supposed to enable one to predict the turn of a card. It is said it works by enhancing a woman's natural intuition."

"A *woman's* intuition?"

He nodded. "According to the monks, it is effective only on women, and not on all women, at that. Only a very few females, those who already possess a high degree of natural intuition, are susceptible to its effects."

Emma grimaced. "Hence the need for experiments?"

"Yes." Edison clasped his hands behind his back. "Apparently Miranda herself is not susceptible to the brew. Hardly surprising, since it is unlikely to work on anyone. Nevertheless, she obviously believes it will be effective on someone, so it appears that she is conducting tests. Perhaps she seeks an accomplice."

"Accomplice." Emma considered the word. "That has a rather nasty ring to it."

He raised his brows. "You do see the problem, do you not? If she believes that she possesses a potion that would allow her to cheat at cards, the possibilities are unlimited."

"Fortunes are won and lost in the games played in the homes of the ton," Emma whispered. "Thousands and thousands of pounds are dropped in the card rooms at balls every week."

"Indeed."

"This is amazing." She shot him a quick, assessing look. "But you said that the elixir is only a single legend from that ancient book you mentioned. Why are you searching for it?"

"If I can find the person who possesses the recipe for the elixir, I may well have found the thief who stole the book."

"Yes, I see. But if the elixir does not work—"

"Understand me well. I have no doubt but that the brew itself is useless. Nevertheless, people have been known to risk a great deal in order to obtain something that they believe to be valuable. Men have died because of this damned recipe. The last one was an apothecary in London."

Her eyes widened in alarm. "Did he die because he drank the brew?"

He shook his head. "I believe that he was murdered by his client, the person to whom he sold some of the special herbs required to make the stuff."

She frowned. "You know the ingredients of the recipe?"

"No. But I do know that it originated on the Isle of Vanzagara. The herbs that grow there are rare and unique to the island. Lorring alerted the handful of apothecaries in London who stock Vanzagarian herbs. He asked them to notify him if anyone attempted to purchase some."

"I see. One of them sent word that he had sold some of the rare herbs?"

"Yes. Lorring is so ill that he can no longer leave his home. So I went to see the apothecary as soon as the message arrived. But I was too late. He had been stabbed. He lived only long enough to tell me that whoever had purchased the herbs was planning to attend Ware's house party."

"My God." A fresh wave of alarm shot through Emma. "Do you believe Miranda murdered the poor man?"

"If she is the one who possesses the recipe, I must assume that it is entirely possible that she killed the apothecary. And, perhaps, others as well. But do not fret, Miss Greyson. You will be safe so long as you play the innocent."

"I am actually rather good at that," Emma muttered. "It is a requirement in my profession."

He gave her an odd smile. "Do you know, until I made your acquaintance, I had no notion that paid companions were so clever and resourceful."

"It is a demanding career, I assure you, sir."

"I believe it." He paused meaningfully. "If you are satisfied with the description of your new duties, there is just one more thing I would like to have plain between us."

"What is that?"

"If you ever do find your way into my bed, Miss Greyson, it will not be because I have paid you to do so."

CHAPTER SEVEN

The following evening, before he dressed for dinner, Edison lit a candle and set it on the floor. He sat down in front of the taper, legs folded into the correct position, and contemplated the flame.

He had long ago discarded most Vanza rituals. But once in a while, when he needed to look deep into his own thoughts, he used the candle.

Meditation with the aid of specially scented and colored candles was an ancient practice on Vanzagara. The monks used it in the temples, and every Vanza master taught his students how to use the flame to focus their concentration.

Traditionally each student received his first candles

from his master. The particular scent and color of the tapers were unique to that particular master. There was an ancient Vanzagarian saying, *To know the master, look at the student's candles.*

It was customary for the student to use the master's candles until he had achieved the Third Circle. At that time he concocted his own meditation tapers, creating them with his personal choice of fragrance and color.

Edison had received his first candles from Ignatius Lorring. They had been a rich, dark purple. He would never forget the exotic scent.

Almost as exotic as Emma's scent.

Where the devil had that thought come from? he wondered. Irritated by his own lack of concentration, he focused again on the flame.

At about the time he would have been expected to craft his own candles, he had stepped outside the Circle. He had never got around to creating his own personal tapers. On the infrequent occasions when he elected to meditate, he used any ordinary household candle that came to hand.

Common sense told him it was not the scent or the color that enabled one to sink into that quiet place where truth existed. It was willpower and concentration.

He gazed deep into the flame. Methodically he went through the process of stilling his body so that his mind could focus more clearly. The cloak of stillness settled on him.

The flame flared more brightly, until he could see into its heart. He looked into the depths while he allowed his thoughts to chart their own course. After a while they took shape and substance.

The decision to bring Emma Greyson into the tangled mystery of the missing book might well prove to be a serious mistake. But after examining it, he was satisfied that his logic was sound. If Lady Ames was the thief and if she had convinced herself that Emma was susceptible to the elixir, then Emma was already ensnared in the web. She might well be in peril at some point in the future, although he doubted that she was in any immediate danger. After all, if he was correct in his conclusions, Miranda needed Emma. She could hardly afford to harm her at this juncture.

By employing Emma to help him in his inquiries here at Ware Castle, he would be in a better position to keep an eye on her, Edison thought.

The flame burned more brightly. Edison allowed himself to be drawn deeper into it, to the place where some truths burned hottest. Here nothing was ever completely clear. At best he could catch only fleeting glimpses of inner knowledge.

Shards of the old rage and pain he had felt as a young man still burned here. So did the abiding loneliness. Here, too, was the source of the unrelenting determination that could have transformed him into a Grand Master of Vanza had he chosen that path. Instead, he had used it to build his financial empire.

He looked past the old truths and concentrated on searching out the flickering glow of the new one that he sensed was there.

He watched closely for a long while. After a time he saw it flare up for an instant, just long enough for him to be certain of it. A second later it vanished back into the heart of the fire. But he had seen enough to know that he must acknowledge its presence even though he had the uneasy feeling that it would haunt him.

Here was the truth in the flame, he thought. He had not employed Emma Greyson merely because he thought she could be useful to him this week. He had not taken her on as a temporary assistant because he wanted to protect her or because he wanted to help her out financially.

What he had done was take advantage of the opportunity to draw her closer to him.

Such a motivation was most unusual for him. Possibly dangerous.

He realized that he did not want to look any deeper into the flame.

"You have won again, Miss Greyson." Delicia Beaumont snapped her painted fan. "I vow, it is most unfair. That makes three times in a row that you have selected the correct card from the pack."

There were other rumblings of discontent from the small circle of ladies who had agreed to participate in Miranda's newest "game."

Emma glanced surreptitiously at the elegant group. She had been aware of the growing irritation of her companions for some time now. It was one thing to tolerate a little nobody in their midst so long as she had the good sense to lose when they played their games; quite another when she habitually won.

Only Miranda seemed content with Emma's streak of good luck. Gowned in a striking black-and-gold-striped evening dress, Lady Ames held court at the card table.

Many of the ladies in the circle gathered around her had continued to drink champagne and brandy after dinner. By the time the men finished their port and came to join them for the dancing, most would be quite drunk.

Emma had stuck to tea, steeling herself when Miranda insisted that she try some more of the special blend. This time she had sipped much more cautiously. The result was that the dizziness was not so strong and she did not feel nearly as ill as she had yesterday. Nevertheless, the sensation she was experiencing was decidedly unpleasant. It was as if her brain were filled with a dark, roiling fog.

"Another round," Miranda said cheerfully as she shuffled the cards. "Let us see if anyone can beat Miss Greyson."

Delicia rose abruptly. "I've had enough of this ridiculous game. I am going to take some fresh air." She glanced around the circle. "Does anyone else care to join me?"

"I will."

"So will I."

"It is really quite boring when one person wins every time," Cordelia Page said very pointedly. She got to her feet with a flounce. "I do hope the dancing begins soon."

Amid a rustle of satin, silk, and muslin skirts, the women departed for the terrace.

Miranda smiled benignly at Emma. "I fear they do not lose well,

Miss Greyson. It is certainly not your fault that you are enjoying a bit of good luck tonight, is it?"

The unhealthy excitement in Miranda's eyes worried Emma. In keeping with her employment agreement with Edison, she had promised to participate in Miranda's games. But enough was enough, at least for now. It was time to lose. Besides, she did not think it would be a good idea for Miranda to grow too confident of the effects of her nasty brew.

"One more round and then I believe I shall go up to my room," Emma said.

Displeasure lit Miranda's expression for an instant, but it was quickly suppressed.

"Very well, Miss Greyson, one more round." Miranda selected three cards seemingly at random from the pack, studied them for a moment, and put them facedown on the table. "Go ahead. See if you can guess the cards."

Emma touched the first card. Through the gently whirling mist that filled her brain she could see a four of clubs as clearly as a sunrise.

"A king of hearts, I believe," she said blandly.

Miranda frowned and turned over the card. "You guessed wrong, Miss Greyson. Swan, pour Miss Greyson another cup of tea."

Swan started forward with the pot.

"No, thank you," Emma said. "I don't want any more tea."

"Rubbish. Of course you do." Miranda gave the footman an angry, impatient look. "I told you to pour Miss Greyson some more tea. Do it now, Swan."

Swan flashed Emma a pleading glance. She did not need any of the tea or her own intuition to realize that the poor man was caught in a difficult situation.

She gave him an understanding smile. "Why not? I believe I will take some more tea, after all. Thank you, Swan."

Gratitude flashed in his eyes. The teapot in his hand trembled slightly as he poured the tea.

When he finished and stepped back, Emma reached for the cup. She pretended to lose her grip on the delicate handle. The cup slipped from her fingers and fell to the carpet.

"Oh dear," Emma murmured. "Now look what I've done."

Miranda looked ready to explode. "Fetch the maid, Swan."

"Yes, madam." Swan fled toward the hall.

"I believe I splashed some tea on my gown." Emma rose. "Please excuse me, Lady Ames. As it happens, I am ready to retire for the evening anyway."

There was a hard glint in Miranda's eyes. "But, Miss Greyson, the night is young."

"As you know, I do not go out into Society very often. I am not accustomed to its hours." Emma gave her a sugary smile. "I doubt that anyone will notice my absence."

"You are wrong, Miss Greyson. I will notice." Miranda leaned forward slightly. A hot intensity radiated from her. "I wish to play another game."

A familiar electricity sparked through Emma. She felt the hair on the nape of her neck stir. A prickly sensation made her palms tingle.

I am afraid, she thought, stunned by the sharp premonition of danger. Mortally afraid. For no obvious reason.

Damn the woman. I will not let her do this to me.

Miranda watched her the way a cat watches a mouse.

Another frisson of fear and warning sizzled through Emma. *What is wrong with me? It is not as though she is holding a gun to my head.*

With a fierce effort of will, Emma collected her nerves and the skirts of her uninspired gray gown. "Good night, Lady Ames. I have had enough of cards for this evening."

She did not dare glance back over her shoulder to see how Miranda had taken the dismissal.

She forced herself to walk sedately away from the card table. En route to the staircase she paused near the open door of the ballroom to check on her other employer. A large number of people had gathered inside the spacious chamber. In addition to Ware's houseguests, many members of the local gentry had been invited tonight.

Chilton Crane had not come downstairs all day, much to Emma's relief. He had sent word to his host that he was nursing a headache.

She glanced around and saw Letty standing with a small group on the other side of the room. She was attired in a heavily flounced satin gown that was cut so low at the neckline that it barely contained her breasts. There was yet another glass of champagne in her gloved hand. Her laughter was growing louder by the minute. She would no doubt be calling for her tonic in the morning, Emma thought. She would certainly not be needing the services of her companion tonight.

Grateful to be free for a while from the demands of both of her employers, Emma started up the staircase.

Of the two careers she was pursuing this week, she feared her duties for Edison would prove to be the most onerous. If it were not for the fact that she had accepted his offer of employment, she would not have taken another drop of Miranda's obnoxious tea.

All the ridiculous talk about a missing book and occult elixirs had given her some serious second thoughts about her new employer. She wondered uneasily if he was mad as a March hare.

But even if that proved true, he was a very rich mad hare, she reminded herself as she climbed the stairs. And if she lasted the week in his employ, she would have triple her usual quarterly wages to show for it. The thought of the money made her more inclined to view Edison Stokes as clear-witted and eminently sane.

She rounded the landing on the second floor and prepared to ascend into the darker reaches above. The staff did not waste many candles lighting the gloomy wing in which her bedchamber was located.

Down below, the music swelled as the dancing got under way in the ballroom. Voices rose in drunken laughter. But the noise was quickly absorbed by the thick stone walls of the old castle.

By the time she reached the third floor and started along the corridor to her room, the sounds from the ballroom were muted, ghostly echoes in the distance. Her footsteps rang hollowly on the uncarpeted stone.

She stopped in front of her door and opened her small reticule to retrieve her key.

Another tiny shiver went down her spine.

That bloody tea. Edison was certain that it could not possibly affect her. But what if he was wrong?

In addition to the fact that it made her head swim, she was beginning to have an uneasy suspicion that it actually worked. She had always been good at guessing games, but her luck with Miranda's cards tonight had been a bit unnerving. Tomorrow she would merely pretend to drink the stuff, she vowed.

She wondered if she should mention her concerns about the tea to Edison. After a moment's contemplation she decided not to say anything to him. It was all very well for her to wonder about *his* sanity, she thought. But she certainly did not want him to question *hers.*

She went into her room and closed and locked the door behind her. The rituals of undressing and preparing for bed did nothing to settle her increasingly agitated nerves. Garbed in her nightgown and a little white cap, she eyed the bed.

She did not think she would be able to sleep.

The urge to take some fresh air before retiring was suddenly overwhelmingly strong. Perhaps such an excursion would help dispel the lingering fumes of Miranda's dreadful tea. A stroll around the top of the old castle walls might do the trick.

Decision made, she took her faded chintz wrapper off the hook inside the wardrobe and put it on. She tied the sash, stepped into her slippers, and dropped her door key into her pocket.

She let herself back out into the corridor, relocked her door out of long habit, and went down the hall to the heavy oak door that opened onto the battlements. When she reached it she had to lean her full weight against it in order to get it open.

Outside, she found herself on top of the ancient stone walls. She walked to the edge and looked out past the battlements. Down below, the extensive gardens, bathed in moonlight, ringed the castle. Beyond the cultivated foliage lay thick, dark woods where the moon made no impact.

She took a deep breath of the brisk air and began to walk toward the far end of the wall. Music and voices drifted up through the night from the ballroom. As she moved farther along the battlements, the sounds of intoxicated revelry receded.

At the end of the south wall, she turned and walked toward the east. The balm of the cool, crisp night cleared her mind of the residual effects of the tea, but it did nothing to lessen the foreboding sensation.

Bloody premonitions. She certainly could not stay out here all night just because she was feeling a bit uneasy.

Determinedly she started back along the battlements. When she reached the door that opened onto the corridor, she used both hands to haul on the ancient iron latch.

She finally got the heavy door ajar. She stepped into the dark shadows of the corridor. Instantly the dark premonition of impending disaster grew more powerful. She was about to force herself to walk toward the door of her bedchamber when she caught the echo of footsteps on stone.

Someone was coming up the spiral staircase at the far end of the hall.

Dread prickled through her. There was no reason for a servant to come into this wing tonight. No reason for anyone except herself to be here at this hour.

She no longer questioned the urgency that flashed through her. She simply knew with absolute certainty that she could not risk going back to her own bedchamber. Whoever was coming up the stairs might well be headed toward that room.

Frantically she weighed her options. Then she leaped for the nearest door. The knob twisted easily in her damp palm. She slipped inside the empty, unused chamber and eased the door closed behind her.

She put her ear against the wooden panels and listened. Her breathing sounded very loud in her own ears.

The footsteps came to a halt. She heard the sound of iron keys rattling on a ring. There was a scraping of metal on metal as one of the keys was fitted into the lock of her bedchamber door.

She closed her eyes and struggled to breathe quietly.

There was a soft curse when the first key failed to unlock the door. She heard another key slide into the lock. Someone had got hold of the housekeeper's key ring, she thought. Whoever he was, he apparently intended to try all of the keys until he found the one that fit her door.

Another key slid into the lock. Another muffled curse. A man's voice, she decided. He was growing impatient.

Then she heard the unmistakable sound of her bedchamber door opening. She shivered. *The intruder was inside her room.* If she had not gone out onto the battlements a few minutes ago, she would have been trapped, perhaps helplessly asleep, in her bed.

"What's this?" Chilton Crane's voice, raised in anger, boomed through the open door. It was loud in the empty hall. "Hiding under the bed, you clever little tart?"

A burgeoning rage dampened some of the fear that had been gnawing at Emma. *The Bastard.* Obviously she had not hit him nearly hard enough yesterday. It was a pity that Edison had prevented her from pushing him down the staircase.

"So you're not under the bed, eh? Then it will no doubt be the wardrobe. It won't do you any good, my dear Miss Greyson. I know you're here, somewhere—" He broke off. "Who goes there?"

Ice formed in Emma's stomach. There was someone else in the hall outside her room. She had been concentrating so fiercely on listening to Crane that she had not heard the second set of footsteps.

Neither, apparently, had Crane.

"I say," Chilton blustered. "What are you doing here? What's this all about?"

There was no response but when Chilton spoke again there was panic in his voice.

"No, wait. For God's sake, put away that pistol. You cannot do this. What are you—"

The muffled explosion of a pistol cut off Crane's protest. A second later a dull thud marked the sound of a body hitting the floor.

Inside the dark, empty room, Emma closed her eyes and tried not to breathe.

After what felt like an infinity, she heard the door of her bed-chamber close. There was no ring of shoes on stone, but after a very long time Emma became convinced that the second intruder had re-treated back down the corridor. She waited several more minutes, however, before she took the risk of letting herself out of her hiding place.

There were no cries of alarm. No sound of footsteps on the main staircase. She was not surprised that no one had heard the pistol shot. The thick stone walls had soaked up most of the noise. The music from the ballroom had no doubt taken care of the rest.

Emma paused outside her bedchamber door. She could not stay here in the hall forever, she told herself. She had to take some action.

She steeled herself to open the unlocked door. It swung inward very slowly.

The smell of death greeted her.

She looked into the moonlit room and saw the body sprawled on the floor. The blood that stained Chilton Crane's ruffled white shirt looked black in the silver light.

This time The Bastard really was dead.

CHAPTER EIGHT

Edison raised the flickering taper so that it cast light on the array of small, opaque bottles he had discovered in the bottom of Miranda's traveling trunk.

He selected one at random and removed the stopper. A vaguely familiar scent, at once crisp and intriguing, wafted out of the container. He could not name the crushed herb inside, but it brought back memories.

He had smelled that curious fragrance years ago in the temple gardens of Vanzagara. It was forever linked to that time in his life when he had worn the gray robes of an initiate in the art of Vanza. It brought back memories. He saw himself as a young man studying philosophy under the guidance of purple-robed monks with shorn heads. He recalled dawn vigils at the place where the lush gardens gave way to the jungle; remembered endless hours of vigorous practice in the ancient fighting arts that were the heart of Vanza.

He pushed the old images aside and put the dark bottle back into the trunk and tried the next one in line. The oddly sweet scent given off by the dried fragments inside it was also reminiscent of Vanzagara.

Ingredients for an occult elixir, no doubt.

There was no sign of the *Book of Secrets*.

He was about to close the lid when his questing fingers touched a leather case. He lifted it out and opened it quickly. The candlelight glinted on a row of bullets. There was also a box of powder. The space where the small pistol should have been stored was empty.

He wondered if Miranda had had the gun in her reticule earlier that night when she had attempted to coax him out onto the terrace. It would be interesting to see the reactions of some of her conquests to the notion that she went about her seductions with a pistol at the ready. The realization would no doubt have a dampening effect on the desire of the average gentleman of the ton. Women and pistols were not a common combination in Polite Circles.

He closed the trunk and rose to cast one more glance around the bedchamber.

"You surprise me, Miranda," he said softly into the shadows. "I would have thought you too clever to put any credence in magical nonsense. Now, I must discover if you can lead me to the *Book of Secrets*."

Muffled laughter sounded in the hall outside Miranda's bedchamber. A woman's low murmur rose and fell. The trysting had begun early this evening, Edison thought.

So much for making his exit in a comfortable fashion. He could not risk having anyone see him leaving this room.

He blew out the taper and went quickly toward the window.

At least he had resolved one question, he thought as he opened the window and vaulted up onto the casement. The evidence was clear.

Miranda had somehow come into possession of the recipe from the *Book of Secrets*, which Farrell Blue had deciphered before his death.

How she had got hold of it and whether or not she knew the whereabouts of the *Book of Secrets* were still open to conjecture. Until he knew the answers to those questions, he would not give away his hand.

He glanced down and was relieved to see no one about in the gardens. Then he reached for the rope coiled around his waist. He tossed one end out the window and secured the other. He tugged firmly a couple of times. The rope held.

Satisfied that he had not forgotten how to tie the Vanza knot, he went through the window. Planting his booted feet against the wall, he gripped the rope in his gloved hands and propelled himself quickly down into the shadows of the hedges.

When he was safely on the ground, he jerked sideways on the rope. The knot at the upper end came free of its mooring. The entire length of the rope tumbled to his feet. He recoiled it swiftly.

Not bad, considering he had not tried that trick in over ten years.

He stood in the shadows for a moment, considering his next move. Music still blared from the ballroom. It was nearly two in the morning, but the partying continued unabated.

If he went back into the ballroom, he would very likely be obliged to fend off Miranda's advances again. He had had enough strenuous physical activity for the evening. It was not as though he were still eighteen.

And truth be known, he thought, the only advances he would be interested in receiving tonight would be from his new employee.

Thoughts of Emma made him smile. It occurred to him that he could certainly summon the youthful vigor necessary to deal with any advances that she might make. Unfortunately, it was highly unlikely that he would be called upon to give a good account of himself in that arena.

The bloody virtue problem.

He made his decision. He went back into the castle via a little-used entrance near the kitchens and slipped quietly up the rear staircase.

On the second floor he turned and went down the hall to his own room. He stopped in front of his door and reached into his pocket for the key. He paused before he inserted it into the lock. The light from the nearby mirrored wall sconce was dim. There was enough of it, however, to allow him to determine that there were no fingerprints in the fine gray powder he had sprinkled on the doorknob earlier. No one had entered his bedchamber after he had gone down to dinner.

It had been a minor and no doubt unnecessary precaution, but Vanza taught that foresight was far superior to hindsight.

He wondered if he should be worried about the fact that the longer this affair continued, the more he fell back on the old habits and ways of his training.

He entered his bedchamber and closed the door.

The soft, hesitant knock came only a moment later, just as he finished lighting the bedside candle.

He groaned. Miranda, no doubt. The woman appeared determined to add him to her list of conquests.

He walked back to the door and opened it only an inch, just enough so that he could speak to her through the crack.

"Miranda, I fear I must plead the headache this evening—"

"Mr. Stokes. Sir, it's me."

He jerked the door wide. "Good God, *Emma*. What the bloody hell are you doing here?"

She lowered the hand she had raised to knock, glanced hastily up and down the length of the hall, and then looked at him with huge, shadowed eyes.

His first thought was that she was not wearing her spectacles. His second was that she did not have the vague, unfocused squint most people who wore eyeglasses got whenever they were without them. Her gaze was clear and sharp and starkly anxious in the candlelight.

"I sincerely regret this, sir, but I must speak with you at once." She clutched the lapels of her wrapper at her throat. "I have been waiting in the closet across the way for what feels like forever. I had begun to fear that you would never return to your room."

"Get in here before someone comes along." He grabbed her arm and hauled her swiftly over the threshold.

As she stumbled past him into the room, he leaned out to check the corridor. Mercifully, it was still empty.

He closed the door and turned to confront her. He could not believe that she was standing there dressed in a nightgown, cap, and wrapper.

"What the devil is going on?" he demanded. "I thought you were concerned about your reputation. What the bloody hell do you think will happen if you are seen entering my room?"

"Unfortunately, I have a more pressing problem at the moment." She hugged herself. "Dear heaven, this is going to be difficult to explain."

He could see that she was badly shaken. Anger sparked within him, so quickly and with such force that he could not tamp it down. He reached for her and seized her by the shoulders.

"Bloody hell. Did Crane make another attempt to force himself on you? I vow, I'll kill him myself this time."

"That will not be necessary, sir." She swallowed heavily. "He is already quite dead. That is why I am here. I have come to ask you for your assistance in getting rid of the body. Or at least shifting it to another room."

"The *body*." He could not have heard her aright. "Are you telling me Crane's body is in your bedchamber?"

"Yes." She cleared her throat. "Unlike last time, I really do not think that I can simply shove him down a flight of stairs and tell everyone he died of a broken neck. There is a rather bloody hole in his chest, you see."

A woman's scream rang out from the top of the staircase. Edison could hear the terrible cry of alarm all the way down the hall.

"Murder. There is murder here. Come quickly."

Emma flinched violently as the shouts of alarm echoed through the castle. "Oh my God, we are too late. Someone has already found the body." She tried to duck away from Edison's hands.

"Hold on, Emma. Where do you think you're going?"

She glanced wildly toward the window. "I must get out of here. I will surely hang this time. Bloody hell, I should have known that sooner or later The Bastard would ruin everything for me." She wriggled in Edison's grasp. "Please let me go, sir. I do not have much time."

"You cannot rush off into the night like this. You're wearing a pair of house slippers, for God's sake."

"I'll get a horse out of the stables."

Chaining her wrist in one hand, he pulled her to the bed.

"What on earth do you think you're doing, sir?"

"You think quickly on your feet, Miss Greyson." He sat down and began to pry off his boots. "But I fear your plan to escape with a stolen horse is not one of your better schemes."

She glared at him as he yanked off the second boot. "Have you got a better one?"

"I believe so."

Edison released her to shrug out of his coat. He unfastened the top half of his shirt while he listened to the turmoil on the staircase. Footsteps and shouts sounded from the landing.

"Sir, what do you—"

"You may not prefer my plan," he said as he finished his preparations. "But it will be infinitely safer for you than your own." He rolled up the sleeves of his shirt. "Come. We must be off."

"Sir. Mr. Stokes—"

He grabbed her wrist and hauled her toward the door.

"Where are we going?" she asked breathlessly.

"To join the other horrified onlookers, of course." He wrenched open the door and dragged her out into the hall. "When we arrive on the scene, we will be just as shocked and surprised as everyone else."

"But Crane's body is in my bedchamber."

"That may be true, but you are not in your bedchamber, are you?"

"Well, no, but—"

"No more argument, Miss Greyson. You are my employee. In situations such as this, I expect you to follow my orders."

She looked dubious.

"I'm afraid you must trust me for the moment, Emma," he said more gently.

Halfway down the hall he saw the lights of several flaring candles cast wild shadows on the staircase. The rumble of dozens of footsteps sounded like thunder in the distance.

They reached the landing a bit behind the bulk of the crowd. No one noticed as they fell in with the others. Everyone was straining for a look at what was happening up ahead.

"Hurry," someone yelled. "Kindly move along up there."

On the third floor everyone turned and stampeded down the dark corridor.

Edison glanced over the heads of the crowd and saw a terrified-looking maid standing in the hall. Her mouth was open and her eyes were wide with fright. The one who had given the alarm, he thought. He wondered what she had been doing on this floor at this hour of the night.

As the throng hurried past, he spotted the heavy silver tray on the floor. Broken bits of a cup and saucer and what had probably been a very expensive china pot were scattered next to it.

Edison pulled Emma closer to his side and inclined his head to speak into her ear. "Did you send for tea earlier?"

"What?" She glanced at him, frowning in confusion. "Tea? No. I was going to go straight to bed after I took a short walk on the battlements. Why do you ask?"

"Never mind. I will explain later." Edison made a note to find the maid after the commotion had died down. It would be interesting to discover who had sent her to Emma's room with a tea tray at that hour.

A shriek went up as the first of the curious guests arrived at Emma's door.

"It's true!" someone shouted. "The man's been shot dead."

"Who is it?" a woman called.

"It's Crane," another man confirmed in a loud voice. "What the devil was he doing up here?"

"Tumbling some poor chambermaid, I expect," muttered portly Lord Northmere. "Man never could keep his hands off maids, governesses, and the like."

"Good God, she must have shot him," a woman cried. "Look at the blood. There's so much of it."

"Stand aside, here." Basil Ware pushed his way to the front of the group. "Kindly allow me to see what the bloody hell is going on in my own house."

There was a short, respectful pause as Basil went through the doorway to survey the scene. Edison felt Emma shudder. He tightened his grip on her arm.

Basil reappeared in the doorway. "It's Chilton Crane and he's certainly very dead. I suppose we shall have to summon the authorities from the village. This is Miss Greyson's room. Has anyone seen her?"

"*Emma!*" Letty's shriek reverberated in the stone passage. "My God, he's right. This is my companion's bedchamber. Where is Emma?"

Heads bobbed and swiveled. A low murmur rippled through the crowd.

"He obviously tried to have his way with the poor creature . . ."

"Miss Greyson shot him . . ."

"Who'd have thought it? Miss Greyson, a murderess."

"She seemed like such a quiet young woman. Perfectly pleasant . . ."

"Turn her over to the authorities at once . . ."

Emma clutched Edison's hand so hard that he could feel her nails bite into his skin. He glanced at her and saw that she was watching Basil Ware's face with a transfixed expression. Then she turned her head very suddenly and shot him a grim, accusing look. No doubt thinking of the horse she had intended to steal from the stables, he supposed.

He tightened his grip on her arm in what he hoped was a reassuring fashion. Then he caught Basil's eyes over the heads of the crowd.

"Miss Greyson is with me, Ware," he said calmly. "Precisely where she has been since she left the party earlier this evening. As she has been quite close to me for some time now, I am in a position to give you my complete assurance that she had nothing to do with Crane's death."

Everyone whirled en masse to stare at Emma. A stark silence fell as the assembled guests took in the sight of Emma in her nightclothes. Then every pair of eyes snapped in unison to Edison. The fascinated gazes swept over his undone shirt and his bare feet. He knew he looked as though he had just got out of a warm bed and had pulled on a few garments in great haste.

The conclusion was obvious but he realized that, in her agitated state, Emma was the last person in the hall to grasp it. She simply stared back at the gaping expressions that confronted her.

Edison gave the crowd a rueful smile and raised Emma's hand to his lips. "Obviously neither of us had planned to make the announcement in this manner. But given the circumstances, I'm sure you will all understand. Allow me to present my fiancée, Miss Emma Greyson. Tonight she very kindly consented to marry me."

Emma sucked in her breath with a distinct, wheezing sound. She gasped and started to cough.

Edison thumped her lightly between her shoulder blades. "I am, of course, the happiest of men."

CHAPTER NINE

D ismiss me?" Emma's voice rose as a new wave of alarm washed through her. She stared at Letty, who was propped up in bed with her coffee. "You're going to turn me off? Letty . . . Lady Mayfield, please, you must not do that. I need this position."

Letty, eyes glinting merrily, wagged an admonishing finger. "Very amusing, my dear. But you cannot expect me to fall for such a ridiculous jest. Imagine trying to convince me that you wish to continue your career as a paid companion now that you are engaged to Stokes."

Emma ground her teeth. The morning was not starting off well. After the magistrate had left, she had spent what little had remained of the night on the cot in the dressing room that adjoined Letty's bedchamber. She had not been able to bear the thought of trying to sleep in her own room. Crane's blood still stained the floor.

Letty had been very understanding, after a fashion. "Of course you cannot continue to sleep in this dismal little room, my dear. You are engaged to an extremely wealthy man. How would it look?"

Emma thought her employer had rather missed the point, but she had not argued.

Letty had glowed very pink when Edison had thanked her for her kindness to his "fiancée."

Emma had tossed and turned fitfully until shortly after dawn. Then she had slipped past the snoring Letty to get herself a cup of tea.

Downstairs she had encountered a strange atmosphere in the warm kitchens. The hum of conversation had ceased immediately when she walked into the room. All eyes had turned toward her. She had not comprehended what was going on until Cook brought her a cup of tea and some toast.

"There now, that dreadful man deserved exactly what he got," Cook said gruffly. "Have somethin' to eat, Miss Greyson. Ye've had a hard night."

"But I didn't shoot him."

Cook winked broadly. "'Course ye didn't, ma'am. Got a perfect alibi, don't ye? Besides, we all know the local magistrate declared it the work of a housebreaker who snuck in while everyone was dancing downstairs."

Emma knew the authorities had been forced to that unlikely conclusion because, thanks to Edison, there had been absolutely no evidence against anyone else in the household.

Before she could think of how to respond, Mrs. Gatten trundled into the kitchens. She smiled cheerfully at Emma.

"Miss Greyson, we just want you to know that we don't hold it against you none, what you did and all."

Emma was still feeling slow-witted from lack of sleep. "I beg your pardon?"

Mrs. Gatten glanced quickly around and then lowered her voice to a rumbling whisper. "We all know the sort Crane was. Ye did warn us. Last night young Polly told me that you saved her from his lecherous ways when he cornered her in a closet up there on the third floor."

"Mrs. Gatten, I assure you, I did not shoot The Bastard, I mean, Mr. Crane. Truly, I did not."

"Of course ye didn't, ma'am." Mrs. Gatten winked broadly. "And ain't no one going to say different, not with you having Mr. Stokes behind ye. He's a kind man, Mr. Stokes, is. Not like some of the fancy."

Emma had abandoned the argument. She had hurriedly gulped her tea and then fled back upstairs.

Matters were deteriorating swiftly, she reflected now. She was about to lose yet another post.

"But it's true." Emma moved closer to the bed. "I do wish to continue in my position as your companion, Letty. Indeed, I have given you no reason to dismiss me."

Letty rolled her eyes. "Do not try to cozen me, gel. It's too early in the day for jokes. You know perfectly well that there is no way on earth you can remain in my employ now that you are engaged to Stokes."

"Lady Mayfield, I beg you—"

Letty gave her a knowing look. "I am proud of you, my dear. You're a credit to me, if I do say so myself. Paid attention, you did. Invested your assets wisely."

Emma stared at her. "I beg your pardon?"

"It's true Mr. Stokes ain't exactly in his dotage. Likely to be around for a good many more years from the looks of him. But there's something to be said for a healthy gentleman in his prime."

"Letty."

"Expect you'll learn to manage him so that you won't have to wait for him to cock up his toes in order to be able to enjoy his fortune."

Emma clenched her hands at her sides. "You don't understand."

"Of course I do, my dear." Letty winked very much the way Mrs. Gatten had earlier. "Your strategy was a bit dicey, in my opinion. Personally, I believe in a gel keeping her assets under lock and key until she's got a wedding ring on her finger. But you did get a public announcement of an engagement out of Stokes. With any luck, that should do."

Emma swallowed heavily. "Do?"

"He's not like so many gentlemen of the ton who'd think nothing of promising a gel marriage in order to seduce her and then abandoning her when she becomes inconvenient. The man's got a reputation for keeping his word."

"Lady Mayfield, I don't know how to tell you this, but—"

"Mind you, some will think it's a bit peculiar that he chose you for a bride. But I believe I understand his thinking in the matter."

"You do?"

"Aye." Letty looked shrewd. "Stokes's known to be something of an eccentric. Word is, he's not easily dazzled by superficial airs and graces. They say he positively loathes the vast majority of the ton because of the unfortunate circumstances of his birth. Yes, I can see where he'd prefer to choose a wife who did not move in Polite Circles."

Emma gazed at her in mounting frustration. It was hopeless. There was nothing she could say that would convince Letty to allow her to remain in her employ. The notion that the new fiancée of the fabulously wealthy Edison Stokes desperately wished to retain her post as a paid companion would strike everyone as ludicrous.

There was only one thing left to do, Emma thought. She braced herself.

"Would you mind very much giving me a reference, Lady Mayfield?"

Letty cackled. "Don't be ridiculous, gel. You've got no need for a reference now." She laughed harder. "A reference, she says. Just imagine."

I'm doomed, Emma thought.

An hour later Emma discovered that the day, which had started out on such a dire note, was about to get worse. Edison sent word via Polly that he wished to go riding.

"For heavens sake, tell him *no,* Polly."

Fresh panic lurched through her. She understood instantly that she was in immediate danger of losing her second post of the day. When Edison discovered that she was no longer in Lady Mayfield's employ, he would conclude that she was no longer in a position to assist him in his investigation.

She needed time, Emma thought. She steadied herself with a deep breath and tried to think of a reasonable excuse to avoid the inevitable.

"Kindly inform Mr. Stokes that I do not possess a riding habit," she told Polly.

Unfortunately, perhaps predictably, given her luck today, the small ruse to avoid the morning ride failed miserably.

Polly returned a few minutes later with a dashing, dark turquoise velvet riding habit and a pair of kid boots. Her eyes danced with excitement.

"Mrs. Gatten found these things," she explained proudly. "They belonged to Lady Ware. Afore she took sick, the mistress was accustomed to ride out every day. I think they'll fit ye close enough."

Emma stared dully at the rakish blue habit. There was, she noticed, even a clever little turquoise hat complete with a blue feather to go with it.

Letty emerged from the dressing room at that moment, a vision in a bright yellow gown with a low, square neckline that framed her ample bosom. She took one look at the habit and clapped her hands. "It'll be absolutely perfect with your red hair, my dear."

Emma realized that there was no point in attempting to stave off the next disaster. There was nothing for it but to ride out and listen to yet another employer dismiss her.

One would assume that sooner or later one would grow accustomed to being sacked, she thought glumly.

Forty minutes later she allowed herself to be assisted into a sidesaddle. She took up the reins, relieved to note that the dainty mare the groom had selected for her appeared quite docile. She feared her skills would prove rusty. She had not ridden since long before Granny Greyson had died.

Edison chose a sleek bay gelding. He vaulted easily into the saddle and led the way out of the yard. He took the path that penetrated the dense woods that ringed the castle.

Within minutes they were deep in the forest gloom.

Fuming, Emma waited for him to bring up the inevitable subject. But he said nothing as they rode deeper into the woods. He seemed intent on his own thoughts.

Under any other circumstances she would have welcomed the opportunity to ride. The morning had dawned bright and clear. She could not deny that it was a great relief to get away from Ware Castle for a while.

She tried for an optimistic view of her situation. On the bright side, she was not in any immediate danger of hanging.

The alibi Edison had provided had some undeniable drawbacks in terms of her career, but it had accomplished what he had intended it to accomplish. She was above suspicion so far as the local magistrate was concerned. He might not believe her story, but there was very little he could do about that.

The village authorities had probably already given up any hope of solving the crime, Emma thought. It was virtually impossible to force the high-ranking members of the ton to answer questions in such matters unless they chose to do so or unless there was hard evidence of guilt.

Emma had a strong suspicion that the servants at Ware Castle were not the only ones who had concluded that she was the one who had killed Chilton Crane. She had seen the avid speculation in the eyes of Ware's guests. None of them would attempt to contest her alibi, of course. That would amount to calling Edison a liar, and she doubted that anyone would be fool enough to take such a risk.

But their respectful wariness of Edison would not keep the jaded members of the ton from forming their own opinions, just as the castle staff had. She could only hope that no one had liked Chilton Crane well enough to try to seek revenge.

Unable to abide the suspense a moment longer, Emma rounded on Edison. "Just who do you think murdered Mr. Crane, sir?"

He gave her a thoughtful look. "The identity of the killer is not important."

"Good God, sir, you think I shot him, don't you?"

"As I said, it's not important. By the bye, I had a word with the housekeeper. She does not know who sent the maid to your room with the tea tray. The instructions arrived in the kitchens via a note. It was unsigned."

"I see." Emma was in no mood to concern herself with irrelevant details. "I suppose you have already heard that I am no longer in Lady Mayfield's employ," she said bluntly.

Edison glanced at her with an expression of mild surprise. "I had not heard that you had left your post."

"I did not leave it voluntarily, sir. I was summarily dismissed."

"Not surprising." Edison's mouth twitched. "Lady Mayfield is hardly likely to employ my fiancée as a paid companion."

Emma's hands tightened abruptly on the reins. The little mare tossed her head in protest. Hastily, Emma relaxed her grip. There was no reason to take out her own frustrations on the poor horse.

"Well, sir?"

"Well, what?"

She glared at him. "You have no doubt realized that I am no longer in a position to assist you in your inquiries. I suppose you intend to dismiss me, too?"

Edison frowned. "Why would I do that?"

"There is no need to beat around the bush or try to tie it up in pretty wrappings. I am well aware that you have brought me out here in order to tell me that I no longer have a post. You probably think that I ought to be grateful for what you did for me last night. And I am. But only to a point."

He watched her with an expression of amused interest. "I see."

"I am well aware that you saved me from the hangman's noose. But now I have lost my position with Lady Mayfield because of your actions, and, as I am therefore of no further use to you, I shall be obliged to look for another post."

"Emma—"

"Which will not be an easy matter, because Lady Mayfield refuses to give me a reference."

"Ah." There was a wealth of understanding in the single soft exclamation.

Emma narrowed her eyes. "She claims I won't need one as I am now your fiancée. I could hardly explain that I am not actually your fiancée without ruining my alibi, could I?"

He looked thoughtful. "No."

"It will be impossible for me to find another post back in London once Ware's guests return to Town and inform their friends and cronies that I was briefly engaged to you, sir, and am very likely a murderess into the bargain."

"Yes, I can see that would raise some difficulties."

"Difficulties?" The anger that had been simmering in her all morning exploded. "That is putting it much too mildly, sir. Once you announce that our engagement is ended, I will be ruined."

"I realize that under the circumstances, a broken engagement would cause a scandal."

"It will be a *disaster*. Thanks to your attempt to provide me with an alibi, everyone believes that, whether or not I am the killer, I am most certainly having an affair with you. Without the protection of a formal engagement, I shall be viewed as little better than a bit of muslin. A woman of easy virtue. No one who learns of this incident will even contemplate hiring me as a companion."

"Ah, yes. The virtue problem."

"I shall likely be obliged to change my name, obtain another wig, and go north to find a post. Perhaps all the way to Scotland."

"A dire fate," he agreed.

A flicker of hope flared in Emma. At least he was not denying his culpability in the matter. "You do see, then, that I face an extremely unhappy situation and it is entirely your fault, sir."

He nodded. "Yes, I suppose one could say that."

Her spirits lifted. She rushed to press her small advantage. "Given the circumstances, I trust you will also agree that it would be grossly unfair of you to refuse to pay me the wages you promised."

"Grossly unfair," he said, readily enough.

"I explained about my sister's school fees."

"Yes, you did."

Relief poured through her. He was not going to be difficult, after all. She may as well try for the rest of it. "I feel that in addition to paying me the amount we agreed upon, the very least you can do for me is write me a reference."

He raised his brows. "A reference?"

"Yes. With a reference signed by a man of your importance, it will be much easier for me to find employment in the North."

"I see."

She quickly pondered the details of her plan. "Luckily, I have copies of my last two references, which I wrote myself. I shall loan them to you, if you like. You may use them as models. I must say, they are excellent."

"Glowing, no doubt."

"Indeed. I am quite pleased with them. I shall fetch them for you as soon as we get back to the castle."

"Kind of you."

"I shall think of a new name for myself that you can use in the reference. I dare not use my own name for a while. Gossip has a way of circulating beyond London. No sense taking chances."

"Emma—"

"If you do not mind," she said briskly, "I would very much appreciate it if you would write it this afternoon. What with all the excitement, I suspect that many of Ware's guests will decide to return to Town quite soon."

"True. Everyone will be eager to spread the gossip about Crane's murder."

"Precisely. It is just the sort of tale that will titillate the ton for several days."

"Indeed." Edison glanced at her, his eyes perfectly unreadable. "I appreciate your offer of assistance, Miss Greyson. But I do not believe that it will be necessary for me to copy one of your references."

"Are you certain? I have had a great deal of experience in the matter. I have learned, for example, that there are certain words that work very well."

He looked briefly intrigued. "Which words?"

Having long since committed them to memory, Emma rattled them off quickly. "Meek, plain, timid, humble, unobtrusive, and spectacles."

"Spectacles?"

"Potential employers are extremely fond of spectacles."

"I see." Edison brought the gelding to a halt. "Odd you should mention them. As it happens, I have been meaning to ask you about your spectacles."

Emma frowned as her mare halted of her own accord. "What about them?"

"Do you require eyeglasses or do you use them to perfect your image as meek, timid, unobtrusive, etcetera, etcetera?"

She shrugged. "I do not need them to see clearly, if that is what you mean. But in terms of my professional career, I do feel they add just the right touch."

He reached out and removed the spectacles very gently. "Do not mistake me, Miss Greyson. I find your eyeglasses rather charming. But in your new post you will not be required to project an air of meekness or timidity. Nor will you need to concern yourself with being unobtrusive. Quite the contrary, in fact."

She blinked. "I beg your pardon?"

"Let me be blunt about this, my dear Miss Greyson. I agreed to pay you triple the wages that you had expected to receive from Lady Mayfield for the quarter. I expect you to continue in my employ at least until you have given me my money's worth."

She felt her jaw drop. "But I am no longer in a position to assist you. I just told you, Lady Mayfield dismissed me this morning."

"It strikes me that, as my fiancée, you will be in an even better position to assist me than when you were Lady Mayfield's companion," he said.

"Have you gone mad, sir?"

"Mayhap." He smiled at her expression. "But it is no concern of yours. Unless, of course, you have some objection to working for a madman?"

"A person in my circumstances cannot be too choosy when it comes to employers."

"Excellent. Then we are in agreement on this. You will play the part of my fiancée and carry on as my assistant until I have completed my inquiries."

Emma shook her head, astonished. "Do you really think your scheme will work?"

"I don't have much choice. In all the excitement last night, there was no time for me to tell you that I searched Miranda's bedchamber and found certain herbs. I am forced to conclude that she actually has got her hands on the recipe for the elixir. Which means that she may be able to lead me to the *Book of Secrets*."

"And you still require my help because Lady Ames thinks the brew works on me."

"Yes."

The prospect of drinking more of the noxious tea was not a happy one. But the thought of looking for another post was even more unpleasant.

"In all fairness, Mr. Stokes, I must tell you that I cannot guarantee satisfaction," Emma said. "It is one thing for me to pose as a companion. I have had some experience in that line, after all. But I have had absolutely no experience as a fiancée and I am not at all certain that I will suit the post."

"On the contrary, Miss Greyson." He leaned toward her and reached out to tip up her chin. "I think you are perfectly suited to the position. All you require is a bit of practice."

He started to bend his head. She realized with a shock that he intended to kiss her.

"One more thing, sir," she whispered breathlessly.

He paused, his mouth inches above hers. "Yes?"

"Given the unusual nature of my post, I really must insist that you write out my reference in advance."

His mouth curved faintly. "I shall see to it in the near future."

Emma noticed the movement in the thick trees behind him just as he started to lower his mouth to hers. A familiar sensation raised tiny bumps on her skin.

Leaves shifted. Sunlight glinted briefly on metal.

"Sir. A pistol."

Edison reacted instantly. He seized Emma's arm, kicked his booted feet free of the stirrups, and hauled both of them off their horses.

He dragged Emma to the ground just as the shot crashed through the woods overhead.

CHAPTER TEN

For a few seconds the rearing, plunging horses created a useful degree of chaos. Birds screeched and took wing, adding to the noise and confusion. Edison used the precious time to haul Emma into the dense foliage beside the path.

By the time the frightened mare and gelding had thundered off into the distance, Edison had Emma safely pinned to the ground behind an impenetrable clump of greenery.

An eerie silence fell on the woods.

"Stay here," Edison whispered. "Don't move until I get back."

"For God's sake, sir, surely you do not mean to go after that poacher?"

"I just want to have a look around."

"Edison, no, you must not take such a risk." She levered herself up onto her elbow and spit out a leaf. "Come back here. He might mistake you for a gamekeeper. There's no telling what he'll do. Poachers can be very dangerous."

He glanced at her. She lay in a tangle of turquoise blue velvet, one stocking-clad leg revealed beneath the hem of the habit. The dashing little blue hat had fallen to the ground, dragging several pins with it. A cloud of fiery red hair tumbled around her shoulders. She glared at him.

It took him a second to recognize the anxiety that glittered in her brilliant eyes. When he did, he felt an odd warmth in his gut. She had just been shot at, yanked off a horse, and dragged into the bushes, but she was worried about *his* safety.

The knowledge that she was genuinely concerned for him came as a distinct but rather pleasant surprise. Since his mother's death, no one except Ignatius Lorring had ever evidenced much concern for his well-being.

"It's all right," he mouthed.

He moved off, staying low in order to take advantage of the concealment afforded by heavily laden tree limbs and thick vines. There was no sound from the woods on the other side of the path.

With any luck, Edison thought, his quarry would choose to stay hidden in the woods on the assumption that no one would come looking for him. What fool would crawl through the bushes in pursuit of an armed man who had just taken a shot at him?

A fool who took great exception to being shot at. And even greater exception to having a lady in his employ put at risk.

The soft sounds of the woods slowly resumed. The birds fluttered and chattered overhead. There was a gentle rustling noise in the nearby undergrowth. A hare, Edison thought absently. Or perhaps a squirrel.

When he was fairly certain that he was out of the line of sight of anyone watching from the other side of the path, Edison rose and moved swiftly into the foliage on the far side. He made his way toward the point where the person with the pistol had been when he had taken his shot.

Stay where you are, Edison thought. *I shall have you in another few minutes.*

His quarry apparently read his mind and realized the imminent danger. There was an explosion of noise as someone abruptly pounded off into the distance.

Once again the birds shrieked and flapped in protest.

"Bloody hell."

There was no point giving chase, Edison thought, disgusted. He was too far away and the woods were too thick to allow him to glimpse the villain.

He moved out from behind a tree trunk. Frustration replaced the anticipation that had been humming through him a moment ago.

"Sir? Mr. Stokes?"

"It's all right, Emma. He's gone."

"Thank goodness." She leaped to her feet and hurried out into the center of the path. "I hope you won't take this the wrong way, sir, but in my opinion what you just did was extremely unintelligent."

He scowled as he walked out of the woods to join her. "That is no way to speak to your only remaining employer."

"Nevertheless, you had no business risking your neck in that fashion, sir. The man did have a pistol, after all. He might have reloaded and taken a shot at you."

Edison looked briefly back over his shoulder to where the villain had hidden himself. Then he looked at Emma. "A second shot, do you mean?"

Her eyes widened as she tried to adjust her little hat. "Good grief. Do you believe that he actually intended to shoot at you the first time, sir? Surely he was merely a poacher who caught a glimpse of the horses and mistook them for deer."

Edison considered briefly. He finally decided not to point out that most poachers used traps and snares. The few who did use guns favored rifles rather than pistols. The latter were far too inaccurate over long distances to make them useful in hunting.

But if he went into a lengthy discussion of why he was almost certain that the bullet had been meant for him, he knew it would only deepen her alarm. In any event, he did not yet know why anyone would want to kill him.

It was not that he lacked enemies. No man could arrive at his position in life without having acquired a few. But he could think of no particular reason why one of them would follow him all the way to Ware Castle to try to kill him. Until he had the answers to those questions, there was no point causing Emma further concern.

"You are quite correct, Miss Greyson. Obviously it was a poacher."

"Of course I'm right." She brushed irritably at the dirt and leaves that had stuck to her skirts. "These woods belong to Mr. Ware. Poachers are his problem, not ours."

He watched her for a moment as she shook out the long skirts of the blue habit. When she reached up to repin the mane of red hair, he stepped closer.

"Emma, I am not quite certain how to say this."

"What is that, sir?" She concentrated on cramming her hair under the turquoise hat.

He took another step forward. He was very close to her now, but she did not seem to notice. She had her head bent forward as she fussed with her hair. He wanted very badly to put his hands into that red fire.

"I have never actually had to thank a lady for saving my life," he began softly. "You must forgive me if I do not do it properly."

"Your *life*?"

She looked up so sharply that he did not have time to step back. The high, peaked crown of her hat struck his chin. The collision knocked the little confection back to the ground. Her hair tumbled once more around her shoulders.

This time Edison could not resist. He reached out to thread his fingers through the bright mane. "If you had not called out the warning, I might well have taken that ball in my back."

Her eyes widened. "Good heavens, do you really think that poacher would have struck you with his shot?"

Edison spared a brief glance for the fresh new scar that marked the tree directly behind her. He calculated swiftly.

"It was not a bad shot, considering he was using a pistol. It would certainly have been a very near thing. In any event, I must thank you."

She cleared her throat. "If you really believe that, then I suppose one might say that we are even now. After all, you saved me from the hangman's noose last night."

He smiled fleetingly. "It would appear that we have forged a very useful association, my dear Miss Greyson."

He tightened his hands in her hair, pulled her closer, and kissed her.

She made a small, soft sound and gripped his shoulders so hard that he could feel her fingers bite into his coat.

"Mr. Stokes," she breathed.

There was a moment's hesitation and then, miraculously, her mouth softened.

The knowledge that she wanted to kiss him almost as much as he wanted to kiss her had a strange effect on his senses. A rush of fierce anticipation flowed in his veins.

Only a taste, he thought, tightening his arms around her. Just the smallest sample. They were, after all, standing in the middle of a country path. This was neither the time nor the place to make love to Emma.

But his customary willpower was not as strong as usual this morning. The memory of how she had looked earlier lying in a tangle of velvet, eyes glittering, scorched through him.

He heard another soft moan and realized that he had his hand on Emma's breast. He closed his fingers very gently around her, savoring the soft curve. He certainly could not put her on her back here in the middle of the road, he thought, but there would be privacy if he carried her deeper into the forest.

Emma abruptly freed herself with a gasp. She stepped back quickly. "Really, sir, I do not think this a sound notion under the circumstances."

He could not seem to follow her logic. He realized that the sudden jolt of desire had muddled his brain.

"Circumstances?" he repeated blankly.

"You are my employer, sir. Indeed, the only one I have at the moment."

"So?"

"Everyone knows that it is most unwise for a lady in my situation to form an intimate connection with the person who pays her wages."

"I see."

She bent low and whisked her hat up off the ground. "The tales of females in my line of work who have been ruined by that sort of liaison are legion." She slammed the little cap back down on her head. "Heavens, I am presently using the very bedchamber of a professional companion who I'm told made the disastrous mistake of getting herself involved with Mr. Ware while she was in service to his aunt."

He frowned. "Are you saying that Lady Ware's former companion had an affair with Ware?"

"That is the gossip among the staff." She did not look at him as she shoved a pin into her hair. "Her name was Sally Kent, I believe. Polly told me that Ware dismissed her after she became inconvenient."

Edison hesitated. "I take it that the fact that you and I are presently engaged in the eyes of the ton does not alter your perception of the dangers of such a liaison?"

"No, it does not." She gave him a cross look. "In point of fact, it only complicates matters dreadfully. But as I do not seem to have much option in matters of employment at the moment, I shall have to make the best of the situation."

He bowed slightly. "Very brave of you, Miss Greyson."

"Yes, it is, actually. Now then, there will be no more incidents such as this." She glanced around. "Perhaps you would be so good as to find our horses, sir. We really should be getting back to the castle, don't you think?"

"You are right. After all, I intend for us to start for London this afternoon. If we drive straight through, we should be there well before midnight."

She glanced at him. "You wish to return to London today? But I thought you wanted to continue your investigation here at the castle."

"As you noted earlier, most of Ware's guests will be only too eager to get back to Town to spread the fresh gossip."

"What if Lady Ames does not return with the others?"

He smiled. "Something tells me Miranda will follow you, my dear Miss Greyson."

She narrowed her eyes. "Have you considered where I am to stay in Town while I pose as your fiancée?"

He grinned. "As it happens, I intend to speak to your former employer about that little matter."

"Lady Mayfield?" Emma looked wary. "What has she to do with this?"

"I am going to ask her for her assistance in introducing you to Society."

Genuine dread lit Emma's eyes. "Oh, no, surely you do not mean to ask Lady Mayfield to . . . to—"

"Sponsor you in the social circles of the ton? Why not? She is perfect for the task. She knows everyone. And something tells me she will enjoy the task immensely."

"Is all this really necessary?"

"Yes, it is." The more he considered it, the better he liked it. "In fact, it's a perfect solution. My plan will enable you to continue to assist me in my inquiries without raising any suspicions."

Emma closed her eyes. "I knew you would be an extremely difficult employer, sir."

"But I pay very well, Miss Greyson," he reminded her in silky tones. "And as you just stated, it is not as if you have a great many options."

"Nevertheless, this post has a very uncertain quality. I really must insist that you write out my reference at your earliest possible convenience."

Chapter Eleven

Two hours later Emma left her packing to slip downstairs. To her great relief the library was empty. She spotted the days' heap of London papers on a table and seized the lot.

She carried them to the window seat and frantically began to search the shipping news. It did not take long to go through the entire stack. She had become quite adept at spotting even the smallest item concerning ships returning to port.

But ten minutes later she was forced to acknowledge defeat. There was still no report of *The Golden Orchid*.

"Stupid, bloody ship."

She folded the last of the newspapers and put it neatly on top of the others. Absently she gazed through the window at the bustling scene in the castle forecourt, where carriages and teams were being readied. Most of the guests were planning to depart immediately after the late breakfast. The rest would no doubt leave tomorrow.

She ought to go back upstairs and finish her own preparations for the trip back to London, she thought. She was not looking forward to the journey.

There was no call to complain, she told herself bracingly. After all, it was not as though she had been enjoying her stay at Ware Castle. In the course of the past two days she had been obliged to drink a noxious brew, got herself dismissed from a very nice post, and had barely avoided rape and the hangman's noose. And then there was that unpleasant incident with the poacher in the woods this morning.

Life in Town would no doubt be a pleasant tonic after the perils of rusticating in the country.

On the positive side, she had managed to obtain new employment, which promised to pay exceedingly well. For a moment she indulged herself in plans for the future. If she succeeded in keeping her new post long enough to collect her wages, she would have enough money to rent a small house for herself and Daphne. If she was careful, she might have a bit left over to invest in another ship.

No. Definitely not another ship, she promised herself. Some other investment this time. Perhaps a property construction venture. A project she could watch over very carefully as opposed to one that could simply up and vanish at sea.

She would fetch Daphne from Mrs. Osgood's School for Young Ladies as soon as the money was in her hands.

Her fingers tightened on the window seat cushion. All of her dreams depended upon keeping her new position as Edison Stokes's fiancée, she reminded herself. She must do nothing to jeopardize this post. She must maintain a suitably professional demeanor at all times.

With what she suspected would prove to be typical efficiency, Edison had already spoken to Letty. Just as he had predicted, Lady Mayfield had been delighted at the prospect of sponsoring Emma in Town. It was clear that she viewed the project as a wonderful new entertainment.

"We must get you out of those dowdy gowns at once," Letty had declared. "You will look lovely in something cut lower at the neckline. My modiste will know just what to do with your bosom."

One thing was certain, Emma thought as she absently watched the carriages. There must be no more heated embraces or passionate kisses with her new employer. That way lay disaster. She would not make that sort of mistake, she vowed. No matter how swiftly her pulse raced when Edison was nearby.

"Miss Greyson," Basil Ware said quietly from the doorway. "I thought I might find you in here."

Emma started in surprise and turned quickly. She summoned a civil smile.

"Good day, Mr. Ware."

He searched her face with somber concern as he walked into the room. "I understand you are to depart today together with most of the rest of my guests."

"Yes. My, uh, fiancé has decided that we should return to Town." She would have to do something about this annoying tendency to stumble over the word *fiancé*. "He feels he should attend to some pressing business affairs."

Basil's mouth curved ruefully. "There is no need to beat about the bush, Miss Greyson. I realize that the sudden announcement of your engagement will create certain, shall we say, complications in your life."

That was putting it mildly, she thought. But she kept her smile firmly fixed in place. She was being paid to act a role and she would do her best. "I have no notion of what you are talking about, sir."

"Come now, Miss Greyson, I understand precisely why and how you have been thrust into this difficult situation."

She frowned in bewilderment. "I see nothing particularly difficult about it."

"Then I fear you have a harsh awakening in store, Miss Greyson."

"I have no notion of your meaning, sir," she said stiffly.

"I think you comprehend me well enough. You are an intelligent woman, Miss Greyson. You must realize that your new circumstances are precarious at best."

With an effort of will, she succeeded in maintaining a serenely blank expression. "Whatever do you mean by that, sir?"

Basil walked to the next bay window and stood looking out over the busy forecourt. His expression was somber. "They are all scurrying back to London like so many bees to the hive. Each hopes to be the first to regale the rest of the ton with an account of Crane's murder and Stokes's sudden engagement."

"The Polite World thrives on gossip," she said neutrally.

"Indeed." He turned his head slightly and gave her a look that combined pity and profound regret. "I blame myself for your unfortunate predicament. Had I been a better host, I would have seen to it that you were protected from the unwanted advances of Chilton Crane. You would not have been forced to defend yourself with an act of violence."

She stared at him. "Are you saying that you believe I shot Mr. Crane?"

"I would not think of making such an accusation." Basil's jaw tightened. "Crane deserved what he got. I, for one, consider that rough justice was done. I only wish that you had not been caught in the coils of the thing. Now I fear you will suffer for your self-defense."

"But I was not caught in any coils, sir. Indeed, I am not involved in any way. My alibi is as solid as the stone walls of Ware Castle. I was with Mr. Stokes at the time of the murder. He explained that quite clearly to your guests last night."

Basil sighed. "Yes, of course. Your alibi is unshakable. And I am glad of it, for your sake. But I must be frank when I tell you that I do not comprehend why Stokes went so far as to announce his engagement to you."

She arched her brows. "I would have thought his reasons were obvious. My reputation was at stake."

Basil shook his head. "Nothing is ever obvious with Stokes. The man plays a deep game. The question is, what game is he playing this time?"

"What makes you think it's a game, sir?"

He turned his head to meet her eyes over his shoulder. There was nothing but gentlemanly concern in his gaze. "If Stokes felt the urge to spring to your defense, all he had to say was that you were with him when Crane was shot."

She struggled to look suitably shocked. "I would have been ruined if he had said such a thing. I was in my nightclothes, sir. Why, your guests would have thought me nothing more than his . . . his current lightskirt." She widened her eyes in what she hoped appeared to be great horror. "They would have assumed that I was his mistress."

Basil swung completely around to face her. "Miss Greyson, please, for your own sake, do not allow yourself to believe that Stokes actually intends to marry you."

"But that is just what he intends to do, sir," she said brightly. "You heard him yourself."

Basil closed his eyes as if in pain. "You are such an innocent."

"Explain yourself, sir. What other plan could Mr. Stokes possibly have in mind?"

"I don't know." Basil's brows came together in a considering frown.

"No one knows Stokes well enough to predict his actions, let alone the reasons behind them."

"May I ask why you feel this great need to warn me about Mr. Stokes's intentions?"

"My conscience pricks me, Miss Greyson. I am aware that I failed in my duties as the master of this house. Because of me, you were put at the mercy of Chilton Crane and now you are at the mercy of Edison Stokes."

"What a peculiar thing to say." She gave Basil a deliberately quizzical look. "I am not at the mercy of any man. Indeed, I consider myself the most fortunate of women. My engagement to Mr. Stokes is the stuff of dreams."

Basil hesitated. Then he inclined his head. "Very well. There is little more I can say except that if things do not work out as you anticipate in these dreams of yours, I pray you will feel free to come to me. I shall see to it that you are provided for, my dear. It is the very least I can do to atone for my negligence as your host."

Before Emma could think of a response, she sensed a movement in the doorway. She turned to see Edison looming very large in the opening. He did not look at her. His ice-cold gaze was fixed on Basil.

"I do not enjoy coming across my fiancée in close conversation with other gentlemen, Ware." He glided farther into the room. "Do I make myself clear?"

"Quite clear, Stokes." Basil gave Emma a small bow. "I apologize if there has been any misunderstanding between us, Miss Greyson. I wish you a pleasant journey back to Town."

He walked to the door of the library and went out into the hall without a backward glance.

Edison looked at Emma.

She was suddenly very conscious of a great silence in the room.

"The stuff of dreams?" Edison repeated with grave interest.

"I thought it had a rather dramatic ring. Perhaps when this business is finished, I shall consider a career on the stage."

Half an hour later Polly slammed shut the lid of Emma's small trunk. "There ye be, Miss Greyson. Yer all packed and ready to set off. I'll go fetch one of the footmen to carry it downstairs for ye."

"Thank you, Polly." Emma glanced around the small, bare bedchamber, assuring herself that she had not forgotten a brush or a garter or a slipper. A paid companion could not afford to be careless with her possessions.

She deliberately avoided looking at the stain on the floor. The servants had tried to scrub out Chilton Crane's blood, but they had not been entirely successful. She turned slowly on her heel, checking the dressing table and washstand.

Her gaze went past the small square of framed embroidery that hung on the wall. She glanced at the open wardrobe. It was empty. The handful of faded gowns she possessed were all safely stowed in the trunk.

The only personal item left in the room was Sally Kent's framed needlework. Emma turned back to stare thoughtfully at the framed picture. *A paid companion could not afford to be careless with her possessions.*

Perhaps, she thought, only another woman engaged in the same lonely, unpromising career could comprehend how very odd it was that Sally had neglected to take the needlework with her when she left Ware Castle.

"Polly?"

"Yes, ma'am?" Polly paused in the doorway.

"Do you think anyone would mind if I took Miss Kent's picture with me? I'll leave the frame behind, of course."

Polly looked at the embroidery with mild surprise. "Do ye really like it?"

"Yes, very much."

Polly grinned. "I'll talk to Mrs. Gatten. But I don't think there'll be any problem. No one here at the castle cares about the thing, and I know Mrs. Gatten would be delighted to give ye a little token of thanks. Go ahead and take it out of the frame."

"Thank you," Emma said.

She waited until Polly hurried off. Then she went to the wall and reached up to take down the little picture. It was surprisingly heavy in her hand. And thick, she thought.

The wooden frame came apart easily. When Emma took off the backing, a letter, several banknotes, and a small, daintily embroidered handkerchief fell to the floor.

Stunned, she bent down to scoop up the notes. She counted swiftly. And then recounted because she could not believe the first sum. *Two hundred pounds.*

"A bloody fortune for a paid companion," she whispered.

It was inconceivable that Sally Kent had left two hundred pounds behind by accident. It was enough money to purchase a small house and have sufficient funds left over for some investments. With such a stake an enterprising person could rent out rooms and live off the income.

Sally Kent could not possibly have forgotten about two hundred pounds hidden in a picture frame.

Emma glanced at the name on the letter. *Miss Judith Hope.* The address was in London. The missive was quite short and had obviously been written in haste.

My Dear Judith:

Please forgive this brief note. I know you are greatly concerned for me. Rest assured that I am well and perfectly safe. My plans are coming along nicely. I have already secured two hundred pounds and am in expectation of receiving another fifty in a fortnight. It is quite in-

credible. Only think of what we shall be able to do with two hundred and fifty pounds, my dear.

Do not be anxious. The prospect of both of us escaping our wretched careers is worth every risk.

I cannot wait until this is finished, dearest. I shall join you within the month. We shall look for a house together.

Yours, Ever and Truly,
S.

P.S.   I made the handkerchief as a gift for you. It is for your collection of unusual blooms. When we have our own cottage, you will be able to plant a real garden.

Emma stared at the letter, dumbfounded, until the sound of voices in the hall jerked her out of the small trance. Polly was returning with one of the footmen.

She hoisted up a handful of her skirts. Hastily she stuffed the letter, the handkerchief, and the banknotes into the pockets she wore tied to her waist beneath the heavy gray bombazine traveling gown.

She let her skirts fall back into place just as Polly appeared in the doorway. A burly footman loomed behind her.

"Albert here will take yer trunk down for ye, Miss Greyson. By the way, Mrs. Gatten says to tell ye to take the needlework with her blessing."

Emma cleared her throat. "Please tell her how very much I appreciate her kindness."

One thing was certain, she thought as she watched Albert heft her trunk. Whatever else had happened the night Sally Kent disappeared from Ware Castle, she had certainly not packed her own possessions. Contrary to what Polly and Mrs. Gatten believed, someone else had performed that task. Someone who did not know about the money hidden behind the framed needlework.

There were very few reasons why a companion who had gotten her-self turned off without references would have left the money behind. None of them boded well for the fate of Sally Kent.

Emma paused at the doorway of the little bedchamber and surveyed it one last time. Her first impression had been correct, she thought. It was not only depressing; there was, indeed, an atmosphere of malevolence about the place.

She hurried toward the staircase, overwhelmingly glad to be leaving Ware Castle.

Chapter Twelve

I knew this would be great fun." Letty swept through the front door of her town house. "Did I not tell you that you had possibilities, my dear?"

"I believe you did say something of the kind," Emma said.

She untied her bonnet strings as she followed her former employer into the hall. Shopping with Letty required stamina. She craved a cup of tea.

"My modiste knew just what to do with your bosom," Letty said with great satisfaction. "I was certain she would."

"You don't think that she plans to cut my new gowns a bit too low?" Emma asked dubiously.

"Nonsense. Low necklines are all the fashion, my dear."

"I shall take your word for it." The cut of her necklines was the least of her concerns, Emma thought.

The gowns had cost much more than she would collect in her wages. She wondered if she could convince Edison to let her keep them when this affair was ended. Surely there must be some way to pawn dresses the way one did jewelry and candlesticks.

"Whatever you say, Letty." Emma started toward the stairs. "If you don't mind, I believe I shall have a tray of tea in my room. I feel the need of some rest. You have exhausted me."

"Run along, my dear. You must get all the rest you can. You will need it. I have accepted at least a dozen evening invitations for you for the next week alone. To say nothing of the afternoon calls that must be paid."

Fortunately, Emma thought as she went up the stairs, she would not have to cope with the rigors of Society for long.

On the landing she turned and went down the hall to her bed-chamber. She opened the door with a sense of relief. Unlike the dismal little chamber at Ware Castle, this room, with its yellow-and-white-striped wallpaper and white curtains, looked cheerful and welcoming. There was even a pleasant view of the wooded park across the street.

She removed her new green pelisse and sat down on the little satin-covered chair near the writing desk. A knock sounded on the door. The tea tray, with any luck, she thought.

"Enter, please."

The door opened to reveal Bess, one of the maids, and two foot-men. All of them were heavily laden with boxes.

"Madam said that I'm to put away all yer lovely new things." Bess was bubbling with excitement. "She says I'm to be yer personal lady's maid."

A lady's maid, indeed. Life had certainly changed in the past few days, Emma thought. She felt as if she were in the middle of a fairy tale.

She eyed the heaps of boxes that were being carried into her bedchamber. She would not get any rest here. Bess would want to examine and exclaim over each new pair of gloves and every cap and petticoat.

A brisk walk would be more refreshing than a cup of tea, she decided. The need to get away from the ceaseless demands of her new post for a while was almost overpowering. And she did have a private matter to pursue, one she had put off for the past two days since the return to London because of her commitments to Edison.

"Very well, Bess." Emma got to her feet and went to the wardrobe to take out the pelisse she had hung there a few minutes earlier. "If Lady Mayfield inquires about me, please tell her that I am taking a walk in the park."

"Will you be wanting one of the footmen to go with you, ma'am?"

"No, I think I can manage to walk across the street without assistance."

Bess's round face crinkled with concern. "But do ye think ye should be walking out alone, ma'am?"

Emma raised her brows as she refastened the pelisse. "Why ever not, for heaven's sake? I have taken many walks in the park."

Bess flushed a dull red and looked extremely uncomfortable. "Aye, but that was before ye was engaged to Mr. Stokes."

Emma stared at her. "Good heavens, Bess. Are you worried about my reputation?"

Bess looked at her toes. "Well, it's just that engaged ladies are supposed to be discreet like."

"Bear in mind that until quite recently I was Lady Mayfield's paid companion, Bess. I assure you, I am nothing if not discreet."

Bess flinched at the sharp tone. Annoyed with herself for having snapped at the girl, Emma sighed, grabbed her reticule, and walked swiftly out the door.

It took her much longer than she had expected to find the address. Eventually, however, Emma came to a halt in front of a small, gloomy little house in Twigg Lane. She opened her reticule, took out the letter addressed to Miss Judith Hope, and verified the address. Number eleven.

This was the place.

She went up the steps and knocked. While she waited for a response, she glanced at the little watch pinned to the bodice of her gown. She could not stay long here in Twigg Lane. Edison would be annoyed if she was not ready promptly at five for the drive in the park. Employers expected punctuality from their employees.

There was a long pause before she heard footsteps in the hall. A moment later the door opened. A sour looking housekeeper regarded her with grim disapproval.

"Please inform Miss Judith Hope that Miss Emma Greyson is calling with a message from a friend."

Dark suspicion scrunched up the housekeeper's stolid features. "What friend would that be?"

"Miss Sally Kent."

"Never heard of her." The housekeeper started to close the door.

Emma stepped nimbly across the threshold and put out a hand to prevent the door from being slammed in her face. She glanced quickly into the dingy hall and saw a flight of narrow stairs.

"You will inform Miss Hope that she has a visitor," Emma said crisply.

"Now, see here—"

A woman's voice, flat and dreary in tone, came from halfway up the stairs. "Is something wrong, Mrs. Bowie?"

Mrs. Bowie glowered at Emma. "I'm just seeing this here lady on her way. She has come to the wrong address."

"I have come to call upon Miss Judith Hope and I will not leave until I have seen her," Emma said loudly.

"You wish to see me?" The woman hovering in the shadows of the staircase sounded bewildered.

116

"If you are Miss Hope, the answer is yes. My name is Emma Greyson. I have a message from Sally Kent."

"Dear God. A message from Sally? But . . . but that's impossible."

"If you will see me for a few minutes, Miss Hope, I shall explain everything."

Judith hesitated. "Show her in, Mrs. Bowie."

"You know very well that the mistress don't want any visitors," Mrs. Bowie growled.

"Miss Greyson is here to see me, not Mrs. Morton." Judith's tone of voice abruptly grew more firm and determined. "Show her in at once."

Mrs. Bowie continued to look mutinous. Emma gave her a cold smile and shoved hard against the door.

Mrs. Bowie reluctantly stepped back. Emma moved quickly into the dark hall and turned to look at Judith Hope. She concluded instantly that the woman had been sadly misnamed. *Hope* was a word that had probably disappeared long ago from her vocabulary.

Judith was very likely in her late twenties, but the grimly resigned lines were already deeply etched in what had no doubt once been an attractive face. She was dressed in a dull brown gown. Her hair was scraped back beneath a plain cap. Only the angle of her chin hinted at a deep core of pride and a grim determination.

She crossed the tiny hall with a rigid spine. "Please come into the parlor, Miss Greyson."

Emma followed her into a heavily draped room and took a seat on the threadbare sofa. There was no fire on the hearth. Judith did not pull the curtains or light a candle. She simply sat down stiffly, folded her hands in her lap, and stared at Emma with an unreadable expression.

"Forgive me for calling on you without an invitation, Miss Hope."

For the first time a tiny hint of emotion flickered in Judith's eyes. "I assure you, I have no objection, Miss Greyson. You are the first visitor I have had since I accepted my current post six months

117

ago. My employer does not encourage social calls. Nor do we go out."

Emma glanced at the ceiling, silently indicating the rooms above, where she presumed the mysterious Mrs. Morton resided. "Will your employer object to me being here?"

"Probably. She objects to everything else, from the taste of the soup to the books I read to her." Judith's hands tightened together. "But I am prepared to risk her wrath if you have news of Sally."

"I am not certain how to begin. The truth is, I do not know anything about Sally. I have never met her."

"I see." Judith looked down at her folded hands. "I am not surprised. I have known for several months that she is likely dead."

"Dead?" Emma stared at her. "How can you be certain of that?"

Judith looked toward the draped window. "Sally and I were friends. We were . . . quite close. I think I would know if she was still alive."

"What makes you believe that she is dead?"

"I have not heard from her," Judith said with stark simplicity. "She would have contacted me by now if she were still on this earth."

"I see."

"As I said, we were very fond of each other. Neither of us has any family, you see. We had planned to save whatever we could and eventually rent a small cottage in the country. But now that will never happen."

Judith's quiet, stoic despair nearly broke Emma's heart. "I am so very sorry."

Judith turned back to her. "You said you had a message from her?"

"Please let me explain. I was employed until quite recently as a companion. A few days ago I accompanied my employer to a house party at Ware Castle."

Judith's face tightened. "That is where Sally went to work as Lady Ware's paid companion."

"I know. As it happens, I was given the bedchamber that once belonged to her." Emma reached into her reticule and removed Sally's letter. "I found this behind a scrap of embroidery. It is addressed to you."

"Dear heaven." Judith took the letter very gingerly and opened it as though half afraid of the contents. She read the note quickly and then looked up. Tears glistened in her eyes. "Forgive me. But now I know for certain that she is dead. He murdered her."

Emma went cold. "What are you saying? Do you mean to imply that Basil Ware murdered Sally?"

"That is precisely what I mean." Judith's hand clenched tightly around the letter. "And he will never be brought to justice because of his wealth and position."

"But why would he do such a thing?"

"Because she had become inconvenient, of course. Sally was very beautiful, you see. She was certain that she could handle Ware. I warned her but she would not listen to me. I think she must have allowed him to seduce her. She had a scheme, which she would not confide to me."

"What sort of scheme do you think it was?"

"I believe that she lied to him, told him that she was pregnant. She probably had some notion of promising to go away if he would give her some money."

"I see."

Judith looked down at the letter. "I warned her not to take such terrible risks. But she was determined to rescue both of us from our dreary careers. Obviously Ware became infuriated by her demands and killed her."

Emma sighed. Judith's logic was extremely weak. Rakes of the ton had no need to resort to murder to get rid of inconvenient lovers. They simply ignored them. It was clear that Judith was so distraught with grief that she felt the need to blame Sally's seducer for her death.

"Even if Sally was involved in a liaison with Mr. Ware," Emma said gently, "he had no reason to kill her, Miss Hope. We both know how these things work. All he had to do was dismiss her from her post when he grew weary of her. Which, from all accounts, is precisely what happened."

"If he threw her out of the castle, where is she?" Judith demanded fiercely. "Why did she fail to post this letter?"

Emma hesitated. "I do not know the answers to all of your questions, but I can tell you that the letter is not all she left behind."

"What do you mean?"

Emma glanced toward the parlor door to make certain that it was closed. Then she quickly lifted the skirts of her new muslin walking dress. She reached into one of the pockets she wore and withdrew the tightly folded banknotes and the handkerchief. She handed them to Judith.

"I don't understand." Judith gazed, slack-jawed, at the notes. Then she lifted her uncomprehending eyes to Emma. "How did you—?"

"Hush." Emma looked meaningfully at the door. On the chance that the housekeeper might have her ear to the panel, she leaned closer to Judith and lowered her voice. "I would say nothing about this if I were you."

"But this is . . . this is a fortune," Judith whispered.

"I found the banknotes and the little handkerchief with the letter. It is obvious Sally meant for you to have the money. Ware must have given it to her, so it was hers to pass along to you."

"But—"

Emma plucked the handkerchief from Judith's hand and unfolded it to reveal an unusual bloom done in crimson and purple threads. "Lovely work. I do not recognize the species, however. I wonder if it was something she saw in Lady Ware's conservatory."

Judith stared numbly at the flower. "Sally embroidered an entire garden of handkerchiefs for me. She knew how much I loved unusual blooms. She always said that one day we would have a real garden with real flowers."

"I see." Emma got to her feet. She raised her voice to a normal conversational level. "If you will excuse me, I must be on my way, Miss

Hope. I am supposed to drive out in the park with my, er, fiancé, this afternoon at five o'clock."

Judith rose slowly. "Yes, of course." She swallowed. "Miss Greyson, I do not know how to thank you."

"No thanks are necessary." Emma lowered her voice again. "I only wish your friend Sally were here so that the two of you could look for that little cottage together."

"So do I." Judith closed her eyes briefly. "My wonderful, reckless Sally. If only she had listened to me."

"I suppose you very wisely advised her not to fall in love with Mr. Ware." Emma sighed. "It is always a mistake to become romantically involved with one's employer."

"Fall in love with him?" Judith's gaze widened. "Whatever happened at Ware Castle, I can assure you, Sally never loved Basil Ware."

"How can you know that?"

Judith hesitated. "Without putting too fine a point on it, Miss Greyson, I can tell you that Sally was not fond of men. It is inconceivable that she would have enjoyed an affair with Ware."

"I see."

"If she allowed him to seduce her, it was because she hoped to acquire some money from him when the liaison ended. She always said we had to do something to change our fates."

"Sally has seen to it that you have enough money to change your fate, Miss Hope. What will you do now?"

Judith glanced up at the ceiling. Then she smiled for the first time. It was a very small, very grim sort of smile, but it was genuine. "Why, I believe I shall hand in my notice."

Emma grinned. "Something tells me that is exactly what Sally would have wanted you to do."

"You have made great progress, Edison." Ignatius Lorring handed Edison a glass of brandy and then lowered his birdlike frame into the other wingback chair. "I had every expectation that you would, of course. There was never another student like you. When I think of how high you could have risen within the great Circle of Vanza—"

"We both know that the way of Vanza would not have suited me forever," Edison said.

The room was uncomfortably warm. There was a roaring blaze on the hearth although the day was sunny and mild. Edison said nothing about the heat. Ignatius wore a woolen scarf around his throat as though he was sitting in the middle of a snowstorm rather than in his library. There was a small blue vial on the table beside him. Edison knew that it contained an opium concoction. Laudanum, perhaps.

Edison glanced around the familiar room. His transition from wild, reckless youth to self-controlled man had begun here. It was in this mirrored chamber with its walls of books that he had first met Ignatius.

Edison had been eighteen and desperate for a post, any sort of post. He had read Ignatius Lorring's papers on Vanzagara and was aware that the intrepid scholar was planning another voyage to that mysterious island.

Edison had approached Ignatius with a proposition. If Lorring would take him along on his voyage as his man-of-affairs, he would work for half the usual wages. Ignatius had immediately hired him. The pair had sailed for Vanzagara and nothing had ever been the same again.

"How are you feeling, my friend?" Edison asked gently.

"I have my good days and my bad ones. This morning I felt well enough to take a walk. But now I am extremely weary."

"I do not intend to stay long. I have an appointment to drive with my fiancée in the park this afternoon at five."

"Ah, yes. The fiancée." Ignatius's silvery brows bounced up and down. A gleam of interest sparked in his pale eyes. "Lady Ames wants her, and you have control over her. Brilliant, Edison. Quite brilliant.

She is a glittering lure with which to hold Lady Ames's attention while you pursue your inquiries."

Edison turned the glass in his hand and studied the golden hue of the brandy. "I do not think of Miss Greyson as bait."

"Nonsense. That is precisely what she is." Ignatius eyed him sharply. "Tell me, did she actually shoot Crane?"

"She denies it."

"Well, she would, of course, would she not?"

"Perhaps. Perhaps not. Miss Greyson is somewhat unpredictable."

"I see."

"I will say this much," Edison continued softly. "If Miss Greyson did not shoot Crane, some interesting questions arise."

Ignatius was silent for a long time. "Yes. I see what you mean."

Edison contemplated the infinity of mirrors that surrounded the fireplace. "Before we make any further moves, I think it would be extremely interesting to find out how Miranda came to be in possession of the deciphered recipe."

"Indeed." Ignatius looked thoughtful. "I do not see how a woman could even know about it, let alone get her hands on it. There are no females involved in Vanza."

Edison thought about the wild shot someone had taken in the woods outside Ware Castle. "Tell me, Ignatius, do you believe it's possible that there are others on the trail of the *Book of Secrets*?"

"I have not heard any rumors to that effect, but it is not inconceivable." Ignatius's thin hands curled very tightly around the arms of his chair. "Why do you ask?"

"I'm not certain yet. But there are a great many unexplained elements in this affair. Some of them would make sense if we knew that there was someone else searching for the book."

"Bloody hell." Ignatius's face was drawn so tightly that his features had a skeletal appearance. "If there is someone else looking for it, he might well conclude that you are in his way. Do have a care, will you?

I should hate to lose the most promising student that I ever had, even if he did eventually go outside the Circle."

"Of course." Edison put down his glass. "After all, now that I am about to become a married man, I must consider my future."

"What the devil do you mean Miss Greyson is not home?" Edison scowled at Lady Mayfield's housekeeper. "She bloody well knew that we had an appointment to ride in the park today."

Mrs. Wilton wiped her hands on her crisp white apron. "I'm sorry, sir, but she went out for a walk some time ago and has not yet returned."

"Where did she go?"

"I couldn't say, sir."

Letty appeared on the stairs. "It's you, is it, Stokes? Thought I heard your voice. Looking for Emma, are you?"

"Yes." He glanced at her. "What's this about her going for a walk?"

"Quite right. Her maid tells me she went into the park across the street."

"I just drove through the park. I did not see Emma."

Letty lifted one shoulder in a small shrug. "Perhaps she went a bit farther."

An uneasy feeling trickled through Edison. "You said her maid told you she'd gone for a walk. Do you mean to say that the girl did not accompany Emma?"

"Apparently Emma wanted to be by herself for a while." Letty came down the stairs. "I believe she is feeling quite overwhelmed by all the excitement. She is not accustomed to it, you know."

It would take a good deal to overwhelm Emma, Edison thought. But it was possible that she had had enough of the demands of her new position for a while and had given herself the afternoon off. Nevertheless, he had sent a message with specific instructions for her to be ready at five.

124

She was only a few minutes late, he thought, glancing at the hall clock. Perhaps he was overreacting. Some women made a point of keeping a man waiting. It was the fact that no one seemed to know precisely where she was that bothered him the most.

It occurred to him for the first time that he did not know all that much about Emma Greyson. She might well have friends here in Town.

Or a lover.

The thought hit him with the force of a thunderbolt. *What if Emma had gone out alone to meet a man?*

And what business was it of his if she had? In spite of the circumstances, she considered him her employer, not her fiancé. And that was exactly what he was, he reminded himself, her employer.

"Bloody hell," he muttered. "She cannot be far off. I shall go and look for her."

"But where will you—?" Letty broke off as the front door opened. She beamed. "Here she is now."

Emma walked through the doorway and came to a halt at the sight of the small group gathered in the hall.

"Oh dear," she murmured a bit too innocently. "Am I late?"

"Yes," Edison said. "Where the devil have you been?" He caught sight of Letty's elevated brow and immediately regretted the tone of his voice. Newly engaged men did not speak that way to their fiancées, he reminded himself. He had to remember his role in this charade. He cleared his throat. "I was a trifle concerned."

"I took a walk," she said airily, heading for the stairs. "I'm afraid I went a little farther than I had planned. Don't worry, it won't take me more than a few minutes to change. I shall be ready shortly, sir."

Edison studied her critically as she dashed up the stairs. She looked slightly flushed, perhaps from her exertions. She had no doubt quickened her pace on the way back to Letty's house because she had realized that she was late.

But that same degree of warmth could have been caused by a man's lovemaking. She had looked just as heated when he himself had kissed her. He caught a glimpse of her kid half-boots as she went up the steps. They were stained with a reddish mud. The paths in the park were covered with gravel.

Wherever it was that she had gone, it had been a good deal farther than the park.

CHAPTER THIRTEEN

Lady Mayfield was right." Edison's mouth curved with icy satisfaction as he led Emma out onto the dance floor later that evening. "You are, indeed, a sensation."

"Do not be deceived, sir. The ton finds me temporarily fascinating only because of the circumstances of our engagement. Most of Lady Ames's guests believe that I really am a murderess. They cannot imagine why you would choose to save me from the hangman's noose."

Edison looked unconcerned. "It will give them something to talk about while we pursue our inquiries."

Who would have thought that she would one day find herself dancing the night away in the arms of the most intriguing man she had ever met? Emma thought. Her gown was a delicious confection of pale green. Her hair was studded with small green leaves fashioned of silk. She was back in the fairy tale.

Edison, of course, was his usual devastatingly elegant self. She wondered where he had learned the trick of looking so formidable and so perfectly attired at the same time. He danced with a powerful, effortless grace. His dark hair gleamed in the light of the chandeliers.

She could not wait to write a letter to her sister telling her all of the details of this night.

It was strange, and a bit disconcerting, to find herself on the dance floor rather than watching from the side of the ballroom. It was even more disturbing to find herself dancing with Edison. The moment would have been a good deal more enjoyable, possibly even thrilling, if it were not for the fact that her employer was in a foul mood. He had been in one all afternoon.

He had kept his expression polite during the ritual afternoon promenade, but she knew that was for the sake of onlookers. After a few polite attempts to make conversation, she had abandoned the effort and ignored him for the duration of the forty minutes they had spent displaying themselves to the ton in the park.

His temper had not improved much by the time he had arrived at Miranda's ball to join Letty and Emma.

The music swelled in the lilting strains of the waltz. Edison swung Emma smoothly into a long, gliding turn. She was intensely aware of his hand, strong and warm, on her back. The expensive gowns of the other ladies on the dance floor whirled past like so many gossamer jellyfish caught in the waves of an invisible sea.

But for Edison's dark mood, it would have been a magical evening. Emma's patience evaporated.

"I vow, you are no better than any of my previous employers," she said.

"I beg your pardon?" He brought her to an abrupt halt near the terrace doors. "What are you talking about?"

"Under normal circumstances it would not matter, of course. No one expects employers to be civil to employees." She gave him a steely smile. "However, in this instance, I feel obliged to point out that you may be ruining the very impression you wish to create."

She saw the glint of irritation in his eyes and knew that he comprehended her meaning perfectly.

"Let's go outside." He seized her arm. "I feel the need of some fresh air."

"Whatever you say, Mr. Stokes."

"Do not, whatever you do, use that tone of voice with me."

"What tone is that, sir?"

"The one that makes you sound as though you are addressing a recalcitrant idiot."

"I assure you, sir, I do not think of you as an idiot, recalcitrant or otherwise," she murmured as he swept her out onto the terrace. "Difficult, moody, and occasionally rude, but definitely not an idiot."

He slanted her an enigmatic glance. "Just one more difficult employer in a long line of the species, is that it?"

"Indeed." She smiled coolly. "By the bye, have you completed my reference yet?"

"No, I have not."

"You did promise to write one straight off," she said reproachfully. "We struck a bargain, if you will recall."

His hand tightened on her arm. "I have not forgotten the terms."

"Ouch."

"Sorry." The line of his jaw was rigid. Nevertheless, he slackened his grip and brought her to a halt at the edge of the terrace. "I've been extremely busy since we returned to Town. I have not yet had time to attend to the matter of writing your reference."

"Are you certain you don't want to borrow some copies of the ones I wrote myself? It really will make it much simpler for you."

He looked out over the night-shrouded gardens. "Miss Greyson, if you want my signature on your bloody reference, you will allow me to pen it myself."

She said nothing.

He turned slightly, braced one mirror-polished boot on the low stone wall, and studied her with unreadable eyes. "Since we are discussing our relationship as employer and employee, I may as well take this opportunity to inform you that I do not want you to go off on your own again the way you did this afternoon."

From out of nowhere anger exploded within her, a bright, hot shower of fireworks that would have done credit to Vauxhall Gardens.

"Mr. Stokes, you go too far. Every employee is entitled to an afternoon off at least once a week. Even the meanest of my previous employers granted that much."

"I hardly think you can complain that I am an overly demanding employer. I doubt that you were so well dressed in any of your other posts." He frowned at the low neckline of her gown. "Although, I will point out that you were a good deal more modestly attired before you took this position."

"Lady Mayfield assures me this gown is in the first stare of fashion."

"*Stare* is a particularly appropriate word, Miss Greyson. Every man in the room has *stared* at your bosom this evening."

"I'll admit that the *livery* you have provided for this post is superior to what I have worn in my other positions, but that does not—"

"Livery?" He gave the jewel-toned silk skirts a meaningful look. "You dare call that gown *livery*? Livery is what footmen wear."

"As far as I am concerned, livery is what an employer requires an employee to wear. The gowns that I am obliged to wear in my role as your fiancée constitute livery so far as I am concerned."

He leaned closer. She could see the dangerous glitter in his narrowed eyes, but she refused to give in to the urge to step back.

"Miss Greyson, am I correct in saying that the gown you have on tonight cost me a good deal more than you received in wages in your last three posts combined?"

"Indeed, it did, sir." She raised a gloved finger. "Actually, that brings up another point I wish to discuss with you. I assume that when I have completed my duties, you will have no particular need of the gowns and bonnets you have purchased for me to wear."

"Of course I won't need them."

"Then I would like to ask you if you would allow me to keep them after I leave your service."

"Do you really think that you will have any occasions to wear a closetful of expensive ball gowns in your next post, Miss Greyson?"

"Highly unlikely." She forced herself not to succumb to the wretched feeling she got whenever she considered the prospect of leaving Edison's service. "But I suspect I may be able to pawn some of them."

"Bloody hell." He sounded genuinely incensed. "You intend to pawn the gowns I bought for you?"

"It is not as if they have some sentimental value, sir."

"I see." He caught her chin on the edge of his hand. "What sort of gift would you consider to have sentimental value?"

"Sir, we are straying from the topic—"

"Answer my question. What sort of gift would you consider sentimental, Miss Greyson?"

He was even angrier than she was. She did not understand it, but she had a feeling discretion might be the better part of valor. He was, after all, her employer. She could not afford to lose this post.

"Well, I suppose I would consider a book of poetry or a pretty handkerchief to have some personal, sentimental value," she said cautiously.

"A book of poetry?"

"I enjoy Byron enormously," she went on hastily. "I am also very fond of horrid novels, especially those by Mrs. York. I vow, she writes the most exciting tales of dark mysteries—"

Something in his eyes made her stop quite suddenly. For an instant she thought she had made a serious miscalculation. So much for trying to placate him. Edison looked furious.

But even as she watched him warily, she could see him apply the full force of his iron control to his temper.

"You're right, Miss Greyson," he said much too evenly. "We stray from the topic. I believe we were discussing my new instructions. From now on, you will not disappear for hours on end. You will make certain that you are accompanied by someone whenever you leave the house, and you will inform the housekeeper where you are going and precisely when you will return."

Her sensible notions of placating him went out the window. She could not remember the last time she had been so furious. "You have no right to give me orders of that nature. My free time is my own. You are not my husband, sir."

"No. I am not your husband. I am your employer." He gave her a grim smile. "And you need this post very badly, so you will obey my instructions. I do not think there is anything else to be said."

"Quite right. You have said more than enough." She whirled and started toward the open doors.

He reached out and caught her arm. "Where do you think you're going?"

"To the ladies' withdrawing room, Mr. Stokes. I trust that meets with your approval. Or are you going to forbid me to attend to matters of a personal nature while I am in your employ?"

His mouth tightened. There was not enough light to allow Emma to tell whether or not he had turned a dull red, but she rather thought he had. Served him right.

Edison inclined his head very formally. "When you return I shall meet you near the foot of the stairs. We have spent enough time here tonight. I do not want Miranda to think that we are so eager for her invitations. Best to keep her uncertain. She is far more likely to give herself away if she remains anxious."

"I understand, sir." Damn his eyes, she thought. She could be just as formal and correct. "I shall look for you near the staircase."

She did not look back as she swept into the crowded ballroom.

•   •   •

A few minutes later she emerged from the withdrawing room and walked back toward the main staircase. She was pleased with herself. She had her emotions back under control and her thoughts in logical order once more.

It worried her that Edison seemed to have an increasingly unsettling effect on her emotions. It was not wise for her to spend any longer in his employ than necessary, she thought.

The sooner he completed his inquiries, the sooner she would get paid and the sooner this entire affair would be finished. It was in her own best interests to do everything she could to assist him.

The music and the hum of conversation reverberated up from the ballroom below. She glanced down the hall and noticed the darkness that marked the servants' staircase. As she watched she saw a familiar figure emerge from a room and disappear into the gloom. Swan.

A flicker of curiosity shot through her.

She wondered why Miranda's devoted footman had not bothered to take a candle to light his way along the darkened stairs.

She paused. It was almost as if Swan did not want anyone to see him, she thought. Which brought up the obvious question of why he was attempting to conceal himself in the very house where he was employed.

Swan was part of the mystery that surrounded Miranda. Emma knew it with a certainty that defied logic. His secretive behavior tonight aroused her intuition. It would not hurt to follow him and see what he was about.

She hesitated a moment longer and then made her decision. Turning, she went quietly down the hall. When she reached the servants' staircase, she peered into the gloom. There was no sign of Swan. He had disappeared into a well of dense shadows.

She gripped the banister firmly and went cautiously down the narrow, twisting steps. When one tread groaned softly beneath her foot, she froze.

But Swan did not loom up out of the darkness to confront her.

After a moment she continued downward, past the ballroom floor, all the way down to the ground floor. She used the toe of her dancing slippers to feel for the edge of each step. It would be extremely embarrassing to tumble headfirst down the servants' stairs here in Miranda's house, she thought. Edison would no doubt be annoyed.

A short time later she emerged in the back hall. There was a door that opened onto the large garden. She could see the dark shapes of the hedges through sidelight windows.

She paused again in the shadows and listened intently. The ballroom was now above her. She could still hear the music, muffled though it was by the ceiling. The voices of arriving and departing guests echoed from the front hall. They sounded very far away.

There was enough moonlight filtering through the windows to allow her to see the door directly across from her. The library, perhaps. Or a study. Just the sort of room where one might hide a valuable book.

She wondered why Edison had not thought to search the house during the ball. Now that the notion had struck her, it seemed an obvious course of action.

There was no reason she could not carry out the task herself. How hard could it be to search a library for an ancient manuscript?

Before she could lose her nerve, she crossed the hall and twisted the doorknob. If there was anyone inside to take exception to her entrance, she could always claim to have gotten lost looking for the ladies' withdrawing room.

She opened the door and slipped inside. Shafts of moonlight poured through a bank of high Palladian windows, creating geometric shapes on the carpet. The walls were lost in dense shadows, but the large globe, the decorative classical busts, and the broad desk told her that she was, indeed, in a library.

There were very few books on the shelves that lined the walls, she noticed. Miranda obviously followed the current fashion, which held that books were not a terribly important component of the properly decorated library.

She decided to start her search with the desk. It stood squarely in a patch of silvery moonlight, and it seemed a likely place to hide a stolen volume.

She hurried across the room. Her kid dancing slippers made no sound on the soft carpet. She circled the desk and opened the first drawer. Disappointment struck immediately when she saw only an array of quills and extra bottles of ink inside.

The next two drawers revealed nothing more mysterious than a stack of foolscap and a scattering of calling cards and invitations.

The last drawer, the one on the bottom, was locked.

Excitement bubbled up inside her. There was something important in the bottom drawer. Why else would Miranda have taken the trouble to lock it?

She reached up to her elegantly dressed hair and cautiously removed one of the green silk leaves. The pin the hairdresser had used to secure the decoration might work on the lock.

It would not be the first time that she had used a hairpin to unlock a desk drawer, she reflected. In the last few months of her long life, Granny Greyson had grown increasingly befuddled and forgetful. She had developed the unshakable conviction that the local vicar was determined to steal her few valuables. Whenever he came to visit, Granny locked her cameos, wedding ring, and the pearls her mother had given her in the drawer of her writing desk. Inevitably she had misplaced the key. She had been fretful and anxious until Emma had picked the lock and retrieved the items.

Emma slid the hairpin into the lock of Miranda's desk.

And went very still at the sound of a footstep in the hall.

Someone was standing on the other side of the library door.

"It's about time you got back, Swan." Miranda's voice was low and tight with anger. "What on earth took you so long?"

135

There was an unintelligible rumble of response. Although the words were indistinct, there was no mistaking the rasping growl of Swan's voice.

A terrible chill shot through Emma. It was a bit too late to get a premonition of danger, she thought. She was already in serious trouble. That was the problem with her intuition. It never seemed to work properly when she needed it.

She straightened quickly. Miranda and Swan were about to enter the library. If one of them lit a taper, they would see her immediately.

Frantically she searched the shadows for a hiding place. There was barely enough moonlight to make out the heavy drapes. They were her only hope. She hurried to the last window and stepped behind a waterfall of dark velvet. Instantly she was enveloped in a stifling, stygian darkness.

She heard the door open even before the fringe on the drapes stopped swaying.

Chapter Fourteen

What do you mean, you found nothing?" Miranda's words were shards of glass. "You had ample time to search Stokes's study. There must have been something there that would tell me why he has taken such an interest in Miss Greyson."

"I did as you instructed, madam." Swan's harsh voice was a river of grinding stones. "I found only books and papers relating to his scholarly pursuits."

"You have failed me, Swan."

"I did as you commanded." Swan sounded pathetically desperate. "You cannot blame me for the fact that there was nothing of interest in Stokes's study."

"There must have been something in that bastard's house

that could have explained his actions at Ware Castle," Miranda snapped. "It is inconceivable that he has engaged himself to Miss Greyson simply because he wishes to marry her."

"Perhaps he is in love with her," Swan suggested softly.

Hah, Emma thought. Not bloody likely.

"Hah," Miranda said aloud. "Not bloody likely. With his wealth and power he could look infinitely higher for a wife. You must have missed something. Go back and take another look. There is still time. He will not return home until dawn."

"Madam, please, it is not easy to get into the house unnoticed. I barely escaped discovery as it was."

"You will go back. Now. Tonight."

"Madam, if I am caught I will be taken up on charges of burglary."

"Then you must be very cautious," Miranda said without any indication of sympathy. "Try his bedchamber this time. Look for anything that will tell me what game he is playing. Letters. A journal, perhaps. Anything."

"His *bedchamber*. I could never get up the stairs unnoticed. Madam, I beg you, do not send me to that house again. The risk is too great."

"Are you refusing to carry out your instructions?"

"Please, don't ask this of me, madam."

"Do you refuse?"

"Yes, *yes*, I must. Don't you see? It is wrong. I could be hung or transported if I am caught. Please, madam, I have done everything you have asked of me until this. It is not fair for you to demand such a task of me."

"Very well, you may consider yourself dismissed from my service."

"*Miranda*."

The single word was a cry of anguish. Emma felt a stab of pity.

"Collect your things and leave this house at once. I shall find someone else to take your place. A servant who is willing to follow instructions."

The door closed behind her.

For a long moment there was only silence in the room. Then Emma heard a strange, burbling sound. She did not recognize it immediately but after a few seconds she realized that Swan was crying.

The horrible, heart-wrenching sobs shook her to the core. It was all she could do not to rush out from behind the curtain and throw her arms around the man.

When she thought she could bear it no longer, the sobs ceased.

"Damn you, damn you, damn you." Swan's anguish had transmuted itself into rage. "Whore. You sleep with all of them but it's me you come back to when you want your satisfaction. You always come back to Swan, don't you? I'm the only one who knows what you need, you bloody witch."

There was a heavy thud. Emma flinched. She realized that Swan had knocked something large to the floor. A classical bust or perhaps the globe, she thought.

There were more crashes and thumps as other objects struck the carpet. Some bounced. Some shattered. Emma held her breath, listening as Swan worked his way methodically around the room.

"They ought to hang you the way they used to hang witches," Swan bellowed softly.

There was a series of muffled thumps. They sounded as though they came from the vicinity of the desk. A boot striking wood?

"Witch. Whore. Witch. Whore." Something crunched loudly. "I'll teach you to treat Swan as though he were your slave. I'll teach you a lesson."

Emma heard papers rustle. Then she heard the sharp, crisp sound of a match being struck. A frisson of panic shot through her. Dear God, was he going to try to burn the house down? Visions of the crowded ballroom engulfed in smoke and flame danced before her eyes.

She could not delay any longer. She had to act.

"Burn, witch, burn in hell. I will never do your bidding again. Do you hear me, witch? Never again. I will break your spell if it is the last thing I do on this earth."

Emma took a deep breath and pushed aside the curtain. She saw flames, but to her great relief, they were safely confined to the fireplace. Swan had only lit a fire on the hearth.

He stood for a while, head bowed and watched the blaze. His broad shoulders and sturdy frame were outlined against the fiery glow. After a time, he turned and stalked toward the door. He moved through a moonlit rectangle and then into shadow.

The door opened and closed behind him.

Emma waited a heartbeat, afraid that he might return. But his heavy footsteps receded down the hall.

She breathed a sigh of relief. She ought to get out of here, she thought. The only sensible thing to do was leave the library as quickly as possible. But she could not resist going to the fireplace to see what it was that Swan had burned in his fury. She hurried across the carpet.

On her way past the desk, she saw that the bottom drawer, the one she had planned to unlock with a hairpin, had been kicked into splinters. Whatever had been inside was now in the flames.

"Oh my God." Emma picked up her skirts and ran to the fireplace.

Two halves of a large leather box lay on the carpet in front of the hearth. The pile of papers that had evidently been stored inside the box were heaped on the flames.

The fire had taken a firm hold but Emma could make out some of the printing on several of the swiftly crisping pages.

Miss Fanny Clifton as Juliet . . .
. . . appear Monday, June 9 and the following week will in Othello
A brilliant performance.

A divine beauty who makes additional lights unnecessary on the stage . . .

Playbills, Emma thought. And reviews. All swiftly going up in smoke.

She took a step, reaching for the poker. Perhaps she could salvage something from the flames. Something crackled under her slipper. She glanced down and saw that some of the papers had fluttered to the carpet when Swan had emptied the contents of the box into the fireplace.

Abandoning the poker, she scooped up the handful of papers. She rolled them up very tightly and stuffed them into her beaded reticule.

Whirling, she started toward the door.

There was no telltale footstep to warn her. She had her hand on the knob when she felt it move beneath her fingers. She sucked in her breath and jerked backward as the door opened very quietly. There was no time to hide behind the curtains again.

Edison glided silently into the room and closed the door behind him. "I wondered where you had disappeared to, Emma."

She was so light-headed with relief, she wondered she didn't collapse. "If you ever startle me in such a manner again, sir, I vow, I shall faint."

"Somehow I cannot envision you fainting." He glanced at the dying fire. "What the devil are you doing here, anyway?"

There was something wrong with his voice, she thought. It lacked all inflection. She told herself she would worry about that matter later.

"It is a very long story," she said. "And I do not think it would be a good notion to tell it here."

"You may be right." Edison put his ear to the door. "There is someone coming down the hall."

"Oh, no, not again."

"Hush." He took her arm and propelled her swiftly toward the windows.

"If you think to hide, I can recommend the curtains at the far end of the room," Emma whispered. "They are quite voluminous."

He glanced at her. The icy glow of the moon turned his features into a cold mask. Belatedly Emma realized that he was furious.

"Forget the curtains," he said. "We are leaving at once."

Edison brought her to a halt and released her to unlatch one of the windows. He bundled her through the opening without ceremony and then followed quickly.

Emma winced as her delicate slippers sank into damp grass. "Now what do you propose to do?"

"We'll make our way around the side of the house to the terrace and back into the ballroom. If we encounter any of the other guests, they will assume that we are merely returning from a stroll in the gardens."

"Then what?"

"Then," Edison said in that same too-even voice, "I shall summon my carriage and take you home."

"But I came with Lady Mayfield in her coach. She intends to stay out until dawn."

"Letty can do as she pleases. You are going home with me. Immediately."

Emma bristled. "There is no need to take that tone with me, sir. I was only trying to assist you in your inquiries."

"Assist me?" He gave her a sharp, raking glance. "I bloody well did not tell you to go into that library."

"I pride myself on being the sort of employee who shows initiative."

"Is that what you call it? I can think of a variety of other terms—" Edison broke off abruptly. "Damnation."

He shoved her away from him and then whipped around.

"What in the world?" Emma stumbled back against a hedge and threw out a hand to catch herself.

She sensed movement at the corner of her eye. She turned quickly. At first she could see nothing at all. And then she noticed the ghostly shadow flowing around a large, bird-shaped topiary. There was a predatory grace evident in the way the figure advanced on its intended prey.

Prey. The full impact of the word seared through Emma. She suddenly knew with a terrible certainty that this was no ordinary house burglar or footpad. The creature was hunting Edison.

She whirled, her mouth open to scream a warning.

The cry died in her throat. It was clear that Edison was fully aware of the danger.

His whole attention was locked on the shadow coming toward him. There was an impossibly calm, waiting quality about him that made no sense under the circumstances.

She thought about shouting for help but she feared that no one would hear her above the noise of the ballroom. She watched in horror as the two men closed in on each other.

It was then that she finally noticed that Edison was moving with the same singularly liquid grace as his opponent. There was a ghostly aspect about him now, just as there was in his opponent. She could not keep track of him. He appeared to exert little effort yet he shifted position in the blink of an eye.

The two men came together in a deadly parody of a dance. The villain made the first move. His leg swept out in a short arc. Edison slipped to the side, evading the blow.

The villain gave a soft, hoarse cry, leaped high into the air, and lashed out with his foot a second time. Edison was too close to avoid it completely. He twisted, taking the blow on the side of his ribs rather than the center of his chest, but it was enough to make him spin backward.

He fell to the ground. In a blur of bizarre, twisting leaps, the dark ghost moved in for the kill.

"No. Don't hurt him." Emma picked up her skirts and made to rush forward. She had no notion of what she could do to stop the attacker. She only knew that she had to do something before he murdered Edison.

"Stay back, Emma."

Edison's command halted her in her tracks. She stared in amazement as he lashed out with his leg and caught his opponent on the side of his thigh.

The dark ghost reeled backward. Edison rose fluidly to his feet. His expression was stark in the cold light of the moon. There was a dangerous aura about him that she had never seen. She knew in that moment that he was wholly capable of killing. The knowledge shocked her.

The villain apparently recognized the same deadly quality and concluded that the tide of battle had turned against him. He spun away, leaped over a waist-high clump of manicured foliage, and vanished into the night.

Edison shifted slightly. Emma was afraid that he intended to pursue the ghost.

"Edison, no."

He had already stopped and turned back. "You are right. It is too late. I fear he is a good deal younger than I am and would no doubt win a foot race."

"Are you all right?" she asked anxiously.

"Yes."

She watched as he ran his fingers through his hair, made a few adjustments to his snowy white cravat, and straightened his coat. When he was finished he looked as elegant as he had before the fight. There were advantages to wearing so much black, Emma thought. The color was extremely well suited to concealing grass stains.

He took her arm and headed back toward the ballroom with a long, swift stride that forced her to trot. She did not complain.

He frowned at her when they reached the terrace. "You are shivering."

She glanced at him and saw that although he appeared to have himself completely under control, the unholy fires of battle still burned in his eyes.

"I cannot imagine why," she said. "Must be a chill in the air."

Chapter Fifteen

Edison held himself in check until the coachman closed the door and climbed up onto the box. When the vehicle jerked slightly and then moved off down the street, he yanked the curtains shut, sank deep into the corner of the seat, and looked at Emma.

She regarded him with an expression of deep concern. "Are you quite certain that dreadful villain did not hurt you?"

"He did not hurt me." Not seriously, at any rate, he amended silently. He would probably have some bruises on his ribs tomorrow, but it would serve him right. He had been a little slow to react. But then, it had been years since he had been in a Vanza skirmish. Certainly the last thing he had expected tonight was an encounter with a student of the art.

But then, nothing about this affair could be termed ordinary. Least of all his new assistant.

He watched Emma, aware of a strange, brooding sensation coursing through him. He did not understand his present mood. He recalled all too well that a violent fight stirred passions that required willpower to control. But what he was feeling now was new to him. He did not comprehend it but he recognized that it was dangerous.

The golden glow of the carriage lamps struck sparks in Emma's hair and turned her eyes into green gems. The urge to reach out and drag her into his arms was suddenly a fire in his veins. He closed one hand into a fist and forced himself to draw a deep, steadying breath.

Except for the telltale shiver he had felt go through her a few minutes ago on the terrace, she appeared as calm as if she had done nothing more adventurous than dance all evening. Her composure annoyed him even as he was forced to admit that he admired it.

"Most of the ladies back in that ballroom would have had hysterics by now," he muttered.

"I cannot afford to have hysterics yet. I forgot my vinaigrette."

Her flippancy was the last straw. The possibility that she had a lover whom she had met secretly that afternoon had gnawed at him all evening. When he had found her in the library, his first thought was that she had again arranged a secret assignation.

He wanted to rip something to shreds, preferably the delicate silks of her green skirts. While he was at it, he wanted to tear the little green leaves from her hair and watch the fiery tresses fall to her shoulders. And when she was quite naked, he wanted to make love to her. He wanted to impress himself on her so thoroughly and so completely that she would never hunger for another man.

He wanted her but for all he knew she had a lover.

A seething wildness swirled within him. Emma's very presence here in the carriage made it impossible to summon the invisible net of internal calm that was his refuge and his armor.

He was, he realized, rock hard and fully erect.

"Are you quite certain that you are all right?" Emma asked uneasily.

"Yes." He shifted his position slightly in an attempt to ease himself.

She frowned. "You have a very odd look about you at the moment."

"What sort of look would that be?"

"I do not know how to describe it. Who was that strange man who attacked you?"

"I have no notion." Edison hesitated. "The only thing I know for certain is that he studied the fighting arts in the same school that tutored me."

"Where was that school?"

"The Garden Temples of Vanzagara."

"Vanzagara?" Her eyes widened in quick comprehension. "Then that villain who attacked you must be involved in this affair, sir."

"Yes." Edison forced himself to think. "He must have been keeping a watch on Lady Ames's house. I think it's safe to say that there is, indeed, someone else after the book. But he seemed too young to be the mastermind behind such an elaborate scheme."

"How do you know that he was young? His face was covered with a cloth mask."

Edison touched his ribs absently. "I am quite certain of it. He moved with the speed and agility of youth. Fortunately, he has not yet learned the tricks one picks up with age."

"This affair grows more complicated by the hour."

"Yes." He contemplated the flaring light of the carriage lamp, trying to focus his concentration. "But I still do not understand how Lady Ames managed to stumble onto such an arcane secret here in England."

"Have you discovered nothing at all about her past?"

"Nothing except what she told everyone when she arrived on the scene at the start of the Season. She claims to be the widow of an elderly gentleman who died in Scotland last year."

"So many questions," Emma whispered. "I may be able to help you with some of them, however."

Edison shifted his gaze from the lamp to her face. "Start with the most important one. What the devil were you doing in Miranda's library tonight?"

Emma blinked. "How did you find me there, sir?"

He shrugged. "I decided to take a look around the library while you were upstairs in the withdrawing room."

"Good heavens. It's a wonder we did not all meet there together."

"All?" Edison felt a nerve twitch in his jaw. He realized he was grinding his teeth. "There was someone else in the library with you before I arrived?"

"As I said earlier, it is a lengthy story." She leaned forward intently and lowered her voice. "You are not going to believe this, sir, but I discovered the most extraordinary facts tonight."

He did not like the excitement in her eyes. He was almost certain it boded ill. "I'm listening."

"After I came out of the withdrawing room, I chanced to notice Swan behaving in a rather suspicious fashion."

"Swan? Miranda's footman? What does he have to do with this?"

"I do not know. But, as I said, his movements appeared strange. So I followed him down the back stairs."

"You followed Swan?" Edison's temper, already smoldering, erupted into flames. This was almost as bad as learning that she had met her lover in the library. *Almost, but not quite.* "Have you gone mad? He might very well be dangerous. What if you had been discovered following him? How would you have explained yourself?"

Her mouth tightened in annoyance. "Do you wish to hear my tale or not?"

He sat forward, too, legs spread, hands on his knees, and schooled himself to a grim patience. "By all means, tell me the rest of this wild story."

"I lost sight of him at the bottom of the stairs, but I noticed the library door. It seemed very convenient. So I decided to take a quick look inside as long as I was in the neighborhood."

"Bloody hell," Edison breathed.

"Of course, I would not have bothered had I realized that you had similar plans." Her brows drew together in sharp disapproval. "I really must insist that in future you keep me better apprised of your intentions, sir. That way we will be less likely to find ourselves tripping over each other while we pursue our inquiries."

"May I remind you, Miss Greyson, that you work for me. I will decide what you need to know and when you need to know it."

"I think you will change your mind when you hear what I learned tonight."

Her expression could only be described as smug, Edison thought. "Just what did you discover?"

"Miranda sent Swan to search your study this evening while you were away from your house. She is determined to discover why you got yourself engaged to me. She does not believe for one moment that ours is a normal sort of connection." Emma sat back. Triumph gleamed in her eyes. "There, sir. What do you think of that bit of news?"

"Very little. I'm not at all surprised to learn that Swan searched my study. I've been expecting him to do something along those lines."

"*Expecting it?*"

"I am well aware that Miranda is very curious about me. After all, as long as you are engaged to me, I stand in her way."

"You knew Swan would go through your study?" She looked crestfallen.

"It was inevitable that she would send someone. Swan seemed a likely candidate for the task." Edison watched her intently. "But how did you happen to learn that he did so tonight?"

"Swan and Miranda came into the library while I was looking through the desk drawers. I was obliged to conceal myself behind a curtain while they talked."

Ice formed in his stomach. She would drive him mad, he thought.

Very carefully, with infinite control, he took his hands off his thighs and reached out to capture her wrists. "Listen to me, Emma, and listen closely. You are never again to go haring off on your own the way you did this evening. You will not take such risks while you are in my employ. Do you comprehend me?"

"No, I do not understand you." She looked deeply offended and somewhat baffled. "Why are you so angry?"

"Because of the risks you took, you little twit. You could have been hurt."

"Highly unlikely. Embarrassed, perhaps, but not hurt. You were the one who was in genuine danger this evening. That dreadful man in the garden tried to do you a terrible injury."

"Would you have cared if I had been injured tonight?"

"Of course I would have cared, sir."

"Why?" He gave her a humorless smile. "Because I am the most generous employer you have had since you began your career and you do not wish to lose your post before you have got your hands on your wages?"

"It is not solely the money—"

"Ah, yes. Perhaps your deep concern for my health and safety stems from the fact that you have not yet got your precious reference out of me."

"I could put the very same questions to you, sir." Her eyes glittered. "Why are you so concerned that I not take any unnecessary risks while I am in your employ? Is it because you need me in good condition so that you can continue to use me to bait your trap for Lady Ames? Am I nothing more than a bit of cheese you intend to use to catch a mouse?"

"If so, you are certainly the most expensive cheese I have ever purchased. I can only hope that you prove to be extremely tasty."

"Sir, you are far and away the most difficult employer that I have had the misfortune to meet up with in the entire course of my career."

"You keep saying that. But the important thing is that I pay very well, isn't it?"

"How dare you imply that my interest in your well-being is entirely mercenary?"

Edison could have sworn that he heard the rumble and roar as the stone wall of his patience gave way. The sound was as loud as the crack of doom.

"Let us discover just how unmercenary your interest in me is, Emma."

He shifted abruptly, moving forward to press her back into the corner of the carriage seat. He used his grip on her wrists to anchor her there, and bent his head.

The instant his mouth touched hers, he knew that Emma's calm demeanor had been as deceptive as his own. She was as close to the edge of this particular cliff as he was.

"Mmmph." After a second or two of stunned hesitation, Emma jerked her hands free and wrapped them very tightly around his neck.

The fierce passions that had been ebbing and flowing between them for the past several minutes exploded. Edison was astonished that the seat cushions did not catch fire.

Emma's lips parted beneath his. Her fingers tightened in his hair.

She might very well have another lover somewhere in London, he thought, but tonight she wanted him.

He fought a short battle with his coat and finally managed to get rid of it. Emma yanked his cravat free with several fierce little tugs.

He braced one foot on the floor of the carriage and crushed her deeper into the seat. The taste of her was intoxicating, lush and spicy and compelling. It was unlike the flavor of any other woman he had kissed in his entire life.

"Edison."

Her silken skirts foamed around his thighs. He tugged at the bodice of her low-cut gown until the firm fullness of her small breasts fell into his hands. He felt one taut nipple press invitingly into his palm. The sweet, hot scent of her body was tinged with the herbs of her bathwater. He had a sudden vision of her bathing in front of a fire and nearly lost what little self-mastery he still possessed.

With a groan he tore his mouth away from hers and bent to take a tight, thrusting nipple between his teeth. Emma shivered and arched herself in his arms.

He was vaguely aware of the sway of the carriage, the muffled sounds of the street, and the clatter of the horses' hooves on the stones. But it all seemed very remote, very distant. Very unimportant.

Emma managed to pry his shirt out of his trousers. Edison felt her fumble briefly with the fastenings and then abandon the task. She slid her hands up inside the garment instead. He shuddered heavily when he felt her fingers on his bare skin. She stopped abruptly.

"Did I hurt you?" she asked quickly. "Is that where the villain kicked you?"

He raised his head to look down into the green seas of her eyes. "If it is, your touch is all I require to heal the bruises. Please don't stop."

"But if he—"

"Don't. Stop. Touching. Me." He lowered his head to her throat. "I beg you."

"Very well." She sounded breathless.

Cautiously at first and then with renewed urgency, she splayed her fingers against his skin. "You feel so strong and warm and so very solid."

He was bemused by the tone of wonder in her voice. "And you are very, very soft."

He scooped up a handful of her silk skirts and pushed them up to her waist. She watched him from beneath half-lowered lashes as he lifted himself slightly to look down at her.

The lamplight turned the skin of her gently molded thighs a creamy gold. Glistening drops of moisture clung to the crisp red curls that marked the juncture of her legs. He heard a ragged sound and realized that it was his own breathing.

"Emma, if you do not want this, say so now."

She slipped her hands out from beneath his shirt and caught his face between her palms. There was a fine trembling in her fingers. For a moment she gazed deeply into his eyes. Then she smiled slightly.

"It feels right," she whispered.

He did not know what to make of her strange words. The desire he saw in her face dazed him. He closed his eyes for an instant, half convinced that he had blundered into an opium den fantasy. When he raised his lashes he saw that Emma was still watching him with a reckless, intense need that matched his own mood.

Hungry desperation swept over him. He surrendered to the powerful forces at work in the carriage. Reaching down, he unfastened his trousers to release his rigid shaft.

He gripped one of Emma's thighs and opened her to his touch. She gasped when he stroked her. She was wet and yielding beneath his palm.

He could wait no longer. He fitted himself to her and pushed deeply, heavily into the tight, moist passage.

She gave a small, half-strangled shriek of protest. Her nails bit through his shirt into his shoulders.

A shock of recognition snapped through him.

"Emma."

He had never made love to a virgin before, but he knew with shattering certainty that that was precisely what he had done tonight. Whoever Emma had gone to meet that afternoon, it was not her lover.

She looked up at him. Passion no longer glazed her eyes.

"I trust this type of activity improves with practice?" She sounded as though she was speaking between clenched teeth.

"Yes." His hands shook. He had made a terrible hash of this. "It does."

"I fear you are much too large to be indulging in this sort of thing, sir."

"Oh, Emma."

With a great effort of will, he held himself very still, allowing her to become accustomed to the feel of him inside her. When he thought he detected a slight relaxation of the tiny muscles that gripped him so snugly, he began to move.

But her body closed around him again, drawing him deeper, trapping him in the damp heat.

He was dimly aware of the perspiration between his shoulder blades and on his forehead. His linen shirt stuck to his skin. He felt Emma shift experimentally beneath him.

"No, my sweet, you must not—"

It was too late. He was lost. Some semblance of sanity returned at the last instant. He managed to pull himself out of her barely in time to spill his seed onto her thigh.

The violent convulsions of his release wracked him endlessly. He shut his eyes, set his teeth, and endured the exhausting pleasure. When it was over he collapsed amid a tangle of green silk. The scent of spent passion was heavy in the air.

He felt the carriage rumble to a halt in front of Lady Mayfield's house.

So much for living in a fairy tale, Emma thought grimly.

She still felt shaky and unreal when she preceded Edison into the library a few minutes later. She gave thanks that Letty was still out and the household staff was conveniently abed. There was no one around to observe her sadly rumpled and stained gown, wildly disarrayed hair, and what she suspected was a very odd expression on her face.

She knew she looked perfectly dreadful. Not at all the way she had envisioned looking after making love with the man she had waited for all of her life.

Of course, she had not known that Edison was that man until tonight. In fact, nothing about the experience had gone according to her very private daydreams. There had been no thrilling courtship, no roses, no declaration of undying love.

No talk of the future.

But there you have it, she thought. When one pursued a career, one could not expect things to go according to the way they did in books.

Glumly she watched Edison light the fire. He looked elegant once more.

It was grossly unfair, the way he had put himself to rights so swiftly and with such negligent ease. He had not bothered to retie his cravat, but other than that, he looked immaculate. She could think of no one else of her acquaintance who could have emerged from the inconvenience of a violent battle and a bout of passion with such aplomb.

He brushed off his hands, rose, and turned to face her. There was a disturbingly somber, decidedly grim expression in his eyes.

"We must talk," he said.

The too-quiet tone of his voice alarmed her as little else could have done in that moment. It gave her the fortitude to pull herself together at last. She gave him what she hoped was a businesslike smile.

"Yes, of course."

He took a step toward her and stopped. "Emma, I do not know where to begin."

Dear heaven, he was going to apologize. She had to stop him. She could not bear an apology, of all things. The fear of having to listen to him tell her how much he regretted their passionate interlude caused her to take an awkward step back. She came up hard against Letty's desk. Her little reticule, which still dangled from her wrist, thumped against the mahogany panel.

She suddenly recalled what was inside.

"Yes," she said. "Yes, of course, we must talk. I am so glad that you reminded me, sir." She hastily opened the reticule and dug out the tightly rolled playbills and papers inside. "I have not yet had a chance to show you what I managed to save from the flames."

"What flames?" Edison scowled at the papers as she spread them out on the desk. "You mean someone tried to burn those in Miranda's library?"

"It was Swan. He and Miranda had a terrible row when she discovered that he had failed to find anything useful in your study. She dismissed him out of hand. It was really very sad."

"What the devil do you mean, it was sad?"

"She did not even give him his quarterly wages, let alone a reference." Emma studied the playbill on top of the pile. "Turned him off without notice. The poor man will no doubt have a difficult time finding another post. But that is not the most unhappy part."

Edison came forward slowly. "What was the unhappy part?"

"I'm afraid Swan made the mistake of falling in love with his employer." Emma cleared her throat and concentrated fiercely on the playbill. "After she left him in the library, he cried. It nearly broke my heart to listen to him."

"He *cried*?"

"And then he flew into a terrible rage. He took a box full of papers out of a locked drawer and hurled them into the flames. I managed to salvage a few after he left the room."

Edison came to stand beside her. He did not touch her as he studied the playbills. "Interesting."

She looked up swiftly. "The violent manner in which Swan tried to destroy these papers made me think that he knew they were very important to Miranda. He was trying to strike back at her for the way in which she had hurt him."

Edison flipped through the small stack. "These playbills and reviews have one thing in common. They all feature an actress named Fanny Clifton."

"There is another thing. Look closely, sir. None of these playbills advertise any performances here in Town." Emma turned over another page. "They feature a company of traveling actors that appears to have performed chiefly in the North."

Edison picked up a review and read aloud.

The glorious Miss Clifton brought a new interpretation to the role of Lady Macbeth. The expression of piercing dread in her fine blue eyes was evident even to those seated in the most remote seats. Her small, graceful form is particularly suited to the elegant costume she wore.

"Fine blue eyes," Emma whispered. "Small, graceful form." She looked at Edison. "Have you reached the same conclusion that I have, sir?"

"That Miranda may have had a previous career as an actress named Fanny Clifton?" Edison tossed the review aside, folded his arms, and leaned back against the edge of the desk. "It would explain why I have been unable to find anyone who knew her before she turned up in London at the start of the Season."

"But she is obviously very wealthy. Actresses are not rich."

Edison raised his brows. "Some have managed to marry extremely well."

"True." Emma reflected on that for a moment. There had been one or two particularly notorious actresses who had succeeded in charming wealthy lords into marriage. "The scandals that ensued have generally made it necessary for the couples to leave Town, however."

Edison met her eyes. "Perhaps Miranda and her husband, the mysterious, late Lord Ames, were obliged to go as far away as Italy."

"Why would she lie and claim that she came down from Scotland?"

"Perhaps because she did not want anyone to suspect a connection to Italy," Edison said slowly.

"If you can prove that Miranda spent some time in Italy during the past year, it would give you a possible link to that Farrell Blue person whom you said deciphered one of the recipes."

"Yes, it would." Edison paused. "Then again, perhaps there never was a Lord Ames."

"A good point." Emma raised her brows. "After all, if I can invent my own references, I suppose another woman might invent a husband. But that would not explain her obvious wealth. It must come from some source."

"Indeed. And the name of that source should prove extremely interesting." Edison straightened away from the desk. "I shall begin making inquiries in that direction first thing in the morning. In the meantime, you and I have something else to discuss."

Emma stiffened. "If you don't mind, sir, I would rather not continue this conversation. It is late and I am quite exhausted."

"Emma—"

"It has been an eventful evening," she said hastily. "I fear I am not accustomed to the, uh, rigors of the social world. I am eager to go to my bed."

He looked as though he would argue. She held her breath. But Edison had apparently reached some private decision.

He inclined his head with awful formality. "As you wish. But do not think that this matter between us can be ignored indefinitely."

"The less said, the better," she muttered. "Good night, sir."

He hesitated. She could see the irritation flicker in his eyes. Again she feared that he would force a conversation. Instead, he turned and went toward the door.

"Good night, Emma." He paused, his hand on the doorknob. "As your employer, allow me to tell you that you went above and beyond the call of duty tonight. Rest assured that you will be suitably rewarded for this evening's work."

She could not believe her ears. And then rage lanced through her. "*Rewarded.* Did you say rewarded?"

"I feel compelled to add an extra few pounds to your wages at the end of your employment in my service," he continued thoughtfully.

"How dare you, sir?" She seized the nearest object, a small globe, and hurled it at his head. "How dare you imply that I would take money for that . . . that stupid incident in the carriage? I am obliged to work for my living, *but I am no whore.*"

He caught the globe with a seemingly absent movement of his hand. "For God's sake, Emma, I did not mean that you were."

She ignored him. She was in the grip of a storm of fury. She cast about for something else to throw and got hold of a vase full of flowers. "I will not take money for what happened between us. Do you hear me? I would sooner starve in the workhouse than accept money from you for that."

She tossed the full vase with all of her strength.

"Damn it, calm yourself, Emma." He managed to catch the vase but he did not succeed in avoiding the contents. Water and flowers splashed him in the face. He grimaced and shook his head once. "I was talking about rewarding you for your investigation in Miranda's library. What you discovered may prove extremely useful."

"Rubbish." She planted her hands on her hips. "I don't believe you."

Anger flashed across his face. "I'm telling you the truth, you maddening, stubborn, featherbrained creature."

He was suddenly roaring at her, Emma thought, nonplussed. She had never heard him lose his temper like this.

"Do you swear that on your oath?" she asked, not bothering to conceal her suspicion.

"Hell's teeth, woman." He glared at her, wet hair plastered to his head, eyes glittering with anger. "If I was in the market for a mistress, I would have chosen a female with a more compliant character and a good deal more experience in the passionate arts than you've got."

Her jaw dropped. "Now you're insulting me for lacking experience in that sort of thing?"

"I'm trying to make it bloody damn clear that I do not view what happened in the carriage as a business venture." With a disgusted gesture he flicked some stray petals from the sleeve of his coat. "The reward I mentioned was for what you discovered concerning Lady Ames, or Fanny Clifton, whatever the case may be."

"Edison—"

He scowled at her as he jerked open the door. "And while we're on the subject, allow me to inform you that if you ever again take that sort of risk, I will never write that bloody reference for you."

"Edison, wait." She picked up her skirts and rushed toward the door. "Perhaps I was a bit hasty in my accusations."

He did not deign to respond. The library door closed very firmly in her face just as she reached it.

CHAPTER SIXTEEN

Edison steeled himself the way he always did on the rare occasions when he was obliged to pay a call on his grand-mother. He even dreaded the simple act of entering the mansion in which she lived, although he could not explain his reaction to the house. By rights it should have pleased his taste in such matters. It was a grand structure in the Palladian style, with classical lines and well-proportioned rooms. But it always seemed oppressive and cold to him. Long ago he had privately dubbed it the Exbridge Fortress.

He crossed the drawing room to the sofa where Victoria, Lady Exbridge sat, a regal, solitary queen of a woman. It was at times such as this, he reflected, that he truly appreciated the usefulness of good manners. They were both sword and shield in the brutally civil skirmishes in which he and Victoria engaged.

"Edison." Victoria regarded him with the austere, imperious air that was second nature to her. "It is about time you got here."

"I believe your note requested me to call at three, Lady Exbridge." He never addressed her as Grandmother. To do so would have been to yield a tiny fraction of the ground he had vowed to defend. She had never wanted him as a grandson, not even after he had salvaged the Exbridge fortune for her. Damned if he would admit that he wished to have her for a grandmother. "It is precisely three now."

He studied his opponent as he inclined his head very formally over her hand. Victoria was, he concluded, in her customary fit fighting form today, perhaps even a bit more eager for combat than usual.

Age had added a few lines and wrinkles to what had once been a strikingly beautiful face, but nothing would ever soften the hawklike glitter in those golden brown eyes. Eyes that were, Edison knew, the mirror image of his own.

Victoria wore the cloak of elegance and style as easily as if she had been born in it. Her high-waisted, silver-gray morning gown with its crisp ruff and full sleeves was obviously the work of an expensive French modiste. It was a perfect complement to her silver hair.

Edison was well aware that her natural sense of style together with her position as the wife of a wealthy viscount had combined to make her a glittering hostess at one time. Her soirees and balls and fashionable salons had once been the talk of the ton. Widowed when her son, Wesley, had been fourteen, she had remained prominent in social circles.

But all that had changed several years later after Wesley's death and the shock of learning that he had gambled away the family estates. She had withdrawn from the social whirl altogether. She rarely went out, preferring the solitude of her conservatory and occasional visits with a handful of old friends.

Not even the restoration of the Exbridge fortune had brought her out of her self-imposed seclusion. What had he expected? Edison asked himself. That she would be grateful to him for protecting her from the shame and ignominy of bankruptcy? As if such a gesture from a bastard grandson could possibly make up for the loss of her legitimate son and heir.

"You should have called to tell me the news of your engagement as soon as you returned to Town," Victoria said, by way of her opening salvo. "I was left to learn the information from Arabella Stryder. It was exceedingly awkward for me."

Arabella was, Edison knew, one of the few friends Victoria still saw regularly.

"I doubt that even a volcano erupting in your drawing room could make you feel awkward, madam." He smiled humorlessly. "Certainly no news of me would have the power to do so."

"One would think that having endured your disdain for the social niceties often enough in the past, I would have grown inured to it. Nevertheless, this time you go too far."

"That is an odd complaint, coming from you, madam. As I recall, it was only last month that you again took me to task for failing to find myself a suitable wife."

Victoria's eyes snapped with anger. "*Suitable* is the key word. From all accounts, your fiancée is hardly suitable."

"You are in no position to form an opinion on the subject. You have not yet met her."

"I have heard more than enough to conclude that you have made a disastrous choice."

"Why do you say that?" Edison asked mildly.

"According to Arabella, your Miss Greyson was employed as Lady Mayfield's paid companion when you met her. Is that true?"

"Yes."

"Incredible. A professional lady's companion? In your position you could easily choose any heiress on the marriage mart."

"I don't know that I can afford to be too choosy, madam." Edison smiled thinly. "We must not forget that I am not exactly a prize myself.

I was born on the wrong side of the blanket, if you will recall. Miss Greyson's parentage, on the other hand, is quite respectable."

Victoria's gaze crackled with anger but she did not take the bait. "I was also told that the reason you announced your engagement to Miss Greyson, in the middle of the night, no less, was because she was in danger of being accused of murdering Mr. Crane."

"That was a factor in the timing of my decision," Edison admitted.

"Everyone who was at Ware Castle believes that she actually did kill Crane. Most of the ton think that you've just engaged yourself to a murderess, of all things."

"It makes no great difference to me, one way or the other." Edison shrugged. "Crane deserved to be shot."

Victoria stared at him. "How dare you sound so blasé. We are speaking of the dreadful killing of an innocent man."

"Chilton Crane was not what anyone would call innocent."

"Have you forgotten that Mr. Crane was a highly esteemed gentleman of the ton? He belonged to all the best clubs. He moved in the most elevated circles. He was connected to the marquis of Riverton on his mother's side."

"Crane was a thoroughly debauched rakehell who preyed on young women who had no one to protect them from his lechery. He specialized in forcing himself on chambermaids, governesses, and companions. He was also a reckless gamester." Edison paused. "In point of fact, he probably had a good deal in common with my father."

"How dare you say such a thing?" Victoria's voice vibrated with fury. This time she did take the hook. "I have told you often enough that Wesley did not force himself on your mother. She was a foolish young woman who got involved with an engaged man well above her station, and she paid the price."

"She was foolish," Edison agreed politely. "Foolish enough to believe my father when he claimed that he loved her. Foolish enough to put her faith in him when he said that he was free to marry her. Foolish enough to think that she had given herself to a man of honor."

"Never forget that she sold her own honor in the process."

He clamped his fingers around the mantel and forced himself to produce a politely quizzical smile. "I am, of course, delighted to discuss family history with you, madam. But I must warn you that I cannot stay long, as I have another appointment at four. If there is something else you wish to talk about this afternoon, perhaps we ought to get to it."

Victoria's mouth was a flat, hard line. As Edison watched she took a visible breath, schooling her raw fury, just as he had done a moment earlier. He wondered if she would retreat to her conservatory after he left. It was what he did when he needed to calm the dark, dangerous emotions such conversations aroused.

He watched her pick up her teacup. The dainty china trembled ever so slightly in her grasp.

He should have been able to take some measure of satisfaction in knowing that he had the power to force her to the brink of her self-control. But as usual, the knowledge that he had done so did nothing to elevate his mood. He wondered again, as he always did, what it was that he wanted from this formidable woman. Why did he continue this bristly, unpleasant association? Why did he not simply ignore her very existence? It was not as if she wanted any attention from him.

"You know very well that I asked you to come here today so that I could hear the truth about your so-called engagement from your own lips," Victoria said icily.

"There is nothing so-called about it. I am, indeed, engaged."

"I refuse to believe that you actually intend to marry this . . . this murderess."

"Have a care with the way you fling that word *murderess* around," he warned her very softly. "If necessary, I am prepared to testify in court that Miss Greyson was with me at the time of Crane's murder."

"Crane was killed in the middle of the night. Arabella said that when you and Miss Greyson appeared to join the others at the scene of the crime, she was dressed in a nightshift, cap, and a wrapper. She appeared to have just got out of bed."

Edison raised his brows. "Your point?"

"My point is that if she is not a murderess, if she was indeed with you at the time Crane died, then it is obvious that she was in your bed. That means she is no better than any other round-heeled lightskirt. You are under no obligation to protect her."

"Neither you nor anyone else," Edison said through his teeth, "is allowed to refer to my fiancée as a lightskirt."

Victoria stared at him. "She can have been nothing more than a brief fling for you."

"She is my future wife." Edison removed his watch and flipped open the case. "I regret to say that it grows late." He dropped the watch back into his pocket. "As much as I hate to cut short this charming conversation, I fear I must bid you good day, madam."

"If you are actually contemplating marriage to this Miss Greyson," Victoria said, "then it can only be because there is some profit in it for you."

"Profit?"

"Your success in matters of business is legendary. You would not make a move as significant as this unless you expected to reap some great financial rewards. Have you discovered that Miss Greyson is about to come into a fortune?"

"Miss Greyson is, so far as I know, as poor as a church mouse. She apparently lost what little she possessed in an ill-fated investment scheme." Edison paused long enough at the door to incline his head in a barely civil gesture of farewell. "But it is always illuminating to learn exactly what you think of me, Lady Exbridge. It is obvious that as the years go by, in your eyes I continue to fall far short of the illustrious example set by my noble sire."

A short time later Edison sank down into the second of two well-padded chairs that flanked the hearth in his club. He absorbed the comforting drone of low voices, rustling newspapers, and gently clinking coffee cups. The small, civil sounds would provide privacy for the conversation he was about to have.

He picked up the coffee cup that had just been set on the table beside him.

Ignatius Lorring was already seated in the opposite chair. Edison was heartened to know that his old friend still felt up to a visit to his club.

Ignatius looked paler than ever, however, and Edison noticed that his chair was set even closer to the fire than it had been on the previous occasion when they had spoken in this room.

Nevertheless, when Ignatius put down his copy of *The Times* and smiled at Edison, there was a flash of the old, familiar brightness in his eyes.

"You look as though you are more in need of a glass of brandy than a cup of coffee, Edison."

"You have the right of it, by God." Edison took a swallow of the coffee. "I have just come from paying a visit to my grandmother."

"Ah, that explains it, of course. I suspect she wanted to hear the details of your recent engagement. Perfectly natural."

"There is nothing natural about Lady Exbridge." Edison put down the cup. "But there is nothing new in that, so we may as well turn to the reason I asked you to meet me here this afternoon."

Ignatius steepled his birdlike hands. "If you are hoping for information concerning Lady Ames, I fear I must disappoint you. I have had no more luck than you did. The woman appears to have sprung into existence like Athena from the head of Zeus, fully armed and gowned for the Season."

"Her finances are a mystery also," Edison admitted. "I have been unable to discover the sources of her income. Nevertheless, my assistant happened across some information that will allow us to reach a little further into her past."

"I am eager to hear it."

Edison leaned back in his chair, stretched out his legs, and contemplated the fire. "We have reason to believe that Lady Ames may have once trod the boards under the name Fanny Clifton."

"She is a former actress? That would explain a great deal." Ignatius pondered that briefly and then shook his head. "But I have attended the London theater quite faithfully for years. Indeed, it is one of my passions, as you well know."

Edison smiled. "I am well aware of your love of the theater."

"Ah, yes. Had I been born in other circumstances, I believe I would have taken quite happily to a life on the stage." Ignatius sighed. "But then I would never have discovered Vanzagara and the philosophy of Vanza, which has given me so much pleasure and satisfaction. In any event, I can assure you that I have never heard of this Fanny Clifton."

"Very likely because she never rose above the level of a player in a small traveling company that performed mostly in the North. And her career may well have been quite short."

"I see." Ignatius bobbed his head in a robinlike motion. "That would explain why I am unfamiliar with her. Very interesting. It will certainly give us a new direction in which to search."

"If we can find a link to Italy and Farrell Blue, we would at least have some notion of how she might have got her hands on the recipe. In the meantime, something else has come up."

Ignatius cocked his head. "Indeed?"

"Before I explain, I must ask you a question, sir."

"Yes, yes, what is it?"

Edison looked at him. "I had an encounter with a practitioner of the art of Vanza last night. He was quite good. And, I think, quite young."

Ignatius's brows rose suddenly. "Are you saying you were attacked? By a student of Vanza?"

"Yes."

"Right here in London?" Ignatius looked flabbergasted. "But that is astonishing. Absolutely astonishing. And, I would have said, quite impossible. I am the only Grand Master in London at the moment. As you well know, I ceased taking on new students some years ago."

"Can I assume from your reaction that he was not in your employ?"

Ignatius snorted. "He most certainly was not. What the devil led you to believe that he was?"

Edison smiled slightly. "The fact that, as you just pointed out, you are the only Grand Master of Vanza in London. I was merely trying to eliminate all obvious possibilities. It did occur to me that you might have set someone to watch Lady Ames's house and that he might not have realized that I was also involved in the matter on your behalf."

"Had I done so, I would have informed you."

"Then," Edison said quietly, "we must assume that this young student of Vanza is working for someone else who is seeking either the recipe or the *Book of Secrets*. Or both."

"You did not question him?"

"Our association was brief, to say the least."

"What do you mean?"

"He quit the contest shortly after he learned that I, also, had studied the arts."

"Hmm." Ignatius blinked as he considered. "You do realize what you are implying?"

"That someone else is searching for the book? Yes. I know what that means."

Ignatius stirred, as though uncomfortable in his chair. He gave Edison an uneasy glance. "We must assume that whoever he is, he is not after the recipe or the book for altruistic reasons. If he had sent a student or come to Town himself for an honest purpose, he would have contacted me immediately. He would have informed me that he wished to participate in the search for the volume."

"Yes."

"The fact that he has not done so can mean only one thing,"

Ignatius said softly. "Whoever he is, he is one who no longer honors the true traditions of Vanza. If he exists and if he wishes to conceal his identity, he will not be easy to locate."

Edison smiled wryly. "I agree that it will not be simple to find a rogue practitioner of the art who wishes to remain hidden. His young student, however, is a different matter."

"What do you mean?"

Edison set down his empty coffee cup and pushed himself up out of the chair. "There cannot be many eager, young Vanza fighters flitting about London. It won't be difficult to find him. When I have him, it should be possible to discover the identity of whoever sent him after the book."

"Bah. Do not waste your time, Edison. We cannot afford to get distracted from our main purpose. The important thing now is to locate the volume before this rogue does." Ignatius tapped his fingertips together. "If we fail, then I will have failed in my last act of true Vanza."

CHAPTER SEVENTEEN

Tell me, Miss Greyson, have you met the Exbridge Dragon yet?" Basil Ware smiled as he took the dainty blue velvet cushioned chair next to Emma.

He had to lean close to make himself heard above the rumble of laughter and conversation. The theater box was crowded at the moment. Letty was holding court. Several aging admirers had appeared during intermission to pay their respects. Each had arrived with a glass of champagne for Letty. They were crowded around her ample bosom, which tonight was framed in scarlet satin.

Emma's own, more discreet bosom was set off by yet another low-cut green gown. This one was trimmed with a great quantity of gold ribbons, several of which were strategically placed to hide her nipples. When she had inquired about the possibility of filling in the neck with a bit of lace, she had been assured by both Letty and the modiste that the style was all the crack.

Emma had put her doubts aside. After all, what did she know about such matters? she thought. She was a former paid companion, not a lady of fashion.

Basil Ware's appearance in the theater box a moment ago had surprised her. When he had arrived she had been occupied watching the scene unfolding in Miranda's box, which was located directly across the theater.

"Dragon? What dragon?" Emma peered through her opera glass and frowned at the sight of Edison bending a bit too gallantly over Miranda's gloved hand.

The notion had seemed quite clever when they had discussed it earlier. Between acts, Edison would visit with Miranda in her box and engage her in conversation in an attempt to draw her out on the subject of her past.

It was all going according to plan, but Emma discovered that she did not care for the way Edison was hovering over Miranda. There was no need for him to sit so close that Lady Ames was able to brush her fingers lightly across his thigh. It was a seemingly careless gesture but Emma sensed that there had been nothing accidental about that little caress. Miranda was trying to spin one of her webs.

"I was referring to Victoria, Lady Exbridge." Basil sounded amused. "Your fiancé's grandmother. She is here tonight. Presumably you are the reason."

Startled, Emma lowered her glass and turned to stare at Basil. "What do you mean? Where is she?"

"She is sitting in the third tier of boxes across the way." Basil angled his head slightly to indicate the direction. "Fourth one from the left. You cannot miss her. She is the lady in pale lavender who has her opera glass trained on you."

"Half the theater seems to have their glasses aimed at me," Emma muttered. And the other half were looking at Edison and Miranda, she thought.

Nevertheless, she looked at the third tier of boxes and counted four from the left. She saw the small but extremely formidable-looking woman in the expensive lavender gown and matching gloves. Lady Exbridge did, indeed, have her opera glass focused in Emma's direction.

"The *on dit*," Basil murmured, "is that she and Stokes despise each other. Unfortunately, after her son died, Lady Exbridge was left with no one except her bastard grandson for a relative."

"And he has no one but her," Emma murmured to herself.

"They have been engaged in a state of war ever since your fiancé stepped in to save the family estates from bankruptcy."

"I am aware that there is some strain in the family relationship," she said cautiously.

"That is putting it mildly." Basil quirked a brow. "Stokes's father was not much interested in financial matters or his estates. In fact, Wesley Stokes succeeding in gambling away his entire inheritance. And then he went and broke his neck in a riding accident."

"Yes, of course, I know the history," Emma said crisply. "I think it was very noble of my, uh, fiancé to rescue the family fortunes after his father's death."

Basil chuckled. "It was hardly an act of virtuous generosity or family feeling. The general consensus of opinion is that he did it to humiliate Lady Exbridge."

"Humiliate her? How on earth could such a gesture accomplish that?"

"I am told that he hoped to force her to acknowledge him in Polite Circles. It was the very last thing she wished to do, of course. After all, he is an embarrassment to her. She chose to withdraw from the social world rather than to be put into the position of having to pretend that she was pleased with the family connection between them."

"How terrible."

"They say that Stokes is the living image of his parent. Every time Victoria sees him, she no doubt sees Wesley and what her son could have been had he been possessed of a different nature. It surely galls her no end."

"How very sad for both of them."

Basil laughed. "Come now, my dear Miss Greyson. You are much too softhearted. You do not understand how these things work in Society. I assure you that neither Stokes nor Lady Exbridge wastes any time feeling sad. They are too busy enjoying the combat."

Emma watched Lady Exbridge lower her glass and turn to speak to a stout matron seated beside her. She could not make out Lady Exbridge's expression, but there was something in the stiff, brittle way in which she moved that told her that Basil was wrong. Lady Exbridge took no pleasure from the war with her grandson. It did not require any great degree of intuition to know that she was a most unhappy and probably a very lonely person.

"I wonder if—" Basil sounded suddenly very thoughtful.

"Yes?" Emma glanced at him. "What is it?"

"Nothing, really. Forget it."

"I can hardly do that when you are acting so mysteriously, sir. Just what did you mean to say?"

"It's none of my affair, of course, but, well . . ." Basil sighed. "Perhaps it is only fair to warn you."

"Warn me of what?"

He lowered his voice and leaned forward with an earnest air. "Please do not take this as anything more than the natural concern of a friend. But it suddenly struck me that you may have become a pawn in the Stokes-Exbridge war."

"What in heaven's name do you mean by that?"

Basil's eyes narrowed slightly. "You may have heard that Stokes's mother was a governess who ruined herself in the affair with Wesley."

"Yes, I know. What has that to do with anything?"

"Whether she likes it or not, Edison Stokes is Lady Exbridge's only blood relative. The offspring of her only child. He is her only hope for carrying on the family name. Stokes has managed to buy his way into respectability. His own children, her future great-grandchildren, will be accepted into Society. She knows that better than anyone."

"What is your point, sir?"

"It just occurred to me that there is very likely nothing on the face of the earth that would annoy Lady Exbridge more than to see Stokes select a wife she considers entirely unsuitable. A woman who, in fact, once held a station in life not unlike that of his mother's. After all, this woman will be the mother of her great-grandchildren."

The shock of his insinuations took Emma's breath. She rallied swiftly, however. After all, she thought, she knew the real reason Edison had announced his engagement to her. It had nothing to do with annoying his grandmother.

"You are mistaken, Mr. Ware."

"Very likely," he agreed graciously. "Please forgive me. I only wished to prevent you from being used in some devious purpose."

"I am not being used, sir." At least, Emma added silently, not in the way you imagine.

"Of course not." Basil looked across the theater and smoothly changed the subject. "I see Miranda is up to her tricks again. She really is a most determined little witch, is she not? With her looks, she is probably not accustomed to failure."

Emma turned her attention back to Miranda's box just in time to see Edison glance in her direction. She thought he frowned when he saw Basil sitting next to her, but it was difficult to be certain from this distance. As she watched he turned back to respond to something Miranda must have said.

Pursuing his inquiries into her past, Emma reminded herself.

It occurred to her that two could practice the fine art of eliciting information.

"You're quite right, Mr. Ware. Lady Ames is very lovely." Emma hoped she sounded casual. "Have you known her long?"

"Not really." Basil raised one shoulder in a dismissive shrug. "We were introduced at the Connerville levee shortly after the start of the Season. I found her to be rather amusing, so I invited her to my country house party."

"Were you acquainted with her husband?"

"Never met the man." Basil grinned knowingly. "But I can hazard a guess as to the cause of his demise."

"I beg your pardon?"

"Lady Ames can be a trifle exhausting, even for a man in his prime. I understand her lord was quite elderly. He probably never stood a chance. I venture to say he expired from overexertion."

Emma felt the heat rush into her cheeks. "I see." So much for her talents as a sleuth. She cleared her throat and turned back to gaze fixedly across the theater.

She saw at once that Edison had vanished from Miranda's box. Another man had taken his place.

"Well, I had best be off." Basil rose abruptly to his feet and bowed deeply over Emma's hand. "Your fiancé appears to be hurrying back to this box. Perhaps he took offense at the sight of me chatting with you."

She knew from the gleam of satisfaction in his eyes that Basil was leaving because he had accomplished his goal. He had amused himself at her expense. It was all nothing more to him than a round of the popular pastime of flirting with another man's lady. The game had no doubt had an extra fillip of interest tonight because of the presence of Lady Exbridge.

"Do stay, Mr. Ware." Emma gave him a steely smile. "I'm certain that Edison will wish to speak with you."

"I have no desire to find myself making a dawn appointment." The laughter vanished from his eyes. It was replaced with something that could have been genuine concern. "I trust you will not forget what I told you at Ware Castle, Miss Greyson. If you should ever find yourself in, shall we say, unfortunate circumstances, you must get in touch with me immediately."

"Really, Mr. Ware, I cannot imagine such a circumstance."

"You have my promise that I will see to it that you are not left destitute and friendless when Stokes has finished his games."

Before Emma could respond, he was gone.

A few minutes later the heavy velvet curtain at the back of the box shifted again. Edison walked in, nodded brusquely at the gentlemen gathered around Letty, and sat down beside Emma. He did not look pleased.

"What the devil was Ware doing here?" he asked without preamble.

Emma tried for an expression of polite surprise. "He merely came by to pay his respects."

"The devil he did. He is determined to seduce you. He won't be satisfied until he's accomplished his goal."

"How very odd," Emma murmured. "Mr. Ware was just giving me a similar warning concerning you and Miranda. He is convinced that Lady Ames has set her snares for you and will not rest until she has made the conquest. I believe he leaped to the conclusion that she lured you into her box tonight."

Edison slanted her a sidelong glance. "You know bloody well what I was doing in Miranda's box."

"Indeed, I do, sir." She smiled brightly. "And were you successful?"

"No." Disgust simmered in his tone. "I can well believe that the woman really is an actress. She has a way of dancing around pointed questions without—"

"Emma dear," Letty sang out from the other side of the box. "A word, if you don't mind."

Emma looked past Edison to where Letty sat amid her cluster of graying admirers. "Yes, madam?"

"Bickle here—" Letty paused to give the portly Bickle a fond glance— "has just invited me to join him in his carriage after the performance. He is going to take me on to the Turley soiree. Would you mind very much if I abandoned you to the care of your charming fiancé for the rest of the evening?" She gave Edison a broad wink. "I'm certain he will take excellent care of you."

Emma tensed. A shiver, half dread, half anticipation, ruffled her nerves. She and Edison had not been alone in each other's company since the night before last, when he had walked out of the library and shut the door in her face. She was not at all certain that she wished to be alone with him.

A part of her was afraid that he would want to bring up what she had taught herself to refer to as the Incident in the carriage. Another part of her was terrified that he would *not* want to discuss it.

She was trapped. "Of course I do not mind. Enjoy yourself, Letty."

"Oh, I'm sure I shall." Letty beamed at Bickle, who turned an unhealthy shade of red. "His lordship is a most entertaining companion."

His lordship, Emma could not help but notice, was also semiaroused. His old-fashioned breeches left little to the imagination.

She looked away quickly, but not quickly enough. Edison caught her eye and gave her a blandly amused look. She studiously ignored him until the curtain rose on the last act of *Othello*.

At the end of the performance, Emma waited in the crowded theater lobby while Edison went to summon his carriage. When he returned to fetch her, she allowed herself to be conducted outside and handed up into the cab. She was aware of the tension in him. It radiated through his hand when he gripped her arm.

Heaven help her, he *was* going to talk about the Incident.

Edison vaulted lightly in behind her and sat down on the opposite seat. "I must speak with you."

Emma braced herself. She was prepared, she thought. Her career as a paid companion had turned her into a woman of the world. She could handle this sort of thing. She determined to carry on as though nothing of any great significance had happened. It seemed the wisest course of action; indeed, the only sensible course.

"I am rather tired, sir," she announced smoothly. "If you don't mind, I would like to go home."

"That is an excellent notion." He sat back, obviously relieved. "I was just about to suggest it but I feared you would argue."

Sudden anger shot through her when she glimpsed the gleam of satisfaction in his eyes. "If you think that I am issuing a . . . a carnal invitation of some sort, you can bloody well think again, sir. I have absolutely no intention of repeating the incident that took place in this carriage the other night."

Oh, nicely done, Emma. Now you have raised the issue of the Incident.

Edison gave her a humorless smile. "Even if I were so fortunate as to receive such a delightful invitation from you, my dear, I would be obliged to refuse it tonight."

"I beg your pardon?"

"Something very interesting has just occurred."

She realized at once that he was talking about a matter entirely unrelated to the Incident. "What do you mean?"

"A few minutes ago when I went outside to summon the carriage, a street urchin was waiting for me. He had a message."

"What sort of message?"

"It's from an old associate of mine, a part-time smuggler named One-Eared Harry. He hangs out around the docks. I occasionally purchased information from him during the war."

Emma was aghast. "Good heavens. What sort of information would a smuggler have to sell to you?"

Edison shrugged. "News of the comings and goings of ships in the waters controlled by the French. Details of the terrain near the coast. Locations of military garrisons. The usual."

She narrowed her eyes. "And just why would you want such information, sir?"

"I am a man with many varied business interests," he said. "I could not allow them to come to a complete halt simply because Napoleon was out to conquer the world."

"Of course not," she muttered. It would probably be best not to pursue this line of inquiry further. She was not certain that she wanted to discover that Edison had practiced a bit of smuggling during the war with France. "Intolerable to imagine letting Napoleon get in the way of one's *financial* interests."

Edison looked amused by her frosty glare. "Occasionally some of the information I gained from One-Eared Harry was also of use to the authorities. I, of course, passed it along."

"I see." So he had once been a spymaster. "You have had a very adventurous life, sir. What sort of information do you think this One-Eared Harry person has for you this evening?"

"I sent word to him yesterday that I would pay for any information regarding the man who attacked us in Lady Ames's garden. Harry has a knack for falling in with bad company."

"I see." She raised her brows. "Since you appear to be on speaking terms with Harry, I assume that you have the same knack."

He grinned fleetingly. "A man with extensive business interests must be flexible."

"That's one word for it, I suppose."

"In any event, I have hopes that Harry has learned something useful." Edison glanced out at the dark street. His jaw tightened. "Lorring told me not to waste my time making inquiries in this direction, but I have a feeling that it may lead to some answers."

A distinct chill went through Emma, similar to the one she had experienced outside the theater a short while earlier. Now she knew that it was not connected to a discussion of the Incident. Something far more dangerous was abroad tonight.

"Where will you meet with this One-Eared Harry?" she asked.

"At a tavern called the Red Demon near the docks."

Another whisper of dread flashed down Emma's spine. "Edison, I do not like this scheme of yours."

"There is nothing in it to alarm you."

She struggled to put into words what she had never been able to explain. "I have a nasty feeling about it. Everyone knows that the neighborhood near the docks is dangerous, especially at this hour of the night."

"Your concern for the safety of your employer is, as always, appreciated." He smiled grimly. "Don't worry, Emma, I'll survive to pay you your wages and write that bloody reference."

Her temper flared without warning. She clenched her gloved hands in her lap. "Mr. Stokes, I have had quite enough of your sarcasm. I happen to be a rather intuitive person and I have a premonition about your plan to meet this One-Eared Harry person tonight. I was merely trying to give you a warning."

"Consider the warning delivered." He leaned forward and caught her chin between his thumb and forefinger. "And in exchange, I shall give you one."

"What is that?"

"Do not allow Basil Ware to get you alone under any circumstances." Edison's expression was as cold as a January storm. "Stay away from him, Emma. He sees you as nothing more than a prize to be stolen in a vicious little game. If he is successful, he will lose all interest in you."

She was suddenly breathless. She fought the unnerving sensation with anger. "Do you think I do not know what sort of man he is? I am an expert in such creatures, sir. I do not require your advice."

"Nevertheless, as your *employer*, I feel obliged to give it."

"I assure you, I can take care of myself. See to it that you heed *my* warning tonight, sir."

"I will."

He released her, sat back, and swiftly unknotted his snow white cravat. She watched with growing unease as he dropped the neckcloth on the seat and pulled up the collar of his greatcoat. He made a few other minor adjustments such as concealing his watch fob.

When he was finished with the simple transformation, he was once again garbed only in darkness and shadow.

"Edison, I mean it," she whispered. "Promise me you will be exceedingly careful tonight."

His smile had a feral edge to it. "Will you give me a kiss for luck?"

She hesitated. And then, in spite of his dangerous smile, she leaned forward and brushed her mouth lightly across his.

He was clearly surprised by the fleeting intimacy. She drew back just as he started to react.

He gazed at her for a long moment with enigmatic eyes.

"You do realize that you cannot avoid forever the subject of what happened between us," he said quite casually.

Emma ignored him. "Concerning my own plans for the evening, I have changed my mind, sir. I will not go home after all. You may have your coachman deliver me to the Smithton soiree. When you have finished your meeting at the docks, you may join me there. I will want a full report of all that you learn from One-Eared Harry."

Chapter Eighteen

The Red Demon exuded the smoky, unwholesome atmosphere that was common to such places. A colorful assortment of dockworkers, villains, prostitutes, and others who eked out a living on the edges of the stews occupied the wooden benches. Mugs of ale and the remains of meat pies littered the tables.

One-Eared Harry sat across from Edison. What remained of his left ear was partially concealed by long, greasy hair and a scarf tied around his head. Edison had heard at least three different versions of the tale involving the loss of Harry's ear. The first involved a fight with a drunken sailor. The second concerned an angry prostitute who had objected to not getting paid for her services. The third had something to do with a gang of thieves who had attempted to steal one of Harry's shipments of smuggled French brandy.

Harry considered Edison a friend but he had never been one to let friendship stand in the way of business. Edison knew he had to remember that the enterprising smuggler sold false information as industriously as he did the more truthful sort. Still, Harry had some standards. And he and Edison went back a long way.

In any event, Edison thought, he could not afford to be overly choosy about his sources in this venture.

"I noticed 'im first on account of 'e moves a bit like you do, Mr. Stokes." Harry cast a wary glance around the smoky room and then leaned across the table. "Smooth and quiet like. Most of the time 'e sort of fades into the woodwork. Ye don't even know 'e's around unless 'e wants you to see 'im. And 'e favors black clothing like yerself."

Edison tried to ignore the sour, musty odor that wafted across the table. He was fairly certain that the only times Harry bathed were on those occasions when he got roaring drunk on French brandy and fell into the river. Such immersions did little good, the river being dirtier than Harry.

"When did you first notice him?" Edison asked.

Harry screwed up his face in what was apparently a considering expression. "A fortnight back, it was. We keep an eye on strangers around 'ere, as ye well know. When I 'eard ye was lookin' for someone who favored dark clothes, kept to 'imself, and was willin' to pay for information regarding yerself, sir, I thought of 'im."

"Describe this man," Edison said.

"Can't rightly say what 'e looks like. Never seen 'im in the daylight."

"How tall is he?"

Harry pursed his lips. "About as tall as yerself, sir. Younger, though, I'd say. Much younger."

"Heavily built?"

Harry looked surprised. "No, sir. Now that ye mention it, 'e's on the slender side. Sort of thin and wiry. Moves like a cat."

"I am not going to pay you for such vague information, Harry. If you cannot tell me what he looks like or where he can be found, then what have you got to sell to me?"

A feverish glint of greed appeared in Harry's eyes. He took a quick swallow of ale, wiped his mouth on the back of his sleeve, and leaned closer. "I think I know where 'e's got 'is lodgings."

Anticipation unfurled in Edison's gut. But he had done enough business with Harry over the years to know better than to allow it to show.

"You can tell me where he lives?"

"Aye. Last night when I was strollin' back to me room above the Fat Mermaid, I noticed 'im goin' into the kitchen door of a pie shop in Oldhead Lane. The widow who owns the shop rents out rooms." Harry paused. "Leastways, I think it was 'im."

"Why do you doubt it?"

"Because 'e was movin' differently from the last time I saw 'im. Not so smooth and easy. Like maybe 'e'd been hurt." Harry clutched at his own ribs and groaned to demonstrate. "Like 'ed been kicked by a 'orse. Or maybe been in a fight."

Edison sat back and thought about it. He was fairly certain he had landed at least one solid blow to the Vanza fighter's thigh and another to his shoulder. "What time did you see him?"

Harry shrugged. "'Ard to tell, sir. Late, that's all I know."

It was possible that this time Harry was selling solid information. On the other hand, it all sounded a bit too helpful.

Edison considered the possibilities for a moment and then shrugged.

"All right, Harry. I shall pay you."

Harry's mouth blossomed into a wide, toothless grin. "Thank ye, sir. I 'ope ye find the bugger. Fair gives me the shivers, 'e does. Wouldn't mind seein' 'im gone from the neighborhood."

He pocketed the banknotes that Edison passed to him under the table, finished his ale, and surged to his feet. He turned, hurried through the crowded tavern, opened the door, and stepped out into the dark street.

Edison waited a moment longer. Then he rose, walked to the rear of the premises, as though on his way to the privy, and slipped outside. Instead of making his way to the jakes, however, he went around the corner of the tavern.

The yellow glow of Harry's lantern glimmered in the light fog that had crawled out of the river. The bobbing light disappeared into a black lane.

Edison followed.

Emma rubbed her arms. "Does it feel cold in here to you, Miranda?"

"Not in the least." Miranda glanced around the crowded ballroom. "It's rather warm, actually. Are you feeling chilled?"

"A bit."

In truth, she had been feeling perfectly comfortable until a moment ago. The sensation that stirred the fine hair on her arms had come out of nowhere, as though an icy wind had blown through the overheated room.

Miranda eyed her with sharp interest. "You have had too much excitement of late. Why don't we go into one of the smaller rooms and sit down for a few minutes?"

The idea held a certain appeal but Emma wished that it had been someone other than Miranda who had suggested it. On the other hand, she told herself bracingly, she was employed to serve as bait. This was a perfect opportunity to try her own hand at probing into Miranda's mysterious past.

It would be quite satisfying to surprise Edison with more information that he had been unable to obtain for himself.

"Excellent notion," Emma said politely. "I believe I would like to sit down for a few minutes."

"It is too bad that I do not have any of my special herbal tea with me. It's very effective for warding off chills and fevers."

It took an effort but Emma managed not to heave a small sigh of relief. "I'm sure one of Lady Smithton's maids could bring us a pot of regular tea."

"Yes, of course."

They made their way through the crush into the hall. One of the footmen ushered them into a small sitting room and went off to fetch a tea tray.

"Poor thing," Miranda murmured as they sat down in front of the fire. "You are not accustomed to the demands of the social world, are you? I expect it is all very wearying for you."

"Fortunately, I have a strong constitution," Emma said brightly. "It was a necessity in my previous career."

"I can well imagine it was. But I suspect that the demands of your engagement to Stokes are proving even more rigorous, albeit vastly more entertaining, than those you encountered as a paid companion, hmm?"

"I beg your pardon?"

Miranda gave her a wink and a knowing smile. "Come now, Emma. We are both women of the world. And it is no secret that you have, shall we say, already allowed your fiancé a taste of the goods."

Emma felt heat flood her cheeks and was furious with herself for the blush. Fortunately, the harried footman returned with the tea tray at that moment. She took the opportunity to recover her self-possession.

"I have no idea what you are talking about, madam," she said briskly when they were alone again.

Miranda gave her shivery little laugh. "Going to play the role of the virgin bride, are you? How delightful. But I must tell you the effect has already been somewhat spoiled by the events at Ware Castle. After all, everyone there did see you in your nightclothes and wrapper. And I must remind you that it was Stokes himself who assured Ware's guests that you had been with him when Crane was murdered."

Emma made a noncommittal response and covered it with another sip of tea.

Miranda's eyes glittered. "Never say that was not true?"

Oh no you don't, you witch. You are not going to trip me up on that point.

"It was all perfectly true, Miranda. But a trifle awkward in terms of my reputation." Emma smiled blandly. "Not, however, as awkward as hanging for murder."

"I understand." Miranda propped her delicate chin on her hand and looked at Emma with a confiding air. "But really there is no need to be coy. As there are only the two of us at the moment, I cannot resist asking you what you think of Stokes's tattoo."

Emma nearly dropped her cup. "His *what*?"

Some of the self-assured certainty vanished from Miranda's eyes. "His tattoo. Surely you have seen it. After all, you have been intimate with him."

"Gentlemen do not have tattoos," Emma said forcefully. "Men who go to sea and pirates have them, or so I have been told. But certainly not gentlemen of Mr. Stokes's station."

Miranda kept her smile but there was a pinched quality to it. "Perhaps in the darkness you did not notice it."

"I have no notion of what you are talking about."

Miranda's eyes widened. "Dear me, do you mean to say that he does not take his shirt off when he makes love to you? How very disappointing. I myself enjoy the sight of a manly chest."

Emma was bloody well not going to admit that the one and only time he had made love to her, Edison had not bothered to remove his shirt. She put the teacup down with great precision and looked straight at Miranda.

"I am well aware that I am new to the ways of the ton, Lady Ames. You must forgive me if I am mistaken, but I was under the impression that it is considered quite vulgar for ladies to kiss and tell."

"I beg your pardon." Miranda's expression hardened. "Just what are you implying?"

"I cannot believe that a well-bred lady would ever discuss such things as tattoos and manly chests. Surely only a certain kind of female, a member of the demimonde"—Emma paused just long enough to give emphasis to her next words—"or perhaps an *actress,* would actually boast of a sexual conquest."

The effect on Miranda was instantaneous. Her jaw dropped. She jerked as if she had been struck. Her eyes turned glassy with malice. Her rage was a palpable force in the room.

"How dare you imply that I am vulgar?" Miranda's voice was a grating whisper. "You are the one who is as common as dirt. You were nothing but a paid companion before Stokes took a notion to save you from the hangman's noose. If I were you, I would start worrying about just why he bothered. You are certainly not the sort of woman a man in his position would ever marry. Why, you are no better than—"

She broke off abruptly, leaped to her feet in a rustle of satin, and swept out the door. The air around her crackled with her fury.

Miranda did know how to make an exit, Emma noted. Yet more evidence that she had once trod the boards. And it was clear that a nerve had been struck with the reference to ill-bred actresses. That will teach you to tangle with a professional companion, Emma thought.

It was only when the spurt of triumph faded that the full realization of what she had just done hit her. *She had as much as told Miranda outright that she knew about her past career as an actress.*

What on earth had come over her? She might very well have put her wonderful new post in jeopardy with her rash words. If Miranda panicked and took flight, Edison would no longer need any bait. He would no longer need *her,* Emma thought.

A cold feeling settled into the pit of her stomach.

Emma clenched one gloved hand into a fist. If only the witch had not made that reference to Edison's tattoo. It was as good as an admission that they had had at least one tryst.

When had it occurred? Emma wondered. At Ware Castle? Or afterward, here in Town? She recalled the way Edison had hovered over Miranda's hand in the theater box earlier that evening. Just how far had he gone in his efforts to learn more about the actress's mysterious past?

Another chill of dread trickled down her spine, jolting Emma out of her grim reverie. The sensation of being touched by ghostly fingers had nothing to do with her unhappy imaginings concerning Miranda and Edison.

Edison was in danger. She was sure of it. But there was not a thing she could do about it.

The unmistakable stench of the Thames was especially strong tonight. Edison would have known where he was even if he had been blindfolded. The river had made London a great trading port. Indeed, he was well aware that he owed a substantial portion of his fortune to it. But it also functioned as the city's sewer. On any given day it was thick with the offal of cesspits and stables, the carcasses of dead animals, and the occasional victim of a footpad.

He stood in the shadows of a fog-shrouded doorway and listened to One-Eared Harry pound on the door of a dock shed.

"Ye'd better be in there with the money ye promised, ye sneaky bastard." Harry rapped harder. "I've carried out me end o' the bargain and I've come for me pay."

This section of the docks was deserted at this hour. Warehouses and storage buildings loomed dark and silent in the swirling fog. The soft murmur of the black water had a hungry sound, as though the river anticipated prey. Vessels of various sizes groaned and creaked and sighed as they shifted gently against the ropes that secured them.

The only light was the weak glow of Harry's lantern. It reflected wildly in the fog, creating an unearthly glare near the shed door.

Harry rapped on the wooden panel. "We 'ad a bargain, damn yer eyes. I've come for me money. No one cheats One-Eared 'Arry."

Hinges squeaked. From where he stood, Edison could see the shed door open partway to reveal a wedge of inky darkness. A voice emanated from the shadows.

"You met with the One Who Went Outside the Circle?"

"Now see 'ere, I don't know nothing about any circle. I met with Stokes, just like we agreed."

"You told him exactly what I instructed you to tell him?"

"Aye. And now I've come for me money. Where is it?"

"If you have carried out your duties, you are of no further use to me."

"What d'ye mean?" Harry stepped back quickly. The lantern in his hand swung wildly. "Now see 'ere, we 'ad a bargain."

"Indeed we did, Mr. One-Eared Harry." The door opened wider. "You have betrayed your friend, have you not?"

"That's a bloody lie," Harry protested. He sounded genuinely offended. "I didn't betray Stokes. Why would I do that? 'Im and me is friends. We've been business associates from time to time."

"Nevertheless, tonight you betrayed him."

"I just relieved 'im of some of 'is blunt, is all. 'E won't miss it. 'E's got more than enough and that's a bloody fact. It was just business."

"On the contrary. You have lured him to this meeting, where he will meet great defeat."

"The devil I did," Harry snapped. "I didn't lure him anywhere. We both know there ain't no pie shop in Oldhead Lane and no rooms above it, either."

"He is no fool. He is One Who Could Have Been Grand Master. He will not go to Oldhead Lane. He will have followed you here. And here his legend will be destroyed forever."

"Now 'old on just one bloody damn minute." Harry took another step back and held up a hand. "If ye think I told 'im those things to make 'im follow me so that ye could get yer bloody 'ands on 'im, yer as mad as a bedlamite."

"I am not mad, Mr. One-Eared Harry. I am an Initiate of the Great Circle of Vanza. Tonight I employed the Strategy of Deception to draw out the One Who Could Have Been Grand Master."

"Why'd ye want to go and do that?" Harry whined.

"When I defeat him in honorable combat, I will prove to my master that I am worthy of being initiated into the next Level of Ascendancy."

"God's blood, yer talkin' gibberish, ye are."

"Enough." The dark figure shifted in the shadows of the doorway. A moment later a second lantern flared to life. "I do not have the time to waste discussing great matters which you can never hope to comprehend."

Edison moved out of his place of concealment, closing the distance between himself and the dark figure who stood in the shed's doorway.

"I think it's time you left, Harry," Edison said quietly.

"What the devil?" Harry raised his lantern, half turning to peer into the swirling fog. "Stokes? What the bloody 'ell are ye—"

The shed door opened wider. A man dressed entirely in black, his features concealed behind a cloth mask, emerged.

The Vanza fighter took two quick steps, leaped high into the air, and lashed out with his foot. The blow struck Harry in the ribs.

Harry gave a muffled grunt and toppled backward over the edge of the dock. There was a resounding splash when he hit the water. The lantern he had been clutching sank like a stone. The light winked out.

Silhouetted in the glare of the lantern he had lit earlier, the Vanza fighter bowed formally to Edison.

"O Legendary One Who Went Outside the Circle. O Great One Who Could Have Been Grand Master, you will honor me by giving me the victory tonight."

Edison winced. "Do you always talk like that?"

The young fighter stiffened. "I speak with respect to one who is still legend."

"Who in blazes told you that I was a legend?"

"My master."

"I'm not a legend," Edison said softly. "I'm an ex-practitioner of Vanza. There is a very large difference."

"My master told me that you could have been a Grand Master."

"To become a Grand Master, one must first call another man Master. I was never very good at that."

The lack of any splashing sounds was starting to concern Edison. He walked toward the edge of the dock.

"My master says that you could have been the greatest Grand Master of Vanza in all of Europe."

"Highly unlikely." Edison risked a quick glance over the side of the dock. There was enough lantern light bouncing off the fog to reveal Harry clinging weakly to a rung embedded in the quay. "By the bye, who is this master of yours?"

"I cannot tell you." The fighter's voice dropped to a reverential tone. "I have taken an oath of secrecy"

"A secret Vanza master? How very odd. Well, I can certainly tell you one thing about him."

"What is that?" the fighter demanded.

"He is not a good master. Any true practitioner of the arts would have told you that there is nothing courageous or honorable about kicking someone like One-Eared Harry into the river."

"You are concerned for this One-Eared Harry?" The young man's voice rose in disbelief. "How can that be? He called himself your friend, yet he betrayed you. He is unworthy of your trust, O Great One Who Could Have Been Grand Master."

Down below in the water, Harry groaned. It was obvious that he did not have the strength to haul himself out of the river.

Edison reached into his pocket and closed his fingers around the pistol he had brought with him. "Nevertheless, as Harry told you, he and I go back a long way. I really will have to fish him out of the river."

"Leave him." The young man went into a fighter's crouch and began to circle. "Tonight you and I meet in honorable combat."

Edison removed the pistol and aimed it casually at the Vanza fighter. "Enough of that. I haven't got time for it tonight."

"What is this? A *pistol*?" The young fighter halted abruptly. His voice shook with outrage. "You would use a pistol? That is not Vanza."

"No, but it's effective. One of the reasons why I went outside the circle is that there is much about Vanza which I found to be exceedingly impractical."

"I will not be denied my victory."

"Take yourself off or we shall both discover whether or not you can achieve your victory over a bullet."

The Vanza fighter hesitated only a few seconds.

"There will be another meeting between us," he finally snarled. "I swear it on my oath as One Who Is Vanza."

"You know, one of these days, you'll get tired of talking as though you were on stage."

But Edison was speaking to the fog. The Vanza fighter had vanished down a dark alley.

CHAPTER NINETEEN

Emma was so relieved to receive the message from the footman that she did not even complain about the manner in which it had been delivered. The only thing that mattered at that moment was that Edison was apparently safe. He had finally arrived at the Smithton house and was waiting for her in his carriage. The fact that it was quite rude for a gentleman to remain in his vehicle while he sent a servant to fetch his fiancée from a ball was not of overriding importance just then.

She clutched her cloak at her throat and rushed down the steps to the waiting carriage. The interior lamps were unlit, she noticed.

A footman opened the door and handed her up inside. Edison was a dark, indistinct shape in the shadows.

"Sir, I have been extremely worried—" She broke off as she sat down and wrinkled her nose. "Good heavens, what is that perfectly dreadful odor?"

"A cologne distilled from the waters of the Thames." Edison pulled the curtains closed and lit one of the lamps. "I doubt that it will become the rage."

"What on earth has happened to you?" She stared at him, appalled, as the lantern sputtered and finally flared.

For once in his life, Edison did not look the least bit elegant.

He looked and smelled as if he had fallen into a cesspit.

He sat ensconced on the opposite seat, swathed from neck to knee in carriage blankets. She realized that she did not want to examine too closely the odd bits and pieces that clung to his wet hair. There was an oily smudge on his cheek that made it appear that he had a black eye.

The expensively tailored trousers, shirt, waistcoat, and coat in which he had begun the evening were bundled into a damp, disreputable heap on the floor. Much of the malodorous smell that filled the cab emanated from them.

She asked the first question that popped into her mind. "What happened to your greatcoat?"

"I was obliged to loan it to a friend who fell into the river."

"Good heavens." She was struck by the sight of his lower legs and feet, which were bare. He had very large feet, she noticed.

"My apologies for the uncivil way in which I summoned you from the ball," Edison said. "As you can see, I am not dressed for Lady Smithton's party."

She realized she was still staring at his feet. With an effort she jerked her gaze back up to his face.

"You look as though *you* were the one who fell into the river, sir."

Edison tightened his grip on the blankets. "I did not precisely fall into the river."

"Do you mean to say that someone pushed you into it? Good God, my premonition of danger was correct. You were attacked, were you not? That man you went to meet, One-Eared Harry, did he do this to you?"

"Actually, I did it to myself in the process of pulling Harry out of the Thames."

"Oh, I see." She was somewhat relieved to hear that. Then a thought struck her. "But how did he fall in?"

"We had an encounter with the Vanza fighter," Edison said softly.

"Dear heaven, are you certain you are unhurt?"

"Quite certain. There is no damage done that a bath will not correct. But the Vanza practitioner got away because I was obliged to see to Harry."

"Did you learn anything useful tonight?"

"All I got out of the affair were more questions." Edison paused. "And confirmation of my suspicion that there is, indeed, a rogue Vanza master operating somewhere in London. He is no doubt after that damned book too."

"What will you do next?"

"I have been giving the matter a good deal of thought. I believe that it would be interesting to find this master and question him," Edison said rather casually.

A fresh frisson whispered through Emma. "How will you do that?"

"It should not be too difficult to draw out the young fighter again. Apparently I am standing in the path of his career advancement. He wants to prove himself by challenging me in ritual combat."

"A duel, do you mean?" Emma's hands went cold inside her gloves. "Edison, you must not even think of such a thing. You could be injured or killed."

"Come now, Miss Greyson. Have a bit of faith in your employer. I admit I am not as young as I used to be, but I have grown more crafty over the years. I have every hope of giving a good account of myself."

"Edison, this is no occasion for jest. It all sounds horribly dangerous. I do not like it."

"I assure you, there is no cause for concern." Edison brushed something that was slimy and green off his leg and settled deeper into his seat. "What about you? I assume you could not resist the opportunity to try to question Miranda at the Smithton affair."

Emma gave a start. "How did you know that I tried to do just that?"

Edison's mouth twitched. "Because you wanted to prove that you could be successful where I had failed, of course. Any luck?"

She flushed. There was no choice, she thought, squaring her shoulders. She had to tell him the truth. "I not only failed, but I did so rather spectacularly."

"I beg your pardon?"

She hesitated. "You will not like this, sir, but I must inform you that I may have ruined your scheme to use me as bait for Lady Ames."

His brows rose. "Ruined it?"

"In my own behalf, I would like to say that it was not my fault that things went awry. I was provoked."

"Provoked," he repeated carefully. "By whom? Miranda?"

"Yes."

"Perhaps you had better tell me the entire tale," he said.

She switched her gaze to the squabs on the cushion behind him. "There is not much to relate. Suffice it to say that Lady Ames made certain indelicate references to our engagement."

"And what, exactly, was the nature of those indelicate references?"

"She leaped to the conclusion that you and I had been intimate."

"What of it?" he asked without any trace of awkwardness or embarrassment. "It happens to be an accurate conclusion. One we fostered ourselves the night Chilton Crane got shot in your bedchamber."

She would not let him disconcert her, she vowed. She, too, could be cool and blasé. She clasped her hands very tightly together and fixed her attention determinedly on the squabs. "The thing is, she asked questions."

Emma knew at once that she had finally got Edison's interest. He narrowed his eyes in the watchful manner that she had come to recognize.

"Questions?" he said.

"About you. Of a particularly intimate nature, I might add."

"I see." A glint of humor lit his eyes. "I have always wondered if women were inclined to gossip about that sort of thing."

Anger unfurled once more in Emma. "They were questions designed, I believe, to imply that you and she have indulged in a tryst."

"What were these questions, precisely?"

"She asked me if I had noted a certain tattoo, of all things, on your person."

"Bloody hell."

She raised her chin. "The implication, you understand, was that she had seen it when the two of you, uh, when you two . . ." She trailed off, unable to say the words. She waved one gloved hand to indicate the obvious.

Edison no longer looked amused. "A tattoo? Did she describe it?"

"No, she most certainly did not." Emma was incensed. "Nor did I invite her to do so. The whole thing was most awkward for me, sir."

"I can well imagine." There was an unholy glint in his eyes.

"Her very personal questions put me in an extremely difficult position."

"Indeed."

She drew herself up. "Therefore, I really do not think it would be at all fair of you to dismiss me from my post merely because I accidentally made an unfortunate remark about actresses."

He looked thoughtful. "You brought up the subject?"

"Yes, I did."

"Hardly a subtle approach," he said dryly.

"I have a feeling that subtlety of any kind is lost on Lady Ames."

"What exactly did you say about actresses?" Edison asked with grave interest.

She cleared her throat. "Something to the effect that only ladies in vulgar careers, actresses, for example, would boast publicly of their sexual conquests the way she did."

"I see." Edison's voice sounded as though he had choked slightly. The corner of his mouth twitched. "Yes, of course. Actresses."

Emma peered at him suspiciously. "Are you laughing at me, sir?"

"I would not dream of doing so."

"You *are* laughing."

He grinned. "Forgive me, Emma, but I would have given a great deal to have seen Miranda's face when you accused her of acting like a vulgar actress."

"It may sound amusing to you now, sir, but you will likely change your mind when you reflect upon the results."

"What do you mean?"

"Don't you understand? After my remarks, she no doubt suspects that we are on to her. Your plans may be in ruins even as we speak."

He raised one shoulder in a shrug. "On the contrary. It may have been an excellent moment to apply certain elements of the Strategy of Redirection."

"I beg your pardon?"

"You have unwittingly used one of the Strategies of Vanza, Emma. You indicated to Miranda that you may be in possession of certain facts about her that she believed to be secret."

"So?"

"So you have, in effect, applied pressure that may force her to move in another direction. Such unplanned changes in a scheme frequently result in mistakes on the part of one's opponent. It will be interesting to see what she does next."

Emma eyed him in silence.

He gave her an inquiring look. "Was there anything else you wished to tell me?"

"No."

"Was there anything else you wished to ask me?"

She hesitated and then looked pointedly away from his gleaming eyes. "No."

"Are you quite certain?"

"Absolutely certain."

"Hmm. Well, just to clear the air between us, I can assure you that Miranda has never had an occasion to see the sign of Vanza on my chest."

She stared. "Are you saying that you do have a tattoo?"

"Such a mark is part of the initiation into Vanza."

"Are you quite certain that Miranda has never seen it?"

"I think I would remember if such an *incident* had ever occurred between Lady Ames and myself."

A great lightness went through Emma. "I see. Well, I wonder why she implied that it had occurred."

"Obviously she was attempting to get you to confirm that I was a member of the Vanzagarian Society." Edison frowned. "Which means that she actually knows about the Society and is familiar with the mark."

"You mean, she may have seen such a tattoo on someone else?"

"Yes."

Emma searched his face. "But who would that be?"

Edison smiled his humorless smile. "Farrell Blue springs to mind."

"Yes, of course." Emma thought quickly. "An intimate liaison be-tween Miranda and Farrell Blue would explain a great deal, would it not?"

"Yes. It would provide an explanation of how she came to be in possession of the recipe for the elixir. She may have stolen it from him."

Emma nibbled on her lower lip while she considered that. "You said Farrell Blue lived in Rome and that he died there in a house fire. If Miranda was involved in an affair with him, then she, too, must have lived in Italy until recently."

"True."

"But she claims she came from Scotland. Even if she is lying about her husband and her life there, those playbills and reviews that we found indicate she lived in the north of England, not Italy."

"The playbills and reviews were dated more than two years ago," Edison reminded her. "Who knows where she has been since then?"

"Excellent point. Perhaps she went to Italy."

"Perhaps," Edison agreed. "There are still a great many questions here, but now that you have prodded Miranda, I wouldn't be surprised to see her make a rash move. Such an action could give us a clue."

Emma relaxed slightly. "Does this mean that I shall remain in your employment?"

"I believe I shall keep you on awhile."

"Thank you, sir. I cannot tell you how relieved I am to hear that you do not intend to dismiss me."

Edison grunted.

"I suppose this would not be a convenient time to remind you of my reference?" Emma asked with what she hoped was great delicacy.

"No."

Silence fell.

Emma studied her hands for a moment. Then she began to twiddle her thumbs.

The silence lengthened.

"What the devil are you thinking?" Edison asked.

She cleared her throat. "I was just wondering why a gentleman would do something so odd as to obtain a tattoo."

"I was nineteen at the time," Edison said dryly. "I think that is sufficient explanation for any odd behavior."

"Yes, of course," she murmured.

He gave her a smile that made her toes curl inside her slippers.

"Would you care to see my tattoo?" He moved slightly, as though he was about to unwrap the blanket.

Emma panicked. *"No."* She glared at him. "Do not be absurd, sir. Of course I do not wish to see your tattoo. It is none of my affair and it would hardly be proper. After all, you are my employer."

"I wonder why I keep forgetting that fact."

Emma was relieved to feel the carriage slowing. She was home at last. She could go upstairs, climb into bed, and go to sleep.

And try very hard not to lie awake thinking of how much she wanted to see Edison's tattoo.

CHAPTER TWENTY

You do realize what you are saying?" Ignatius gazed broodingly into the fire. "If what you have told me is true, a trusted member of the Society has not simply gone outside the Circle. He has established his own Circle."

"So it would seem."

Edison glanced at the library windows. One of them stood wide. He realized that it had been opened before he arrived in an effort to air out the room. He could still smell the faint residue of the opium-laced smoke.

Ignatius was using more and more of the drug lately, and he had begun to take it in a variety of ways. The pain must be getting worse, Edison thought.

"It is a deplorable development." Ignatius's eyes glittered

with indignation. "One that must be dealt with properly by the officials of the Vanzagarian Society. He certainly must not be allowed to get his hands on the *Book of Secrets*."

"I doubt that he is any closer to locating it than we are." Edison leaned back in his chair. "That is why he sent his student to spy on me."

He had decided not to mention the complication of the young fighter's ritual challenge. Ignatius had enough on his mind at the moment.

"It occurs to me," Ignatius said slowly, "that this rogue master may be employing the Strategy of Distraction in an attempt to interfere with our search—"

He broke off on a hoarse grunt, closed his eyes very tightly, and put one hand on his stomach. Stark lines of pain deepened around his mouth.

Edison got swiftly to his feet. "Shall I ring for someone to bring you more of your medicine, sir?"

"No, thank you." Ignatius opened his eyes and took an unsteady breath. "I will wait until you leave. I cannot think clearly when I am under the influence of the stuff. Now, where were we? Oh, yes, the rogue master. Good God, what if he gets to the book first?"

"Calm yourself, Ignatius. You must not become agitated."

"Such a thing would shame the Society forever in the eyes of the Vanzagarian temple monks. It would be the worst betrayal of all." Ignatius sagged weakly against the arm of his chair. "It must not happen."

"I give you my oath that, whoever this rogue master is, he will not get his hands on the *Book of Secrets*."

It was time to leave, Edison thought. Ignatius needed his medicine.

Half an hour later Edison walked up Lady Mayfield's front steps and banged the knocker. While he waited for the housekeeper to respond, he glanced idly over his shoulder.

With its stands of trees and extensive hedges, the park across the street offered ample concealment for anyone who might be following him. He wondered if the Vanza fighter was watching him even now from the shelter of a bush.

This entire affair seemed to center on baits and lures of one sort or another, he reflected. He and Emma were both playing similar roles now.

He smiled to himself as he recalled how flustered she had become last night when he had offered to show her his tattoo. He was almost certain he had seen the gleam of womanly desire and sensual curiosity in her brilliant eyes.

The door opened. Mrs. Wilton bobbed a curtsy. She looked wary. "Good day to you, Mr. Stokes."

"And to you, Mrs. Wilton. Will you be so good as to tell Miss Greyson that I am here?"

Mrs. Wilton cleared her throat. "Well, as to that, sir, I'm afraid Miss Emma is out at the moment."

"Out? Again?" The pleasant sense of anticipation Edison had been indulging vanished between one breath and the next. "Damnation. She knew bloody well I was planning to pay her a call this afternoon."

"I'm sorry, sir, but something unexpected like came up."

"Where the devil did she go?"

"She got a message from someone named Lady Exbridge about an hour ago asking her to call this afternoon," Mrs. Wilton said. "Miss Emma said you'd understand."

Edison's first thought was that he had not heard the name correctly. Then he went cold. "Lady Exbridge? Are you certain?"

"Yes, sir."

"Bloody hell." Anger swept through him. A lot of it was directed at himself. "I should have considered this possibility. The old bat could not get at her through me, so she has gone around me."

A terrible vision of Emma forced to confront his formidable grandmother alone crystallized in his brain. Victoria would be merciless.

Emma, for all her spirit and determination, would not stand a chance against her.

Edison swung around and hurried back down the steps. He could only hope that he would get there in time to save Emma from the worst of Victoria's fury.

Twenty minutes later he rapped furiously on the front door of the Exbridge Fortress. Jinkins, the butler, opened it with an expression of pinched disapproval. Edison was familiar with it. He had always suspected that Jinkins had adopted the look from his employer's repertoire of expressions reserved for her sole relative.

"Tell Lady Exbridge that I wish to see her immediately, Jinkins."

Jinkins did not trouble to conceal the gleam of triumph in his eyes. "Lady Exbridge has given strict instructions to tell all callers that she is not at home."

"Get out of my way, Jinkins."

"Now see here, sir, you cannot simply barge into a private house."

Edison did not bother to respond. He walked through the front door, forcing Jinkins to scamper aside.

"Sir, come back here this instant." Jinkins pursued Edison gamely down the hall.

Edison glanced at him as he came to a halt in front of the drawing room door. "Do not interfere, Jinkins. This is between Lady Exbridge and me."

Jinkins hesitated uncertainly but he appeared to know that he had lost this skirmish. He hovered angrily in the hall behind Edison but made no further attempt to stop him.

Edison resisted the almost overpowering urge to charge into the room and snatch Emma out of Victoria's clutches. He assumed the cloak of his hard-earned self-mastery and forced himself to open the door in a quiet, controlled manner.

The effort was wasted. Neither woman heard him enter. Seated at the far end of the room, they were intent only on each other. The tension between them filled the air with a dangerous electricity.

"... nothing more than a paid companion," Victoria said coldly. "How could Edison possibly be serious about marriage? Clearly he is using you in some dark scheme."

"Since you are his grandmother, I realize that you consider Edison's happiness your paramount concern."

"Nonsense. Happiness is fleeting and ephemeral, to say the least. It is not a goal that encourages a sense of duty and responsibility. The pursuit of it produces the sort of licentious, frivolous behavior that destroys families and fortunes."

"Ah." Emma sipped tea with a meditative air. "I understand.'"

Victoria bristled visibly. "What is it that you think you understand, Miss Greyson?"

"Your concerns regarding Edison's sense of duty and responsibility are entirely misplaced, Lady Exbridge. You must know as well as I do that he is not the wastrel and rake his father was."

A hush fell.

"How dare you," Victoria whispered. Her teacup clattered loudly in the saucer. "Who do you think you are to talk about Wesley that way? He was descended from some of the finest families in England. He was a nobleman who moved in the most exclusive circles."

"It is sad, is it not, how a man's bloodlines have so little influence on his sense of honor."

Victoria's outrage was palpable. "Are you saying that Wesley Stokes was not an honorable gentleman?"

Emma shrugged. "From what I have heard, your son's notion of honor had much in common with that of other gentlemen of the ton."

"I should think so."

"In other words, he did not allow it to get in the way of his pleasures," Emma said.

Victoria's mouth worked. "I beg your pardon?"

"Lady Mayfield informed me that in the course of a short but extremely active life, Wesley managed to lose the family estates, engage in at least two duels, bedded any number of his friends' wives, and preyed on young women who lacked protection from their employers and families."

"You know nothing of my son."

"Ah, but I do. Lady Mayfield, as it happens, remembers him well."

"And I remember her," Victoria snapped. "Thirty years ago Letty was nothing but a lowborn adventuress who managed to seduce that doddering old fool, Mayfield, into marriage."

"Forgive me, madam, but Lady Mayfield was, until quite recently, a kind and generous employer. I will not allow you to speak ill of her. She is a lady who looks after her staff, and I can assure you that makes her a paragon of virtue in my eyes."

"Which only goes to prove how very low your notions of virtue are."

"I will admit that my career as a professional companion does, I mean, *did,* provide me with an unusual perspective from which to view the world," Emma said. "I learned very quickly to be aware of the true nature of others, especially rakes, scoundrels, and those who are inclined toward cruelty and debauchery."

"Did you, indeed?" Victoria said in freezing accents.

"Oh, yes." Emma inclined her head in a confiding manner. "My very livelihood depended upon such observations, you see. It is always the employee, no matter how innocent she may be, who suffers when there is an Incident. But then, I'm sure you are well aware of that, knowing, as you do, what happened to Edison's mother."

Victoria turned a violent shade of red. "I do not allow that subject to be discussed in this household."

"I understand. It must have been heartbreaking for you to realize what an irresponsible son you'd raised."

"Irresponsible."

"You no doubt blamed yourself. And then to realize that your only grandchild was doomed to illegitimacy—"

"Be quiet. I forbid you to speak another word."

"It must have been an enormous relief to you," Emma continued blithely, "to learn that Edison takes after you rather than his father."

Victoria's mouth opened and closed like that of a fish on dry land. It took her several seconds to recover. "Edison? Takes after *me*?"

Emma contrived to look mildly astonished. "I would have thought the similarity was obvious. Only a man of bone-deep fortitude and determination could have gone out alone in the world and fashioned a fortune from nothing. Only a man with a deeply ingrained sense of honor and responsibility would have rescued the family estates from their creditors."

"Now see here, Edison bought back the family estates as a way of avenging himself. There was nothing of honor involved."

"If you believe that, madam, then you have allowed your grief to blind you to your grandson's true nature," Emma said gently. "If Edison had sought vengeance, he would have allowed you to suffer the humiliation of bankruptcy. Instead, you are sitting here today in your lovely mansion with all of your fine clothes and your servants."

Victoria searched her face as though Emma had gone mad. "He wants me to feel obligated to him. That is why he saved me from bankruptcy. It was an act of arrogance. A way of showing me that he does not need me or the family connections."

"Rubbish." Emma set down her teacup. "But I suppose that statement is proof positive that you two are very much alike in another way. You are both inclined to be amazingly stubborn."

"Of all the nerve. See here, Miss Greyson—"

Edison decided he had heard enough. He straightened away from the door frame and walked into the room.

"Forgive me for interrupting this delightful little tête-à-tête, but I'm afraid that Emma and I had an appointment this afternoon."

"Edison." Emma turned swiftly, her eyes lighting with a warm glow of pleasure. "I did not hear the butler announce you, sir."

"That is because Jinkins did not announce him." Victoria scowled at Edison. "What did you do to the poor man?"

"I merely told him to stay out of my way." Edison smiled as he came to a halt beside Emma. "It is advice that I frequently give to people who get between me and what I want. Are you ready to leave, Emma?"

"Yes." She rose quickly, searching his face as if wondering how much he had overheard.

He would let her wonder for a while, he thought. She deserved it for stirring up all of these odd sensations inside him with her impassioned defense of his honor.

"Then let us be off." He took her arm and walked her out of his grandmother's cold house.

CHAPTER TWENTY-ONE

Are you ever going to speak to me again, sir?" Emma untied the strings of her bonnet as they walked into Letty's hall. "Or do you plan to remain mired in forbidding silence for the duration of our association?"

Edison said nothing. He stalked through the door behind her.

"I vow, you put me in mind of a character in a horrid novel," Emma said.

She was deliberately goading him. It was no doubt a mistake but she had decided she had had quite enough of this mood of brooding menace.

The interview with his grandmother had done enough to lower her spirits for the day. She had seen few sights as sad as the elegant, austere Lady Exbridge reigning like some doomed queen in a castle of self-imposed loneliness.

She gave a small shiver and thought of Daphne. She and her sister were infinitely more fortunate than Edison and his grandmother, she thought. True, she and Daphne had to struggle for money, but at least they could take comfort in each other. They were not completely alone in the world. There was no impenetrable wall between them the way there was between Lady Exbridge and Edison.

Edison tossed his hat to Mrs. Wilton. "You should not have gone to Lady Exbridge's today, Emma."

They were the first words he had spoken since leaving his grandmother's house. She did not know if he had refrained from quarreling with her on the drive back to Letty's house because of the presence of his groom or because his rage had made him bereft of words.

"Amazing." Emma handed her bonnet to Mrs. Wilton. "He speaks at last."

"Bloody hell," Edison said.

She rounded on him. "And just what was I supposed to do when I received a summons from your grandmother?"

"You should have ignored it."

"I could hardly do that, sir. She is your grandmother, after all. She had every right to expect to meet me, and as you had not bothered to arrange a proper introduction—"

"There was no need for an introduction."

Emma felt the heat rise in her face. Of course there was no need for her to be properly introduced to his only close relative. She was not truly engaged to him, after all.

"You and I may understand that, sir, but I assure you, Society takes a different view of the matter," she said stiffly. She was suddenly very much aware of Mrs. Wilton's presence.

Edison's eyes narrowed dangerously. "I do not give a bloody damn what Society thinks."

"You have made that quite clear." Emma tried frantically to signal him with her eyes and remind him of Mrs. Wilton. It had been Edison's idea, after all, to maintain the charade of an engagement in front of everyone, including the household staff.

Edison spared a sharp glance for the housekeeper, who hovered uneasily, Emma's bonnet in her hands. Then he turned back to Emma.

"While we are *engaged,* Emma, you take your instructions from me. I am, after all, your future husband. You may as well get into the habit of obeying me."

That was too much. Emma consigned Mrs. Wilton to perdition. "Sir, you go too far."

"Not far enough, it would seem, since I neglected to make my instructions concerning my grandmother perfectly clear. Henceforth your orders are to stay away from Lady Exbridge."

Emma spread her hands, exasperated beyond measure. "What on earth are you worried about?"

"She's a dragon," Edison said bluntly. "Given half a chance, she'll eat you alive."

"I assure you that I can take care of myself, sir."

"Nevertheless, I do not want you seeing her alone. Is that understood?"

"It's all well and good for you to give your instructions now, but as you were not around to issue them two hours ago when Lady Exbridge's message arrived, I fail to see how you can hold me accountable."

Mrs. Wilton coughed. "Beggin' yer pardon, ma'am, there's a message for ye."

Emma frowned. "Another one?"

"Yes, ma'am." Mrs. Wilton picked up the silver salver that sat on the hall table. A folded sheet of paper rested on it. "It arrived a couple of hours ago. Right after you left. The boy who brought it to the kitchen door said to tell ye that it was urgent."

"I wonder who could have sent it." Emma picked up the note, aware that Edison was still seething.

She ignored him while she opened the missive.

She read the note quickly.

Miss Greyson:

From your remarks about actresses last night, I must conclude that you know more about this affair than I had supposed. I have given the matter a great deal of thought since we last spoke. It is obvious I underestimated you. We are both women of the world. I have decided to be open with you. It is imperative that we speak privately as soon as possible. I must explain certain facts to you.

I assure you, Miss Greyson, it is in your best interests to meet with me today. I have a proposition to put before you, one that I think you will find extremely interesting and very profitable.

Please come alone to my house as soon as you receive this note. I must warn you that delay of any sort could be dangerous. Tell no one that you intend to visit me. I will remain at home for the rest of the day in anticipation of your visit.

Yrs.

M.

"Good heavens." Emma raised her eyes and saw that Edison was watching her very intently. "It is from Lady Ames."

"The devil you say. Let me see it."

Edison snapped the sheet of foolscap out of her hand and glanced at the message. When he looked up again, Emma saw a familiar gleam in his eyes.

She suspected that there was a similar excitement in her own gaze. They both knew what the note meant. Miranda had clearly succumbed to the pressure of knowing that Emma was aware of her career as an actress.

Conscious of Mrs. Wilton standing nearby, Emma kept her expression polite and composed. "Interesting, is it not, sir?"

"Very. The Strategy of Redirection appears to have worked."

Emma glanced at the clock. "It is not yet four-thirty. There is still time to call upon Lady Ames."

"A moment, if you please," Edison said sharply. "I wish to consider this development more closely before you go haring off."

"There is no time for lengthy consideration." Emma snatched her bonnet back from Mrs. Wilton and plunked it on her head. "Excuse me, sir, but I must be off."

"Damnation, Emma, hold on here." He cast an uneasy glance at the hapless housekeeper. "I have not yet decided how best to deal with this."

"You may accompany me to Lady Ames's house," Emma said as she sailed through the doorway. "We can discuss the matter en route."

"You can be bloody well certain that I will accompany you." His tone was ominous as he followed her down the steps. "I have a number of things I want to discuss with you before you speak to Miranda."

"Yes, of course, sir." Emma surveyed the busy street. "First, be so good as to hail us a hackney."

"Why would you wish to bother with a dirty public coach?" He glanced across the street to where his groom stood waiting with the gleaming phaeton and team. "We shall use my carriage."

"No, Miranda might see it in the street and recognize it."

"What of it?"

"In her note she specifically says that I am to come alone. If you accompany me to her address, you must stay out of sight. The hackney will be anonymous. If you remain in it, she will not see you."

Edison looked dubious but she knew that her logic was sound. It did not take him long to see that too.

"Why is it that every time I manage to convince myself that I am giving the orders around here, something like this occurs?" he muttered.

Nevertheless, he quickly flagged down a passing hackney carriage and handed Emma up into the cab. She wrinkled her nose at the smell, a mix of ancient, dried vomit and soured wine. Experience had taught her not to examine the stains on the floor of any hackney coach too closely.

Edison climbed in behind her and sat down. He eyed the interior of the hackney with ill-concealed disgust, but he refrained from comment.

He looked at Emma. Her own excitement was bubbling so high that it took her a few seconds to notice the dark expression in his eyes.

"Listen to me, Emma. We must assume that Miranda has panicked," he said.

"Indeed." Emma reflected quickly on the possibilities. "She believes I am aware of her past, but she cannot possibly tell how much of it I know."

"Which means she has decided that you are no longer a simple pawn," Edison said evenly. "You have become potentially dangerous to her. You must be very, very careful when you speak with her this afternoon. Do you comprehend me?"

"I believe you are right in saying that Miranda has decided I can no longer be easily manipulated, but I doubt that she views me as dangerous. She mentions a proposition in her note. Perhaps she wishes to make me a partner in her scheme to use the elixir."

"It makes sense."

"Such a partnership may have been what she intended all along. After all, she could not hope to dupe me into winning a fortune for her at cards. Sooner or later she would have had to take me into her confidence."

Edison hesitated. "There is another possibility."

"What is that?"

"Before I explain, I must ask you a direct question. And you must tell me the truth."

"What is the question?"

He held her eyes. "Did you shoot Chilton Crane?"

She was so outraged, she could barely speak. "I told you, I did not kill him. I am not sorry that he is dead, but I most certainly was not the one who shot him."

He studied her for a long moment. Then he inclined his head, as though satisfied.

"Very well, then," he said. "If that is true, then I think it's safe to say that Miranda never meant to take you on as an equal partner. I believe she intended to force you to assist her in her card-cheating scheme."

"What does this have to do with whether or not I shot Crane?" Emma scowled. "And how could she possibly coerce me into helping her cheat at cards?"

"By blackmailing you."

"Blackmailing me?" Emma was floored. "But in order to do such a wicked thing, she would have had to find something to hold over my head. Something that would have made me afraid to defy her."

"Perhaps she did find something to use in just such a manner," Edison said. "But I snatched the weapon out of her grasp."

"Whatever are you talking about, sir?"

"Chilton Crane."

Emma felt her jaw drop. *Chilton Crane?*

Edison sat forward and rested his elbows on his thighs. His expression was coldly intent. "Crane's death never bothered me but the time and place of it did raise several questions. What if it was Miranda who encouraged him to go to your room that night? She may have intended for the two of you to be discovered together."

Emma shuddered. "In which event, I would very likely have been dismissed by Lady Mayfield."

"You would have been desperate. Perhaps desperate enough to allow Miranda to coerce you into participating in her card-cheating scheme."

"But it did not turn out that way. I was not in my room when Crane arrived. I told you, someone followed him down the hall and shot him dead."

"If you did not shoot him," Edison began thoughtfully.

"I swear I did not."

"Then someone else did," he concluded.

She looked at him. "Miranda?"

"Perhaps."

"Why on earth would she kill him?"

"Perhaps she followed him down the hall that night, intending to be the one who discovered him in your bed. But things went wrong. You were not around to be compromised."

Emma swallowed heavily. "Do you really think that when she realized that I was not in my bedchamber, she shot Crane? Are you saying she hoped I would be put under suspicion of murder?"

"It's possible that when she saw her plan was about to fail, she realized there was another way to accomplish her goal. She knew you would be the most likely suspect if Crane was found dead in your bedchamber."

"You think she may have planned to step in to offer me an alibi and thereby save me from the hangman's noose?"

"If she had done such a thing, you would have been forced to do whatever she demanded of you."

His calm, well-schooled logic sent a shiver through her. She hugged herself as the frightening possibilities cascaded through her mind. If she had not gone to Edison that night, if he had not implied to all and sundry that she had been in his bed when the murder occurred . . .

"Wait." Emma turned sharply back to face Edison. "According to your version of events, Miranda would have had to come to my bedchamber prepared to kill Crane that night. How could she possibly have guessed that her scheme would go awry because I wasn't in the room? Are you saying that she brought a pistol with her on the off chance that things would not go according to her plan?"

"I think it very likely that Miranda is in the habit of carrying a pistol in her reticule," Edison said. "When I searched her chamber at Ware Castle that night, I found a pistol case. There was extra powder and some balls in it but no weapon."

222

"Then she may, indeed, have had it with her," Emma whispered.

"Yes. She probably went downstairs after she shot Crane and waited for the body to be discovered. But nothing happened for some time."

"So she grew impatient and sent the maid to my room with the tea tray to precipitate the discovery."

"That is how it appears," Edison said.

Emma drummed her fingers on the seat. "When did this notion that Miranda was the killer first occur to you, sir?"

He shrugged. "It crossed my mind as a possibility at the time because of the pistol. But there were other, equally plausible explanations for Crane's death."

She slanted him a reproving look. "Including the possibility that I had killed him?"

Edison smiled faintly. "I told you, I had no great objection to the notion that you had shot Crane, but it did present certain difficulties. First and foremost, I had to make certain that you did not trip yourself up and ruin the alibi I had supplied. I admit that my attention was concentrated in that direction until we were well clear of Ware Castle."

"What makes you think you can believe me when I tell you that I did not kill Crane?"

He watched her with gleaming eyes. "I do not think that you would lie to me now. Not after what you so charmingly term the incident that took place between us."

She stared at him. "Are you saying that just because we have been . . . been *intimate,* you now feel you can trust me?"

"Actually, I think I had come to trust you even before we made love," he said thoughtfully. "But I had not asked you since then about Crane's death because there was no need to confirm that you did not kill him. Until now, that is."

"Do you mean to say, sir, that you never once concerned yourself with the possibility that you had employed a murderess?"

Edison smiled. "Not as long as the victim was Chilton Crane."

A rush of unexpected warmth went through her. "I am touched, sir. Quite . . . quite touched, indeed. You are certainly unique in my long string of employers."

He shrugged. "I have always had a certain tendency toward eccentricity."

The pleasant warmth faded. "I see. So it is only your eccentric nature that enables you to employ a possible murderess?"

"Umm."

Annoyed, she pressed on. "Would any murderess do? Or is it only a certain species of murderess you are willing to employ?"

His eyes gleamed. "I am very selective."

She decided her only option was to abandon the topic. "Let us return to the matter at hand. You still cannot be certain that Miranda actually shot Crane. We are speaking of murder, after all, sir. Surely Lady Ames would not risk such a dangerous deed merely to . . . to—"

"Secure a fortune? On the contrary, I think it's possible that Miranda is a reckless opportunist who has already killed once to obtain the deciphered recipe from the *Book of Secrets* and, perhaps, the book itself."

"Farrell Blue?"

"Yes. If that is true, why would she not kill a second time?"

Emma turned back to the window, her thoughts whirling. "I remember how stunned she appeared when you announced your engagement to me there in the hall that night. I assumed it was because it struck her and everyone else as a terribly unlikely alliance. But I suppose she might have worn just such an expression if she had suddenly realized that her plans had gone awry a second time that evening."

"She had risked committing murder and had nothing to show for it. The prize was denied her."

Emma made a face. "I do not care to think of myself as a prize, sir."

He looked distinctly uncomfortable. "I did not mean that the way it sounded," he muttered. "It was a poor choice of words."

"Yes, it was." She sighed and straightened in the seat. "Nevertheless, I suppose it is no worse than thinking of myself as bait."

His brows drew together in a grim line. "Emma—"

"Returning to our current problem," she interrupted smoothly, "I do not think anything you have said alters the way in which I shall deal with Miranda."

"I thought I made it clear, she is dangerous. Very likely a murderess twice over."

"Yes, but only consider, sir." Emma gave him a determinedly bright smile. "I am the one person she dares not kill. She desires my help in her scheme."

Edison sat back slowly. His eyes never left her face. "That fact no doubt gives you some protection from her venom. But you must not take any undue risks, Emma. Listen to her. Hear her proposal. Learn as much as you can, but do not provoke her temper."

"Believe me, sir, now that the evidence of two murders is mounting against her, I shall make it a point not to do anything foolish or reckless."

"I would feel infinitely more reassured about the matter if I did not fear our definitions of the term *reckless* differ greatly."

"Any man who associates with known smugglers and who does not hesitate to meet a villain at a dockside rendezvous in the middle of the night is in no position to lecture me on the subject."

Edison grinned reluctantly. "You really are much too impertinent to make a successful career as a professional companion, you know."

"With a bit of luck, my finances will soon come right and it will not be necessary for me to go back into service after this post." She peered out the window. "The carriage is slowing. We have arrived in Miranda's street."

Edison glanced out at the row of handsome town houses. "I realize that I'm starting to sound like you when you have one of your premonitions, but I do not like this."

"What can possibly go wrong?"

"I would rather not contemplate the entire list of things that could go wrong, if you don't mind. It is far too extensive." Edison's jaw was set in rigid lines. "Very well. I will wait here in the carriage while you meet with her. But, Emma, you must promise me that if you feel in any way uneasy, you will not hesitate to leave at once."

"I give you my word on it."

The carriage drew to a halt, as Edison had instructed, several doors down from Miranda's house. Emma alighted quickly and walked the rest of the way.

The neighborhood looked vastly different this afternoon than it had on the night of the ball. On that occasion, Emma recalled, the street had been clogged with carriages. Miranda's front steps had been thronged with expensively garbed guests. Lights had glowed from every window of her house. Music had echoed from the ballroom. An almost feverish air of activity had animated the scene.

There was no such lively aura about Miranda's residence today, Emma thought as she went up the steps and banged the knocker. In fact things seemed almost unnaturally quiet.

A cool sensation shivered through her. She felt her palms tingle in a too-familiar way. *No, please,* she thought. *Not another premonition. I have had quite enough of that sort of thing of late.*

She glanced over her shoulder as she waited for someone to respond to her knock. The other town houses appeared subdued and silent. Of course, it was nearly five o'clock, Emma reminded herself, the hour to see and be seen in the park.

At this very moment most of the Polite World, seated astride spectacular mounts or driving elegant equipages, were parading along sylvan paths. It was the sort of scene in which Miranda no doubt gloried. That she had chosen to wait in her house all afternoon in hopes that her request for a visit would be heeded said a great deal about her sense of urgency concerning this situation.

No one came to answer the door. Emma flexed her gloved hands to rid herself of the prickling sensation. It did not work.

She knocked again and waited, listening for the sound of footsteps in the hall.

A few minutes later she was forced to conclude that no one was going to respond. Perhaps Miranda had gone out after all, she thought. Still, someone should have answered the door. Although it was entirely possible that the household staff had seized the opportunity to enjoy a bit of leisure time.

The uneasy twinges continued to plague her. She stepped back to survey the windows. The curtains were all drawn tightly closed.

She sighed. It was impossible to ignore the whisper of dread. Something was very wrong inside Miranda's house.

She turned and hurried back to the waiting hackney. It was time to take more forceful action. She hoped Edison would not be difficult.

CHAPTER TWENTY-TWO

Edison scowled. "Break into Miranda's house? Have you gone mad?"

"I think something is wrong." Emma peered out through the hackney window. The steps in front of the town house were still quiet. No one had come or gone in the few minutes she had been arguing with Edison. "There are not even any servants at home. Miranda has a great number of them, if you will recall. Surely there should be a maid or a footman around."

"Bloody hell." Nevertheless, Edison leaned forward to study the scene. "I knew this was a bad notion."

"Well, sir? Are we going to investigate or not?"

Edison hesitated a moment longer. Then he switched

his attention back to her. She saw the grimly intent expression in his eyes and knew that he was as concerned as she.

"*We* will not do anything," he said. "You will wait here in the coach. I'll go around back and see if there is anyone about in the gardens."

"I will accompany you," Emma said firmly. "If there is something wrong, it will be better if there are two of us to deal with it."

"No, Emma." He made to open the door.

"Wait." She grabbed his sleeve. "Listen to me. If you go in alone, someone may mistake you for a housebreaker."

"Which is precisely what I will be if things are as you describe. I don't want you involved."

"Nonsense. If we stick together, we can claim that we were invited to pay a social call and became concerned about Miranda's safety when no one answered the door. Which is only the truth."

"A bit thin, I think." Edison opened the door and got out. He turned to look back at her. "You are to stay here, do you understand?"

He slammed the door without pausing for a response and started around the corner.

Emma waited until he was out of sight before she followed him.

As soon as she turned the corner, she saw at once that she had waited a little too long. Edison was nowhere to be seen. He had already vanished down a shadowy alley that ran between two rows of walled gardens. Leafy vines and an assortment of flowery creepers cascaded down the high stone walls. Tree limbs projected out over the alley on both sides. The late spring foliage was thick and heavy, creating a canopy of green overhead.

She hurried into the shaded alley and then paused, trying to orient herself. From this side it was difficult to tell which gate opened onto Miranda's garden. She tried to recall how many town houses she had passed when she had gone to knock on Miranda's front door a few minutes earlier. Four? Or was it five? She had not counted.

She stopped in front of the fourth gate and hesitated again. Things could become exceedingly awkward if she accidentally entered the wrong garden, she thought.

"One would think," Edison said softly from the top of the garden wall, "that I would eventually learn that you do not take orders well."

She jumped back and looked up quickly. *"Edison."*

She searched frantically for him amid the overhanging foliage. It took her a few seconds to spot him. He was almost invisible in the tangle of greenery that flowed out and over the wall.

When she finally saw him, she glared. "Do not ever do that again, sir. You gave me a terrible start."

"Serves you right. Well, as you are here now, you may as well come into the garden. It is obviously wiser to have you close at hand where I can keep an eye on you than it is to leave you to your own devices."

He disappeared. A moment later the gate opened with a soft squeak. Emma slipped quickly into the garden. Hedges blocked her view of the back of the house.

"Follow me," Edison said.

He avoided the paths, leading her through a maze of greenery until they emerged near the kitchen door. He surveyed the house for a moment.

There was an ominous quality to the silence that emanated from the depths of the town house. She realized that, although she had insisted on coming this far, she did not want to enter the place.

"Stay here," Edison whispered.

She waited in the shadow of a hedge and watched as he went up the back steps to try the door.

It opened easily. Edison glanced back at her. She knew that he was going to proceed inside. She drew a deep, fortifying breath and hurried up the steps to join him.

The foreboding silence outside the house was nothing compared to the gloom-filled interior. There was no one about in the kitchens, but there was a general air of readiness. The workbenches had been freshly scrubbed. Vegetables filled a nearby basket, awaiting preparation for the evening meal. A pile of cleaned and plucked pigeons was heaped in a pan.

"It does not look as if she took a notion to suddenly close up her house and leave town," Edison observed.

"No."

Emma trailed after him through the kitchens into the rear hall. She recognized her surroundings instantly. This was where she had stood the night she had followed Swan down the back staircase. She glanced across the way and saw that the library door was closed.

Another terrible chill lanced through her. She could not take her eyes off the door.

"Edison, the library."

He gave her an odd look but did not ask questions. He crossed the hall and opened the door.

Emma caught her breath at the sight of the chaos inside. The library had been turned upside down. But that was not what brought her stomach up into her throat.

The essence of death was unmistakable.

She reeled back a step. Instinctively she reached into her reticule for a handkerchief to put over her mouth. Breathing shallowly through it, she stared in horror at the figure that lay sprawled on the library carpet.

"Oh my God, Edison. Is it . . . ?"

"Yes. It's Miranda." Edison walked into the room and came to a halt beside the body. "Shot dead."

Emma took a reluctant step into the room. She could not look away from the terrible bloody stain that soaked the bodice of Miranda's afternoon gown.

"How could this happen in her own home?" Emma asked. "Surely the servants would have heard the shot. Where are they, anyway? Why did no one sound the alarm?"

"Perhaps she sent them away before the killer arrived." Edison moved to a nearby table and studied the objects that lay scattered on the floor beside it. "She appears to have been expecting you, however."

Emma forced her gaze away from Miranda's body and focused instead on the items lying on the carpet beside his gleaming Hessians. There was a jar of herbs, a teapot, and a single cup. Next to the tea things was a deck of cards that had fallen and partially fanned out across the rug.

"She obviously planned to give me another one of her tests." Emma looked at him. "But why would she do that? She was already convinced that I was a suitable candidate for the elixir."

"Yes, but if she intended to talk you into going into partnership with her, she would have needed to persuade you that you really could read the cards under the influence of the elixir."

"I suppose that explains why she sent the servants away for the afternoon," Emma said slowly. "If she intended to give me a demonstration of the effects of her elixir and talk to me about the details of her scheme, she probably thought it best to be private."

Edison slowly examined the shambles. The few books Miranda had used to decorate the shelves lay on the floor. Papers littered the carpet. The globe had fallen from its stand. The drawers of the desk stood wide.

"I suppose this could have been the result of a burglary," he said.

"You do not sound very convinced of that."

"I'm not." He went to the desk and glanced into the drawers. "I think, under the circumstances, we must assume that whoever did this was looking for the recipe for the elixir or the *Book of Secrets*."

"Do you think he found anything?"

"There's no way to be certain." Edison studied the room. "But he may have found something because he obviously decided that he no longer needed Miranda."

"Dear God, Edison. What should we do now?"

"The answer to that is obvious. We should get out of here. As quickly as possible." He reached for her wrist.

Alarm shot through her. "Edison?"

"The last thing we need at this point is for you to be connected to a second murder."

Emma's stomach lurched violently. "But how could anyone possibly link me to this crime?"

"I do not know and I do not intend to find out." He hauled her out the door into the hall. "We must get out of here before one of the servants returns."

"I will not argue with you, sir."

"That makes a pleasant change."

They retreated from the house along the same path they had used to enter it. Emma did not realize how tense she was until they reached the alley and found that it was still deserted. Then a light-headed sensation swept over her.

"Are you all right?" Edison glanced sharply at her. "You look a little pale."

"Of course I'm all right. It's not as though I have not seen murder before. This is my second one in less than a fortnight." Emma took a breath. "At this rate I shall soon grow quite accustomed to the business."

"How very fortunate for you, my dear. I, on the other hand, may have to resort to carrying a vinaigrette."

They hurried down the alley and stepped out onto the street. Emma saw the hackney waiting at the corner. The coachman was slumped in his seat, snoring peacefully. The horse dozed, one hoof cocked.

Edison rapped on the side of the coach. "Rouse yourself, coachman. Your customers have returned. We wish to be off immediately."

The coachman jolted awake. "Aye, sir." He took up the reins with a long-suffering sigh. "Typical of their sort," he muttered to the horse. "Always changin' their bloody minds. First they tell ye to wait until yer finally settled into a nice little nap and then they wake ye and tell ye they're in a terrible hurry to get somewhere."

Edison yanked open the coach door and bundled Emma inside. He got in behind her, shut the door, and drew the curtains.

Emma hugged herself. "Who would want to murder Miranda?"

"Personally, I do not doubt that there are any number of people, including a few jealous wives, who would cheerfully have shot her." Edison sat back and looked at Emma. "But in this instance, I think we would do well to assume that whoever killed her was involved in this damnable affair of the missing book and the recipe."

"Yes." Emma reached up to massage her temples. "But, Edison, you mentioned jealousy as a motive."

"What of it? I do not think it a likely explanation in this case."

"You are forgetting that there is someone who did, indeed, have good cause to be jealous of Miranda's many lovers."

There was a short, brittle pause.

"Indeed," Edison said softly. "It might be best if we found Swan before the authorities leap to the same conclusion. I have some questions for him."

"What makes you think that he will answer them?"

Edison smiled his enigmatic smile. "I will offer him a bargain. In exchange for giving me the information I seek concerning Miranda's past, I will lend him my assistance in evading the authorities, should they decide to try to arrest him for her murder."

Emma froze.

Edison watched her. "What's wrong?"

"Nothing."

"Damnation, Emma, I am in no mood for games. Tell me what is bothering you about my plan."

"It is of no great importance, sir. It merely struck me that the bargain you intend to offer Swan strongly resembles the one you made with me."

He looked both irritated and baffled. "The devil it does."

She shrugged. "Salvation from the noose in exchange for assistance in your inquiries? It sounds familiar enough to me. But I must warn you, I do not think it will work in Swan's case."

Anger crackled briefly in Edison's gaze. It was gone almost instantly, concealed beneath the layer of icy control that he wielded so effortlessly.

"There is nothing about what I am proposing that is akin to the arrangements you and I have made," he said evenly. "Leave that aside and tell me what makes you think it won't work?"

"I believe that he really did love her," Emma whispered. "He may have killed her. But I do not believe that he will sell you any information about her that will besmirch her memory, not even to evade the hangman's noose."

"You sound very certain of that."

She tightened her hands in her lap. "I am."

"Your faith in true love is quite touching," Edison said. "But it has always been my experience that most people are extremely practical about things such as life and death and finances."

"Mark my words," Emma said. "You will not be able to bribe Swan. But if he is *not* the one who killed her, you might be able to secure his assistance by making him a promise."

"What sort of promise?"

"Give him your oath that you will try to find the person who actually did murder the woman he loved."

CHAPTER TWENTY-THREE

Y ou will not credit it, Emma, but everyone is saying that her exceedingly odd servant, Swan, returned to the house yesterday afternoon and shot Miranda dead," Letty announced with ghoulish relish.

Emma put aside the stack of daily papers she had been perusing in hopes of discovering news of *The Golden Orchid*. As usual, there was no report of a late ship returning with a fortune for its investors. She studied Letty, who was glowing with excitement.

The news of Miranda's death had struck the Polite World shortly before breakfast. It was uncanny, Emma reflected, how gossip traveled through the ton.

"Are the authorities certain that it was Swan who killed her?" she asked carefully.

Although she had suggested precisely the same thing to Edison, she was not entirely satisfied with the explanation. In fact, the more she considered the possibility that Swan had murdered Miranda, the less she liked it.

It was not that she could not imagine Swan killing Miranda in a fit of rage and jealousy, she thought. Intense passions had been known to provoke dangerous reactions in unstable people. The problem was that such a ready answer did not feel right in this case. It struck her as too simple and a bit too convenient, given the bizarre affair of the *Book of Secrets*.

She suspected that Edison held the same opinion, although he was determined to find Swan and talk to him.

"Indeed. In fact, Calista Durant informed me that Basil Ware was talking about hiring a Bow Street Runner to track down Swan and bring him to justice." Letty helped herself to another cup of tea and sat back on the yellow sofa.

She had removed her bonnet a few minutes earlier when she had rushed through the front door with her news of murder most foul and titillating. But she was so eager to impart the latest *on dit* that she had not taken the time to change. She was still dressed in the gown she had worn when she had set out to pay her afternoon calls. It was a purple and yellow muslin confection trimmed with a neckline that dipped so low her much vaunted bosom threatened to spill out of it.

Emma had spent the day at home waiting impatiently for word from Edison. It was nearly five and he had still not arrived with news of the results of his search for Swan.

"Do the gossips say why Miranda's servant would wish to kill her?" Emma asked.

Letty's eyes gleamed. "According to her housekeeper, it was no secret that Miranda dallied with the man on a regular basis. Difficult to believe, is it not?"

"Not particularly," Emma said dryly. "When I took up my career as a companion, I was amazed to learn how many ladies of the ton enjoy a fling with a handsome footman."

"Yes, of course, dear, that is common knowledge. Swan, however, was anything but handsome." Letty broke off and pursed her lips as she contemplated the matter. "Nevertheless, I will admit that there was something quite fearsome about him, which might well have appealed to a woman such as Miranda."

"A woman such as Miranda?"

"I always thought her tastes tended to be somewhat low when it came to that sort of thing."

Emma raised her brows. It was not so very long ago, she reflected, that Letty had hailed Miranda as "all the crack" and "the very mirror of style and fashion." It sounded as though the ravenous jackals of the Polite World were already turning on their newest victim. One could not even die in Society without becoming a subject of unpleasant gossip.

"You were saying, Letty, that Miranda and Swan had an affair?"

"Oh, I wouldn't go so far as to dignify that sort of casual sport as an affair, dear. But, yes, apparently she invited him into her bed from time to time when she had no other lover conveniently at hand."

"That does not explain why he would kill her."

"Word has it that she became angry with him and dismissed him out of hand on the night of her ball. Turned him off without a reference, apparently. The servants report that he packed his things and left the house before dawn. They all claim that he was in a seething rage."

"I see."

"The assumption is that Swan has been lurking near Miranda's house ever since, awaiting his opportunity for revenge. Yesterday, when he saw the servants leave for the afternoon, he ran inside, shot Miranda dead, and stole the silver."

"Hmm." Emma forced herself to pour a cup of tea in what she

hoped appeared a calm, steady manner. "I wonder why Miranda sent her entire staff off for the afternoon. Rather odd, don't you think?"

"Oh, there is no great secret about that. The butler told the authorities that Miranda gave her staff the time off to go to the fair."

"How very generous of her," Emma murmured. "And so very unlike her."

Letty chuckled. "If you want my opinion, I suspect Miranda wished to entertain her newest lover in private, so she got rid of the servants for the afternoon."

"Why would she insist on privacy for a tryst? She never sought to hide any of her other lovers. In point of fact, she was inclined to boast of her affairs."

"Perhaps it was her new lover who insisted on complete secrecy," Letty said.

It was clear that the gossips of the ton had already worked the entire plot out to their satisfaction. Poor Swan did not stand a chance, Emma thought. She hoped for his sake that he had had the good sense to leave Town.

Then again, perhaps he had not yet heard that his beloved Miranda was dead. In which case, Emma thought, Edison might be able to find him before Basil Ware's Bow Street Runner did.

"Why the devil should I believe you this time?" Edison folded his arms and leaned back in his chair. He looked at One-Eared Harry with something less than enthusiasm.

It was not the fact that Harry had recently sold him out to the Vanza fighter that annoyed Edison. He knew his old associate well enough to expect that sort of thing from time to time. What irritated him this afternoon was that Harry had just come from the docks. He had brought with him a great deal of mud and muck, which he had managed to deposit on the expensive Oriental carpet that covered the floor of the library.

Harry had turned up on Edison's doorstep within hours after the word had gone out that it was not only Bow Street who was looking for Lady Ames's ex-servant.

He shuffled his feet on the other side of the desk and had the grace to look abashed. "I know yer probably a bit put out by what 'appened the other night. But I swear to ye again, Mr. Stokes, I never knew the bugger meant to kill ye. It was just a business deal, ye see."

"Of course."

"I knew ye'd understand." Harry managed a weak, gap-toothed smile. "I was just tryin' to make a bit sellin' information to two parties what seemed to 'ave a mutual interest in each other. 'Ow was I to know that cove meant to beat ye to a pulp?"

"Forget it, Harry. I do not have any time to waste on your apologies, heartfelt though I'm sure they are."

"That they are, I swear it on me mother's 'onor."

"Well, I suppose that is a step up from your sister's honor. Is she still making money hand over fist with that brothel she opened last year?"

"Doin' real well," Harry assured him. "Thank ye for askin' after 'er. The whole family is right proud of Alice. Any'ow, I know I owe ye for pullin' me outa the river. A man's gotta repay a debt like that and that's why I'm 'ere."

"I assume you came in response to my inquiries?"

"Right ye are. And there'll be no charge for the information, which should tell ye I'm serious about gettin' things square between us."

Edison was interested now. "What have you got for me?"

"'Eard ye was looking for a cove named Swan what used to work for a dead lady."

"Well?"

"I think I know where 'e is," Harry said earnestly. "Leastways, where 'e was early this mornin'."

"And where was that?"

"Down at the docks. 'E was askin' around for work. I didn't think

241

nothin' of it at the time. Told 'im I didn't need any 'ands. But later when I got word ye was lookin' for 'im, I tried to find 'im again."

Edison's instincts and experience told him that Harry was telling the truth this time. "Were you successful?"

"Not exactly. But Moll at the Red Demon told me she saw 'im later. She said 'e looked real strange, sort of angry and sad at the same time. Swan told 'er 'e was leavin' town right away. Something bad 'ad 'appened, 'e said, and 'e'd likely get the blame for it."

Edison frowned. "Did he say where he was going?"

"No." Harry turned his greasy cap between his fingers. "But 'e did tell Moll that 'e 'ad to see a lady afore 'e left."

Edison flattened his hands on the surface of his desk. "Did he mention a name?"

"No. Just said a lady."

An ominous chill went through Edison. He got slowly to his feet. "Did he say why he had to see this lady before he left town?"

"Moll told me Swan said somethin' about 'ow 'e'd promised 'imself that he wouldn't risk 'is neck for any other female ever again as long as 'e lived but this one was different. She'd been nice to 'im, 'e said. And she was in danger."

Late that afternoon, having not had so much as a word from Edison, Emma retired to the privacy of her bedchamber to reread the letter that had arrived in the morning post. She did so with a mounting sense of unease. She knew her younger sister very well. Daphne was definitely on the brink of doing something rash.

My Dearest Emma:

Your latest letter tells me that you will soon have all the money we need. I pray you are correct because I vow I cannot remain here at Mrs. Osgood's School for Young Ladies much longer.

I must tell you, Mrs. Osgood grows odder by the day. You will never believe what happened last night. I was unable to sleep so I went downstairs to fetch a book. (Mrs. York's latest horrid novel arrived yesterday and we have all been taking turns reading it aloud.)

As I went down the hall to the library, I noticed that the door was closed and I saw a gleam of light beneath it. I put my ear to the panel and heard the most peculiar noises. It sounded as though some wild animals had got inside and were rooting about among the books.

The most dreadful grunts and groans issued forth. And then I heard a terrifying shriek. I feared that Mrs. Osgood was being murdered so I took my courage in both hands and opened the door.

The sight that met my eyes was even more astonishing than the fireworks we saw two years ago at Vauxhall Gardens.

Mr. Blankenship, a respectable widower who owns a farm in the neighborhood, was on the sofa. He was lying on top of Mrs. Osgood, if you can imagine. His trousers were down around his ankles and his very large, very bare backside was in the air. Mrs. Osgood's equally bare legs were flung out on either side.

Fortunately neither of them noticed me. You may be certain that I closed the door with great haste and rushed back upstairs.

I must tell you, dear sister, that I suspect that what I witnessed was what is known as lovemaking. If so, I fear that all the charming poetry and novels we have enjoyed and even Byron's exciting tales have sadly misled us both. It was, I assure you, the most ridiculous sight. . . .

Emma refolded the letter and looked out the window at the park on the other side of the street. She had not felt at all ridiculous in Edison's arms, she thought wistfully. Those moments of passion in the carriage would warm her for the rest of her life.

A brisk knock on her bedchamber door brought her out of her reverie.

"Enter," she called.

The door opened. Bess, the maid, bobbed a brisk curtsy and held out a small slip of paper. "I've got a message for ye, ma'am. A boy brought it to the kitchen door a moment ago."

Excitement unfurled inside Emma. With any luck it would be news from Edison. Perhaps he had made some progress. She leaped to her feet and rushed across the room to seize the note.

"Thank you, Bess."

She opened the paper and read the short, inelegantly scrawled message.

Miss Greyson:

Please come into the park. I must speak with you. You are in great danger.

> *Yrs.*
> *Swan.*

"Good heavens." Emma looked up. "I am going to take a walk in the park, Bess. If Mr. Stokes comes to call, kindly ask him to wait for me."

"Yes, ma'am."

Emma hurried past her through the doorway. She dashed downstairs, grabbed her bonnet off a hook, and let herself outside. She went down the steps, crossed the street between two lumbering hay carts and walked swiftly into the park. A crisp little breeze ruffled the leaves.

She came to a halt when it occurred to her that she had no way of knowing where Swan was. She assumed that he was hiding in the nearby foliage. He had very likely been watching the house, she told herself. He would have seen her come down the steps a moment ago.

"Miss Greyson."

She spun around at the sound of the rasping voice.

"Swan."

She frowned at the sight of him standing in the shelter of a leafy

244

tree. He was a sad picture. He no longer wore Miranda's spectacular blue livery. Instead, he was attired in an old ragged shirt and a tattered coat and pants. He had a sack slung over one shoulder. She suspected that it contained all of his worldly possessions. It was obvious he had not shaved for several days.

But it was the expression of despair in his eyes that wrung her heart.

She went toward him quickly and stopped directly in front of him. Impulsively she put a hand on his stained sleeve. "Are you all right?"

"They've set a Runner on me, Miss Greyson." Swan rubbed the back of his hand across his brow. "But I reckon I can stay out of his sight until I'm on the road north."

"Did you kill Miranda?"

"God help me, I thought about it for a while after she sent me away." Swan squeezed his eyes shut briefly. When he opened them a second later, his gaze was stark. "But I swear I did not do it. Someone else murdered her."

"I see."

"You were kind to me at Ware Castle, madam. You weren't like the other ladies. You didn't laugh at me or ask Miranda if you could borrow me for a night. That's why I came to warn you, Miss Greyson."

"Warn me about what?"

"You are in grave danger. You must believe me."

"*Me?*" Emma stared at him. "Why on earth would I be in danger?"

Before Swan could reply, the bushes behind him rustled softly. He gave a startled gasp and whirled around. His pack slid off his shoulder and fell to the ground.

Edison stepped out of the cover of a leafy copse. His eyes were cold and watchful.

"Yes, Swan. Tell us why Miss Greyson is in danger."

CHAPTER TWENTY-FOUR

I did not kill Miranda, I swear it." Swan fell back a step. He put out a trembling hand as though to ward off the devil himself. "Please, you must believe me, sir. I'm no murderer. I don't deserve to hang."

Emma gave Edison a repressive frown. Surely he could see that if he frightened Swan too much, they would learn nothing. Edison ignored her. He continued to pin Swan with a relentless stare that clearly intimidated the younger man.

"You had what some would call an excellent motive, did you not?" he asked much too casually.

They would get nowhere this way, Emma thought. She took a step forward, putting herself between Swan and

Edison. "Mr. Stokes does believe you, Swan." She glared at Edison. "Is that not true, sir?"

Edison hesitated. Then he shrugged. "I'm willing to consider other possibilities. *Convincing* possibilities."

Swan did not look reassured. Emma slanted Edison a speaking glance before giving Swan another determined smile.

"Mr. Stokes is going to find the real killer," she said.

Swan's eyes widened. "He is?"

"Yes, he is. Now you must help by answering his questions."

Edison kept his gaze fixed on Swan. "I did not ask you if you killed Miranda. I asked you why you think Miss Greyson is in danger."

"But that's what I was trying to explain to her, sir." Swan's huge, grimy hands knotted and unknotted in a spasmodic manner. "I fear the same person who murdered Miranda will be after Miss Greyson next."

"But why would he want to kill me?" Emma demanded.

Swan glanced briefly at her. "You misunderstand, ma'am. I don't think he'll want to murder you. At least not right off. I think he may try to use you somehow."

"Vastly reassuring," Emma said dryly.

"Bloody hell, man." Edison caught Swan by the collar of his ragged shirt. "Who is after Miss Greyson?"

"That's ju-just it, sir," Swan stuttered desperately. "I don't rightly know who he is. I only know that Miranda was afraid of him and now she's dead and I th-think he wants to get his hands on Miss Greyson."

"Why?" Edison asked.

Swan looked as though he might faint. The panic in his eyes was too much for Emma. She touched the hand that Edison had clamped around the young man's collar.

"Let him go, sir. Surely you can see that you are making him exceedingly anxious."

"I do not care about the state of his damned nerves. I want answers."

"Well, you will never get them this way." Emma tightened her fingers around Edison's arm. "For heaven's sake, sir, you have him by the throat. I doubt if he can even breathe, let alone talk to you in this state. Release him. Then he will speak with us. Won't you, Swan?"

"Y-yes." Swan did not take his frightened, wide-eyed gaze off Edison.

Edison hesitated. Then, with a disgusted twist of his mouth, he took his hand away from Swan's collar. "Very well, you are free. Talk. And be bloody quick about it."

Emma smiled reassuringly at Swan. "It will be easier if you start at the beginning. Tell us about Miranda."

Swan blinked several times and then dragged his eyes away from Edison. He looked at Emma. "What is there to tell? I was foolish enough to think that she loved me. Me, her footman, no less." He wiped his brow with the back of his big fist. "When I look back on the time with her now, it is as though I see myself in a terrible dream."

"When did you first meet her?" Emma asked gently.

"At the beginning of the Season. When she arrived in town she had no staff of any sort. She hired an entire house full of servants from an agency. I was one of them." Swan sighed. "I aspired only to work in the kitchens or gardens. I was astounded when she gave me a fine suit of livery and told me that I would be her personal footman."

"How long did it take you to go from footman to lover?" Edison asked bluntly.

"Not long." Swan looked down at the toes of his battered boots. "I think I fell in love with her the moment I saw her. She was so beautiful. I only wanted to serve her. When she invited me into her bed, I thought I was in heaven with an angel."

"I would have said she had more in common with a witch," Edison remarked.

Swan did not look up. "You have the right of it, sir. But I did not see that until much later. It took me a long time to realize that the only reason she favored me was because I amused her. Rather like a pet spaniel, if you see."

"Oh, Swan," Emma whispered.

He raised his eyes to meet hers. "She only wanted me in her bed when she was bored with her fine gentlemen lovers. I should have known better than to fall in love with a lady."

"Oh, Swan," Emma said again. "Those of us in service must be so cautious about that sort of thing."

Edison gave her an irritated look and then turned on Swan. "Let us move on to more important matters than the state of your heart. How did you discover that Miranda was once an actress?"

Swan looked genuinely startled. "You know about her career on the stage?"

"A little," Edison said. "Tell us what you know of it."

"There is not much to tell," Swan said. "I don't think she intended anyone to know about it. But one night after she came home from a ball, she was in a strange mood. She had had a great deal of champagne. She talked a lot about what fools the members of the Polite World were. How easy it was to pull the wool over their stupid eyes."

"Is that when she told you that she had once been an actress?" Emma asked.

"Not exactly." Swan blushed. "First she wanted me to make love to her. Right there in her library. On top of her desk, if you can believe it."

Emma stared at him. "On the *desk*?"

"The better sort get odd notions at times," Swan explained.

"Yes, but a *desk*?"

"Once she insisted that we do it on the stairs," Swan confided, turning a deeper shade of crimson.

"Good heavens."

"It was bloody uncomfortable," Swan admitted.

"I can imagine. All those hard steps. I mean, how could one possibly—"

"We seem to be straying from the topic," Edison interrupted grimly. "What happened after the, uh, incident on the desk, Swan?"

"Like I said, she was in an odd mood that night. She wanted to talk to someone. She had her fine gentlemen lovers and all her fancy friends, you see, but I think she was lonely."

"Lonely like a spider waiting for prey," Edison muttered.

Emma gave him another quelling glance. "Go on, Swan."

"She told me she'd once been a great actress. She talked a lot about how everyone loved her when she was on stage. She told me that there was nothing to compare to the feeling she got when the audience broke into a frenzy of applause. Then she unlocked a drawer in the desk and showed me a box full of old playbills and reviews."

"Did she tell you how she made the transition from actress to lady of the ton?" Emma asked.

Swan hesitated, brow furrowing in thought. "It was all quite vague, really. But I got the impression that a wealthy gentleman fell in love with her and married her against his family's wishes. They went to live in Scotland because his father cut him off without a penny. But later, after his parents died, he came into his inheritance."

"That would be the late, unlamented Lord Ames?" Edison asked.

Swan nodded. "Yes. In any event, Miranda said something about him having died shortly after he collected his inheritance."

"Convenient," Edison observed. "And you're right about the vague aspect of the tale. I have made some inquiries but I was unable to locate any family connected to Miranda. There is a Lord Ames in Yorkshire but there is no relation."

"Miranda told me that her husband had no other relatives," Swan said.

Edison raised his brows. "So Miranda got the entire inheritance, is that it?"

"She said she used the money to return to England and take her place in the ton." Swan looked at him. "That's all I know about her past, I swear it. Except—"

"Except what?" Emma prodded.

Swan frowned. "I don't think she inherited a vast fortune. Just enough to see her through one Season, in fact."

"That would explain why I was unable to discover any information concerning her investments," Edison muttered. "She didn't have any."

"What made you think she possessed sufficient funds for only one Season, Swan?" Emma asked.

"Because she was obsessed with some scheme to make more money," Swan said. "She hinted that if it worked, she would never have to worry about her finances again. I don't know the details of her plan, but I do know that it involved you, Miss Greyson."

Edison looked thoughtful. "When did you conclude that Miss Greyson was necessary to Miranda's scheme?"

"During the house party at Ware Castle," Swan said. "Something happened there that convinced Miranda that she would soon be richer than Croesus. I don't know what it was. I only know that she was convinced that she required Miss Greyson to make the plan work."

Edison glanced at Emma and then returned his attention to Swan. "Did Miranda ever mention a special book or manuscript?"

Swan's brow puckered again. "No. Miranda didn't have much interest in books and the like."

"What do you know about her special tea?" Emma asked quickly.

Swan moved one hand in a dismissive fashion. "Only that she was forever serving it to her new lady friends when she invited them to play cards. She claimed it was a fine tonic, but I don't think she ever drank much of it herself, to tell you the truth."

"Did she say where she acquired the recipe?" Edison asked.

"No. Maybe it was something she learned when she lived in Scotland. I've heard that they eat and drink odd food there."

"Do you think Miranda and her husband ever traveled to the Continent?" Edison asked.

"She said that they had never had the money to travel." Swan frowned again. "But I did wonder once—"

"About what?" Emma asked in a coaxing tone.

"It's nothing really. But one time, Miranda lost her temper with a maid who spilled some tea on one of her fancy lady friends. She cursed the girl in a language I'd never heard. Afterward the guest laughed and complimented her on what she called her excellent command of the Italian tongue."

Emma saw a familiar gleam appear in Edison's eyes. She knew what he was thinking, but she shook her head slightly, warning him to keep silent. She gave Swan another smile.

"Many people learn Italian as well as French and Greek," she said.

"I doubt that many actresses learn all those languages," Edison said. "Especially those who never made it out of a traveling company."

Emma paid him no attention. "Swan, did you conclude that Miranda lived in Italy for a time simply because she happened to know a few Italian curse words?"

"When her guest teased her, Miranda said something about a childhood tutor. But the guest said no tutor would teach such gutter language. Miranda merely laughed and changed the subject. But I could see that the question had made her uneasy. I wondered about it at the time." Swan paused. "But why would she have lied about whether or not she had ever traveled abroad?"

"Why, indeed?" Edison repeated softly. "Tell me, what were you looking for the night you searched my study?"

Swan blanched. Fresh panic flashed across his face. "You know about that? I swear I did not steal anything, sir. I only looked around a bit."

"I know you did not take anything. What did you hope to find?"

"I don't know. That was the problem, if you see what I mean."

"A rather odd way to conduct a search," Edison mused.

Swan licked his lips and gave Emma a pleading glance. Then he turned back to Edison. "I told you Miranda took odd notions from time to time. After we returned from Ware Castle she was obsessed with employing Miss Greyson in her scheme. I think she went so far as to try to force Miss Greyson into her service. But she said you stood in her way, sir. She wanted to learn more about you."

"Did she murder Chilton Crane in an attempt to make Miss Greyson lose her position with Lady Mayfield?" Edison asked.

An unhappy, bewildered expression creased Swan's features. "At the time, I told myself that my beautiful Miranda wouldn't stoop to murder to further her plans. But now I'm not so certain. I do know that she was furious that night after you and Miss Greyson announced your engagement, sir. The next day she told me you had ruined everything, but she would not say how."

"She was convinced the betrothal was a fraud," Emma said. "So she sent you to search Mr. Stokes's study to find some proof."

Swan sighed heavily. "When I returned with no helpful information, she flew into a rage and told me I was useless to her. That was when she dismissed me."

"Was it you who took a shot at me in the woods that day outside Ware Castle?" Edison asked very casually.

"Shot at you?" Swan was clearly shocked by the question. "No, sir, I swear, I never did such a thing, sir."

Emma glanced quickly at Edison. He looked briefly meditative and then he inclined his head, apparently satisfied at some inner logic.

"It was most likely Miranda, then," he said as though the incident in the woods amounted to nothing more than a brief, irritating encounter with a pesky insect. "A desperate effort to get rid of me before we all returned to Town."

"She did know a thing or two about pistols," Swan allowed. "She always carried one with her, although it did her little good in the end. I asked her once if she feared footpads or highwaymen. She told me that it was another sort of villain who worried her these days."

"Did she describe this other sort of villain?" Edison asked.

Swan shook his head. "No. I don't think she knew who he was. She merely hinted that someone might be after something she possessed. In the end, she was right to be afraid, wasn't she? He murdered her."

Edison looked dubious but he said nothing.

"It's the truth, I swear it, sir. She never wanted to talk about it. And as much as I wanted to protect her, I could hardly force her to tell me, could I?" Swan swallowed heavily. "I was only her footman, after all."

Edison watched him closely. "Why do you think this mysterious, unnamed villain may be after Miss Greyson now that Miranda is dead?"

Swan hesitated.

"Tell me," Edison pressed.

"Well, sir, it's just that after I heard about Miranda's death, I got to thinking. The only thing she cared about was her secret scheme to make a fortune."

"So?" Emma prompted.

It was Edison who answered. "Swan has leaped to the obvious conclusion, Emma. If Miranda needed you to make her scheme work, it stands to reason that whoever killed her for the secret might also need you."

That bloody tea recipe, Emma thought. "I see."

Swan gave her a wretched look. "I'm sorry, Miss Greyson."

She put her hand on his sleeve. "You must not feel guilty about any of this, Mr. Swan. It's not your fault."

"I should have listened to the others," he said wearily. "Everyone from the groom to the housekeeper gave me the same advice, but I paid no attention."

"What advice was that?" Emma asked.

"They all warned me that there's nothing more foolish or hopeless than falling in love with your employer."

CHAPTER TWENTY-FIVE

A short while later Emma stood in the shadows of a tree, folded her arms beneath her breasts, and watched Swan disappear down one of the wooded park paths. In a moment he was lost to sight.

"We were right. She must have been Farrell Blue's mistress in Italy," Edison said quietly. "She probably killed him after he succeeded in translating the recipe for the elixir."

"As his mistress she had probably learned enough about Vanza to suspect that someone else would likely come looking for the volume."

Edison nodded. "So she set the fire and tossed the book into the flames, hoping to cover her tracks. It all fits together."

Emma listened to the leaves rustling in the branches above, very conscious of Edison beside her. He had one hand braced against the trunk of the tree near her head, the other was thrust under his coat, planted on his hip. He, too, watched the space where Swan had vanished, his expression deeply thoughtful.

She glanced at him. "It was very kind of you to send Swan to your estate in Yorkshire."

"Kind?" Edison frowned. "There was nothing kind about it. Sending him away was the only practical thing to do."

She hid a fleeting smile. "Yes, of course, sir. I should have realized instantly that when you told him to take himself off to your estate, you were just being practical, as usual. Sheltering a man who is wanted for the murder of one of the most popular figures in the ton is such an eminently commonsensical thing to do."

He slanted her an irritated look. "Swan will be safe enough at Windermere until I sort things out here in Town. More important, he will be out of my way."

"Meaning you will not have to worry about him while you go about your affairs."

"I do not need any more distractions than I already have." He tapped one finger against the tree trunk. "Matters are complicated enough as it is."

"Yes, of course." She cleared her throat. "Speaking of complications—"

"What of them?"

She braced herself. "It has just occurred to me that I have become one."

"What the devil do you mean by that?"

"You employed me to act as bait to hold Miranda's attention while you searched for the missing book," she said very steadily. "Now that she is dead, I no longer have a task to perform for you. I assume you will not be needing me any longer."

"Damnation, Emma—"

"I quite understand, sir," she assured him. "It's just that our arrangement has obviously been terminated in an unexpected fashion."

"I suppose murder could be classified as unexpected."

"Which means, of course, that certain details not attended to in a timely manner have now become rather pressing."

"Pressing?"

"You kept saying you would take care of it," she said reproachfully. "But you never got around to it. And now our business together is finished and I really must insist that you fulfill your part of the bargain."

He turned his head to look at her. There was an ominous light in his eyes. "If this is about your bloody reference—"

"You did promise to write one."

"Contrary to your assumption, you have not completed the tasks I engaged you to fulfill."

"I beg your pardon?"

He kept his hand on the tree trunk beside her head and leaned very close. "I still need you."

His mouth was only an inch or two away from hers. She suddenly found it difficult to breathe.

"You do?"

"Yes, Miss Greyson, I most certainly do."

He removed his hand from his hip and wrapped it around the nape of her neck. He moved so swiftly she did not realize his intention until she felt herself crowded back against the trunk of the tree. By then, it was much too late to protest, even had she wanted to do so. His mouth came down on hers, hard and fierce and urgent.

The explosion of sensation was as sharp and intense as it had been on the other occasions he had kissed her. So much for her theory that one grew accustomed to this sort of thing, Emma thought. She gave a soft little sigh and twined her arms around his neck.

He trapped her legs between his thighs. Deliberately he deepened the kiss. Her knees trembled. She gasped when he ended the embrace a moment later. When she opened her eyes she found him watching her with a dark, enigmatic gaze.

"Now all I have to do is find a way to protect you," he said.

She was aware of her mouth opening and closing at least twice before she managed to pull herself together. His kisses had a positively devastating effect on her brain, she thought.

A sudden, dreadful thought occurred to her. Life would become considerably less exciting when her term of employment ended and she no longer had Edison's kisses to warm her senses. She did not want to contemplate the prospect.

"Protect me?" She knew she sounded like an idiot, but she was still having trouble collecting her thoughts.

"It's possible that whoever murdered Miranda was after the *Book of Secrets,* in which case you are probably not in jeopardy. But it's also conceivable that whoever killed her was simply after the deciphered recipe. And if that is the case—"

"And if he knows about Miranda's little experiments on me, the killer may think that I can be of use to him." Emma wrinkled her nose. "Lovely. But you keep saying the recipes in the book are nothing more than meaningless occult gibberish. Who would believe they actually worked?"

"Miranda, for one, apparently."

Emma groaned. "Yes, I suppose so. But who else would be so gullible as to put any credence in such arcane lore?"

"A member of the Vanzagarian Society," Edison said bluntly.

"But surely the members of the Society are educated gentlemen such as yourself, sir. They would know better than to believe that the recipe was anything other than an interesting bit of ancient history. Surely none of them would commit murder to obtain it."

"You don't know the gentlemen of the Vanzagarian Society. Most are merely enthusiastic students of Vanza. But some are so deeply into the philosophy that they have lost all perspective. They are inclined to believe the most amazing occult nonsense." Edison looked past the tree toward Letty's town house. "And in this case, one of them has gone so far as to kill because of his convictions."

Emma suppressed the uneasy sensation that shot through her. She certainly did not need any more premonitions of danger, she thought grimly. She was already quite worried.

"Well, we must look on the bright side, sir. If this mysterious person killed Miranda for the recipe and thinks he needs me to employ it, he is highly unlikely to try to murder me."

"True, but he may well hatch a plan to kidnap you."

"Oh." Emma thought about that. "I suppose you would find such an occurrence a trifle inconvenient?"

His mouth quirked. "More than a trifle." The smile was gone as quickly as it had come. "The thing is, I do not think that I can keep you safe in Lady Mayfield's house any longer."

"What do you mean?"

"I intend to hire a couple of Runners to keep an eye on you. It will not be possible to do that without informing Lady Mayfield about what is happening."

"Where is the problem in that?" Emma rolled her eyes. "If I know Letty, she will quite enjoy the excitement."

"She may enjoy it, but she will be unable to keep quiet about it. The tale will be all over Town by midnight tonight. If my inquiries are made public, the killer will be warned and will likely disappear before I can find him."

Emma winced. He was right. Letty's love of gossip would soon overwhelm any promise she might make to keep silent about events. "I see what you mean."

"I must find a more secure place in which to keep you."

"I wish you would not talk about me as though I were a valuable bauble that must be stored in a safe," she muttered.

"Ah, but you are an extremely valuable commodity, Miss Greyson. And I do not intend to lose you."

She could not decide whether or not he was teasing her, so she decided to ignore the remark. "Do you propose to pack me off to one of your estates, the way you did Swan?"

He shook his head. "No, that will not do. If I sent you away, the killer would likely conclude that I am on his trail. He may well be provoked into doing something rash or into leaving the country altogether."

She spread her hands. "It seems that I have become a serious complication for you, sir. What will you do with me?"

"The most practical thing," he said slowly, "would be to move you into my own town house."

She stiffened. "No. Absolutely impossible. You cannot be serious, sir."

He eyed her speculatively. "Why not?"

"Why not? Have you gone mad? A gentleman does not move his fiancée into his town house. I would be transformed into your mistress in the eyes of the ton. No reference, no matter how brilliantly written, would overcome that stigma."

"Emma—"

"Why, I should be obliged to change my name, dye my hair, and invent a whole new past for myself. That would present a host of difficulties. I have my sister to consider, after all. I cannot simply up and disappear off the face of the earth."

"Emma, listen to me."

"No, I will not listen to you try to talk me into such a dreadful plan. I do not care how much more money you offer to pay me. I will not move into your town house and that is final."

"If it is the thought of being branded my mistress that distresses you so," he said in a strangely neutral voice, "you could move in as my wife."

"Your *wife*?" She threw up her hands, exasperated beyond all reason. "You are, indeed, a candidate for Bedlam."

"I think the notion has possibilities."

She seized the lapels of his coat and stood on tiptoe to glare into his shuttered eyes. "Try to think more clearly, sir. It is not like you to be so obtuse. When this affair is finished, it would be even more impossible for me to conceal my identity if I have posed as your wife."

"What if we made the charade a reality?" he asked very softly.

The rage that surged through her was so powerful that she did not trust herself to speak. How dare he make light of such a subject? Her heart was in danger of being broken and he had the gall to jest.

Very deliberately she unclenched her fingers and stepped back. She turned her back to him and stared fixedly at the street.

"This is hardly an appropriate time to mock me, sir," she said very coolly. "We have a serious matter on our hands."

He was silent for a long moment behind her.

"I beg your pardon," he said eventually. "You are right, of course. This is no time to jest."

"I am glad you realize that."

"It does leave us with the problem of where to put you until this matter is ended."

She forced back the anger and pain that had threatened to swamp her. Think, she ordered her beleaguered brain. Think quickly or there is no telling what idiocy he will suggest next.

The idea popped into her mind wholly formed. One moment it did not exist, the next it was there, complete and obvious. There was a sense of rightness to it that told her it had sprung from the intuitive side of her nature. She considered it for a moment, examining it from all sides, and then she turned back to Edison.

"Lady Exbridge," she said.

"What about her?"

"I will go to stay with her."

"What?"

"Think, sir. It is the obvious thing to do. Indeed, what could be more appropriate in the eyes of the world than for your fiancée to move in to your grandmother's house?"

It was his turn to stare at her as though she had lost her mind. "That is the most insane, the most ludicrous, the most outrageous notion I have ever heard."

"Why? You can tell her exactly what is going on. She will not gossip. Her sense of family responsibility will ensure that she will keep your secrets."

"You have no notion of what you are talking about," he said. "Even if I were to agree to such a plan, she would refuse."

Emma shrugged. "Ask her."

Hands clasped behind his back, Edison stood at the window of his grandmother's drawing room. He gazed out over the forecourt to the massive gates that protected the entrance to the Fortress. He was quite aware of Emma sitting quietly, her hands folded demurely in her lap.

"I see," Victoria said after a long moment of deep contemplation.

They were the first words she had spoken since Edison had explained the situation to her.

He still could not believe that Emma had talked him into coming here to ask for his grandmother's help. He braced himself for Victoria's refusal. She would reject the request out of hand, of course. The notion of cooperating with him in this plan to protect Emma was ludicrous.

Things would have been so much simpler if Emma had agreed to move into his house, he thought. Instead, she had refused to even consider the possibility.

The alarm he had seen in her eyes when he had suggested that she marry him had made him feel strangely empty and cold. A moment before, she had returned his kiss with a passion that had threatened to melt his bones. And in the next instant she had refused to even consider marriage.

He wondered when he had himself first begun to consider it. It was as if the idea had been there, buried somewhere in his brain, since the first moment he had met her.

"I'm sure it's a great relief to you to know that my engagement to your grandson is, indeed, a fraud after all, Lady Exbridge," Emma said encouragingly. "I have only been acting a part to help him catch a thief."

Edison suppressed a strong urge to cross the room, haul her up out of the chair with both hands, and tell her that there was nothing fraudulent about the passion they shared.

"For obvious reasons," Emma continued blithely, "I could not explain the details when you invited me here to tea. But with Lady Ames's death, matters have become somewhat untenable."

"To say the least." Victoria's voice was very dry.

Edison turned around abruptly. "Damnation, I told you this would never work, Emma. Come, we must be off. We do not have any more time to waste."

She made no move to rise. "Really, sir, the least you can do is grant your grandmother a few minutes to contemplate the situation. We have sprung this on her without any warning. She needs a moment or two to think about it."

Victoria gave her an odd glance. "You say my grandson employed you to assist him in locating this missing book?"

"Yes, madam, I was to be the bait." Emma smiled ruefully. "At the time, I was in urgent need of a new position, so I accepted the post in exchange for handsome wages and a proper reference."

Victoria frowned. "A reference?"

"I'm quite certain that a reference from a gentleman of Mr. Stokes's stature would open many doors for me, and as I do not know how much longer I may have to wait for certain financial investments to come to fruition, it is possible I will need to seek another post—"

"Emma," Edison said through his teeth. "You are straying from the subject."

"Yes, I am," she agreed. "Well, madam, as I was saying, it has all become a great tangle. Now Mr. Stokes says that we require the assistance of someone we can trust if we are to continue with our scheme. Naturally, we thought of you."

"Hrumph."

"Lady Mayfield is a good-hearted soul and, unwittingly, of course, she has been exceedingly helpful," Emma plowed on gamely. "But we dare not take her into our confidence. I'm sure you understand."

Victoria gave a ladylike snort. "Letty could not keep a secret if her life depended upon it. She is an inveterate gossip."

"I fear you are right, madam."

Victoria flicked an enigmatic glance at Edison. "And just why, may I ask, have you decided to come to me for help in this matter?"

"Mr. Stokes felt, quite rightly, that he could entrust a secret of this import only to a member of his own family." Emma paused. "And as you happen to be the only relative he's got, we came straight to you."

Edison turned back to the view of the gates. He waited for Victoria to announce in ringing accents that she was under no obligation to help him in any way.

"The first thing we must do," Victoria said crisply, "is get you to a good modiste, Miss Greyson. The only thing worse than Letty's tendency to gossip is her taste in fashion. The neckline of the gown you are wearing is cut far too low."

Chapter Twenty-Six

I told you she would help us." Emma smiled smugly as she stepped into Edison's arms later the following evening.

"So you did." He glanced across the crowded ballroom to where Victoria stood with a small cluster of expensively dressed matrons.

Emma followed his glance. Victoria was resplendent in a silver satin gown trimmed with silver flowers and a matching turban. As Emma watched she fanned herself languidly with a handsomely decorated silver fan.

"I vow, that gown is wonderful on her," Emma said. "She outshines all of the other ladies in her vicinity. Your grandmother certainly has a gift for fashion."

"I will allow her that much." Edison raised his brows

and glanced meaningfully at Emma's neckline. "I knew those gowns Letty chose for you displayed far too much bosom."

"You must not criticize Letty. She has been extremely helpful. She did exactly as you wished her to do, even if she did not know about your scheme."

Letty had been amazed to learn that Victoria had invited Emma to move in to her house.

"Who would have thought the old stiff-necked gel would unbend so far?" Letty had chuckled that afternoon when Emma had explained the situation. "But it's wonderful news for you, my dear. I cannot wait to tell everyone that the rift between Victoria and her grandson has been healed at last. I vow, it will be *the* topic at every soiree and ball tonight."

She had rushed straight off to spread the fresh gossip while Emma was whisked away to a dressmaker to have the necklines of her gowns raised. Edison had gone about his own mysterious business. He had disappeared for the remainder of the afternoon only to reappear in time to escort Emma and Victoria to the Broadrick ball.

"Now that you have me settled at your grandmother's, what are your plans, sir?" Emma asked as they circled the floor.

"I have hired two Runners to watch the house day and night. One of them will also accompany you if you go out without me."

"Don't you think the villain may notice a couple of Bow Street Runners hanging about all the time?"

"They will be disguised as stable grooms when they are working."

"Hmm." Emma considered the situation. "And what of you, sir? How do you plan to proceed with your inquiries?"

"The next step, now that I have someone to keep an eye on you, is to draw the mysterious Vanza fighter out into the open again. Once I have my hands on him, I will make him tell me the name of the master he serves."

"You believe that this rogue Vanza master is the killer, do you not?"

"I'm not yet positive that he is the murderer, but I am convinced that he is deeply involved in this affair. When I learn his identity, I believe that I will have a key that I can use to sort out the rest of the business."

Emma watched him uneasily. "Something tells me it will not be that simple."

"On the contrary, I think it will all work out very nicely. Most things do if they are planned and carried out in a logical, intelligent manner."

"And, pray tell, what am I to do while you are playing this dangerous game with the Vanza fighter?"

"Nothing."

"Nothing?" Emma frowned. "But I am supposed to assist you. Indeed, you have employed me to do so. I must insist on being allowed to perform my duties."

"Your task consists solely of staying out of trouble," Edison said. "I do not want to have to worry about you while I search for that damned Vanza fighter."

His casual dismissal of her responsibilities in the investigation was too much. "Now see here, Edison, I am a professional person. I will not tolerate being treated like so much baggage to be stored in a closet until needed. You know very well that I have been extremely useful to you thus far."

"Very useful."

The condescending tone made her see red. "Damnation, Edison, if you don't allow me to fulfill the duties for which I was employed, I shall quit immediately."

"You cannot quit your position. You have not got your reference yet."

"This is not a joke, sir."

He brought her to a halt a few feet away from where Victoria waited. There was no glint of amusement in his eyes.

"Your duties consist of acting the part of my bride-to-be," he said. "I suggest you concentrate very hard on that task, because you have not quite got the hang of it."

Emma was so outraged it was all she could do not to shriek at him like a fishwife. She barely recalled in time that they were standing in the middle of a crowded ballroom.

"Not got the hang of it," she whispered tightly. "Not got the *hang* of it? How dare you, sir. I have given an absolutely dazzling performance in the role of your fiancée."

"There, you see?" He shook his head with an air of deep regret. "As my fiancée, you should be all sparkles and smiles and sweetness and light. Instead, anyone watching us at this moment is no doubt gaining the impression that you would like to throttle me."

She gave him her most charming, brilliant smile. "Anyone watching would be absolutely correct, sir."

She turned on her heel and stalked off to join Victoria.

Edison was still brooding over the quarrel an hour later when he left his club. He did not understand how the storm had blown up with virtually no warning. The last thing he had intended to do this evening was engage in a bitter argument with Emma. His only goal was to keep her safe until he had found the killer.

A thin fog swirled through St. James Street. Edison did not bother to search the mist for the one he knew was watching him. He could feel the other's presence as a cold prickle of sensation on the back of his neck. It had been like this for the past two days. The young Vanza fighter was following him.

Carriage lights glowed in the mist. Edison started walking, absently aware of the familiar sounds of a busy London night. The muffled clatter of hooves and the jangle and squeak of harness leather echoed in the darkness. The drunken laughter of several fashionably dressed rakes grated on his ears.

Out of the corner of his eye, he watched the dandies disappear into a narrow lane. He knew that they would spend the rest of the night seeking various forms of debauchery and unsavory excitement. Deep in those narrow streets and alleys, they would encounter smoky gaming hells and brothels that offered all manner of perversions.

Edison felt the old anger twist inside him. His father had lived just such a careless, wasted life as those young rakehells who had vanished into the black maw of that lane. The relentless pursuit of meaningless, unwholesome pleasures had been paramount for Wesley Stokes.

He thought about what he had overheard Emma say to his grandmother the day Victoria had ordered her to come to tea. *It must have been heartbreaking for you to realize what an irresponsible son you'd raised.*

Emma was right. Victoria must have been well aware of the truth about his father. She was too intelligent not to have known that Wesley had been, at heart, an incurable gamester and a feckless wastrel. However much she had doted on him, she must have been deeply saddened by the inescapable knowledge that her son and the family's sole heir had been doomed by his own uncontrolled passions.

Emma was right about the rest of it, too, Edison reflected. Victoria would have blamed herself. Every time she looked at Wesley's portrait in her drawing room, she had to face the fact that she had failed.

Just as he would blame himself if his own son turned out badly. His own son.

He looked into the fog and saw a future he suddenly ached to bring into existence, a future in which Emma held their baby in her arms.

The vision was so real that it brought him to a halt. He shook himself free of the image and glanced around. He was mildly surprised to notice that he had walked farther than he had intended. The realization brought him back to the business at hand.

For a moment he had almost forgotten his purpose this evening. Such lapses could be dangerous. He had not come out into the night with the goal of pondering the past, the present, or the unknowable future. It was not good for the spirits to dwell on what could not be altered. He thought he had learned that lesson long ago.

He glanced at a passing hackney and contemplated hailing it. He had used just such a public coach to come to St. James Street earlier after having left his own carriage for Emma and Victoria. The two Runners he had hired that afternoon would serve as coachman and groom. They would see the women safely home from the ball.

In the meantime, he had plans of his own. They required his full attention.

He turned at the corner and walked down a fog-clogged lane. At the end of the narrow passage, he could see the fiendish glow of a gaming hell's windows. In a nearby doorway a man huffed and groaned hoarsely in the throes of sexual release. The prostitute he had pinned up against the wall murmured something encouraging. Her giggle sounded brittle and utterly false.

Edison continued walking toward the fiery lights of the underworld that lay at the end of the alley. He did not turn to glance back over his shoulder. There was no need. He heard no footsteps behind him, but he knew the watcher had followed him into the lane.

The Vanza fighter would not be able to resist such an opportunity. He was too young to have learned the virtues of the Strategy of Patience.

Edison unfastened his greatcoat as he walked steadily toward the fires of hell. He slipped his arms out of the sleeves and draped the heavy garment over his shoulders as if it were a cloak.

The young fighter was good. The attack, when it came, was swift and virtually soundless. If he had not been expecting it, Edison thought, he might have missed the telltale whisper of an in-drawn breath altogether.

As it was, it told him the fighter's exact position.

Edison moved, gliding to the side and spinning around. The lights of the gaming hell glared in the fog, providing just enough illumination to enable him to see the masked figure closing in from the side.

Realizing he had been spotted, the Vanza fighter lashed out swiftly with his booted foot.

Edison slid out of range. "What's this? No formal challenge this time? I am offended. Where is your sense of tradition?"

"You do not honor the ancient traditions, therefore I do not challenge you in the old way."

"A very practical decision. Congratulations. There may be hope for you yet."

"You mock me, O Great One Who Has Stepped Out of the Circle. But you will not do so for long."

"I would take it as a favor if you would stop addressing me as though I belonged in some ancient legend."

"Your legend ends tonight."

The fighter danced closer. He swung his leg in another brutal arc that failed to find its target.

"Take off your coat," he snarled. "Or do you intend to try to use your pistol to even the odds again tonight?"

"No. I don't plan to use a pistol." Edison stepped back. He let the greatcoat fall from his shoulders.

"I knew that you would eventually accept the challenge." Satisfaction laced the fighter's words. "I was told that even though you have gone outside the Circle, your honor is still Vanza."

"Actually, my honor is my own."

Edison dodged another kick and moved in beneath it. He snapped out a blow that caught the fighter on the ankle. The man gasped and lurched to the side in an unbalanced move that left him vulnerable.

Edison seized the opportunity. He rained a series of short, sharp blows designed not to cause injury but to keep his opponent reeling.

The young fighter abandoned the effort to maintain his balance. He threw himself to the ground and rolled toward Edison.

It was a deft recovery. Edison was impressed. The move was an old one from the Strategy of Surprise.

He opted for a move from the same Strategy. Instead of falling back, he leaped over the rolling figure, twisted in midair, and came down on the other side.

The fighter realized too late that his attack had been thwarted. He struggled to get back to his feet, but there was no time.

Edison was on him. He pinned the young man to the damp paving stones with an unbreakable hold from the Strategy of Restraint. He felt the fear and rage that shuddered through his victim.

"It's over," Edison said softly.

There was a moment of tension during which he worried that the fighter would fail to yield. He would have another kind of problem on his hands if the young man made such a decision. He sought for the formal words that would allow his opponent a face-saving way out of the impasse.

"Even though I have gone out of the Circle, my honor is un-questioned by any in the Society or on Vanzagara itself," he said. "I de-mand from you the respect that a student must show to a true master. Yield."

"I . . . yield."

Edison hesitated a few seconds and then released his captive. He got to his feet and stood looking down at him. "Get up. Take off that ridiculous mask and move closer to the light."

Reluctantly the fighter hauled himself up off the stones. He limped slowly toward the glare of the gaming hell windows. Then he stopped and reached up to pull the scarf away from his face.

Edison looked at him and stifled a bone-deep sigh. He had been right. The fighter was no more than eighteen or nineteen at the most. No older than he himself had been when he had sailed for the East with Ignatius Lorring. He looked into the sullen, haunted eyes and saw a mirror that reflected his own past.

"What is your name?" he asked quietly.

"John. John Stoner."

"Where does your family live?"

"I have no family. My mother died two years ago. There is no one else."

"What of your father?"

"I am a bastard," John said flatly.

"I should have guessed as much." The tale was so close to home that it made him shudder. "How long have you studied Vanza, John Stoner?"

"Nearly a year." There was a desperate pride in the words. "My master says I learn quickly."

"Who is your master?"

John looked at his own feet. "Please, do not ask me that. I cannot tell you."

"Why not?"

"Because he told me that you are his enemy. Even though you have defeated me in honorable combat, I cannot betray my master to you. To do so would be to sacrifice all that is left of my own honor."

Edison moved closer. "Will it make it any easier for you to give me his name if I tell you that your master is a rogue? He has not taught you true Vanza."

"No." John's head came up swiftly, his eyes stark. "I will not believe that. I have studied hard. I have served my master faithfully."

Edison considered his options. He could probably force the name of the renegade out of John, but to do so would deprive the young man of the only thing of value he had left, his honor. Edison remembered too well what it felt like to have only that one commodity to call his own.

He contemplated the scene through the gaming hell windows. The fiery glare revealed the figures of the debauched men inside, men who drank too much and risked too much. They were men who had nothing left to lose, not even their honor. It would be all too easy for John to become one of them after his failure tonight.

Edison made up his mind. "Come with me."

He turned and walked toward the entrance of the fog-shrouded lane. He did not look back to see if John had obeyed him.

The fog had lifted by the time Edison arrived at the docks with John in tow. The cold light of the moon revealed the outlines of the ships that bobbed gently in the water. The familiar stench of the Thames filled the air.

There had been only one brief stop en route. That was to collect John's entire assortment of worldly possessions from a dismal little room above a tavern.

"I don't understand." John hitched his bundle higher on his shoulder and stared, bewildered, at the creaking masts of the *Sarah Jane*. "Why have we come here?"

"You have been a nuisance on occasion, John, but you have succeeded in convincing me that you are serious in your quest to learn true Vanza. I take it you have not changed your mind in the past hour?"

"Changed my mind? About Vanza? Never. Tonight I have failed but I will never cease to search for the balance that brings knowledge."

"Excellent." Edison clapped him lightly on the shoulder. "Because I am going to give you a chance to study Vanza the way it should be studied. In the Garden Temples of Vanzagara."

"Vanzagara?" John swung around so quickly that he nearly dropped his bundle. The lantern he carried revealed the stunned expression on his face. "But that is not possible. It lies across the seas. Is it not enough that you have defeated me? Must you continue to mock me?"

"The *Sarah Jane* is one of my ships. She sails at dawn for the Far East. One of her ports of call is Vanzagara. I will give you a letter to give to a monk named Vora. He is a man of great wisdom. He will see to it that you receive instruction in the true ways of Vanza."

John looked at him as though afraid to believe him. "You are serious."

"Very."

"Why would you do this for me? You owe me nothing. I did not even tell you the one thing you wished to know, the name of my master."

"Your ex-master," Edison said. "And you're wrong. I do owe you

276

something. You reminded me of someone I knew when I was much younger."

"Who?"

"Myself."

Edison saw the elated John safely aboard the *Sarah Jane*. He had a word with the captain, informing him that his new passenger was to be put ashore in Vanzagara, and then he returned to the small room John Stoner had called home for the past year.

There was very little left in the tiny chamber. But the remains of John's most recently used Vanza meditation candle were still in a dish on the table. Edison had noted them earlier but he had said nothing about them.

He walked across the small room and hoisted the lantern to spill light on the cold, melted bits of beeswax. The candle had been tinted a dark crimson. Edison pried one of the pieces off the plate and inhaled the scent.

To know the master, look at the student's candles.

When he found the man who had given John the crimson tapers, he would find the rogue master.

CHAPTER TWENTY-SEVEN

So, you have managed to win over the Exbridge Dragon." Basil's mouth curved with dry humor as he brought Emma to a halt at the edge of the dance floor. "My congratulations, Miss Greyson. You must be something of a sorceress."

"Nonsense." Emma glanced toward Victoria, who was chatting with two women who appeared to be old friends. "Lady Exbridge was kind enough to invite me to stay with her until the marriage."

Basil looked thoughtful. "Until tonight, no one in Society would have believed that the Dragon would ever have deigned to recognize her bastard grandson's choice of bride."

Emma raised her chin. "She is his grandmother, when all is said and done, sir."

Without waiting for a response, she whirled and walked briskly away from Basil. She had not wanted to dance with him in the first place. She had not wanted to go back onto the floor with anyone after Edison had left. She had been too busy worrying about his plans for the evening.

But Basil had materialized the moment Edison vanished, and Lady Exbridge had urged her to accept his invitation to waltz.

It was really very difficult trying to please Victoria, Emma reflected as she moved back through the crowd. In the short time she had spent with her, she had learned that her gowns were not only cut too low, they had too many flounces. She had been told that the particular shade of green Letty had decreed for most of the items in her wardrobe was not the right one. In addition, she had been informed that Lady Mayfield had allowed her to accept too many invitations from the wrong people in the Polite World.

All in all, Emma thought, she was very glad that she had not had the misfortune to have been employed by Victoria as a lady's companion. She had no doubt that Lady Exbridge would have proved to be every bit as difficult an employer as her grandson.

A liveried footman went past with a heavily laden tray. Emma seized a glass of lemonade and paused beneath a potted palm to down the entire contents. Dancing, she had discovered, was thirsty work.

So was worrying about Edison. She glanced out the window into the night. He was out there somewhere pursuing his scheme to lure the Vanza fighter out of hiding. She was still annoyed with him for refusing to take her with him.

She was searching for a place to set down the empty glass when she heard Victoria's voice drift through the branches of the palm.

"I have no notion of what you are talking about, Rosemary. Murderess, indeed. What utter rubbish."

Emma went very still.

"Surely you've heard that Crane was found shot dead in her bed-chamber," the woman named Rosemary said.

"I assure you," Victoria snapped, "that if my grandson's fiancée actually did shoot this Chilton Crane person, he most certainly deserved it."

Rosemary gave a shocked gasp. "Surely you jest, Victoria. We are speaking of the murder of a gentleman of the ton."

"Really?" Victoria sounded coolly astonished. "If that's true, then it was, indeed, a memorable event. After all, there are so very few true gentlemen in the ton. It would be a pity to lose one. However, I do not believe there is any cause for alarm in this case."

"How on earth can you say such a thing?" Rosemary demanded, clearly scandalized.

"From everything I have heard, Chilton Crane was no gentleman and no great loss to the world."

There was a short, stunned pause and then Rosemary abruptly changed tactics. "I must admit that I was amazed to see that you have given your approval to your grandson's choice of brides. Even if one ignores the fact that her name is connected to a murder, there is no getting around the business of her former career."

"Former career?" Victoria repeated vaguely.

Sensing an opening, Rosemary pounced. "Heavens. Has no one told you that Miss Greyson made her living as a lady's companion until the night she became engaged to your grandson?"

"What of it?"

"I would have thought that you would have preferred a daughter-in-law from a more elevated station. An heiress, surely."

"What I prefer," Victoria said crisply, "is precisely what I have got. A future daughter-in-law who shows every sign of being able to help my grandson reinvigorate the family tree."

"I beg your pardon?"

"Family bloodlines are not unlike horse bloodlines, you know. To keep the breed strong and robust, one must look for spirit and intelligence in a prospective daughter-in-law, just as one would in a mare."

"I cannot believe—"

"Look around you," Victoria said. "Don't you think it's a pity that so many families in the Polite World show evidence of weakness in the bloodlines? Poor constitutions, a sorry tendency to frequent the gaming hells, and an inclination to debauchery. The Stokes family line will be spared that fate, thanks to my grandson and his bride."

Emma managed to restrain herself until she and Victoria were on the way home in the carriage. When the vehicle, guarded by two sturdy-looking Bow Street Runners, set off into the late night traffic, she looked at the older woman.

"Weakness in the bloodlines?" she murmured.

Victoria's brows rose in a manner that was strongly reminiscent of Edison. "So you overheard that, did you?"

"It's a shame Edison was not present. He would have been extremely amused."

Victoria turned her head to look out the window. Her jaw was set in rigid lines. Her shoulders were stiff and very straight. "No doubt."

There was a short silence. Emma looked at Victoria's gloved fingers. They were tightly folded on her lap.

"It was very kind of you to lend your assistance to him in this venture, madam," Emma said quietly. "It is very important to him because he feels a great debt of gratitude to his friend, Mr. Lorring, and to the monks of Vanzagara."

"How very odd."

"Perhaps. Nevertheless, he is committed to finding the villain who stole the book and the elixir recipe. After the events that transpired today, he had nowhere else to turn except to you."

"Astonishing." Victoria gazed fixedly out into the darkness. "Edison has certainly never needed any help from me before."

282

"Oh, but he has. The thing is, he did not know how to ask for it. And you, I am sorry to say, were not very good at offering it."

Victoria's head snapped around. Her fierce, strangely desperate eyes pinned Emma. "What do you mean?"

"As I told you, the two of you have much in common when it comes to stubbornness and pride." Emma smiled wryly. "They are no doubt a few of those delightful traits that you mentioned. The sort that are passed down through family bloodlines."

Victoria's mouth tightened. Emma braced herself for a blistering scold.

"Are you in love with my grandson?" Victoria asked instead.

It was Emma's turn to go rigid and focus on the scene outside the window. "An acquaintance of mine recently reminded me that it is most unwise for anyone in service to fall in love with his or her employer."

"That is not an answer to my question."

Emma looked at her. "No, I suppose it is not."

Victoria searched her face. "You *are* in love with him."

"Do not concern yourself, madam. I assure you, I will not make the mistake of assuming that he loves me." Emma sighed. "That is how the disasters always seem to come about, you see. False assumptions."

It was not yet dawn when Emma heard the light, rapid *ping, ping, ping* on the window of her bedchamber. She was still wide awake. Her thoughts had been churning ever since she had climbed into bed. A part of her was waiting but she did not know why.

Ping, ping, ping.

Rain, she thought. But that made no sense. The moon was out. For the past two hours she had been idly tracking the band of silver that was moving so slowly across the carpet.

Ping, ping, ping.

Not rain. Pebbles.

"Edison."

She scrambled out of bed, grabbed her wrapper, and hurried to the window. She opened it quickly, leaned out, and looked down.

Edison stood in the garden directly below. He had his greatcoat hooked over one shoulder. His cravat hung loose around his neck and his head was bare. The moonlight cast cold shadows around him as he watched her window.

She was so relieved to see him safe and sound that she felt slightly dazed.

"Are you all right?" she called softly.

"Yes, of course. Come downstairs to the conservatory. I want to talk to you."

Something was wrong. She could hear it in his voice.

"I'll be right down."

She closed the window, tightened the sash of her wrapper, and went to the table to pick up the candle.

She let herself out into the hall, tiptoed past Victoria's door, and descended the back stairs into the kitchen hall. She walked quickly to the conservatory door and opened it. She saw at once that she would no longer need her candle.

Moonlight flooded the glass-walled room with a radiance that etched the plants in silver. Palm fronds loomed against the backdrop of the night outside the windows. Broad leaves cast strange shadows. Massed flowers, stripped of their exotic hues, lined the benches. An earthy mix of exotic scents floated in the air.

"Edison?"

"Here." He moved out of the dark place between two leafy trees and came toward her down a moonlit aisle. "Keep your voice down. I do not want to wake the household."

"No, of course not." She blew out the candle and set it aside. "What happened? Did you find the Vanza fighter?"

Edison came to a halt in front of her. He tossed his greatcoat over the nearest workbench. "I found him."

The neutral quality of his voice alarmed her as nothing else could have done at that moment.

"What is it?" She swallowed uneasily. "Did you . . . were you . . . forced to kill him?"

"No."

"Thank heavens for that much. What did you do with him?"

Edison leaned back against one of the pillars that supported the glass roof. He folded his arms and looked past her into the darkness outside the windows. "I put him on a ship bound for Vanzagara."

"I see." She hesitated. "Was he as young as you suspected?"

"Yes."

"So that is the problem. He reminded you of yourself at that age."

"Sometimes you are entirely too perceptive, Emma. It is an irritating habit in an employee."

"It was a logical conclusion," she said apologetically.

"You are right." Edison exhaled deeply. "He reminded me of the fact that I was not the only young man who ever found himself adrift in the world. He also reminded me of how desperately young men search for ways to prove to themselves that they are men. How those of us who were born as bastards seek some semblance of personal honor. Yes, he reminded me of myself at that age."

She touched his arm. "What troubles you now? Do you doubt that you did the right thing?"

"By sending young John Stoner off to Vanzagara? No. If there is any hope for him, it lies there. As much as I may scorn the metaphysical nonsense spouted by the members of the Vanzagarian Society, I must admit that it was my experience on the island that gave me what I needed to find my place in the world."

"Did you discover the identity of the rogue master from this John Stoner?"

"No. But I will know the rogue when I find him. It's only a matter of time now."

He sounded remarkably unconcerned about that aspect of the situation. She knew that his thoughts tonight were centered on the past. The encounter with John Stoner had awakened too many memories. She ached to comfort him but she had no notion of how to get past the wall he had built long ago to protect himself.

"I'm sorry," she whispered.

He said nothing. He simply looked at her.

"I am so sorry that tonight you looked into a mirror and saw yourself as a young man."

For a moment he did not react.

"I do not think of myself as so very old yet," he finally said very dryly.

"Oh, Edison." She did not know whether to laugh or cry.

Impulsively she put her arms around his waist and pressed her face against his chest. With an uncharacteristically brusque, almost jerky movement, he wrapped his arms fiercely around her.

"Emma." His mouth came down on hers as though the world might end in the next five minutes.

It was not comfort he sought, she realized. It was something else, something more primitive and far less civilized. It was her turn to hesitate. This was the second time she had stood on this particular precipice. On the first occasion she had learned just how dangerous it was.

But the hunger in Edison ignited a blaze within her. The gentle urge to comfort him was transformed into a desperate need to respond to the desire in him.

His mouth never left hers as he lifted her off her feet. He used one hand to force her lower body against his own. He was fiercely aroused.

"I had to see you tonight," Edison whispered roughly against her mouth.

"Yes." She pulled her head back an inch or so and lifted her hands to rake her fingers through his hair. "Yes, it's all right, Edison. I am glad you came to me."

"Oh, God, Emma."

He lowered her slowly to her feet as though the feel of her was both a pleasure and a keen agony. Then he picked up his greatcoat and tossed it on the floor. He turned back to her, shrugged out of his black evening coat, and cast it aside. He met her eyes.

"Emma?"

"Yes. Oh, yes, Edison."

She took a step toward him. With a husky groan he pulled her close again and then he drew her down. The heavy woolen greatcoat could not disguise the hardness of the stone floor, but the garment was warm and it carried a faint hint of Edison's scent. Emma inhaled deeply. Excitement and need poured through her.

Edison gathered her to him.

This was right, she thought as the heat of his body enveloped her. It had to be right.

She shivered when she felt his hand slide between her thighs.

"This time," she whispered, "you will kindly remove your shirt."

"This time," he promised as he yanked at the fastenings, "I will do anything you ask of me."

He got the pleated white shirt undone, but before he could wrestle himself free of it, Emma spread her fingers across his bare skin. She could not see his chest because he was leaning over her, his broad shoulders blotting out the moonlight. But she could feel him. The texture of the crisp hair and the shift of his muscles enthralled her.

"You are magnificent," she said softly. "Strong and beautiful."

"Oh, Emma. You do not know what you are doing to me. I promised myself that I would remain in control tonight."

She smiled. "Surely your training in the art of Vanza taught you some useful exercise that can be applied at moments such as this."

"One of the great drawbacks to the art of Vanza," he muttered against her throat, "is that it teaches that all strong passions are to be avoided."

"Then it is obvious why you are not well suited to the philosophy. You are a man of great passions."

287

AMANDA QUICK

"The odd thing is, I did not realize just how strong my passions were until I met you."

He kissed her again, his mouth hot and rough against hers. But his hands were incredibly tender. The contrast left her breathless.

She felt his fingers cup the exquisitely sensitive place between her legs. A great heat rose within her.

"Edison?"

"This time we will not rush the matter," he vowed. "This time I want you to feel something of what I felt last time. Surely even a portion of that pleasure would make you understand."

"Understand what?"

But he did not answer. Instead, he held her more tightly and stroked her slowly, going deeper into her with each movement. She trembled under the flood of passion that assailed her. She clutched at him as the aching, yearning, wanting sensation built within her. She was vaguely aware of her own breathing. It sounded ragged and uneven.

When she began to twist against his hand, silently pleading with him for a culmination to the intense feeling, Edison gave a soft, hoarse groan. But he did not open his trousers, slide between her legs, and fit himself to her body as she expected.

Instead, he slid down the length of her, eased her legs farther apart, and pushed aside the skirt of her lawn nightshift. Then, astonishingly, he put his mouth on her.

"*Edison.*" Emma knew that her small scream of shock and surprise would have awakened the entire household, indeed, the entire neighborhood, had it not got caught and partially strangled in her throat.

She was shocked by the strange caress. Shocked, amazed, and unbearably thrilled. Everything in her lower body went very tight. She flung out her arms, seeking something, anything, to anchor herself. Her fingers brushed against the iron supports of the workbenches on either side of the narrow aisle. She gripped them and held on as though they could keep her safely bound to earth.

But a few seconds later when the release sang through her, she knew that nothing could restrain her to the cold ground. She was flying.

Edison was suddenly on top of her, crushing her into the warm greatcoat. He drove himself into her and groaned as she contracted fiercely around him. He was too big, but she did not care. All that mattered was binding him to her, making him hers for whatever time the fates allowed.

"*Hold me.*" He moved within her, sinking deeper with each thrust.

He arched his back and went rigid.

Energy rippled through his taut muscles as he poured himself into her.

Emma held on to him with all of her strength.

It seemed an infinitely long time later when Edison opened his eyes and gazed up into the full glare of the moon. The fact that he and Emma were still lying in the glow told him that in truth very little time had passed. It had just seemed as if he had floated there for an eternity.

He tightened his arm around Emma. She stirred against his chest. He felt her hand flatten on his bare stomach and smiled slightly. He had got his shirt unfastened but he had not managed to get it off entirely.

Next time, he promised silently.

Next time.

There had to be a next time. A lot of them. His future was with Emma. Surely she would comprehend that now.

"Emma?"

"Good heavens." She sat up swiftly and looked around with a dazed expression. "We are in your grandmother's conservatory, of all places. We must get out of here before someone discovers us."

"Calm yourself, my sweet." He put one arm behind his head to pillow himself and looked up at her. "You are no longer a respectable lady's companion who must be constantly concerned with the virtue problem."

She made a delicious picture, he thought. The little white nightcap was askew. Her hair was a cloudy tangle around her face. The wrapper was unfastened and the bodice of her shift was open.

"Nevertheless, it would be horribly embarrassing if we are found here, sir."

He winced at the sir. Old habits died hard, he reminded himself. "No one has burst in on us thus far. I think we will get through this undiscovered."

"We should not take any more risks."

She scrambled to her feet. He was amused when she lurched and flung out a hand to steady herself. He watched her for a moment while she struggled to set herself to rights.

"Hurry, sir." She glared down at him. "It is nearly dawn. The servants will soon be up and about."

"Very well." Reluctantly he got to his feet. When he started to refasten his shirt, he realized that she was gazing at him with an odd expression. "What's wrong?"

"Nothing," she said quickly. Too quickly.

He frowned. "Are you all right?"

"Yes. Yes, of course. It's just that, well, I have only now realized that I still have never actually seen you without your shirt."

He grinned slowly. "Allow me to show you my tattoo, my dear."

He relit the candle she had brought with her, gave her a mocking bow, and peeled back the wings of his unfastened shirt.

"*Edison.*" His name was a choked gasp on her lips. She stared at him as though he had turned into a monster in front of her eyes.

He raised his brows. "Obviously you are not as impressed as I'd hoped you'd be. Next time I shall leave the shirt on."

"Oh my God, *Edison.*"

He was ruefully aware that he was hurt by her lack of appreciation of his bare chest. He stopped smiling.

"I would remind you that a few minutes ago you were not complaining." He started to refasten his shirt.

"Wait. Your tattoo." She seized the candle and stepped closer.

"I trust you do not intend to set fire to the hair on my chest," he murmured.

She ignored him. For a long moment she stared fixedly at the place near his shoulder where years ago the mark of Vanza had been etched.

He glanced down. "It is called the Flower of Vanza. Were you expecting a more interesting design, perhaps?"

She raised her stark eyes to his. "I was expecting a design that was completely unfamiliar."

He stilled. "What are you saying?"

"I have seen that mark elsewhere, Edison."

"Where?"

"Sally Kent's embroidered handkerchief."

Edison was at a loss. "Who?"

"She was the paid companion who attended Lady Ware during the last months of her life. It was Miss Kent's bedchamber I occupied during the country house party at Ware Castle, remember?"

"Forgive me, Emma, but I am not following the thread of this conversation very well."

She licked her lips and drew a deep breath. "Sally Kent embroidered a picture of that mark into a handkerchief that she left hidden together with two hundred pounds. I found the money and the handkerchief and a letter to Sally's friend Judith Hope concealed in Sally's old bedchamber."

"Go on."

"It was obvious that Sally had intended that the money and the needlework go to Miss Hope. I took them to her shortly after we returned to London. You recall the day, do you not? You were quite out of sorts with me because I was a bit late returning to Lady Mayfield's."

He looked at Emma. "About this Sally Kent—"

"Edison, she vanished after she had an affair with Basil Ware."

"Bloody hell."

Silence fell while Edison swiftly resorted and refit the pieces of the puzzle.

Emma eyed him uneasily. "I suppose you are thinking that I should have thought to mention Sally Kent and her needlework to you long before now."

"What I was thinking," Edison said, "was that we are victims of the virtue problem."

"What on earth do you mean?"

"You would have noticed the resemblance between my tattoo and Miss Kent's embroidery design much earlier on in this affair if we had made love much sooner and with greater frequency."

CHAPTER TWENTY-EIGHT

He was too late. The house was empty. Only the house-keeper remained. Edison stood alone in the study of the man who had called himself Basil Ware.

He walked to the desk and examined the bits of melted wax that lay in the bottom of the candle holder. They were crimson in color, the same shade of red as the remains of the taper he had discovered in John Stoner's room.

He snapped off a small chunk and held it to his nose. It had been scented with the same herbs. *To know the master, look at the student's candles.*

Emma heard Edison in the hall shortly after one o'clock that afternoon. She put down her pen, pushed aside the letter she had been attempting to write to her sister, and leaped to her feet.

"He has finally returned, Lady Exbridge."

"I am well aware of that, my dear." Victoria looked up from her book, removed her spectacles, and glanced toward the door of the library. "I do hope he has some news that will ease your nerves."

"There is nothing wrong with my nerves."

"Indeed? It is a wonder that you did not drive me to Bedlam today with your anxious forebodings and your endless pacing. You have acted like the heroine of a horrid novel all morning."

Emma gave her a dark look. "I cannot help it if I am inclined toward premonitions and forebodings."

"Nonsense. I'm sure you could curb the tendency with a bit of fortitude and an application of willpower."

The door opened before Emma was obliged to come up with a response. Edison walked into the room without giving the long-suffering Jinkins a chance to announce him. His eyes went first to Emma. Then he inclined his head briefly to his grandmother.

"Good day to you both," he said.

"Well?" Emma hurried around the corner of the desk. "What did you discover, Edison?"

"Basil Ware has packed up and left Town."

"Gone. Hah. He knows we are on to him."

"Perhaps." Edison walked to the desk and leaned back against it, his hands braced on either side of his thighs. "The housekeeper informed me that he has left Town to rusticate at his country estate. I have sent one of the Runners to Ware Castle to check, but I doubt that he will find Ware in residence."

Victoria frowned. "Emma has told me most of what has happened in the past few hours. What do you think is going on now?"

"I don't yet know the whole of it," Edison said. "But I think it's safe to say that Ware was once a member of the Vanzagarian Society.

Nothing else would explain the tattoo of the Flower of Vanza that Sally Kent apparently noticed."

"Poor Sally Kent," Emma whispered. "I wonder if he killed her because she discovered the tattoo."

"I doubt it," Edison said. "The tattoo would have meant nothing to her."

"But she was blackmailing him for some reason," Emma said. "She may have attempted to extort money from him by pretending that she was with child, but such a ploy would have been doomed to failure. Yet in the end she actually got money from him, so she must have learned something about him that was far more damaging—" She broke off, recalling Polly's tale. "Yes, of course."

"What is it?" Edison demanded.

"Murder. I think she witnessed *murder*. Dear heaven."

Victoria stared at her. "Whose murder?"

"Lady Ware's." The logic of the thing came together quickly in Emma's mind. "That explains everything. Polly the maid told me that the night Lady Ware died, she saw Basil emerge from the bedchamber. He told her that his aunt had just succumbed and then he went on down the hall to inform the household. Polly went into the room and saw Lady Ware's body. As she pulled up the sheet, Sally rushed from the dressing room looking as though she'd seen a ghost, and fled."

Edison looked at her. "You think she saw Basil kill his aunt?"

"My former employer was given Lady Ware's old bedchamber when we stayed at the castle," Emma said. "The dressing room adjoins it in such a way that it would be quite possible for someone to be inside without anyone in the outer room being aware of the fact. I'll wager Sally was in there that night when Basil went to see his aunt for the last time."

"If she saw Ware do something to hasten the woman's death, that would explain the blackmail," Edison said slowly.

"Indeed. Nothing else does. In my experience paid companions who are so foolish as to become involved in Incidents with their employers or a member of the employer's family rarely get paid for their efforts. They are far more likely to be dismissed." Emma shot Edison a sidelong glance. "Without so much as a reference, let alone two hundred pounds."

Edison scowled. "This is no time to bring up that particular subject."

Victoria looked politely puzzled. "What on earth is going on here?"

"Nothing of any great importance," Edison muttered. "All we have at this point is speculation and deduction. Perhaps we will know more when the Runner returns from Ware Castle. In the meantime, I have taken some other precautions."

Emma paused to peer at him. "What other precautions?"

"I have some influence in certain quarters down at the docks. I have offered a reward to any ship's captain who reports a man of Ware's description booking passage on board any vessel either here in London or in Dover. In addition, I have sent word out to the various members of the Vanzagarian Society to watch for Ware."

"What if he travels north?" Emma demanded. "Or alters his looks and changes his name?"

Edison shrugged. "I did not say it would be easy to find him. But in time we will get him."

"Hmm." Emma paused beside the desk. She drummed her fingers on the polished mahogany. "He is a very clever man. Now that he knows we are on his trail, he may easily disappear."

"You are assuming that he left town because he realized we were closing in on him," Edison said. "But there is another reason he may have chosen this particular moment to vanish."

"What do you mean?"

"He may have accomplished his goal," Edison said softly. "Perhaps he found the recipe or the *Book of Secrets*. We still do not know which one he was after."

Victoria met Edison's eyes. "Do you think he will still want to get his hands on Emma?"

Edison did not answer immediately. He turned to study Emma as though she were an interesting problem in scholarly logic.

Emma did not like the expression in his eyes. She stepped back and held up her hand. "Now, hold on one moment here. Let's not get carried away with wild imaginings. At this very moment Basil Ware is either scurrying off to the Continent with his stolen book or he is busy attempting to elude you in some other fashion, sir. Either way, he has a good deal more on his mind than kidnapping me."

"I do not think we can depend on that," Edison said.

Emma closed her eyes and flopped down into the nearest chair. "You cannot keep me cooped up forever in this house, you know. I will go mad."

"There is an alternative," Edison said casually.

Emma opened one eye. "What is that, pray tell?"

"We could keep you cooped up in my house."

"I don't think so." Emma opened the other eye. "I wish to preserve what little is left of my reputation, tattered and torn though it may be."

"Quite right." Victoria closed her book with a snap. "I, however, am free to come and go, and I think that I might be very useful to both of you in this little drama."

Emma and Edison stared at her.

"How?" Edison asked.

Victoria gave him a cool smile but there was an anticipatory gleam in her eyes. "Gossip flows through the ton like water through a sieve. Why don't I go out this afternoon and pay a few social calls? Perhaps I shall learn something useful. Who knows? Basil Ware may have accidentally dropped a hint of his intentions to someone in Polite Circles, someone who would have had no notion of what he meant."

Edison hesitated. Then he nodded once. "It's worth a try. I, in turn, will take myself off to my clubs to see if I can pick up any information in that quarter."

Emma made a face. "What of me?"

"You can finish your letter to your sister." Victoria got to her feet with brisk enthusiasm. "Now, if you will excuse me, I believe I shall go upstairs and change my gown. One needs to be properly dressed for this sort of thing."

Emma waited until the door closed behind Victoria. Then she looked at Edison.

"I do believe that your grandmother is enjoying this adventure."

His mouth curved slightly. "You may be right. Astonishing."

"Obviously this unfortunate taste for excitement runs in the family."

My Dearest Daphne:

I have good news and some bad news. First, the good. It appears that my current employer will not be requiring my services much longer

Emma stopped abruptly and gazed sadly at what she had written. The thought of the impending end of her term of employment with Edison was not good news. It was the most unhappy news imaginable. She could hardly bear to contemplate the prospect of the lonely life she would be obliged to endure without him.

Dear heaven, she had fallen in love with the man.

Enough. She had to pull herself together, for Daphne's sake, if nothing else. Determinedly she dipped her quill in the blue-black ink.

I have every expectation of receiving the final portion of my wages within a few days. I am having some difficulty securing a reference from him, but I think, in the end, I will manage to do so. Please try to carry on there at Mrs. Osgood's School for Young Ladies for just a while longer.

Now for the less cheerful news. There is still no word in the newspapers regarding The Golden Orchid. By all accounts it has, indeed, been lost at sea, yet I cannot seem to abandon the notion that

the ship will eventually return. Perhaps it is only that I cannot bring
myself to believe I was so foolish as to invest in a doomed

Carriage wheels clattered in the drive. An unpleasant shiver shot through Emma, startling her with its intensity. She looked up from the half-finished letter to her sister and glanced at the tall clock. It was nearly five o'clock.

She peered out the library window and caught a fleeting glimpse of a dark red and black carriage pulled by a team of handsome grays. Lady Exbridge's town coach. Victoria had returned from her afternoon calls.

Of course it was the Exbridge carriage, Emma thought. Edison had given strict instructions that no other coach was to be allowed through the gates until he returned. Even the milk wagon and the fishmonger's cart had been barred for the day. Cook had been obliged to go to the end of the drive to buy the items she required for the evening meal.

Victoria would no doubt have interesting gossip. Emma tried to breathe a sigh of relief, but it got stuck in her throat.

This was ridiculous. There was no call for this sense of panic. Edison had left one of the Bow Street Runners to watch the house. Nothing would get past the man.

Outside, the carriage halted on the paving stones. Emma's sense of foreboding deepened. She tried to force herself to write another line or two to Daphne while she waited for Victoria to come down the hall to the library.

She gripped the quill too tightly. It snapped in her fingers. Annoyed, she tossed it aside. She was starting at shadows, she thought. The tension of the past few days had obviously begun to affect her nerves.

Victoria must be in the hall by now. Straining to listen for the butler's greeting, Emma opened the center drawer of the desk to search for a fresh quill. And saw the small knife that Victoria used to sharpen the nibs of her pens. She removed the cap and saw that the blade was fashioned of good, stout steel with a keen edge.

A low murmur of voices echoed in the hall. The butler sounded anxious.

"Sir, I really must insist that you leave. Lady Exbridge has given instructions not to allow anyone except members of the family and the staff into the house."

"Calm yourself, my good man. I assure you that Miss Greyson will see me." Basil Ware opened the door of the library. "Won't you, Miss Greyson? After all, Lady Exbridge would be positively crushed if you refused to join us in her carriage."

"Mr. Ware." Emma stared at him and knew that all of her forebodings had been accurate.

"Do say you will come, Miss Greyson." Basil's eyes glittered with malice but his smile did not slip. "It's nearly five. We are going for a drive in the park. Your future mother-in-law thinks that it will be just the thing to show the Polite World that you have her seal of approval."

"What the devil do you mean, you let him walk right into the house and take her away?" Edison slammed the hapless Runner up against the wall of the library. "You were supposed to guard her. I *paid* you to protect her."

The ruddy-faced man's name was Will. He had come highly recommended from Bow Street, but at that moment Edison was close to strangling him.

"I'm sorry, sir," Will said earnestly. "But it's not my fault they got yer lady. Ye don't understand. Miss Greyson insisted on going with Lady Exbridge. And I didn't have no instructions regarding Mr. Ware."

His own fault, Edison thought. It had never occurred to him that Basil would walk right up to the front door. The Strategy of the Obvious.

"The very least you could have done was follow the damned carriage," Edison growled.

"Well now, I don't expect it will be too difficult findin' that fine vehicle," Will said soothingly. "Someone will 'ave noted which direction it went."

"You idiot, he probably abandoned my grandmother's town coach as soon as he was out of sight of the house. Switched to a hackney or something else equally anonymous, I've no doubt."

"Give up a 'andsome carriage like that?" Will stared at him as if he'd gone daft. "But it's worth a bloody fortune."

"He couldn't care less about the damned coach." Edison tightened his hands on Will's collar. "It was Miss Greyson he wanted. And now he's got her, thanks to your bloody incompetence."

Will's face twisted in bewilderment. "What's *incompetence* mean, sir, if ye don't mind my askin'?"

Edison closed his eyes briefly and breathed. He forced himself to release Will. Then he took a step back from the Runner and turned away.

He would accomplish nothing if he did not regain his self-control, he thought. His only hope now was logic and strategy. He had to start thinking the way Basil Ware thought. That meant he had to begin thinking in the way of Vanza.

He unfolded the note that had been waiting for him when he returned to Victoria's mansion and reread the message.

Stokes:

They are both safe and will remain unharmed providing you arrange to transfer the recipe to me. Instructions regarding where and when to deliver it will be sent to you sometime during the next few hours.

He was dealing with a student of Vanza, Edison reminded himself as he crumpled the note in his fist. A man who had sunk himself so deeply into the Strategy of Deception that he had escaped detection as a former member of the Vanzagarian Society. *A man who was so deeply into Vanza that he evidently believed in the efficacy of the occult elixir.*

Basil Ware would place his faith in the Strategies. All of his planning would be done according to those tenets.

Sending messages regarding the delivery of a valuable item while keeping oneself and one's hostages hidden was no simple task, Edison reflected. It would certainly not be easy to manage from a distance. Time was a factor. Once the game was in play, Ware would want things to happen as swiftly as possible. The longer the entire process went on, the greater the risk for him.

Therefore, Ware was still somewhere in London. He would be deep into the Strategy of Concealment now.

That particular Strategy taught that the best hiding place was the place one's opponent considered the least likely for the simple reason that he believed it to be secure and under control.

"You're a fool, Ware." Emma looked at Basil with disgust.

The nondescript hackney in which they rode had been waiting in a nearby lane. Basil had closed the curtains, but a few minutes ago Emma had caught a whiff of the river. The stench told her they were in the vicinity of the docks.

"You have no room to talk, my dear." Basil sat on the opposite seat. He had put away his pistol after one of his men had secured Emma's and Victoria's hands behind their backs. "Had you taken my offer at Ware Castle, you could have enjoyed a pleasant position as my, shall we say, associate. Instead, you chose to cast your lot with Stokes."

Realization dawned. "It was you who shot Chilton Crane in my bedchamber, not Miranda."

"I kept a close eye on Miranda while she was at Ware Castle. When she tried to involve one of my staff in her scheme to send Crane to your bedchamber that night, I realized her intentions."

"She wanted me to be found in bed with Crane."

"Indeed. She believed that if you were thoroughly compromised, she would be able to control you by offering you a post. But you are a most determined female, Miss Greyson. I was almost certain you would find your way out of such a simple tangle."

"You followed Crane to my room, saw the opportunity, and murdered him so that I would be facing the specter of the hangman's noose, not merely unemployment due to a soiled reputation."

Basil inclined his head. "I am Vanza. I believe in making a thorough job of such things."

"Miranda must have assumed that I really did kill Crane," Emma said.

"Probably. But she was dumbfounded, not to say furious, when Stokes came to your rescue in such a gallant fashion. She assumed that he must be after the recipe." Basil smiled. "And I confess I leaped to the same obvious conclusion."

Victoria glowered imperiously. "Why on earth would my grandson need some ridiculous occult potion that can only be used to cheat at cards? Why, he can make more money in one successful shipping venture than he could in several months in the gaming hells."

"Besides," Emma added, "Edison is a man of honor. He would never cheat at cards."

Basil shrugged, unruffled by the implied accusation. "Perhaps he believes that the recipe will lead him to the *Book of Secrets*."

"Aren't you interested in the book?" Emma demanded.

"Not particularly. I do not think it exists. I suspect it was consumed by the fire in Farrell Blue's villa. Even if it escaped the flames, it is useless to me."

"Why do you say that?" Emma asked.

"Now that Blue is dead, I doubt that there is anyone alive today who can decipher any more of the recipes. And as it happens, I am interested in only this one, very special elixir."

"And in my future daughter-in-law," Victoria said grimly.

Emma was startled to hear herself called a future daughter-in-law, but she decided this was not the time to question Victoria's choice of words.

"Oh, yes." Basil's mouth twisted in irritation. "I'm afraid I do require her services. At least until I find another woman who responds to the elixir. Unfortunately, females who are susceptible to the potion are not very thick on the ground, as Miranda discovered. It took her months to find you, Miss Greyson."

"How did you discover that Miranda possessed the recipe?" Emma asked.

"I have spent the past few years in America, but I have kept in touch with my contacts in the Vanzagarian Society. When I returned, I heard the rumors about the theft of the *Book of Secrets,* of course. However, I paid little attention to them because I was busy with my own project."

"Hastening the death of your aunt?" Emma said grimly.

"My, you have been busy." Basil chuckled. "You're quite right. It was obvious she intended to take her own sweet time about the business of dying, so one night I took matters into my own hands. Or should I say I took a pillow into my hands?"

Emma took a deep breath. "And Sally Kent saw you do it. She then tried to blackmail you for it."

He inclined his head in an approving fashion. "Very astute of you, Miss Greyson. I gave the little fool some money to keep her silent while I considered how best to get rid of her. And then I saw to it that she disappeared."

"Why did you go after the recipe for the elixir?" Emma asked. "You had just come into an inheritance."

"Unfortunately, I did not discover until after the old woman was dead that the Ware estate was very nearly bankrupt," Basil admitted. "There was enough money to keep up appearances for a while, but not for long. I was forced to consider new measures."

"I suppose you set out to find yourself a wealthy widow or an heiress," Victoria said. "That is the usual means by which gentlemen repair their finances."

"As it happens, I preferred a widow to an heiress. I did not want to be obliged to go through the negotiations and the business of settlements with a young lady's father, you see. The truth about the state of my own finances might have surfaced."

Emma suddenly understood. "You limited your search to widows and Miranda was on your list."

"She appeared a likely prospect at first," Basil agreed. "But I had no intention of becoming the victim of someone else who was playing the same game as myself. Naturally I conducted a discreet but extremely thorough investigation of her background."

"And you turned up the fact that she was an adventuress," Victoria said.

"I was about to strike her off my list when, quite by chance, I stumbled onto the fact that she had lived in Italy for a time and that she was now in the habit of serving a rather vile tea to her female acquaintances. I put that information together with the rumors about the theft of the *Book of Secrets* and the fire at Blue's villa, and suddenly all was clear to me."

"I must say it was very clever of Miranda to invent the identity of Lady Ames and move straight into Society," Victoria remarked. "She must have stolen some valuables from this Farrell Blue person. Enough to cover the cost of at least one London Season."

Basil smiled grimly. "But not for a second or a third. She had to find a way to make the elixir work. I thought it best to allow her to take the risk of conducting the experiments. It would have been vastly more difficult for me, a gentleman, to find a way to feed the potion to an endless string of unsuspecting females."

Emma narrowed her eyes. "You killed Miranda, didn't you?"

"As a matter of fact, I did not."

"You're lying," Emma said. "It must have been you."

"I admit that I fully intended to get rid of her. I went to her house the other afternoon when I was informed that she had sent her servants away for the day. I suspected that she had begun to panic."

"You knew that she had sent a message to me?" Emma asked.

"The person I employed to watch her house warned me that she had done so. I feared that she intended to tell you everything, perhaps even offer to make you a partner in her venture. I could not allow that. But when I got there, she was already quite dead. And the recipe was nowhere to be found."

"I don't understand." Emma stared at him. "You must have been the one who killed her. There is no one else . . ."

"Ah, but there is, Miss Greyson. Your fiancé."

Emma was incensed. "He did not kill Miranda."

"Of course he did." Basil's eyes glittered. "What's more, I believe he found the recipe. The library had been most thoroughly searched."

There was no point arguing with him, Emma thought. "You believe that Edison will hand over the recipe for the elixir in exchange for Lady Exbridge and myself, don't you?"

"Yes. I think he will do precisely that. Unlike me, he is weakened by his notions of Vanza honor."

Victoria stirred and tried to adjust her position on the small wooden stool. "No doubt Edison will blame me for allowing that despicable Basil Ware to kidnap you."

"Ware kidnapped both of us, not just me." Emma tested the strength of the knots that bound her wrists behind her back. "But you're quite right. Edison will not be pleased. He does not like it when things do not go the way he intends."

In the end it had been horribly simple for Ware, she thought. He had ordered two of his men to stun Victoria's coachman and groom with blows to the head while they sat waiting for their mistress outside a fashionable address. When Victoria had finished with her visit, the villains, dressed in the Exbridge livery, had carried her off before she had even realized what had happened.

Basil Ware had held a pistol on her while the carriage was driven back through the mansion gates. When one of the grooms had failed to recognize the coachman, she had been instructed to inform him that it was none of his affair if she wished to employ a new man.

With Victoria forced to give the orders, Basil Ware had had no difficulty entering the house.

Emma gave up struggling. The rope that one of Ware's men had used to secure her was stout and firmly knotted. She looked at Victoria.

"Is there any slack in your bonds, madam?"

"There is some give because that dreadful man left my gloves on when he tied my hands." Victoria paused to twist against her restraints. "They are not so tight as to make my fingers go numb but I do not think that I can free myself."

Emma surveyed their surroundings. Ware's men had kept both women under guard in a room above a dingy shop until nightfall. Then they had driven them in an anonymous hackney to the docks. A short while ago they had finally been deposited and left alone on the second floor of an abandoned warehouse.

Large crates and several barrels loomed in the shadows around Emma. Coils of thick rope sat on the floor like so many plump snakes. A layer of dust cloaked the lot. The grime on the windows was so thick it blotted up the fitful moonlight.

Emma was uncertain of the time but she knew that she and Victoria had been gone from the Exbridge mansion for several hours.

"I wonder why he brought us to the docks?" Emma mused as she inched her way closer to Victoria.

"Perhaps because he intends to sail as soon as he has the recipe in his hands. He appears to be convinced that Edison possesses it."

"I cannot believe that Ware actually thinks Edison murdered Miranda in order to get his hands on some silly bit of occult lore."

"It does raise the issue of who really did kill Miranda." Victoria paused. "What on earth are you doing?"

"Trying to get behind you so that you can reach into the pockets beneath my skirt."

"What have you got in your pockets?"

"The knife from your desk drawer is in one of them. We may be able to use it to cut through these ropes."

"Astonishing," Victoria said. "What in heaven's name made you think to bring along a penknife?"

"The notion came to me when I heard Basil's voice in the hall."

"I wish ye'd sit yerself down," One-Eared Harry said. "Yer makin' me dizzy with all that prowlin' back and forth. Yer like some great caged beast waitin' to be fed. Here, 'ave some ale. That'll settle ye."

Edison ignored him. He came to a halt at the narrow window and looked down into the pinched lane. He and Harry had been waiting in the small, dark room above the Red Demon for hours. One of Harry's men had finally returned to the tavern with a useful rumor an hour ago.

Still, Edison had waited. The Strategy of Timing taught that the more impatient one was, the longer one should delay before making the attack. But he dared not hesitate too long. The message from Ware had been very specific. The recipe was to be left in the appointed alley on the other side of town within the hour.

Ware would have men watching the location, which meant there would be few guards left to keep an eye on his prisoners.

"'Ow many men d'ye think he'll have with 'im?" Harry asked conversationally.

"Only one or two at the most. He's far too arrogant to concern himself with a couple of women." Edison smiled grimly. "The fool will not have the good sense to realize what he is dealing with when it comes to Emma and my grandmother."

"Difficult, are they?"

"You do not know the half of it. But that is one of the reasons we must get to them while Ware is distracted by his anticipation of acquiring the recipe. If we wait too long, Emma and Victoria are quite likely to take matters into their own hands."

"I'm ready whenever ye say. The sooner the better, far as I'm concerned."

Edison pulled his watch out of his pocket and flipped it open. "It's time."

"Thank the lord." Harry banged down his mug and surged to his feet. "No offense, but I don't think I could've stayed in the same room with ye for much longer. Yer startin' to make me right edgy."

Edison closed the watch and started toward the door. He took his pistols out of his greatcoat pockets to check them one last time. Both were loaded. The powder was dry.

Chapter Twenty-Nine

Emma felt the last strands of the rope part. Euphoria gripped her briefly.

"You did it, madam. I am free."

"Thank heavens. I thought I would never get through those bonds."

Emma stretched her arms cautiously. Then she rubbed them briskly. She was stiff and sore from having been confined for so long, but she could manage. She turned quickly and picked up the knife.

"I'll have you out of these ropes in a moment."

"No doubt," Victoria said dryly. "But have you given any thought to what we should do after that? The only way out of this room is back down the stairs. Ware and his men will be waiting for us."

"There is another way out." Emma sawed the small blade across the thick strands. "The window."

"You intend to climb down to the street?"

"There is a great quantity of rope lying about on the floor. We can use it to descend to the pavement."

"I am not at all certain that I can manage such a feat. But even if we both succeed in escaping, we are in one of the most dangerous sections of London. Two women wandering around the docks at night could well meet with an extremely nasty fate."

"Have you any other suggestions?"

"No," Victoria said. "But there is one thing—"

"Yes?"

"My grandson is well known around these parts," Victoria said quietly. "He does a great deal of business here."

"Yes, of course." Emma's spirits lifted immediately. "We shall invoke his name if we are accosted. And the name of his friend One-Eared Harry too."

Victoria gave a long-suffering sigh. "What can Edison be thinking of to associate himself with men who bear names such as One-Eared Harry? If only I had taken that boy into my care all those years ago. Tell me the truth, Emma. Do you think I would have ruined him the way I ruined Wesley?"

The pain that lay beneath the simple question wrung Emma's heart. She chose her words with the same care she would have used to handle a fragile blossom.

"My grandmother was a very wise woman. She told me once that parents can take neither all of the blame nor all of the glory for how their offspring turn out. In the end, she said, all of us must take responsibility for ourselves."

"Edison did that very well, did he not?"

"Yes," Emma said. "He did."

The thud of footsteps on the stairs came just as Emma finished cutting through the ties that bound Victoria.

"There is someone coming," Victoria whispered. "He will likely check our bonds and see that we are free."

Emma turned on her heel and scooped up the heavy stool upon which she had been recently perched. "Stay where you are, madam. If he opens the door, try to distract him for a moment."

"What are you going to do?"

"Have no fear. I am really very good at this sort of thing, although I am more accustomed to using a bedwarmer than a stool."

She hurried across the room, her soft kid shoes making only the slightest patter on the heavily timbered floor. She reached the door just as the footsteps halted on the other side. Taking a deep breath, she raised the stool high over her head and waited.

The door opened abruptly. A candle flared.

Victoria spoke sharply from out of the shadows, her voice as imperious as though she berated a servant. "It is about time you got here. I trust you have brought us something to eat. We have been without food or water for hours."

"Be bloody glad you're still alive." The man stalked into the room and raised the candle. "Where the devil is the other one?"

Emma slammed the stool down onto his head with all her might. The villain did not even cry out. He simply fell to the floor with a heavy thump. The candle flew from his hand and rolled in the dust.

"Emma, the candle." Victoria started forward.

"I've got it." Emma picked up the taper and blew out the flame. "We must hurry now. Someone will come looking for him."

"Yes." Victoria had seized a coil of rope and was already dragging it to the window. "But I do not know if I can manage to climb down a length of rope."

"We shall tie some knots in it. Our gloves will protect our hands. We are only one floor above the ground, Victoria. We can do it. I will go first so that if you slip I can help break your fall."

"Very well." Victoria jerked open the window and tossed out one end of the rope. "We can but try. I see no one down below. I suppose that is a good sign."

"A very good sign," Emma said. "I was afraid Ware might have posted more guards."

She tied two large knots in the heavy rope, but she dared not take the time to fashion more. She secured one end of the rope around a heavy barrel.

When she was ready, she hoisted her skirts, swung one leg over the windowsill, gripped the rope in both of her gloved hands, and prepared to descend into the narrow street. It struck her that the lane below appeared much farther away than one would have expected.

"Be careful, my dear," Victoria whispered urgently.

"Yes," Edison said quietly from somewhere above Emma's head. "Be very careful. I have not gone to all this trouble just to have you break your ankle at this point in the game."

Emma barely managed to stifle a small shriek of surprise. She looked up swiftly. There was nothing overhead except the night sky. Then she realized that there was a shadow dangling just above her.

"My God. *Edison.*"

"Hush. Go back inside. There's no point doing this the hard way if we can avoid it."

"Yes, of course."

Emma scrambled back off the windowsill and turned to watch him follow. If she had not known he was there, it would have been impossible to see him, she thought.

Garbed entirely in black, he was only a dark shape against the night. The length of rope he had used to lower himself from the roof dangled in the opening behind him.

Emma rushed toward him and threw her arms around his waist. "It's about time you got here, sir."

"Sorry for the delay. It could not be avoided." He hugged her briefly.

Victoria gazed at him in astonishment. "How did you find us?"

"It's a long story. Suffice it to say that one of the least practical aspects of Vanza is that if one has studied the Strategies and then stepped back outside the Circle, one can generally predict what another student of the arts is likely to do. Ware assumed that I would conclude this was the last neighborhood in London he would select for a hiding place."

Emma frowned. "I would have thought that Ware would have anticipated the possibility that you would second-guess him."

"Just to be on the safe side," Edison said dryly, "I put out the word that I was willing to pay a good deal of blunt for information regarding his whereabouts or the whereabouts of his henchmen. Nothing speaks as loudly as money in this section of the city."

"Yes, of course. Very shrewd, sir, if I may say so."

"Thank you." Edison looked at the man lying on the floor in a patch of moonlight. "I see you have been up to your old tricks, Emma."

"Victoria and I made a good team." Emma glanced toward the door. "I am awfully glad to see you, Edison, but we really should be getting out of here."

"I agree. But I think it would be easier for all of us to depart by the stairs, rather than by ropes." Edison crossed the floor to the door. "Wait here. I will only be a moment."

"Edison, you mustn't," Emma said.

"It's all right," Edison said. "Ware is, at the moment, a victim of the Strategy of Distraction. He is unable to concentrate on everything at once. From what I was able to discern earlier, he kept only two men here with him. You ladies have taken excellent care of one of them. My friend Harry and I dealt with the other earlier. The rest of Ware's henchmen are on the other side of the city, waiting for me."

"Nevertheless," Victoria whispered urgently, "Ware himself is downstairs and he's got a pistol. You'll run straight into him."

"Think of it as him running straight into me." Edison opened the door and glided out into the hall.

Emma looked at Victoria. "He really is the most difficult employer

I've had in my entire career. I probably should have made him write my reference before I let him go downstairs."

He had never put all of his trust in the Strategies, Edison thought, but he had to admit that there was some value in the Strategy of Timing, if only because of the element of surprise.

He removed his pistol from his belt and stepped out of the darkened hall. He went to the doorway of the lantern-lit room that served as an office. Basil paced the floor inside. A pistol dangled loosely in his hand.

"I regret that I have kept you waiting, Ware," Edison said.

Basil jerked violently and spun around. His mouth worked furiously when he saw Edison.

"Damn you, Stokes." He raised the pistol and pointed it at Edison. "Damn your bloody eyes."

He pulled the trigger without a second's hesitation. The explosion was thunderous in the small room.

Edison was already moving. He slipped to the side of the doorway and listened to the ball crash into the wall behind him. Then he moved swiftly back into the opening. Ware was at the desk, seizing the second pistol that lay there.

Edison was obliged to shift position again. Ware's second ball shattered wood somewhere in the darkness.

"Where are my men?" Basil raised his voice in a commanding scream. "*He's here,* you fools."

A faint tremor went through the wooden floor beneath Edison's feet.

"Bloody hell." Too late he realized that he and Harry had miscalculated. Ware had kept a third villain to guard his back.

Edison dropped to the floor but not quickly enough. There was a flash of light from the dark space behind the stairwell. He felt the fire slice across his ribs as cleanly as a knife blade.

"Kill him," Ware yelled. "Make sure he is dead."

Edison turned onto his back and fired at the hulking figure who loomed in the shadows. The man jerked and reeled back against the staircase. His pistol crashed to the floor.

The wooden floor shuddered again. Edison realized that Ware was coming up from behind in the best tradition of the Strategy of Surprise. The appropriate response, according to the teachings, was to roll to the side and use the opportunity to regain one's feet.

Instead, Edison twisted once more, ignoring the pain that lanced through him. He grabbed Ware's booted foot as it arced through the air toward his head. He yanked violently, wrenching the boot and the ankle inside with all of his strength. Ware yelled, toppled backward, and went down hard.

Edison surged to his feet and started toward his prey.

Basil had already struggled to his knees. He glanced past Edison, eyes narrowing.

"Shoot, you idiot," he shouted. "Do it now."

It was an old trick. Perhaps the oldest of all. But a disturbing sensation tingled down Edison's spine. He did not bother to turn his head to see if there actually was someone with a pistol behind him. He threw himself to the side and rolled swiftly behind a post.

Fresh pain ripped through his wound. He clawed at the second pistol in his pocket.

The wounded villain had lurched back to his feet. He had a pistol in his fist. It roared out of the darkness.

Edison got the second pistol out of his coat but he saw at once that there was no need to fire it.

The gun fell from the villain's hand. He clutched at the wound in his shoulder and stared at Edison. He blinked his eyes several times.

"Now look what ye went and made me do. Ye moved, ye bloody bastard. Now I'll never get me pay."

He toppled headlong onto the floor.

Edison pulled himself to his feet with the aid of the post. He looked at Basil, who was lying facedown in a pool of blood. The bullet that had been intended for Edison had struck him in the chest.

"*Edison,* are you all right?" Emma flew down the stairs in a swirl of skirts.

Victoria was right behind her. "Good Lord, there were shots. Is Ware dead?"

Emma ran toward him. "I thought you said everything was under control."

Edison put his hand to his side. "I made one slight miscalculation. However, the mistake has been rectified."

"Dear God, Edison." The soft, anguished cry came from Victoria.

He saw that she was staring at him, her hand at her throat.

"You're bleeding." Emma stopped in front of him. Her eyes were huge.

Her shocked exclamation reminded him of the fire in his side. He looked down. The lantern light from the office gleamed on the damp spot that stained his black shirt. He realized that he was feeling numb. He fought the light-headed sensation with every ounce of willpower at his command.

"I'll be all right. It's just a crease. I think. Go outside and call Harry. He's waiting for my signal."

"I'll fetch him." Victoria gave Edison a fearful look as she hurried toward the door. "Edison, there is so much blood—"

"Go find Harry, Grandmother," he said very steadily.

Victoria fled.

"Sit down, Edison." Emma lifted her muslin skirts and started to tear a strip from her petticoats.

"I told you, I'm all right," he muttered.

"I said, sit down." She came toward him with a grimly determined expression.

He sank down onto the second-from-the-bottom step. He was amazed at how weary he suddenly felt. "I suppose you're worried that I might not survive to write that damned reference for you."

"It's not that, sir." She gently peeled aside his torn shirt to reveal the wound. "It's that I have my professional standards to maintain. In the course of my career I have had some unfortunate situations arise, but I have never yet lost an employer. I do not intend to begin with you."

CHAPTER THIRTY

Twenty minutes later Edison settled himself gingerly into the cushions of the hackney coach Harry had secured. He had been right. The wound in his side was superficial, but it hurt like the very devil.

Victoria sat down across from him and studied him with grave eyes. "How bad is the pain, Edison?"

Her obvious anxiety made him feel awkward. "Tolerable, madam."

It was not the fire in the vicinity of his ribs that annoyed him, it was the strange, light-headed sensation he was experiencing. He gritted his teeth and vowed he would not humiliate himself by fainting.

Emma followed Victoria into the coach and sat down

next to him. One-Eared Harry climbed up onto the box to join the coachman. The vehicle jolted into motion.

"The bleeding has stopped very nicely," Emma said, fussing with her makeshift bandage. "We shall get you some laudanum as soon as we get home."

"You can forget the bloody laudanum." Edison sucked in his breath and braced himself against the sway of the coach. "I prefer brandy for this sort of thing."

"What about those villains we left bound at the warehouse?" Victoria said. "All except Basil Ware are alive."

"Sooner or later they will get themselves free." Edison's head was spinning now. It was getting difficult to think. "When they do, they will disappear back into the stews."

"We should have seen to it that they were taken up by the magistrate," Victoria said.

"I do not care what happens to them." Edison breathed deeply, trying to stave off the darkness that threatened to cloud his brain. "Ware is dead. That is all that matters."

"Speaking of Basil Ware," Emma said, "your grandmother and I have a great deal to tell you about him. He gave us many of the details of his scheme. He murdered the apothecary to cover Miranda's tracks, by the bye, but he claimed that he did not kill Miranda. I did not believe him but it is odd that he would lie about that murder when he willingly confessed to the other killings."

"I believe him." Edison closed his eyes and leaned his head back against the seat. He could not hold out much longer. A great weariness was about to consume him.

"What do you mean, you believe him?" Victoria asked. "Why wouldn't he lie—?"

"Good heavens," Emma breathed. "Look."

"At what?" Victoria asked.

Edison could not bring himself to open his eyes.

"That ship. The second one tied up at the wharf."

Edison listened to her scramble about on the seat. Her next words were slightly muffled, as though she had her head stuck out the window.

"It's *The Golden Orchid*," she called. There was a joyous lilt in her voice. "I don't believe it. Can you see it?"

"Yes, yes," Victoria said brusquely. "It is nearly dawn. There is enough light for me to read the name of the ship. *The Golden Orchid*. What of it?"

"Stop the coach," Emma shouted up to the driver. "I want to have a closer look."

Edison groaned. "It's just a ship, Emma. If you don't mind, I really could do with some brandy."

"Yes, of course. I'm so sorry. What was I thinking? Harry, tell the coachman to continue on to Lady Exbridge's address."

"Right ye are, ma'am," Harry called.

"I shall come back later this morning to get a better look." There was more commotion as Emma settled back into the seat. "I knew it would return. I knew it all along."

"Why on earth are you so concerned about that ship?" Victoria asked.

"That ship," Emma announced, "is the stupid, bloody ship in which I invested all of the money that my sister and I got when we sold our house in Devon. Don't you see, Lady Exbridge? *The Golden Orchid* is home safe and sound. She did not go down at sea after all. And I'm now quite rich."

"Rich?" Victoria echoed.

"Well, perhaps not as rich as Croesus or you or Edison. But I can tell you one thing, madam, I shall never again be obliged to work as a lady's companion." Emma's exuberance bubbled up and overflowed like fine champagne. "We shall have enough blunt to lure a dozen suitors to Daphne's feet. She shall have her choice of husbands. She'll have the freedom to marry where her heart leads. And she'll never have to work as a governess or a lady's companion."

"Astonishing," Victoria murmured.

Edison stirred but he did not open his eyes. "I believe that Lady Mayfield may have mentioned to you that I was hoping to secure a good match for myself this Season."

"What's he talking about?" Fresh alarm sharpened Victoria's query.

"Perhaps he's hallucinating." Emma put her hand on Edison's brow. "The pain and the shock of the night's events may have affected his brain."

"Now that you're rich and as we're so conveniently engaged into the bargain . . ." Edison paused to gather his strength. Emma's hand felt very good on his forehead, but he could not seem to get his eyes open. "I cannot think of any reason why we should not go ahead and get married."

"Hallucinations, without a doubt," Emma whispered. "He's worse off than I thought. When we get home we must send for the doctor."

It occurred to Edison that she sounded far more anxious now than she had the night she believed that she would hang for Chilton Crane's murder.

"There is no point arguing with a man who is having hallucinations," he pointed out. "Will you marry me?"

"Quite right," Victoria said. "Do not argue with him, Emma. There is no telling what sort of effect it might have on him while he is in this condition. We do not want him to become agitated. You may as well tell him you will marry him."

There was a crackling pause during which Edison was keenly aware of the passage of eternity. After an endless moment when nothing appeared to be happening, he groaned and put his hand on his bandaged ribs.

"Very well," Emma said quickly. "I shall marry you."

"Thank you, my dear. I am honored." He slipped down toward the waiting darkness.

The hushed voices of the two women followed him deep into the shadows.

"I doubt he will recall any of this in the morning," Emma said.

"I wouldn't be too certain of that if I were you," Victoria murmured.

"Nevertheless, madam, I must have your word that you will not take it upon yourself to remind him that he actually proposed marriage tonight."

"Why ever not?"

"Because he might feel obligated to go through with it." Emma sounded oddly desperate. "I certainly do not want him to get the notion that he is now honor-bound to marry me."

"It is past time he married someone," Victoria said with an air of practicality that Edison could only admire. "I rather think you will do, Miss Greyson."

"Promise me you will say nothing of this to him, Lady Exbridge."

"Very well," Victoria soothed. "I shall keep silent. But I do not think it will change anything."

"Nonsense. When he awakens he will forget the entire affair."

Not bloody likely, Edison thought, hovering on the very edge of oblivion.

"I wonder what it was about my mention of that bloody ship that brought on the hallucinations," Emma mused.

"I expect it had something to do with the fact that he owns the bloody ship," Victoria said.

He awoke at once when Emma poured brandy into the raw wound.

"For God's sake, don't waste it all on the damned bullet hole." He reached for the decanter. "Let me have some of it to drink."

Emma allowed him a swallow. Then she retrieved the brandy. "Go back to sleep."

He lay back down on the pillows and put his arm over his eyes. "I won't forget about it, you know."

"You're still suffering from hallucinations." She finished binding up the bandage. "You're a bit warm but the wound is clean and it should heal nicely. Go back to sleep."

"On the off chance that I'm actually quite lucid, promise me that you'll still be here when I awaken."

She tried to squelch the wistful longing that threatened to film her eyes with tears. "I'll be here."

He groped for her hand. She hesitated briefly and then gave it to him. He gripped it fiercely, as though afraid she would slip away.

She waited until she was sure he was asleep.

"I love you, Edison," she whispered.

There was no response. Which only made sense, she thought. He was asleep after all.

The sound of the covers being tossed aside and a short, bitten-off oath brought her awake shortly before noon. She opened her eyes to a room full of sunshine. She was cramped and stiff from having spent the past several hours curled up in the large reading chair.

Edison was sitting up on the edge of the bed, studying her with the old, enigmatic gaze. He had a hand planted somewhat gingerly on the bandage that covered his injured ribs, but his color looked normal. His eyes were clear and as watchful as ever. He was bare to the waist. The sheet flowed around his thighs.

Emma was struck with a burst of shyness. The rush of heat to her cheeks annoyed her. She cleared her throat.

"How are you feeling, sir?"

"Sore." He smiled faintly. "But otherwise quite well, thank you."

"Excellent." She pushed herself briskly up from the chair and tried not to wince when her stiff legs nearly gave way beneath her. "I'll ring for some tea and toast for you."

"Have you been sitting in that chair since we got home at dawn?"

She glanced uneasily at the mirror and groaned when she saw her rumpled gown and chaotic hair. "It shows, does it not?"

"I know I made you promise to be here when I awoke, but I did not mean that you had to sleep in that chair. I would have been satisfied so long as you remained somewhere in the house."

She opened her mouth but could not find any words. After a few seconds she made another attempt.

"Tea and toast," she got out. "I trust you're hungry."

His eyes held hers. "I was not hallucinating last night, Emma. And I have not forgotten anything. You promised to marry me."

"Why?" she asked baldly.

For the first time he looked baffled. "Why?"

"Yes, why?" She threw up her hands and began to pace back and forth in front of the bed. "It's all very well for you to say you want to marry me, but you must see that I have a right to know precisely *why* you wish to marry me."

"Ah."

"Is it because you feel obligated to do so?" She shot him a glowering look. "Because if that is the case, I assure you, it is not necessary. Thanks to the return of *The Golden Orchid,* I am no longer in any financial difficulties."

"No, you're not," he agreed.

"And my reputation is of no great concern because I do not intend to move in Society. Lady Exbridge has kindly offered to sponsor my sister, Daphne, for a Season. But I shall stay in the background and everyone will forget about my brief stint as a suspected murderess and fiancée."

"My grandmother assured you that such minor peccadilloes could be swept neatly under the carpet, did she?"

"Yes, she did." Emma came to a halt at the far end of the room. "So, you see, there is no need for you to feel obliged to marry me for the sake of honor or whatever."

"Well, that certainly narrows things down a bit."

"What do you mean?"

He smiled. "Apparently I have only one reason for marriage left."

"If you think to convince me that you actually need the profits from my one, single share in the cargo of *The Golden Orchid,* sir, save your breath. Whatever amount of money I realize from my investment can be only a drop in the bucket to a man of your resources."

"I love you."

She stared at him. *"Edison."*

"I sincerely hope the feeling is mutual."

"Edison."

"Just before I fell asleep for the second time, I could have sworn I heard you say something to the effect that you loved me." He paused. "Or was I hallucinating again?"

"No." She unstuck herself from the floor and flew toward him. "No, you were not."

She threw her arms around him and hugged him with all of her strength. "Edison, I love you so much it hurts."

He sucked in his breath very sharply. "Yes," he said. "It does."

"Good heavens, your wound." She released him and stumbled backward, horrified by what she had done. "I am so sorry."

He grinned. "I'm not. It was worth it. Now I won't have to write that bloody reference for you."

The captain of *The Golden Orchid* arrived the following morning to make his report. Emma was obliged to cool her heels with Victoria in the library while he was closeted with Edison.

"I've a good mind to tell him how many problems he caused me," she fumed as she poured tea.

"Look at the positive side, my dear." Victoria peered at her over the rims of her reading glasses. "If it had not been for Captain Frye's problems at sea, whatever they were, you would never have met Edison."

"Are you quite certain that you consider that a positive thing, madam?"

"Rest assured," Victoria said quietly, "nothing so positive has happened to me in a good many years."

Emma felt warmth flood through her. "I am so very glad that you and Edison have grown closer in recent days, madam."

"Yes, indeed," Edison said from the doorway. "Nothing like a little theft, murder, and kidnapping to bring a family closer together, I always say."

Emma shot to her feet. "You should not be out of bed, sir."

"Calm yourself, my dear. I feel perfectly fit." He winced as he walked into the room. "Or very nearly so."

Freshly shaved, a crisp white shirt covering his bandaged ribs, his Hessians newly polished, he looked as elegant as ever. It really was most unfair, she thought. If one did not know better, one would have thought that he had done nothing more onerous during the past two days than drop in at his St. James Street club.

"Well," she said gruffly, "just what did Captain Frye have to say for himself?"

"*The Golden Orchid* was blown far off course, got becalmed for several days, and was forced to put into an unscheduled port in order to take on fresh food and water."

Emma folded her arms beneath her breasts. "I would like to have had a word with Frye. That man caused me no end of trouble."

Edison took the cup of tea Victoria handed to him. "Frye assures me that the contents of the cargo will more than make up for any inconvenience the investors have suffered. In fact, it exceeds even my expectations."

Emma decided not to hold a grudge against Frye after all. "This is wonderful news. I must write to my sister immediately."

"I look forward to meeting her," Edison said.

"So do I," Victoria murmured. "It should prove quite entertaining to shepherd a young lady through her first Season. A new experience for me."

Edison raised his brows. "If Daphne is anything like Emma, the experience will no doubt prove memorable." He put down his cup. "If you will excuse me, I must be off."

"What on earth are you talking about?" Emma demanded. "Surely you do not intend to carry on with your usual business affairs. You must rest."

He met her eyes. The lightness that had infused his mood a moment ago was gone. In its place was a bleak determination.

"I will rest after I have finished the affair of the missing book."

"Finish it?" For a moment she was lost. Then it struck her. "Oh, yes, you did say that you were inclined to believe that Basil Ware told the truth when he claimed that he did not kill Miranda."

"Yes." Edison turned to walk toward the door. "Until that issue has been settled, we cannot close the door on this matter."

She suddenly knew where he was going. "Wait, I will come with you."

He paused in the opening. "No."

"I have been as deeply involved in this as yourself, sir. I insist upon seeing it through to the end."

He appeared to give that considerable thought. Eventually he inclined his head.

"You have that right," he said.

Victoria glanced at each of them in turn. "What is going on here? Who are you going to see?"

"The man who murdered Lady Ames," Edison said. "And who also brought about the deaths of several other people into the bargain."

CHAPTER THIRTY-ONE

"Forgive me for not rising, Miss Greyson." Ignatius Lorring remained in his chair and bowed his head with a grace that belied his frail condition. "This is not one of my better days. Nevertheless, it is a great pleasure to make your acquaintance. I have long been curious to see what sort of lady Edison would choose when the time came."

"Sir." In spite of herself and all that she and Edison suspected about this man, Emma gave in to habit and dropped a little curtsy.

She thought that she had been prepared for this encounter, but she was nevertheless dismayed by the sight of the obviously ill man. Edison had been right, she thought.

Ignatius could not possibly have long to live. He was so pale that he appeared almost translucent.

Ignatius gave her a rueful smile as she rose from the curtsy. "Yes, my dear. I am, indeed, dying. I suppose I ought to be grateful for the privilege of having had a long and eventful life. But I cannot seem to accept my imminent demise with equanimity."

Edison went to stand in front of the fire. "Was that why you went to such an effort to obtain the *Book of Secrets*? Did you hope to find a magical elixir that would prolong your life in that damned manuscript?"

"So you have reasoned it all out, have you?" Ignatius settled deeper into his chair and contemplated the infinity of libraries reflected in the mirrored wall. "I assumed that was the case when my butler announced you a moment ago. In answer to your question, I, and many others in the Vanzagarian Society, are convinced that the mysteries of the ancient occult sciences are not magical in nature. They are based upon a science different from the one we practice today, but they are not magic."

"You must have known that sooner or later I would understand that you were deep in the Strategy of Distraction."

"Quite right. I knew it would be only a matter of time before you came to realize that I was at the heart of the matter. Tell me, what was it that gave me away?"

"The business of the candles," Edison said. "Ware was not the type to bother himself with the training of a student. But if he had taken one on, he would never have given him meditation candles that were crafted with the same herbs and colors as his own. The risk was too great. He was using the Strategy of Concealment, after all. He would have known that another practitioner of Vanza could easily make the connection between himself and Stoner."

"To know the master, look at the student's candles." Ignatius nodded.

"Someone had given Stoner his candles. And then planted the remains of identical candles in Ware's study." Edison looked at him.

"Only someone who knew that I was already suspicious of Ware would have laid that trail for me."

"I worried a bit about the candles. But I thought I could get away with it long enough to get my hands on the book."

"You believed that you could decipher the recipes in the *Book of Secrets*?"

"Oh, yes." Ignatius flashed him a look of icy humor. "If Farrell Blue could work out the key to the recipes, I certainly could have done so also. I am twice the Vanzagarian scholar that he was."

"Why did you involve me in the search for the book in the first place?"

"It was a grave risk." Ignatius's mouth crooked grimly. "But you were my last hope of finding it. You were the best student of Vanza that I ever had. I know your capabilities better than you do yourself. I know how very dangerous you are. But it was worth the gamble. I had nothing left to lose, you see."

"You masterminded the entire affair." Edison looked at him. "You arranged for the theft of the book from the temple. But whoever you hired for the task betrayed you."

"Indeed. The bastard secretly sold the book to Farrell Blue. My people were closing in, but by the time they got to Rome, Blue was dead and his villa lay in ashes. There was no sign of the book."

"Most likely it went up in flames."

Ignatius tightened his pale hand into a trembling fist. "I could not allow myself to believe that. To do so was to abandon all hope."

"You scoured Rome for rumors and you realized that at least one of the recipes had been deciphered."

"Servant talk. But it was all I had. I concluded that the fire was no accident. I assumed it had been set to conceal the murder of Blue and the theft of the book, or, at the very least, the recipe." Ignatius raised one frail shoulder in a small shrug. "But I was growing weaker by the day. I needed the assistance of someone who was intelligent enough and objective enough to continue the search on my behalf.

Engaging your help was a calculated risk, Edison. But I was a desperate man."

"Why did you kill Lady Ames?" Emma asked.

"Time was running out. Edison had told me that she had the recipe but he wanted to apply the Strategy of Patience to the situation. Unfortunately, that was a luxury I could not afford. I was certain that she either possessed the book or knew where it was. I went to see her that afternoon immediately after she sent the message to you, my dear."

Edison eyed him closely. "She opened the door to you? A stranger?"

Ignatius's pale eyes glittered. "I have not lost all of my skills. I assure you, the little adventuress never heard me enter the house. She was not aware of my presence until I confronted her and demanded that she turn over the recipe and the book."

Edison looked up from the fire. "She gave you the recipe but she could not give you the book because she did not possess it."

"She told me it had burned when Farrell Blue's study went up in flames, but I did not believe her." Rage gave Ignatius's face a brief vestige of color. It did not last long. His thin body spasmed. He gasped and then succumbed to a wave of wracking coughs. "I knew she was lying. She *had* to be lying."

Emma saw Edison tense but he did not leave his position at the mantel.

The dreadful coughing eventually ceased. Ignatius took a snowy white linen handkerchief from his pocket and wiped his mouth.

"I was so certain that she was lying," he repeated dully. "I confess I lost some of my self-mastery when she refused to give it to me."

"In your frustration and anger, you shot her," Edison said. "Then you tore apart her library hoping to find the damned book."

"Yes." Ignatius sighed. "The library and her bedchamber both. My search was interrupted by the arrival of Basil Ware. I took the recipe for the elixir and retreated to the garden to keep watch. Ware did not stay long inside. When he emerged, he did not give the alarm. I realized then that he was playing his own game."

Emma was incensed. "You must have known that Ware might very well be after the recipe. Yet you did not warn Edison."

"By then things had grown more complex," Ignatius conceded. "Edison had already learned that there was a rogue involved in the business."

"You," Edison said flatly.

"Yes. I was relieved to know that my young student, John Stoner, had not betrayed me. Nevertheless, I thought it best to provide another distraction for you, Edison."

"You took the remains of a meditation candle from the batch you had created for John Stoner to Ware's house. You left the melted bits in his study for me to find," Edison said.

"I hoped it would confuse you for at least a while longer."

"The candles you crafted for Stoner were not the same color or scent as the ones you used when I was your student. When did you change the formula?"

Ignatius's mouth twisted. "When I began to explore the darker secrets of Vanza. I wanted new candles to light my new path."

"Why did you steal the elixir recipe from Miranda?" Emma asked. "Even if it worked, it was not the sort of potion that could help you."

"Quite true, my dear Miss Greyson. The last thing I need at this point is more money. I took the recipe with me in the faint hopes of using it to lure whoever has the *Book of Secrets* out of the woodwork. After all, if the book is still out there, whoever has it is no doubt having a great deal of difficulty deciphering it."

Emma frowned. "You thought you might be able to convince whoever possesses it that you had some sort of key to the other recipes?"

"It was worth a try," Ignatius said. He leaned his head against the back of the chair and closed his eyes in unutterable weariness. "But it appears that my time has run out."

"Where is the recipe?" Edison asked.

"Here." Ignatius opened his eyes and sat up slowly.

He opened a leather-bound journal that lay on the table beside him and removed a sheet of paper. "Take it. I obviously have no further use for it."

Edison took the page from his hand. He studied what was written there for a while and then he shook his head with infinite regret.

"Utter nonsense," he said. "Ignatius, you are not yourself these days. Otherwise you would know that your entire scheme was for naught. There is nothing of value in the *Book of Secrets*. It is an historical curiosity, nothing more."

"Do not be too sure of that, Edison." Ignatius leaned back in his chair and closed his eyes again. "The deepest secrets of Vanza have been locked in that book for generations. Who knows what can be learned from them?"

There was a long silence. After a while Edison took his hand from the mantel and walked back across the room to join Emma.

"Come," he said. "It's time to leave."

"By the bye," Ignatius murmured from the depths of his chair, "what did you do with my young, eager acolyte?"

"John Stoner?" Edison paused. "I put him on a ship bound for Vanzagara. There he will be able to study the true way of Vanza."

"I am rather glad that you did not kill him." Ignatius smiled faintly. "He reminded me of you at that age."

Edison took Emma's arm. "We have our answers. The affair is finished."

"What's this?" Ignatius did not bother to open his eyes. "Surely you intend to have me taken up on charges of murder? Where is your sense of justice, man?"

"You are a master of Vanza," Edison said quietly. "And you are dying. Justice will be served without my interference."

Ignatius said nothing. His eyes remained closed. His chest did not appear to move.

Edison led her to the door. Something made Emma glance back over her shoulder just as they were about to walk out into the hall.

She saw Ignatius toss the sheet of paper containing the deciphered recipe from the *Book of Secrets* into the heart of the fire. The flames leaped to consume it.

Edison was at his desk in his study later that day when he got the news that Ignatius Lorring had taken his own life with a pistol.

He read the note twice and then, very slowly, he refolded it.

After a while he went down the hall to the conservatory. He was in the midst of repotting a golden orchid when Emma burst through the door.

"Edison, I came as quickly as I could. What's wrong?"

He watched her hurry toward him. She was flushed and breathless. Red curls bobbed wildly from beneath her cap. She had not taken the time to put on a bonnet. The soft slippers on her feet were the sort that ladies reserved for indoor wear.

"You look as if you have run the entire distance between the Fortress and this house," Edison said.

"Not exactly." She came to a halt in front of him. "I hailed a hackney."

"I see." He started to touch her cheek and belatedly recalled that his fingers were dirty from his work among the plants. He lowered his hand. "What makes you think something is wrong?"

"I just had a feeling." She searched his face. "What is it, Edison?"

"Lorring put a bullet through his head this afternoon."

She said nothing. Instead, she put her arms around him and leaned her head against his shoulder.

Edison felt something inside him ease. He gathered her close, seeking the warmth she offered.

Neither moved for a long time.

CHAPTER THIRTY-TWO

The wedding was the event of the summer. Lady Exbridge insisted upon making a splash. It was not difficult because everyone in the Polite World was more than eager to witness the gala conclusion to the Season's most outrageous betrothal. Invitations to the elaborate wedding breakfast held after the service were much sought after.

When Emma walked down the aisle in her gown of white and gold, she wore a wreath of golden orchids in her hair. She caught her sister's eye and winked.

Daphne grinned. Emma's heart swelled at the happiness in her face. Her younger sister had taken to life in London with an exuberant enthusiasm that showed no signs of waning. Thus far she appeared vastly more interested in the city's museums, theaters, and fairs than she did in her upcoming Season. The Fortress was now a house filled with warmth, light, and activity as Victoria supervised preparations for bringing her out.

Edison had endured the elaborate wedding arrangements with stoic patience. "It would have been a good deal more practical to get married by special license and be done with it," he said on several occasions.

But Emma knew that he had tolerated the cheerful chaos because of Victoria, who glowed with joy and a renewed pleasure in life these days.

Edison turned to watch Emma walk toward him. She did not need her intuition to see the love in his eyes. It dazzled her senses. She gave him a radiant smile as she joined him at the altar.

The words of the wedding service echoed in her heart. She knew beyond a shadow of a doubt that the vows would sustain them both during all the years of their lives.

I thee wed . . .

Much later that night Edison stirred beside her in their moonlit bed.

"I very much appreciate your taking me on in this post," he said humbly. "I know that I have had no prior experience as a husband, but I want to assure you that I will endeavor to give satisfaction."

Emma smiled dreamily in the shadows. "Rest assured, sir, you give *complete* satisfaction."

"If you require references, I fear I must tell you that I cannot present any."

The warmth of the abiding love they shared between them blossomed into laughter. Emma raised herself on her elbow and leaned across his broad chest. She looked down into his gleaming eyes.

"If I require any references from you, sir, I shall write them myself. I am quite good at it."

"Indeed. How could I possibly forget your great talent for references?"

He pulled her closer so that he could kiss her again.